Chasing Roses

ALSO BY JEAN M. GRANT

A Hundred Breaths
A Hundred Kisses
A Hundred Lies
Letters to Nobody
Seeker
Silent Creek
Soul of the Storm
Will Rise from Ashes

Chasing Roses

JEAN M. GRANT

Chasing Roses

Book cover and scene break art by AK Westerman, AK Organic Abstracts | OA Graphic Design.

Print ISBN 979-8-9923754-4-2

Digital ISBN 979-8-9923754-3-5

www.jeanmgrant.com

DEDICATION

To plant lovers everywhere.
It's completely normal to talk to your flowers.
Really.
The bees understand you, too.

One

Olivia

I was stuck.

Again.

Not cornered by a bear or something. Not wedged in a slot canyon dying of thirst or being forced to cut my arm off. *Eek.* My dad always said I had a colorful imagination. Note to self: stop watching suspenseful movies at midnight when I couldn't sleep.

Stuck could be so many things. No bear, no canyon. That was good, at least.

I wasn't stuck in my personal life, as in trapped in a stale relationship, either. A man who sticks around, what's that? I wasn't metaphorically or metaphysically or even emotionally stuck—though my stepmom would beg to differ on the last one.

Oh, I was *stuck*-stuck. Locked-in-my-attic stuck. At least I wasn't afraid of enclosed spaces. It could be worse.

For crying out loud. This was the second time I'd done this! At least the last time Logan had been home. Damn that ancient gate latch on an even older door! If not propped open correctly, the door swung shut, and using gravity for the latch mechanism, locked me in.

The musty odor made my head spin. A sneeze escaped my throat like a squeak. My allergies were triggered mostly by dust mites and mold these days and, well, I was in mold-city right now.

I could try to scrape off the two layers of paint around the sash of the window. But some idiot had painted it shut. Oh yeah, that was me. Oops. I had gone through a home security kick two years ago, removing options for another burglar to find their way into my home. Even if a person did decide to break in this way, they couldn't go farther. Case in point. At least I knew my simple fortifications worked.

I had painted the window shut outside, too, for good measure.

Floorboards moaned with each of my crouched steps. Maybe I'd fall through the floor. Problem solved...and another thing to repair. I wiped sweat off my brow with the back of my hand. It wasn't summer yet, so I wouldn't suffocate up here.

Good job, me, for picking the right time of year to get stuck.

Using a screwdriver I found sitting abandoned beside an empty toolbox, I chiseled a path along the bottom sash of the old, angled witch's window, nearly as old as the 1850s farmhouse itself.

The screwdriver slipped, sliding off the sash and catching my left thumb in the process. Tears burned my eyes. Sucking on my sliced thumb, I ran my other hand along the window frame.

This damn window was not going to budge. The path of freedom teased me through the clouded glass: scramble down the shingled roof, shimmy onto the old maple tree with the tire swing, escape into the sunset...

No one in their right mind would come up here. Then somebody did. Me. I'd decided, foolishly, to take the mold issue into my own hands. I panicked at seeing a dead mouse, kicked the door stopper...and so it shut, automatically locking me in. The door opened out into the stairwell, so I didn't even have hinges I could try to loosen.

I fell onto an old chair cushion. A plume of dust shot into the already stagnant air. I sneezed again. Lifting my phone—thankfully I'd had that in my pocket—I entered "how to open a painted-shut window" into my browser search bar and received a list of tools I did not possess in the attic: box cutter, putty knife, hammer, sandpaper. All I had was a screwdriver. I kicked it. Even if I could scrape the paint away on the inside of the window, that didn't help with the painted-shut exterior.

"Great."

I scanned my list of phone contacts again.

If Logan were not in school, I would try him first, but I didn't want him to get detention for phone use. My finger hovering, I glanced at the last message from him. The GIF of a cat eating pizza laughed at me.

Come August, Logan would be gone. What would I do without him here? College was taking him an hour away, but it could just as well be across the country.

Secretly, I hoped he didn't get the position with Senator Reuben Cordova. I needed this last summer with my son. We had a road trip planned along coastal Maine in July. But, if he got the congressional internship, the trip was off.

I contemplated calling Irina, but with a glance at the time, that option was out. My stepmom was in the middle of her weekly radio show and wouldn't be able to tear herself away for another hour. Besides, she would probably badger me for the umpteenth time about joining her team in the biennial Great Garden Race of New England.

What good would I be on this race anyway? I'd managed to kill most of the plants she brought over to fill the flower beds. A few still hung on for dear life, resolute little things emerging from the soggy March ground after this week's freak warm weather. Old Man Winter would be back next week to kill them. Mark my words.

There was nothing wrong with flowers. Heck, I loved to draw them, and I was taking a floral watercolor workshop at the library. Flowers were simple, joyful. The rose arrangements my father chose for my monthly deliveries were beautiful, and I commemorated each one in my sketchbook.

I blew out a sigh, reeling in my errant thoughts. Okay, so no Logan, no Irina. If I called the town's non-emergency number, no matter who answered, word would spread through dispatch like wildfire, and my coworkers would not let me live this one down. Our crew was small and mighty...and gossipy.

One plus to working with the regional dispatch team was it kept me informed of criminal activity in the area. Last week, we took a call about a break-in, and my hopes had risen. False alarm. It wasn't *him*.

So, no calling dispatch.

I tapped a finger on my phone. What about my friend Alexa? No, she was teaching kickboxing class.

Logan should be home around dinnertime, since he would likely be in the library after school to work on his AP U.S. government research paper. Dinner was only...

Seven hours away. Could my sanity...and body—damn that morning coffee—make it that long?

Though it wasn't large enough to squeeze through, I popped the attic vent loose. At this point, what harm was there in more damage up here? Fresh air bathed my face. The extra sunshine was a welcome contrast to the dimness in the attic. The air and sun did not help my mood though.

I looked around as frustration swept over me. Thanks to a massive leak during the heavy rains this past fall, mold coursed across the beams and ceiling like a rampant heat rash. How was I going to pay for this? Logan's first tuition bill was due in August. I pinched pennies as much as I could already, and my boss, Glenn, reluctantly allowed me to work overtime. Though dispatchers made good money in big cities, they didn't fare as well in central suburban Massachusetts. My copyediting side job helped, barely. Dad had left me a little money, but it wasn't enough to cover four years at UMass Amherst, even with Logan's scholarships. Loans were the only way for us to fill the gap.

I collapsed onto the floor near the pried-open vent.

The contractor Logan insisted I hire to install central air-conditioning—something he had secretly saved for over the past year with part-time work, oh, my sweet son—had stumbled upon a hot mess of an attic and roof situation upon inspection. The verdict: I needed a new roof *and* mold remediation before they would even consider installing central AC. I could try minisplits instead. Regardless, Logan's money was a drop in the bucket for the cost of these repairs.

Settling in for the long haul, I repositioned myself on the floor cushion, played on my phone and scrolled through social media for a little while, then, as my battery drained, shifted to looking through a box of baby stuff. The tears welled again. I closed the box after tucking one of Logan's old onesies back in it.

When the driveway camera app pinged on my phone a few minutes later, I nearly jumped out of my skin.

It was the fifteenth of the month. Of course! Walt!

I opened the video app. A Park's Petals delivery van idled in my driveway, the lemon-yellow circlet of blossoms in the logo a smiling beacon. Saved by the flowers! I sent a look up to my moldy and water-damaged rafters, tears of relief blurring my vision. "Thank you, Dad!"

Via the app, I watched Walt lean into the van, which he had parked farther down the driveway today. His habits had become a bit off lately. Once, he came to the garage door instead of the front. Another time, he'd delivered me someone else's get-well-soon basket. Regardless, I looked forward to seeing him each month, and especially today. "Saved by Walt!" I said to myself.

In my euphoria—or mental exhaustion—the phone slipped from my hands. I scrambled on my hands and knees for it.

The doorbell rang and the video showed just the top of his uniform's blue cap. I must have nudged the camera by mistake when changing the porch lightbulbs yesterday. He was holding this month's arrangement of roses. I squinted. Yellow roses. I loved yellow. Dad knew. He always had.

Two years now, and the flowers kept on coming through the Rose of the Month Club membership, a little gift he'd left behind. *Roses for my little Olivia Rose*, Dad would say to me as a girl, gifting me the flowers every year for my birthday. My dad had been the sentimental type. He said he got teased awfully for the surname, and later in life he went by J.R. instead of Jerry Rose. I sighed, my heart welling with an aching sadness.

Then I spoke through the app on my phone. "Thank God you're here! I'm stuck in my attic. Can you come inside? I'll open the garage door for you to come in that way."

"Uh...okay," Walt said, his voice sounding different, almost mangled, through the mic.

I smacked the side of my phone, an old habit that did no good. The Wi-Fi up here sucked. The video on my phone froze just as Walt turned to wave at the camera. My screen gave me a fixed picture of the baseball cap and his dark face, both a blur of pixels. I shook my phone again fruitlessly.

I'd done a lot of settling for good enough through the years. A single paltry income did that to a person. But I'd spent good cash on this security camera kit. So, I didn't have the heart to blame it for any malfunction. For now, I would call it a Wi-Fi issue.

I swiped my screen to another app and opened the garage door. The low rumble of it rolling up the tracks was an indication that at least something in this house worked. I found the screwdriver and began a light thump on the attic door so he could locate me in the rear hallway. "Here, Walt. Here."

Heavy footfall. "Ms. Rose?" His deep voice was muffled through the thick door.

That was weird. Walt always called me Olivia. He also knew Dad...*before*. Before life went to hell in a handbasket.

I yelled, "I locked myself in the attic. I need you to open it."

"Okay."

I heard his steps on the slender creaky stairs.

I stepped back as he opened the door.

Hallway light poured into the dim attic. I blinked and breathed in non-gross air. Just as I was about to smother him with gratitude, I swallowed a cry.

The man standing on the steps and staring with utter confusion on his face was not Walt.

A weakness in my legs raced up my thighs and skipped like a stone through my stomach. Queasy with alarm and disorientation, I tripped on the cushion, fell back, and knocked my head on something.

Two

Olivia

I awoke on a couch and moaned. Pain throbbed as if someone had taken a bat to my skull.

"Easy, Liv. I need to check your pupils. You took quite the blow to your head when you fell," my coworker Yasmine said.

Three pairs of eyes stared down at me. Glenn hovered close. What the hell was he doing here? Yasmine, an EMT, worked a blood pressure cuff around my arm. Third, a stranger in Walt's uniform, the man who rescued me from the attic, stood in the corner, worrying the hat in his hands.

The hardly used leather couch squeaked as I attempted to sit up.

Not here. I can't be in this room. Not where Dad...

My throat began to tighten.

Yasmine spoke firmly but softly. "You beaned your nut badly there. Just ease yourself up. Is it okay if I check your eyes?"

I nodded and regretted it.

Glenn bent to lay a wool throw blanket on me. I waved him and it away, trying to keep my vision focused on the people in the room. Despite having been bolted shut this morning, all the windows were open, including the one with the drab drapes always pulled closed. *Not that damn window.* "Can we move to the kitchen or living room? Who opened my windows? It's cold." It wasn't cold, but March's weirdly mild air swirled old papers on the desk in the corner of the family room, and gooseflesh rippled along my arms.

Yasmine shined a bright penlight into my eyes while talking over her shoulder to our boss. "Glenn, grab her some juice."

"I didn't faint," I insisted.

"Just a precaution. You're not diabetic or—"

"No. You would know this already, Yas."

She turned to the stranger. "Could you please shut the windows? Carbon monoxide detectors were good. She didn't pass out from carbon monoxide poisoning."

"I didn't pass out!"

Back to me, she said, "Sit a moment longer, Liv. Let me finish." She tucked the penlight into her upper pocket. Her curly black hair was held back with a hot-pink headband today, and she smiled at me with a pacifying look. "You gave us a scare, chica."

Scare? That man in the corner had given me one. So much that I'd freaked out and thwacked my head. I was usually as steady as a resting heartbeat; it came with my job. I had felt pretty good with my security setup in the house and was doing more with getting out, living—but then I saw a stranger in my home, and it tumbled me back.

All I wanted in this moment was routine, the normal, predictable stuff of the boring life of a forty-two-year-old single mom. I thought I had moved past my crap!

"You're not Walt," I said to the man.

At first glance via the video on the security system, this man *had* looked like my friend and beloved floral delivery person, but upon closer inspection he was most certainly not him. Blue cap, blue shirt, male build, yes. But this man wore round, black-framed glasses—that complemented his bone structure well—and had only the slightest hint of time wrinkled around the corners of his almond-shaped eyes and looked to be at least twenty-five years younger than Walt. Closer to my age. His skin tone was lighter than Walt's, a deep umber brown. Instead of Walt's usual cheery smile, this man's face held a frown, carved deep from his forehead to the sparse black beard along his jawline. A frown of concern, not irritation. He had a Park's Petals hat, shirt, and name badge. The badge read *Holden*. Not *Walt*.

I should have noticed that in the video, but my elation at being helped had overruled my common sense. And the video had been lagging.

"No, I'm not Walt."

The shirt fit this man tighter, in a flattering way. Bald Walt had a beer belly. This man was fit and his hair, which had been obscured by the cap earlier, was closely cut and black, edged with a hint of gray. He returned my assessment. It sent shivers down to my toes.

"This isn't Walt," Yasmine repeated, her eyes narrowing.

I blinked. "I know that. I meant to ask *where* is Walt?"

Realization softened this guy's dark brown gaze. "Walt retired two weeks ago. I took over his route."

"Impossible. I would've known. He wasn't going to retire until fall. That's what he told me. Bought a condo in Florida."

Was Walt's strange behavior a sign of early dementia? He didn't even say goodbye. My heart squeezed with hurt.

Glenn offered me a glass of orange juice. I didn't want juice. I wanted out of this room. I stood on wobbly legs.

Glenn said in his no-nonsense tone, as if he was talking about the weather, "This is Holden James. He works at Park's Petals. He called 911 when you passed out. You got a bit of a bump there."

I reflexively felt the small lump on the crown of my head. "I didn't faint. I tripped and hit my head." Had I fainted? That moldy air *had* been getting to me.

The man stiffened. "She let me in, like I told you."

Glenn nodded, his look still trained on me. "Right. She did, but Liv is uh..." He shook his head, not sharing my personal business.

My lips quivered. *Do not go there, Olivia. Zap that right out of your headspace!*

I sipped the juice, wetting a very dry throat.

The man shifted from foot to foot, clearly ready to leave. "I've been doing his route for two weeks now," he repeated.

Yasmine unclipped the pulse oximeter from my finger. "All clear. No immediate sign of a concussion, that I can tell, but have Logan keep an eye on you tonight, okay? He needs to watch for signs of concussion that can pop up. You need rest. Limit screentime and reading. Drink fluids."

"Okay."

"Everything else is fine. I want you to follow up with your doctor anyway."

This man, Holden James, stepped a few paces toward the doorway, slapping his cap back on. "I'll go now if everything is okay?" Sweat beaded at the top of his brow.

Just then Officer Nick Cartwright came into the room. Having my boss here and a police officer felt like overkill.

All I did was lock myself in my attic and hit my head. They didn't need to treat me like a porcelain doll. Two years ago, I was a headcase, but I got over that...mostly. I had a few weird coping mechanisms, but didn't everyone? I gave Nick a wave and he smiled back.

"Hey, Olivia."

"Hey, Nick. They really did send everyone, huh?"

"Slow day for us," Nick said with a smile.

Glenn held out his hand to shake Holden's. "We're good now. Thanks again. We appreciate you helping Olivia and calling us."

My voice shook a little. "Thank you for calling for help, Mr. James." *And pulling my incapacitated body from the attic.*

"Holden," he corrected. "No thanks needed." With that he was out the door.

Glenn turned to me. "Okay, I won't expect to see you tonight."

I opened my mouth to protest but clamped it shut. I never won a battle with all five foot six of Glenn. Where genetics had been lacking in the height department, it made up for in fortitude. My boss was hard as nails but could be soft, too. I gave a tiny nod, already mourning the overtime I desperately needed and would not get tonight. Oh well. I could use the time to finish the manuscript I was copyediting for Courier's Cozies, the mystery-genre publishing house. The manuscripts were a twisted way for me to find morsels of how perps operated, and a good way to make use of my associate's degree in English. These authors did serious research. I envied their skills. But Yasmine said no reading.

Logan burst into the room. "Mom! Mom!"

"Hey, sweetie."

"I saw the ambulance and, and..."

Those baby-blue eyes flashed. The more that Logan grew into a man, the less I saw of his father in those eyes.

"I'm fine. I just clocked my head in the attic. I got locked in and the floral deliveryman came to my rescue. Hey, why are you home?"

"Early dismissal. It was a half day." Logan took in the vase of yellow roses on the coffee table—which I just now noticed—then turned back to me. "Where's Walt? I saw a different guy leaving in the delivery van."

I chuckled. "I asked the same thing. He retired early."

"Geesh, Mom. First you argue with the technician about the central air, and now you're going up in the attic. For what? Just let the pros handle it." He glanced around at Yasmine, Nick, and Glenn. "Let's go to the living room, okay?" He was already looping an arm around me.

At least my son understood my dislike of this room.

Assured I was fine, everyone saw themselves out. Yasmine paused in the foyer, shooting me with her piercing gaze. "See you Saturday?"

I nodded obediently. I looked forward to Saturday coffee with Chloe and Yasmine, and the occasional kickboxing class at the gym with Alexa when she could get me a free pass. If I was grading myself, I would give a C, maybe a B minus, in my efforts to get out there more, discover new interests, socialize. It's not like I didn't mind going places, doing things. I liked being around friends. I just...lacked the desire to do so these days. Returning home caused panic to seep in sometimes. The coming in, opening the door. The memory. The less I went out, the less I had to deal with *that*.

Why leave the house when I could order everything online, even grocery delivery? Technology made everything easier.

My trip with Logan was coming up. I'd already done ample research on the hotels and locations. We used to love our road trips and excursions, no matter how small, and though this hit the bank account, it would be worth it. I eased onto the soft leather couch in the living room as I thought about how little time remained with Logan this year before he went to college. *I will not be a hermit once he leaves!*

I stared back through the foyer that connected the living and family rooms. The roses were fresh and crisp in the purple vase on the other coffee table. They were sunshiny and beautiful with buttery-yellow petals, prickly and glossy stems, toothed leaves. My fingers itched to see what morsel of wisdom or memory from Dad was on the card this time.

I would distract myself this afternoon by drawing the arrangement in my sketchbook.

Logan followed my gaze. He strode over to the family room, picked up the arrangement, and after closing the door to the room behind him, brought them over in front of me. He placed them on the table.

I turned to him. "How was school?"

"Good."

"Is Maya coming for dinner?"

Logan ran a hand through his wavy hair. "I asked her if you and I could have dinner alone tonight." He paused. "Remember that internship I applied for with Cordova's campaign?" His lips fought the smile. but a sad hesitation moved in his eyes.

How could I forget? It's all he talked about. My summer's fate hinged on it.

Speaking past the grief that knotted my stomach, I asked, "When do you start?"

"Right after graduation."

Three

Holden

After finishing my last delivery of the day, I couldn't wait for a relaxing night. This week's highlights included an encounter with a man answering the door in his underwear, a dog that chased me off the property, getting lost twice, and then this woman locking herself in her attic. My new job sure held adventure.

Picking up Walt's route meant overtime for me until Jin and Zach hired another driver. I didn't mind. The hours were long but padded my bank account—barely. The job got me closer to moving forward. Valentine's Day had kicked my butt though. I'd never seen so many roses in my life. Why did men always send red roses? Tash had preferred bling over blossoms.

Instead of my usual evening of streaming a movie or reading, or the occasional going out with my buddy Paul to catch a game at the bar, Sunday night was dinner with the family. Maybe Paul and I could plan a fishing day soon;

we'd go before dawn for a few hours before both heading off to work at nine.

I yawned and stretched a crick in my neck. I used to love going to Mom and Pop's, especially when Tash and I were together, but lately, each visit was more painful than the last. It wasn't the company. It was the lying to them that festered in my conscience.

Pixie trilled and rubbed against my calf, circling for both love and food. She was like a shark: first the brushes against the leg, and if I didn't appease her after two or three passes, her teeth gave me a subtle reminder. I bent down and rubbed her behind the ear.

Honestly, Pixie was the only good thing to come out of my divorce and a very lousy previous year—and I was determined to make this year better.

Tash had wanted a cat, so she got one. She enjoyed the kitten phase of our uniquely colored fluffball. Pixie's body was a mix of white and brown splotches, and she had a clear divide down her face: half white, half brown. It was ridiculously cute.

Pixie had gravitated toward me, and away from Tash. She didn't like that, and the kitten phase had run its course. Now Pixie was my only girl.

"Dinner?" I asked her. She followed me to the kitchen on light, happy paws, her tail high. As she yowled pleasantly, I cracked open a can of wet food and microwaved a few scoops for fifteen seconds. Pixie only ate her food warm. It probably stank my microwave up to high heaven, but I wouldn't know. "Fish tonight. Spoiled girl." She stood on her rear paws, stretching to try to get inside the fridge. I swiped my hand down her soft coat. "Alright, one olive."

It was so weird. She loved green olives. With the sound of the lid popping open, the slide of fork against glass, she came barreling in from her hiding places.

After filling her dish with wet food and one olive, I removed my glasses and rubbed the bridge of my nose. Wiping tired eyes, I trudged to the bathroom, where I stripped and turned on the shower, meditating as steam filled up the room.

All week, while I familiarized myself with Walt's route, I could not get that incident with the woman in the attic out of my mind. At first, I had thought she maybe fainted or passed out from some fumes. No alarms had been blaring inside her home, so I *wanted* to presume all was well. But...presuming gets people into trouble. No more presuming allowed in my lifetime. No, sir. After carrying her to the family room, and catching my own breath, I'd opened every window I could while waiting on the ambulance to show up. Carrying her outside would have given me a heart attack. She wasn't heavy, but my formerly fit body was turning flabby and weak. Paul invited me to do some mountain biking with him this summer. Maybe I'd take him up on it, get myself back into shape. I'd become lax with a lot of things this past year.

Adrenaline had kicked in, and I got the woman to the couch safely without throwing out my back or anything. She had been *out*-out for a few minutes. Eyes closed, cheeks rosy—either naturally or from the wallop to the head—and hair a bit disheveled. I never touched a sleeping person because, uh, creep factor. But, after I laid her on the couch, her long hair covered her face, so I quickly brushed it aside.

Shaking my thoughts away, I stepped into the shower and scrubbed my skin extra hard, working the soap into a lather, hot water ricocheting off my body and, thick with suds, swirling at my feet. I had been the only one around to help her. The one person they would blame if something more serious had happened.

I shivered, the warmth of the water no longer soothing on my tired body. I turned the faucet off.

Showered and changed into crisp jeans, an undershirt, and a soft blue collared shirt, I went into the kitchen to prep a salad and to finally sort the stack of mail from this week.

A strong mug of coffee would be needed to dig through the pile. Alyssa and Paul wouldn't arrive at Mom and Pop's for another hour, and their house was only ten minutes away on foot. Alyssa always assigned me the salads to make—with specific instructions. Chefs were particular. My sister was an artist in the kitchen, and she knew it. As the coffee brewed, I washed spinach, then added pecans, spring greens, goat cheese—checking the date first—and pears. I still had the homemade poppyseed dressing Alyssa brought me last weekend.

There was no more delaying, so I sat to handle the inevitable. I chucked the junk mail and set aside the bills momentarily. I'd turned off most of my autopayments when I got slapped with negative-balance fees.

I rubbed my knuckles as I pondered which pain first: the envelope from my lawyer or the one from my college. After fortifying myself with a sip of black coffee, I opened the college one. Every time I looked at the letterhead, it made me sigh. Like one of those deep-from-your-diaphragm, tired-with-life sighs. This letter said the same thing the last emails I'd opened had: the deadline for re-enrollment was fast approaching. I needed to confirm my intent to stay in the program by July fifteenth if I wanted to return in the fall.

Though my credits could be transferred if I chose another university, my place in the engineering program and the associated financial aid would be forfeited.

I'd been on a leave of absence for a year now. Fifteen credits shy of finishing my master's seemed like so little...and so much, especially at my age. Plus, I had my thesis to finish. Mom had gone back to school in her forties to get the career she had put off while raising me and Alyssa, and I was doing the same, although I hadn't put it off for kids. I was starting a new career for...other reasons. And I needed a bit of a miracle if I were to scrape the money together by the deadline.

I couldn't let this opportunity slip. Mom always says that when life knocks you down, you have two choices: stay down or get up. Sometimes life was a bit of a boxing match against Muhammad Ali though.

I was not going to let it keep me down.

I rubbed the bridge of my nose again, then took off my glasses and cleaned them with the hem of my shirt. I lacked money to pay the tuition bill thanks to envelope number two—lawyer's fees. I opened his letter next. My lawyer had set up a payment plan, but even that was a stretch. You didn't make much as a floral deliveryman. The bank had refused my application for a home equity line of credit. There was no way I could put the school tuition and lawyer fees on a credit card. I'd never dig out of that debt. Student loans were still an option, but I really didn't want to take on that burden either or risk not having enough even with the loans.

I folded both letters and set them aside. Shrugging into a light jacket, I grabbed the salad, dressing, and a bottle of sriracha sauce, and headed for my parents' house.

I entered through the back, wiping my boots on the doormat and allowing the porch door to ricochet the way I always had as a kid to announce my presence. Smack, smack, smack.

Alyssa was sitting at the kitchen island, scrolling on her phone, her curly hair swept up into her signature pineapple hairdo. She played with the petite gold cross hanging from a slender chain around her neck as she looked up. "Hey."

"Hey." I gave my sister a quick hug.

She wrinkled her nose. "What did you bathe in?"

I tugged at my shirt collar. "Uh, soap? Orange mint or something?"

"Your clothes reek, Holden. Like mildew or something?" Her pulled face made her look ten, not forty. "Have you lost more weight? I'm hugging bones here."

My clothes shouldn't stink. The water drain trap in the front-loading washing machine probably needed cleaning again. Or I had forgotten to move the wet clothes over to the dryer quickly enough. "Guess I should try washing my clothes, huh? Not wear them inside out like I did in college when they got dirty?"

"Sorry. Long week at the restaurant. I wasn't thinking. I didn't mean—"

I grinned and she laughed in return, knowing I was just yanking her chain. "It's fine, Alyssa. Thanks. Can always count on your sniffer." I waved the apology away and flicked a look at the mess on the kitchen island. Alyssa may be a genius with her kitchen tools, but she left a debris field in her wake. I brought two dirty bowls and a few utensils over to the sink. "What are we experimenting with this week?"

"Blackened salmon—for you." She smiled with the winning smile that snagged her my high school best friend, Paul. She shifted her attention to the oven timer. "Almost done. Creamed Swiss chard, the salad you brought, and spicy tomato orzo. I put extra heat in it."

I sprayed the counter and began wiping it down. "Sounds delicious." Four place settings and one kid's plate lay stacked on the kitchen table. "Paul couldn't make it?"

"Overtime at the office. One of their accountants is sick."

"We'll see him after Tax Day," I said.

"Yup. I'm used to being a tax season widow."

"Think he could make time to go fishing?"

"For you? Of course." Bending and pulling out a pan from the oven, she whiffed the steamy air. "I hope you like this one. My eyes are tearing up just smelling this." She turned her head over her shoulder and sneezed.

Alyssa always made one portion spicier for me. I took the sriracha out of my jacket pocket and set it with the dinnerware.

She looked horrified. "No, Holden! Come on, this is extra, *extra* spicy. I pulled out the big guns. You don't need that."

I pushed my glasses up on the bridge of my nose. "We'll see about that. You a doctor now? Found the cure?" I gave her a teasing look.

"One of these days I will win this contest, and yes, I know more than your doctor does," she said, thrusting her chin out and crossing her arms.

Believe me, I wanted her to win, to out-spice my defective olfactory bulb. She hadn't yet, but I humored her in each week's battle, complimenting my perfectionist sister on a meal well done. Not only did she see this as a challenge, but sometimes, she came off affronted that I couldn't enjoy the dishes that had garnered her prestigious culinary awards. I'd accepted the smell-taste thing and had moved on, Alyssa, not so much.

"Where's everyone?"

She returned to the stovetop to check on two simmering pots. "In the living room. Bring this chardonnay out with you, please. I'll make yours a spritzer." She winked.

"Well, I do love some bubbly, don't I?" I winked back. "I want a cherry, like Jayla's Shirley Temple, please."

She rolled her eyes.

Grabbing a handful of pretzels on the counter to munch on, I made my way to the living room. I loved texture. Bubbles on my throat, the crunch of a pretzel, and that hit of sriracha. It worked.

Now, booze? When you're lacking seventy-five percent of your tasting ability, you get drunk fast. Real fast. Liquor was water on my palate. I usually went with seltzer and lime. Tonight, I would accept one glass of wine to lightly imbibe because my mind needed it. When time allowed, Paul and I liked to go brewery hopping. He would indulge in a local ale and tell embarrassing stories from our high school days, while I marveled at the brewery's inner workings. It was fascinating stuff.

Giggles trickled through the doorway from the living room.

Jayla was tickling Pop, who dodged her poking fingers. Mom sat on the couch by the coffee table, enjoying her pre-dinner tea and watching the two of them. Her eyes lit when she saw me. "Holden. How're you doing, sweetheart?"

I scrubbed my jawline, wondering if I should shave. Tash always liked me clean-shaven, thus me growing my facial hair out recently. I had to be a rebel sometimes. I leaned down to hug Mom, knowing she wouldn't complain about my clothing's stench or scruffy chin. "What are you working on there?" I pointed to the purple pile of yarn on the coffee table next to her crochet hook.

"A little something for Evelyn's grandbaby."

I nodded hello to my dad at the same time Alyssa called from the dining room, "Dinner's ready."

I scooped Jayla up with a tight squeeze.

"Giddy-up!" she said with a giggle.

We did a little switcheroo, and I carried her to the table piggyback-style. "How's my favorite love bug?"

She hugged me around my shoulders. "Good! I lost another tooth today. Bit into an apple and—gush! All this blood came out!"

"Wahoo. A big one?"

I lowered her carefully to the floor. She smiled at me, showing the empty spot in her teeth. "Yesss! I hope I get two dollars from the tooth fairy for this one. Can I come visit Pixie soon?"

"You bet."

As we sat at the table, my phone rang. I pulled it out to silence it, and Pop looked over my shoulder as he took his seat beside me.

My lawyer. Why was Earl Bachman calling me on a Sunday? Did this month's payment not go through? I wasn't unfamiliar with those calls from his billing department.

"Why do you have a lawyer calling, and on the Lord's Day no less? Not Tasha bothering you still?" Dad asked, his tone irritated.

I really should rename the caller ID to something else.

Pop eased himself into his chair, the cringe not hidden on his face. He blew out his breath and then lifted a glass of iced tea to take his daily dose of medication. His back pain flared at night, so Mom always laid a pill beside his dinner drink. After setting a pillow against his lower back, he held my gaze.

Wrong lawyer, Pop. Not the divorce lawyer. The other one.

"No, it's not Tasha. It's for work. Just a holdup on one of the new construction sites." I silenced the phone and plunked it back into my jacket. Alyssa cast me a look. I avoided her gaze. *Not tonight, Alyssa. Not tonight. How could I tell them?* I needed her to save me from this conversation, not silently dagger-eye me into telling my parents the truth.

I was hoping to have been done with my degree by now, to have found a new job, so that Mom and Pop didn't need to worry...or know the truth about what happened and how I was let go—thrown under the bus, more like it.

Alyssa took my hint and began to talk about some new fiasco at the restaurant.

We joined hands and Pop led grace.

After an amen, I shook hot sauce on my salmon and dug in.

Four

Irina

Zooming past Ethan, our station director, who gave me an irritated "late again?" glare, I made my way down the hallway toward the little girls' room in the back of the radio station. This bladder wasn't going to hold it until the end of my hour-long show. With a chipper wave over my shoulder, I said, "Morning, Ethan! Violet wasn't feeling well, and the vet only had an eight o'clock appointment."

Not waiting for his response—likely an eye roll—I dropped the container of moustokouloura, my grandmother's famous grape molasses cookies, on the communal kitchen table before darting into the bathroom. The toilet seat was up again. I sighed as I grabbed a tissue and lowered it with a thwack. The station was run by mostly men who hadn't grown out of the awful habit by the age of twenty like they should have.

Pressure eased, I washed my hands, adjusted my scarf—the dog-paws-and-spring-flowers one, my favorite—then walked into the air studio faster than one could say, WCWE 93.3 FM *Community Radio, catching you on the threes!*

My show was slotted between Tom's *Motown Moves* and Khadir's *Happy Thoughts, Happy Body.* I still had twenty minutes before airtime, but Ethan was a stickler for punctuality and liked DJs to arrive thirty minutes ahead. Mr. Cranky Pants would load up a pre-recorded show at the tick of ten minutes before, just to be safe. Then he'd have a meltdown. He should see my doctor who told *me* that I needed to do less, slow down. If people couldn't keep up with me, then that was their problem. Life was short, and I wanted to live mine to the fullest. Age was just a number.

In the studio, I flopped onto my seat, and it spun in response. Tom was sick this week, so a previous episode of *Motown Moves* was playing according to the screen. Green lights on the top of the soundboard indicated we were live on the airwaves and cyberwaves. I set my thermos of English breakfast tea off to the side and dropped my handbag on the extra chair in the corner.

Both computers hummed quietly, ready and waiting. I glanced at the monitor to double-check the time slots for the underwriters. All was well in the land of radio in downtown Worcester.

Just as the overhead clock ticked to 9:45 a.m., the phone rang. "Irina here at WCWE 93.3 FM Community Radio." I already knew it was Sam calling to complain about one of his elderly roommates at Living in the Pines.

Sam said, "This morning Gretchen was watering her succulents again the wrong way. Told her how she was *supposed* to do it, but she still doesn't listen to me. And she doesn't water her cacti from the bottom either. Tried to explain the patina of the terracotta pots to her and she looked at me like I was from Mars."

"Sam, nice to hear from you."

"She never listens."

"How are *your* plants doing, Sam? How is that rabbit foot fern?"

He coughed, loud and phlegmy. "It's fine. Taking care of it just like you said. But, Gretchen, she—"

A knock on the door and a throat clearing drew my attention. Ethan poked his head in. "Irina, he's here."

I covered the receiver with a palm as Sam continued to whine about his neighbor.

"Send him in. Is he prepped?"

"Why wouldn't he be?" Ethan snapped.

Strike me pink, he was a rabid dog today. I was ten minutes late. Whoop-de-doo. Not once in five years of running *Your Gardening Hour* had I missed an episode. I had lots of pre-recorded episodes on standby, but come hell or high water or snowstorm, I was here. I didn't renege on my responsibilities. Not even when Jerry was sick. We'd worked around his doctor's appointments.

"Sam, honey. I can't wait to hear more about it next week. We have a special guest, and I need to prep him before getting on the air. Talk soon?"

Sam mumbled an "okay" and hung up.

I did a quick touchup of my mauve lipstick, assessed my cheeks, overly pink thanks to rosacea, and sighed. Then I resigned myself with a fluff of my wispy bangs and straightening of my scarf. I pulled out my notecards.

Douglas Francis came through the door. "Irina..." he said, leaning forward with a hand outstretched.

"Doug, you know I don't shake hands." I stood, walked around the desk, and leaned in, giving him a hefty hug. It elicited a chuckle from the handsome man in a suit that probably cost more than my minivan. "How's the family?"

I gestured for him to sit on the other side of the desk, in front of mic two.

Douglas possessed a formal air, with a well-groomed beard like a softer George Clooney, who was in his sixties now and still as sexy as ever. Douglas was fit, not round. He had oozed confidence, but lacked arrogance, during our previous encounters, but today he had a deer-in-the-headlights kind of look and was balling his hands. Maybe the studio intimidated him.

"Good, good." He blinked rapidly, high cheekbones a bit flushed. He added, "Just found out that my daughter, Katy, is pregnant again. Due in August. Another boy."

I pressed my lips together with a smile. "Nice to hear. Babies are precious."

"And yours? Your grandson, uh, Liam, is it?" Douglas asked.

"Logan. He's off to college this fall," I said proudly, fighting the pain that wanted to knot my stomach into a tight ball. Logan had been eight when I came into the Rose family picture, and unlike his mother, Olivia, he welcomed me with muddy fingers, sloppy kisses, and so much...love.

Douglas lifted a dark eyebrow. "Botany?"

I chuckled. "Political science. He might go to law school afterwards."

"Impressive."

Only if it's what he really wants, I wanted to say. Logan had loved geology like his grandfather, but after...well, after Jerry's death...Logan shifted his interests. I understood why. Regardless, it was sad to see a young man give up on his dreams out of a feeling of obligation. Logan wanted to heal his mother's spirit, crushed by the loss of her father. Olivia was getting better-ish now. Or so she claimed.

I put my headphones around my neck and gestured to Douglas to do the same. "We're going to do this live, as we spoke about on the phone. Just speak naturally into the mic. I will do the rest. I know in the past we've done pre-recorded interviews, but there is just something about being live, and in honor of the twenty-fifth anniversary of the race, no less. We may take questions from callers at the end if time permits. You okay with that?"

He nodded, his face growing ruddier by the moment. He crossed, then uncrossed his arms.

"Pretend we're at my place, having tea and chatting. There are even cookies in the kitchen for after."

That got a grin. He had a handsome grin. "Those are cute," he said, pointing to my display of heart-shaped rocks and minerals along the back wall.

Jerry had loved hiking, even with his bad knees. "Thanks. My husband gave them to me. Each of the DJs here put a little something on his or her area of the wall to make it feel like our own office. Know my favorite?"

"That pink one, rose quartz?" His smile widened as I saw the tension loosen from his shoulders.

I smiled back. "Bingo."

I walked him through the logistics. "We'll keep it easy and breezy. You've already read through the questions I'll ask. These mics are very sensitive. They can even pick up the sound of the CD trays opening, so have some water and get the fidgeting out of the way now," I teased. I handed him a water bottle from my stash below the desk. "This is going to be a fabulous year for the race, Doug. Just follow my cues and you'll be fine. Take your time, enunciate." I winked. I queued up my fade-in music and the first underwriter promo on the computers.

I slid my headphones on. My fingers did the rest as the earlier show faded out. Lights illuminated the soundboard with a few flips of switches. I tapped my foot to the upbeat rhythm of the theme song. Next, the underwriter promo played.

Douglas shifted in his seat, then took another sip of water. He dabbed at a sweaty brow, though the temperature was kept a bit cooler in here because of the equipment. He also slid on his headphones.

I wound up my radio persona. "This is Irina Georges-Rose, with *Your Gardening Hour,* catching you on the threes where I make gardening a breeze. Today's guest is a special one. We are speaking with Mr. Douglas Francis, president of the Francis New England Botanical Conservancy. That's right, friends. We're talking about races today. Races for flowers, that is."

I moved the button on the soundboard, playing the rest of my theme music. I gave Douglas a thumbs-up.

As the music ended, I turned my mic back on, as well as mic two for Douglas. "There's something special in the air this year, and no, it's not pollen or mayflies, though they're already making an appearance here since it's mid-April. It's race season, my friends. Every two years, the Francis New England Botanical Conservancy hosts a race with a prize of one hundred thousand dollars. This year, though? They've upped the ante in honor of their twenty-fifth anniversary. That's right. A cash prize of two hundred fifty thousand dollars. And—" I drew out the suspense. "—some surprises, I am told. Welcome, Douglas. Let's talk first about the legacy of the Great Garden Race. I understand the race was created in honor of your grandmother?"

I pointed to him.

"That's right, Irina. My grandmother, Rosamund, loved her rose gardens, and really, all plants and flowers. She had a magical touch."

"Those gardens *are* exquisite. I visited the estate on Brookhaven Island once. What a charming place. Plant lovers can get lost there."

"Her favorite was the rugosa rose, uh, some call them beach roses."

"Oh, those are quiet beauties. When was the first race?"

"My grandfather held the first race in 1975, on a whim. Some say it was on a bet. The lure of the race caught on faster than he anticipated, and he decided early on to run it biennially—uh, that's every two years—because it takes a lot of time to plan." Slowly, as he grew comfortable speaking, Douglas leaned forward. A soft gleam lit his blue eyes. A gleam of fondness. He clearly loved his grandparents and the race.

"Tell me, Doug. Why a race?"

"Pardon?"

Shoot, I caught him off guard. "Well, you said your grand-father did it on a bet. Why commemorate your grandmoth-er's passion for flowers with a race, specifically?"

"My grandmother had a competitive edge. She'd enter pie baking—Key lime was her favorite—or quilting contests at the local fair."

"Was she athletic, too?"

"Definitely! She'd beat you in a foot race or a swim across a pond. My grandfather liked to row crew. I think, that's where, between the two of them, they got the idea of a race."

"But not your typical race," I said. "A garden race?"

He nodded. "Yes. First, out of their love for flowers, they created the conservancy. The purpose was to share and celebrate gardening traditions in New England, while fostering protection of wildflower areas. They would host an annual Easter egg hunt at the conservancy. This evolved into an annual summer picnic and botanical scavenger hunt on the property grounds. Then, a friend had dared my father to make the competition bigger—the prize, too. Challenge accepted. And now we have the Great Garden Race which is a scavenger hunt for botanical items on a larger scale, across a state." Douglas beamed, pleased with his answer.

"I'm sure Rosamund loved it."

"She did, and she even participated in the first few races. After that, my grandfather passed the torch on to my father, and he expanded the race. And then, in the 1990s, the Rosamund Francis Scholarship Foundation was born for aspiring botanists. Donations seed those scholarships."

"There you have it, folks. A sensation. They brought a renewed love to the gardening world and supported young botanists, in turn."

Douglas nodded. "Yes, and she valued the bond of friendship above anything else, and this race can truly bring about new friendships."

Or make enemies. I'm speaking to you, Dottie Jones. Her weekly podcast always happened to go live during my radio show. If that wasn't intentional, then I don't know what was.

But now was not the time to ponder my nemesis. Instead, I thought about the friendships I'd formed in my four races, the first three with ladies from the garden club, and Jerry of course, and last time with Jin and Zach. This was even more reason why Olivia should join our team this year. She needed more friends and connection. And my current team needed a fourth. Olivia could use the money, too. Logan told me about the attic repairs.

But Olivia was...well...Olivia. As stubborn as a stone. She pretended she was fine, but she hadn't been since Jerry died.

I gave Douglas another thumbs-up. "Can you tell us what may be different about this year's race?"

"N-nothing, really." He averted his eyes for a moment, then brought his gaze back to me. "Though it may feel grander this year, it will follow the same rules as previous years."

I wondered why he fumbled on that question. Perhaps he was hiding something about this year's race? I chewed my lip, determined to get to the bottom of that.

I said, "Each year you pick a state in New England. Once, the race was a coastal route along Cape Cod up to the North Shore. The last race was in New Hampshire, and before that, Vermont." Given that the Francis estate was in Maine, I suspected in honor of the anniversary, that state would be chosen this year.

"Need to spice it up," he said.

"So...no hints about this year's race, Douglas?" I said coyly. "I heard there might be surprises?"

He chuckled. "Let's just say yes, a surprise or two. Pleasant ones. But my lips are sealed, even for you, Irina."

"Hmm, Doug. I do love a good secret. So, there *are* indeed a few things different this year. In the challenges?" I pressed.

"Not exactly. Like I said, all will be pleasantly surprised, including the competitors."

"Well, what's more pleasant than a quarter of a million dollars?" I said with a breezy laugh.

Douglas laughed but didn't elaborate.

Hmm.

Was the prize more than that? Were they awarding cars or trips from sponsors? In previous years, they had given some material prizes, small trips, and gift cards.

It looked like Douglas was done spilling the tea. "You have our interests piqued now. Okay, let's chat about the nitty-gritty of the race..."

We spent the rest of the segment discussing the rules and taking phone calls. Douglas stumbled over one call about the rumors of cheating competitors, but we got through it. Despite the efforts the organization put into setting clear rules and monitoring teams and vehicles, the race had its fair share of sneakiness. In past years, teams had been disqualified for cheating, mostly by using unauthorized use of technology or forming alliances, since neither was permitted in the race.

Before we knew it, it was time to wrap up. "How will those following the race know what's going on?"

"We'll give daily updates on the website and social media as teams check in nightly at their hotels and at the stops along the route. Each night at nine p.m. we'll have our daily YouTube discussion, sometimes interviewing the team that was cut or one of the top finishers."

That was my cue. "For more information, go to the Francis New England Botanical Conservancy's website—" I looked at Douglas and he recited the URL.

I added, "As always, thank you for supporting FM 93.3, a station where we put the 'we' in WCWE. Next month we'll be hosting our Fabulous Fun Drive at The Blue Room Brewery and celebrating you, our listeners. Stay tuned for details." I clicked off the mics and ran another underwriter promo. I sipped my water. "Great job, Doug!"

"Thanks. Sorry for my nerves." He finished his water. "Looking forward to seeing you there again, Irina."

I fussed with my scarf. "You're too kind. I've got a great team lined up."

"Jin Park and Zach Westerlind again?"

I nodded. "And my stepdaughter." It was barely a fib, just premature. *This year, our team will finally take first place.* If I could just convince Olivia to join.

I escorted him out with a goodie bag of molasses cookies and got a smile—was *that* a smile?—from Ethan. Another successful *Your Gardening Hour* in the books.

I stopped in the kitchen, chatted briefly with our station custodian, invited her to one of the gardening workshops, ate a cookie, and then was off. I needed to walk Violet and Lily and had a salon appointment this afternoon. Then, after a quick dinner, I had an evening workshop at Park's Petals with Zach.

Tomorrow, I would give Olivia another call.

I had plenty of friends I could ask, but I wanted Olivia on our team. Jerry had been our fourth wheel, a helpful stabilizer. In his place, it didn't feel right to bring another friend into the circle when I could bring my stepdaughter—my family.

Five

Zach

Music floated through my earbuds while I assembled the floral arrangement. The citrusy scent of tulips wafted up to me as I did a little head bob, feeling the beat thrumming in my chest. I situated stems in a foam block. Paused. Tilted my head while inspecting the design. Took a few stems out and readjusted. There. Better.

Eleanor had loved tulips, so I had mixed them, sweet peas, and statice into the funeral arrangements. I was torn between the Italian Ruscus or myrtle for greenery. It had to look perfect.

Selena, my floral design assistant, tapped my shoulder. I popped out my earbuds.

"What do you think, Zach?" She pointed to the arrangement she had been working on beside me.

I eyed the basketball-net-shaped vase holding the arrangement that I would deliver to one of the kids supported by Flower Child. "Those white daisies and orange carnations are so pretty together. Fab find on that vase, Sel. Taylor's going to love it."

"Thanks."

"Oh, here are the orange lollipops." I pushed over the bag. Maybe Jin would join me for the delivery tomorrow. Though Jorge and Holden made most of our deliveries, the ones for the pediatrics wing at the hospital were my thing.

Selena finished adding the lollipops, then moved on to sorting the supply delivery we received this morning, which currently sat in boxes behind our workstation.

Meanwhile, I returned to my own arrangement. I clipped a few more stems.

A crash reverberated from the back room.

Water droplets fell as I paused in pulling a tulip from the hydration bucket. Another crash, a sickening thud of something large hitting the floor—

Jin cried out.

Selena gasped, and a customer by the grab-and-go flower fridge jumped, nearly losing the bouquet in his hand.

Both stared at me. I dropped my branch cutters and the tulip on the workbench and dashed toward the workshop, my heart in my throat. What the hell happened? I pushed through the swinging door, expecting the worst. "Jin!"

Jin moaned from beneath a pile of boxes, a ladder, and other debris. "Shit!" he said through gritted teeth. Then he cursed in Korean, words that would make his mother faint. My boyfriend only dipped into his pot of flavorful swear words when he was in real trouble. Like the time he careened into a tree on a mountain bike trail in Vermont, or when he lost his balance on a rock climb in the White Mountains and broke three fingers.

A quick assessment showed his leg at a godawful angle. Ripping my gaze away, I shifted it to his scrunched face, which wasn't any better. I slipped my hand into my back pocket for my phone. Empty. "Jin?" I said shakily as I crouched beside him, pulling the hefty ladder off his body. "You know what happens when you go all parkour in the back room," I teased. But pretending life was a big bowl of gummy bears when it came to my partner being injured was a challenge.

He cursed again as I dropped the ladder off to the side, trying not to break more vases that had fallen from the second shelf. Glass shards sparkled in the bright overhead lights like a hundred teeny ice cubes spread across the floor.

"Be right back." I turned around to run out but collided with Selena instead. "Can you call 911, please?"

She nodded and hurried back to the front counter.

I returned to Jin and pushed more of the mess aside. Twice now, he had complained to me about the supplies being piled too high on the new shelves. Even with this renovated area, space was sorely lacking. We needed extra money to outfit the other back room with a fridge, shelves, and tables. We needed the HVAC updated, too. That cost a lot. So, I shoved the supplies into any space I could find.

A monthly edition of *From Faux to Fabulous* poked out from beneath his prone body. "You didn't need to take your frustration out on *Faux to Fab*, you know. I could've moved the magazines," I said with a wink.

He moaned again but didn't move. Trying to put on a tough front despite his pinched expression, he said, "I'm a lucky man to have someone so buff to rescue me...even if he's more concerned about his flower magazine than his boyfriend."

I rolled my eyes. "Hey, flowers are the epitome of chic. And you know how I've read this magazine since I was a kid."

"...and you had to hide them from your mother, I know, I know. And your grandma Bea encouraged it by taking you to her flower clubs or something. You give me that sob story every time I ask you to clean out your hoarder's collection in here." He grimaced.

To distract him from the pain, I kept chattering. "These old editions are like a good vintage wine or dress. They never go out of style. They spark creativity." Soberly, I said, "Jin, what *were* you doing? I had prep work for tonight's class under control. I thought you were back here crunching numbers."

I found a bolt of crinoline and slid it under his head. I tried not to look at his torn-up right pant leg. Blood made me squeamish.

Jin flinched as he gently prodded his ribs. "You didn't have any of the supplies out, and Irina will be here any minute."

I gritted my teeth. "I had it under control, Jin. Don't be such a drama llama."

"No, you didn't, and you know it. You were having a fit over that order from Jarvis Funeral Home. The flowers *will* be perfect. You don't settle for less. Eleanor would have loved anything you design."

I mumbled, "Nobody likes a sloppy florist, especially Jarvis Funeral Home. The only sloppy that dares enter my presence are my turkey Sloppy Joes."

"And even those you eat with a fork." He snorted.

"Because messy finger food is for cavemen."

"That's your mom talking."

I pursed my lips. Jarvis could be a huge client. They usually used Dottie Jones's shop, The Happy Hibiscus, for their orders. Not this time. Because we had known Eleanor Campbell personally, her family asked Jarvis Funeral Home to have us make the spray and basket arrangements for the wake, funeral, and burial. Eleanor had been a dedicated patron in our small shop, visiting our not-so-affluent area of Worcester almost weekly to get a bouquet to brighten up her kitchen window or dining room table. She loved to chat. "Eleanor deserves nothing less than perfect."

Jin spoke through pinched lips. "It's why I love you. Your eye for detail, except for when it comes to storage shelves...and hoarding." He made a stab at a smile but sweat beaded on his high forehead below a beautiful swath of black hair. "Beauty and books."

I was by no means the handsome one in our relationship, but whatever. I sighed and ran a hand through the close-cropped hairstyle I'd kept from my swimming days. "So that means you stick to the books, 'kay? No more climbing shelves. Stick to the numbers—just don't tell me about them." I laughed, though our numbers were dismal. Jin knew how much I relied on him for that part, how I could get lost in the creative side of the biz. "Let me handle this mess. Maybe Holden can design more functional shelving. He's good with that stuff. And he'll find a home for my *Faux to Fab* collection. Which is not the dumpster," I added with a lift of my eyebrow.

He was quiet as I stroked his hand.

Overall, Jin and I complemented each other: analyst and dreamer, organizer and artist, adventurer and one who went along for the ride. But lately things had been...strained. There's a reason people advise against working with your romantic partner. Maybe our vacation this fall would bring that spark back. Love sometimes got buried beneath the stress of a business. We just needed to dig ourselves out of this hole.

"Zee. This hurts like hell. Distract me."

I had already been trying to do just that. I passed a glance around, desperate for something lighthearted to say. "At least you didn't hit the plants?" I pointed to the boxes of air plants and succulents waiting to be used in this evening's class. We shared a laugh at the explosion of flower shrapnel everywhere: shattered glass, foam rings, grapevine hearts, thorn strippers and branch cutters, and ten thousand picks to name the million things scattered on the floor.

"Or the helium tank," he added, pointing to a few inflated mylar balloons in the corner.

"Strategic landing. See? It was a good thing *Faux to Fab* was here to cushion your fall. Guess no bungee jumping in November," I said, only half teasing. No crazy sports when we ventured to New Zealand? That would be a prayer answered!

Jin had planned out every detail for our vacation in six months, including speedboats, bungee jumping, ziplining, spelunking in caves with glowworms, hair-raising hikes, and who knows what else. My stomach twisted as I thought about the adrenaline adventure. At least I managed to coax him out of booking shark cage diving. This morning's matcha threatened at the back of my throat.

Jin waved a hand. "Oh, there *will* be bungee jumping."

I wiped slick hands on my jeans. "We'll see. Let's just get you taken care of."

Silence filled the workshop as I gave him sips of water, dabbed at sweat on his forehead, and tried to keep him comfortable.

We didn't mention the obvious implications of Jin's broken leg. How long would he be laid up? Most of his job was deskwork, so he could manage with a cast at least. But depending on his pain and recovery, he might need me on hand to help with that, too.

Eff me. The race!

Would Jin be able to participate? We still only had three people on our team. Were we now down to two? I did these races for *him*. My adventure-junkie partner consumed competitions like a drug. They were my bane. I *loved* flowers, but that was the extent of it. This would be our second Great Garden Race, after coming in second place last time. Jin had signed us up without asking me, assuming I would be fine with it, since I never said I wasn't.

But...

Glory seeking aside, we needed the prize money and publicity. After three years of running the business Jin inherited from his parents, we were not yet in a comfortable place. The exposure from the race would boost sales during the slow summer months to take us to the fall and winter holiday season. I kept putting off our wedding date because...well, weddings were not cheap. Neither were renovations.

A siren wailed through the silence, and relief poured through me.

Winning first for once would feel awfully nice, too. I supposed I still had some of that glory-seeking bug in me from my days of swimming.

"My dad's going to be pissed," Jin said as paramedics came in.

"Why? What for? He's retired." I shook my head. Of course, Jin would go right to that. It's why he worked so hard. To be honest, it's what connected us sometimes, or at least was the commonality that reigned over the other things that connected us: this need to please our overbearing parents.

I moved out of the way of the paramedics as they knelt beside Jin. They began checking his vitals and assessing his injury.

I fidgeted with the hem of my shirt, feeling helpless. "Want me to bring you a pumpkin spice latte at the hospital?"

He snorted, then grimaced. "Zee, it's May."

"*This* drama llama will search high and low to find you one!"

He smiled, that soft upturn of his lips that made my insides quake. The smallest dimple deepened on the right side of his mouth.

"I'll be right behind the ambulance with your java fix."

"Holy cannoli. What happened here?"

I turned to see Irina in the doorway.

"Earthquake?" Jin said with a chuckle, then a wince.

I stepped out of the room. Irina gave me a side hug. "Oh, Sugar. Don't worry about the class. I've done these Mother's Day baskets a hundred times."

She was already reaching for a broom behind the front counter as I followed the paramedics with Jin. Selena gave me a sympathetic look on our way out. Over my shoulder, I said, "Just put the Campbell flowers in the fridge. I'll finish them tonight." If I came back. Would Jin be able to go home from the hospital, or would he need to stay overnight?

I scrubbed hands through my short, bristly hair. Seriously, could things get any worse?

Hours later, I sat in my parked car in the parking lot of the shop. I inhaled. Leaning back in my seat, I closed my eyes and let the hit of nicotine and dopamine from my vape wash over me.

"Zachary? Are you still there?" the stern voice asked.

If only I wasn't. I turned the volume down on the speaker of my cell phone. She would not relent. How long had I been living here? Years. And she persisted in getting me to return home, to resume a life I did not want. "Mom, I don't want to move back to San Francisco," I said through gritted teeth, as I turned my car off. I needed to wrap up this call and get inside the shop to finish work. It was already nine p.m.

Earlier in the evening when I'd shot off a text to Mom, expecting empathy, I got the response: "*Out with the ladies, message Sandy.*" Sandy, as in her assistant.

Frustrated, and desperate for someone to talk to, I called her on my way back here to the shop. Big mistake. Now I was getting an earful. Why did I continue to try? Because sometimes, my mom was nice, sometimes she was good. And sometimes her Spanx were wound so tight, they squeezed the heart from her.

"Your little hobby can wait. Come back home for a while. Bring Jin. He'd love to see—"

"The flower shop isn't a hobby, Mom. It's my career."

"Pfft."

I vaped again, allowing the sensation to smother a scream clawing its way up my throat.

"Coach Martelli said he could meet with you again—"

"Mom. No. I'm good here." Besides, thirty-two was too old for starting over in swimming.

"You were the best of the best. 'The best in the West.' You can't let one mistake—"

A mistake? I nipped that conversation point quickly. "I'm happy here, Mom."

"You can't let this little hobby derail your dreams."

Your dreams, Mom. Not mine. Before she could say more, I ended the call.

Then I just sat in the quiet darkness of the flower shop parking lot and vaped a little longer, allowing it to numb all the pain.

I was surprised to find the lights still on when I dragged myself through the shop door, its bell jingling. Our classes ran from five to seven, and Selena would have closed at eight.

A warm, herbal scent wafted through the air, cutting through the mash-up of floral and earthy aromas. Soft voices conversed in the back room. I poked my head in, yawning. The room was spotless, like the accident hadn't even happened. The floor was swept clean. Everything had been reshelved or put into drawers or bins. Even the class components were put away.

"Oh, Zach. Why aren't you at home?" Irina said, looking up from her mug.

She sat with Holden at the main workbench.

I gave Irina a hug, holding in a sob. I would not break, not here, and not in front of anyone. My parents had driven that mindset into me—not because of who I was, but who my family was. Defeat was not in the Westerlind vocabulary. Yet, around me, situations seemed to contradict that fact: a floundering business, a relationship where I was too gutless to disagree with my partner or tell him the truth about why I didn't exactly love these adrenaline adventures...

Irina's hug was like a soft peanut butter cookie right out of the oven. I inhaled and pulled back from the embrace reluctantly. "Can you live here?"

"Violet and Lily would miss me, but I'll consider it, Sugar."

I laughed. She never called anyone else Sugar; just me. Zachary meant "sugar" in Greek, and given her upbringing and passion for baking, the moniker had stuck. It made me feel special. Sometimes I wished she was my mom.

She handed me a tissue and looked me over. I smelled the ghost of her musk perfume on my T-shirt. It was one that always lingered in that mom way. The *Ini Presence*, I called it. I shifted to my cheerful persona. "Looking snatched, as always, Ini." The woman was serving looks on a refined platter. Today's scarf had happy dog faces on it—for a bit of spunkiness—paired with a striking cobalt-blue, ruffled chiffon blouse. Gold hoops, salon-fresh ashy blonde bob, and styled acrylics completed her look.

She waved my compliment away.

"What are you doing here, Sugar? Why aren't you home taking care of Jin, or catching up on some Z's?" She grabbed another mug and poured some of her delicious tea for me. She topped off Holden's. He gave me a silent nod of hello. Never one for words, Holden.

I pushed out a smile. "The Campbell arrangements." Feeling the itch to finish the arrangements, I clenched and unclenched my aching hands.

"That can wait until tomorrow. What's the verdict?" Irina blew on her tea.

"Broken leg. Bruised ribs. He's staying overnight. Might need surgery. His mom is with him tonight." I fell onto a stool beside Irina.

"It'll be okay, Zach." Irina shuffled papers into a pile to put away in a folder. I saw a few maps, a bullet-point checklist, and another with the Francis New England Botanical Conservancy rose insignia on it. Was she talking about the race with Holden?

Holden.

Why hadn't I thought of him?

Holden had been with us for six months now. His résumé was way overqualified to be a delivery person. He had a bachelor's degree in construction management and occupational health, had recently left a safety officer position at Whitlock Construction, and was going for his master's in civil engineering. Holden turned out to be a whiz at so many mechanical things around here that Jin and I were clueless about. Though he wasn't a flower guy, he was a good driver and hardworking employee.

"Zach? You okay, Sugar? You spaced out there." Irina pushed the tea closer to me.

I sipped. Honeyed, just how I always took it. Irina was the best.

"Working on the race planning, Ini, now that we have Jin's replacement?" I asked, pointing to the pile of papers, then smiling at Holden. He gave me a nod of agreement and the flicker of a smile.

Irina had charts. And lists, folders of info! You would think this race was her full-time job.

She smiled at me deviously. "Always."

"Oh, I know that look. Spill the tea. What do you know about the race this year?"

"We can talk about it later. You, my dear, need rest. Do take that with you." She pointed to a covered container. "Holden's sister sent over leftovers from her restaurant. Shrimp scampi and corn salsa. He brought them for me, but you look hungrier. And take a few of the kourabiedes I brought."

Jin loved her orange blossom almond teacakes. "You sure?"

She and Holden both smiled at me.

I looked at my employee with a tired smile. "Welcome to the team, Holden." I turned to Irina. "So, is Olivia confirmed? Do we have our team of four?"

Six

Olivia

I pulled up to the curb at the bottom of a winding driveway.

The modest colonial home was set back among large pines and birches. Yellow siding, brick chimney, lovely wraparound porch. Quaint, quiet, wooded. It would seem impregnable, right? Wrong. Sitting at the end of a cul-de-sac, it was the perfect spot for a perp to break in unnoticed. One had done so a month ago, according to the dispatch logs.

After bending down the sun visor, I flipped up the mirror and did a quick face check. Makeup subtle, long hair brushed. Like I had done on previous inquiries into home burglaries, I wore my dispatcher uniform, consisting of the light blue department-issued polo with cloth nameplate and WRECC logo, so I appeared official.

A call to Marta Neil with my questions would have been simpler, but calling meant a phone record and another reprimand from Glenn. I already had one strike last year.

One very big strike. One that had put me on mandatory leave.

My phone pinged with a message from Irina. I swiped it away. *No, I am not doing this garden race!*

Inhaling, I ran through my spiel again in my head as I walked up the driveway. A new-looking *Secured by Emergency Exit* sign stood rigid and commanding in one of the tranquil flower beds of daffodils along the footpath. Stickers on the lower-floor windows stated *Secured by EE.* Emergency Exit was a good home security company. Two years ago, they were in my top choices as well.

A dog barked from inside, setting my already frayed nerves on edge. *Stick to the story. Keep it quick.*

This would be the last visit. I had stopped this nonsense a year ago...but then the whole stuck-in-the-attic-and-letting-a-stranger-into-my-house thing triggered something in my brain in March. A professional therapist would label this visit as regressive behavior. I acknowledged it was morally gray, and if Glenn found out, I'd be in hot water. Again. Or out of a job.

Yet.

Here I was.

It's not like I was an addict. But maybe the thirst for justice, to find the man who broke into my home and sent my life down a bad path, *was* an addiction? Or just an unhealthy obsession. Between my mental state after the attic fiasco and then this recent burglary that just happened to have his footprint all over it, I couldn't help myself. I needed to check it out. To ease my mind...to right a wrong...or both. I didn't know.

I was like an alcoholic who worked in a liquor store.

Now here I was again, convincing myself this visit was fine. I was helping them, too, wasn't I? I genuinely wanted to follow up on the leads; I knew how important closure was to some people.

I tucked my clipboard under my armpit and rang the doorbell before I lost courage.

This needs to happen. He needs to be caught. I am doing good for our community. Those statements steadied my mind.

I could see the dog's small profile through the glass pane. Marta Neil didn't mention a dog in her report. This pup was new. Why not a German shepherd or Belgian Malinois or even a Labrador retriever? A big dog that could take a bite out of a leg or arm.

I had yet to get a dog, so who was I to talk?

A woman's voice grumbled behind the door. I felt the pause, as if she was entering a code into the alarm system, and I smiled at the door, certain she was looking at me through the spyhole. I straightened my posture, making my nameplate obvious. A few locks and clicks, and the door opened.

"What do you want?" asked a woman in her seventies, wearing a loose T-shirt and jeans. Despite the casual attire, her shoulder-length platinum hair was shiny and styled. I bet she went to Irina's salon. She eyed my uniform.

"Mrs. Marta Neil?"

"Yes?" Terser now, through a contracted mouth, dozens of wrinkles appearing around unadorned lips. If a one-syllable word could be even more terse.

The dog beside her, a little brown terrier, sniffed my black shoes, then circled back behind Marta's feet. Sharp nails scratched the foyer's hardwood floor.

"I'm Olivia Rose from the Wellford Regional Emergency Communications Center. I had a few questions about the incident you reported on April sixth." I offered my smile, tremulous as it may be, and professional tone. *Look at the nameplate.*

ROSE, *dispatcher.*

She looked at it with a tilt of her head. "Could you have not called? I-I don't like unannounced visits, even from authorities."

I don't blame you. "Yes, ma'am. I tried multiple times, but I think your phone number was incorrect in the report." I recited her phone number, reversing the last two digits.

She pursed her lips. "Yes, you have the three and four switched."

I clicked a pen and jotted it down. "That would explain it."

The dog yapped. Could the dog smell my lies? I began to sweat. I hated these polos. And I hated myself a little for doing this. *Last time. Last time.* Even addicts could have a relapse.

"Prissy, stop!" she snapped. She turned to me. "Will this be quick? She needs her dinner."

I was happy Marta didn't invite me in. In the past, sometimes people did, but I never crossed the threshold. That took it too far.

This isn't taking it too far, Olivia?

I moved my eyes over the clipboard. pretending to read. "We only had a few more questions. It will be quick."

She crossed her arms under a large bosom. "When the police came, I already answered their questions."

I tapped the pen, urging my pulse to slow down. "Right. Just a few more for clarification."

Marta grabbed a dog biscuit from a jar in the foyer and tossed it to the dog. It took the treat and scampered down the hallway. "I got Prissy here after the break-in. She barks up a storm at the slightest breeze. She hates the mailman and loses her mind when packages get delivered. Her barks trigger my headaches, but she's worth it."

"Smart idea, after the B and E, uh, burglary. She is good to have. And you? Are you doing okay?"

Surprise lit Marta's eyes. "As good as I can be, I suppose. Our HOA created a community watch program."

"Ah, that's good. The car you mentioned in the report. You said it was an orange Subaru hatchback?"

"Yes. One of those crossover sporty type cars. I think a Subaru. It was dark out at the time. It was parked in the cul-de-sac, and originally I assumed it was a friend of Christopher's. The car model reminded me of my daughter's and she has a sportswagon."

"Christopher..." I pretended to scan my memorized notes. I already knew everything about this case. The stolen items included diamond and ruby rings, gold earrings and necklace, a designer watch, a few personal documents, one television, spare cash on the counter, and prescription drugs, of which this couple had the motherload. "That's Mr. Foley, your neighbor?" I pointed to the closest house to the right. "He didn't see anything else?"

"Yes, he's my neighbor. Isn't that in your report? He saw nothing unusual."

"You're certain the vehicle you mentioned was the perpetrator's vehicle?"

"I know everyone on this street." She screwed up her face in a frown and her pointer finger began a fast tap on her elbow, her arms locked across her chest. "Yes. After I got home, I-I came home...I came home and he was here...in my house..." She lifted her hand to the diamond crucifix at her neck and rubbed a thumb over the dainty cross.

"You were the only one home?"

She nodded. "Herbert was off with his friends that night, playing poker. I came back early from a dinner out with friends. I had a headache." Her pale skin grew paler despite the evening glow of the porch light. "Like I told the police, I think this guy was watching my house. He targeted us! I saw that car once before and thought nothing of it. It's like he...he knew my schedule. Do you know how violating that feels?" Her hand shook and she drew it down to her side.

Yeah. Actually, I did.

My mouth went dry. These assholes exploited people's vulnerability. It was sick, and I wanted to hug Marta right now. Her lower lip trembled. I shifted away from the raw emotion of the event. "Do you remember any distinguishing features on the car? A roof rack or tow hitch, perhaps?"

"A roof rack or hitch?"

"Like the kind to put bikes or skis on top or a hitch for towing trailers?"

She balled her hands, her face going slack. "'Fraid not. Sorry. But no, I don't think it had either of those." Her shoulders slumped.

Damn. Her perp probably wasn't *him*. That guy, the man who had broken into *my* home, had been driving an orange hatchback with a bike roof rack. I knew the rack design, because I owned a similar one...back when Dad, Logan, and I used to ride the local trails. That seemed like eons ago. Like Marta, I had also seen the vehicle—conspicuous; there weren't many orange hatchbacks with bike racks in the area—and thought nothing of it at the time. The thief was cocky, but that hadn't stopped him.

Still, still. This *could* have been him. What if he had taken the rack off? Two years was a long time.

Maybe he sold his car. Maybe he moved. Maybe, maybe, maybe. This was futile. I shouldn't have come here.

To fight the trembles in my hand, I scribbled a few pretend notes. I had to ask the last question, even if the car might not be a match.

"It says here the person wore a dark hoodie and some sort of mask over his face. Did you see any distinguishable tattoos or unique birthmarks? Anything else that we could use to identify him?"

She blew out her breath. "I already answered these questions. No. He was dressed head to toe in pants, sweatshirt. Besides, it was dark. I saw nothing. A shape, really, as he ran for my back door. I'm sorry."

I tucked the pen into my pocket as my heart thudded dully in my chest. I swallowed a painful lump, then assembled a thoughtful and kind expression. "Thank you for your time, Mrs. Neil. We'll keep you abreast of any updates."

As she stepped back, she gave me a guarded look. "Thank you, uh…" She looked at the nameplate. "Rose. I'm sorry you came all the way out here for nothing."

My smile weakened.

"Thoughtful of you to come and check on me, though. The police these days, I swear they do nothing. Take my name, write my number down wrong, ask pointless questions, then drop it. Herbert got himself a gun. I got Priscilla and an alarm system. We won't let another degenerate break into our home again. That watch he stole? Herbert got it when he retired. It meant a lot to him." Her scowl returned.

She closed the door behind her with a loud thump.

Seven

Olivia

There was a reason I always took first dibs on overnight shifts at work, and after speaking with Marta Neil, I could have used a night shift to distract me. The darkness, the creaky old house, Logan's graduation this weekend, his impending departure, memories of what happened...they were too much at once.

I gave up on scrolling social media and streamed food shows instead. After a few hours, the streaming app gave me one of those annoying "Are you still watching?" reminders and I selected "yes" with just a bit too much aggressiveness...and a yawn. Then a sneeze. Perhaps the mold from the attic—still not remediated, because with what money?—was migrating down to the living areas now.

The upbeat intro theme played from the television. I loved watching *Harry's Harried Hoedown*. Chefs, professional or self-taught, competed to prepare unique but wickedly delicious food for a cash prize. I was drawn to the plating styles and decorative touches. Which reminded me:

I just finished the weekly watercolor art class at the library. On my phone, I scrolled to the library's website and found the events page. Oh! August classes were up. A few taps and I signed up for Still Life with Colored Pencils and Cookie Decorating with Cathy. Though I'd missed out on having an art career, I held no regrets about dropping out of college. Logan had been worth it. I found other ways to fill that void.

Fine, I had a *little* bit of regret. I never complained, though. When, less than a year away from graduating with a double major of English and fine arts, I found out I was pregnant with Logan, Eric had seen the plus sign on the pregnancy test and panicked. He refused to talk about any option other than "getting rid of it," and so he cut and ran when I decided to have the baby. Years together, we'd planned to get married, and he was gone without a thought.

Had he even loved me? Certainly not more than he loved himself and his family's name. He went on to be a bigshot finance analyst in Boston. I moved back into my childhood home with Mom and Dad.

Even with my associate's degree in English, I'd jumped from job to job until landing the dispatcher position eight years ago. I had come upon the copyediting side hustle by luck—I had a friend who worked at the small publishing house, and she threw me a bone. My parents helped a lot when Logan was little, but I hated taking their handouts. After Mom died, Dad met Irina and they married and moved into a home of their own. He left the house, mortgage-free, to me ten years ago. Living here rent-free helped.

I wanted more out of life, but how could I do that when I used coupons, shopped sales, neglected house repairs, and still came up short every month? Even if I did find the time and money to pursue art full-time, the paycheck might not be enough. Which was more important: financial security or chasing a dream?

Trying to distract myself, I searched for the perfect fat cat GIF. I found one doing a stretch and falling off the table and sent it to Logan. He always slept with his phone on silent, but he'd see it when he woke up. My son was familiar with my insomnia, so it wouldn't surprise him to see the timestamp.

After *Harry's Harried Hoedown* ended, I grew restless. Sipping my now cold herbal tea, one that Irina dropped off last week from a British sampler set, I clicked off the television.

The sketchbook stared back at me, its cover a gloomy gray, its contents gloomier. I had banished the sketchbook into a box in the closet a year ago. Spurred by my visit to Marta Neil, this evening I found myself digging it out.

I flipped open the sketchbook.

There he was. The man who'd broken into our home. The scumbag.

Drawing him over and over in the notebook had been very unhealthy. I knew that now.

Marta Neil had the right ideas. Gun, dog, alarm system...better ways to cope. But I was not a gun person, nor a dog one either. Yasmine once suggested we try a shooting range, and I chickened out.

Would a gun or dog have even helped me?

Would either have saved Dad?

If only we'd stayed out later that night. I had felt like I had been coming down with a cold, so Dad drove me home early while Logan and Irina finished the movie at the theater.

My throat tightened. This punk had been casing my place, too, just like Marta's.

Dad and I had walked in to find this perp in my living room. Dad never should have been here the night of the break-in. But I had offered him a cup of coffee after he dropped me off.

Tears pricked my eyes as my memory burned. The perp's words, in that young voice with its thick Worcester twang.

Take it easy, lady. Nobody's gonna get hurt.

Then it happened in a blur.

Dad gripping his chest in agony. Dad falling to the floor.

The thief took our phones. Refused to let me call 911.

He never laid a hand on any of us, but he might as well have.

He ran out the back door, leaving our ransacked home...and me doing chest compressions on Dad. We had an old landline, but my call was too late.

My dad died under my palms.

He had been fit as a fiddle, he loved to say. No under-lying heart issues. He was healthy! Hearts do weird shit when under stress. A home invasion qualified as stressful.

The guy had made off with our phones, Dad's prescription pain medicine he'd left at the house after his knee surgery, Mom's diamond ring and the emerald birthstone pendant Dad gave me when Logan was born, some extra cash, Logan's laptop...and my entire world.

I lost my dad and a part of me that night.

I wiped at tears and pulled myself from the flashes of memory, of pain.

My drawing emphasized the man's broad shoulders, rounded like he worked out. He was probably in his mid- to late-twenties. Fit legs in denim. Pale complexion, blue eyes. A hint of brown hair poked out beneath the black ski mask. The smallest inky design of a tattoo could be seen just under the left side of his jaw and down the neck. A flower stem. The hint of petals. Thorns. Like a rose.

The irony was not lost on me.

So many roses in my life. Dad's deliveries...I'm sure he didn't intend for them to be a bittersweet punch each month. I wished I knew how he had set them up before his death, complete with a personalized note, no less. Seriously, did the man have a premonition? I scoffed. Not Dad. Not level-headed, rational Dad.

I could ask Irina, but that would require a conversation, and I avoided those with her as much as possible.

I flipped through the sketchbook, studying each drawing I'd made since that night. Some were full body—in jeans, navy-blue hoodie. A few were from behind, an outline. Other sketches included the windows, with the pushed-in air conditioner smashed on the floor, the curtains flapping in the breeze. Or a close-up of his cold blue eyes.

I slammed the sketchbook shut and put it on the coffee table. I needed to burn this book. Today's visit to Marta Neil? Over-the-top recklessness. No more of that nonsense, either. It was time to get my shit back together. I was allowed one bad day. And today was it. Time to move on.

What I couldn't move on from, though, was the other regret. Putting an AC in a downstairs window? Stupid. Someone in my vocation should have been more prepared. I wasn't an officer, but damn it, I knew criminals! How many calls had I logged in over the last eight years working at WRECC? How many crimes had been committed in our area? Plenty. Criminals looking for an easy score came to the nicer neighborhoods.

I ground out a loud sigh.

Tonight, I felt as blocked as a constipated elephant. What more could I do? The only options I could see were options

I know I shouldn't take, so basically, there were no options at all. I was stuck with no answer, no hope of justice.

I went to warm up my tea again. The wee hour of three a.m. glowed on the microwave clock. Curling back onto the couch with a blanket, I opened my laptop to read emails. I had no projects right now from my editing clients.

I grabbed and flipped open my second sketchbook: my flowers. Nearly two dozen drawings made since I received the first arrangement from Dad starting the month after his death. Unlike the other book, this one was bright, beautiful, and joyful. Another delivery would arrive tomorrow—or rather, today, like just a few hours from now. Always on the fifteenth.

I missed Walt. This new delivery guy...well, I don't know. He was new. A stranger to me. He had been nice, but a bit standoffish, during the April delivery, probably still perplexed after the attic fiasco in March. He had told me a silly flower pun, and I wrote it down in my sketchbook. I re-read it.

What's a flower's favorite kind of story?

A budding romance.

I almost snorted. I was a sucker for puns.

Summoning a happier spirit with my flower sketchbook was not working the way I hoped, but the heaviness in my chest lifted a smidge upon recalling Holden's friendliness. I liked his effort.

I turned to my third notebook. This one contained hand-copied information from the dispatch records. Our regional call center used a CAD system which created and maintained a detailed electronic repository of all calls. Technically, I was allowed to review the reports as needed and even print them...for internal use only.

Technically, I wasn't allowed to bring any of that home. But, oh yes, I had transcribed information from multiple reports into my small notebook. During the first year after Dad's death, I'd parsed information from incidents that even vaguely matched activity, crime, or person to my own incident. The man who had broken into my home was still at large.

Even though our department collaborated with the police and fire departments, and I knew our town's employees, I felt like they dropped the ball on my case. Like they didn't care.

Dead ends, limited resources, no leads, they claimed.

Sometimes you needed to take matters into your own hands. So I had.

It's not like I was doing unauthorized searches on these punks in the Criminal Justice Information Services—CJIS—system. Deliberate searching for *him* would plunk me right back into murkier waters...resulting in termination or federal charges.

So, I didn't cross *that* line. Last year I did a few house visits and had, yes, copied some information and brought it home. But I stopped! I had stopped. I never specifically searched for this scumbag in the databases. Never.

The call logs didn't give much information though. It was the additional database searches that yielded the best criminal information. If requested by officers during a dispatch incident, or by Glenn or our senior scope operator, Jason, we were authorized to run searches in the NCIC—National Crime Information Center—database at our terminal. This extended to the fingerprinting and criminal histories databases. Sometimes Jason ran follow-up searches after filing the incident reports. I memorized a few details from some searches of people with similar criminal histories, but never ever printed anything. I would memorize and add it to my notes at home.

I also never looked for *him* in the databases. But any other information I acquired was fair game, and I had a decent memory.

Glenn had given me a very stern talk when he learned about what I had done. I had been put on a month-long unpaid leave. That was a swift kick to my butt to stop this nonsense, so I stopped.

Until my little trip to Marta Neil's.

I slammed the notebook shut. What was I doing going down this path again?

A shiver chilled me to the core. Pulling up the blanket, I lay back on the couch.

Finally, insomnia released me from its grip, and I fell asleep just as the sun began to brighten my family room.

I awoke with a loud groan at the light streaming in through the windows. Blinking away blindness from what had to be near-noon sun, I sat up to find someone standing in front of me.

Covering my heart, I chastised, "Logan! Geesh!"

He grimaced, making his youthful face seem harder, older. He pointed to the notebooks beside me.

I shoved two of them under the blanket. "I was working late."

He flapped the remaining book—the one of Scumbag's sketches, dammit—out in front of me.

"This is work? Mom, what the hell is this? I thought—after last year—that you stopped this?" He chased a hand through his unruly neck-length brown hair.

Hope rested in his eyes. Hope that his mom wasn't a lunatic or at least returning to bad coping mechanisms.

I watched the bob of his hard swallow.

"Mom?" he said, softer, sadder. He sat next to me on the couch with a flop. I couldn't turn away. I had no words.

Logan didn't need this stress. He had so much else to handle, with college coming up, and first that internship he was so excited about but which would also be challenging—his first time living away from me.

Wetness blurred my vision. "I haven't been...I was just...remembering. You know, with the anniversary coming up."

"Mom. It wasn't your fault. And you're not doing anything that can get you in trouble again?"

I shook my head. "No! I'm not. I couldn't sleep. Was just thinking about Grandpa, ya know? I brought them out to throw away. Promise." And I did promise it. I was going to toss the Scumbag sketchbook and reports notebook.

He gestured toward the coffee table, where my newest floral arrangement sat beside a steaming cup of coffee and some sort of biscuit. "The new guy from Park's delivered your flowers. He asked how you were doing."

Pretty peach roses surrounded by white ranunculus. A card stuck out from the spray. Last month's note included a memory about our trip to Acadia when I was a kid. I wondered what this month's would say.

"He told me to ask you, 'What do you call a flower that runs on electricity?'"

Oh, another pun. "What?"

"A power plant."

I chewed my lip, feeling lighter again at Holden's effort to make me smile. With a sigh, I said, 'Look, Logan, we can talk about this..." I gave a wave to the Scumbag sketchbook now sitting beside the bright floral arrangement.

He shook his head. "Don't want to. Mom, you need to let this go. You need to move past this."

I nodded. "I am. I have."

"I need you to be okay before I leave. Promise me, Mom?"

"Promise, sweetie." That was the truth. I squeezed his hand.

"Gram Ini dropped off the cake and reminded us to be at her place by two o'clock so we can carpool for graduation. Dinner reservations got moved to seven thirty. Maya and her parents are going to join us, if that's okay?"

"Sounds good."

"Gram also dropped off that paperwork for the race." He pointed to the stapled pile beside the roses. "It'll be good for you. You should do it."

"I'll think about it." That was a half-truth. I could use the money—winning was a long shot though. And it meant two weeks alone with Irina and two others on this team that I didn't know well.

Irina and I...well, it was complicated. I was still mourning the loss of Mom when Dad married Irina. The more she pushed, insisting she was helping me, the more I pulled away.

When she came to plant flowers here, I felt woefully inadequate at home maintenance. When she took me to her fancy salon for a fresh style, I got the feeling she didn't like how I styled my hair. She sent baked goods over with Logan all the time.

Well, those I liked. I was a decent baker but preferred the decorating aspects.

I think I was just tired of Irina "helping" me, as if I were faulty and needed fixing.

We were opposites that just never got on.

That alone was enough to dissuade me from doing this race.

I downed a gulp of the coffee in front of me. "Let's go get ready for graduation, hmm?" I smacked my knees, stood up, and went over to the sofa table.

The smile returned to his eyes.

I retrieved the memory card from a charger, loaded it into the digital camera, and snapped a photo of him. Today was about Logan. Not me and my messed-up coping mechanisms.

I needed to put the past behind me...and embrace today. For Logan. For myself.

Eight

Olivia

The deluxe ergonomic chair creaked with my deep stretch. Nearing the end of a twelve-hour shift, I released a yawn, my vision glazing over. I blinked at the monitors in front of me. At least there were a few perks—like nice chairs—to the newly remodeled Wellford Regional Emergency Communication Center, or WRECC, or as we jokingly called it, WRECK. Working here wrecked your psyche and sleep schedule, but we had nice chairs.

"Hamstrings?" Chloe asked from the call station beside me.

"Always." I pushed the chair back, stood, and adjusted my desk to a higher level with a flip of a switch. I rubbed my lower back, then reached my arms behind me for a twist.

Glenn popped his head into the room, a coffee mug in his hand, his face neutrally composed. "Olivia, I need to talk to you when you get off shift."

I nodded and turned back to my screen, my mind immediately going to Marta Neil. But that was a month ago.

No way did Glenn know about it. I'd been on the straight and narrow since. I had followed through on my promise to Logan. I was actually feeling better again, chasing all those bad thoughts away with busyness. I had banished the Scumbag sketchbook and reports notebook back into the depths of a closet. Hadn't quite burned them yet, but banishment was good.

Glenn probably just needed to discuss more of my overtime requests.

I blinked away my concern and turned back to my home away from home...my keyboards, radio dock, two color-coded phones and seven monitors. I could keep track of everything under the sun: camera feeds on the main thoroughfares, the local airport alerts, mapping system, incoming calls and transfers, EMS incidents, resources, responders, and radio channels... It might seem overstimulatory, but I liked it.

Our team of just under thirty call takers, dispatchers, supervisors, EMTs, and paramedics operated out of a complex shared with the police and fire departments that serviced four towns. We managed calls about wellness checks, disputes, drunks, rowdy teens, domestics, car accidents, medicals, wildlife issues, runaways...and the occasional B and E or larceny. Today there were two call takers and one dispatcher, me. The three of us could swap roles when needed though.

I listened to radio chatter on active cases, responded to a few PD and fire personnel, and closed out more incidents.

"I got a coupon for that new hot Pilates place. Come with me next week?" Chloe asked.

I smiled. "Don't we sweat enough?" Chloe was a few years older than me and already dealing with hot flashes. I'd had a taste of one or two—not fun.

"Well, the owner is pretty hot..." she said with a smirk.

I chuckled.

She blew a breath over her hot tea. In the dimmed overhead lights, her dark purple gel manicure looked black. My chewed-down nails looked sad even with the bright coral polish I got this weekend on our girls' day out. We also purchased some clothes and books at a local thrift shop, and had gone on a five-mile walk around Malden Lake. It had been rejuvenating.

"Wanna grab a bite at Taco House after shift?" Chloe gestured toward the large and bright 17:21:45 on the clock across the communication room. The clock was sandwiched between a sign that read "*Emergencies are never predictable*" and three television screens with subtitles that showed the news, weather, and the food channel, which provided a sense of non-urgent normality during the calm snatches in our days.

"Probably not today. Logan's got some free time this weekend, and I want to bake him a treat." I loved cake decorating and had made it a tradition to make his birthday cakes every year, and to decorate cookies for him whenever I had the chance. The artist in me loved the fine detail work; the mom in me loved to see him smile when he saw the end result.

He had moved into a teeny, shared apartment in Boston for the summer so he could be closer to the Cordova campaign headquarters. In August, he'd move again, toting the remaining boxes in my garage to Amherst for college.

In a few weeks, I would spend Father's Day alone. Last year, the first Father's Day without Dad, Logan and I commemorated him with a long hike on his favorite mountain trail in New Hampshire. Dad had been like a foster father to Logan. Though Logan denied his grandfather's death was the reason he switched college majors, I knew otherwise. Logan wanted to see justice, too, but at the political level.

We had a lull in activity, so I found myself pulling up the NCIC database at my terminal after getting another coffee. The log-in screen taunted me. Daily. I could run my own scope work if I wanted.

Chloe was busy with something at her workstation, and Sharon, the other call taker, at hers.

My finger hovered over the mouse.

Stirred by the memory of Marta Neil, of those damn sketchbooks, I stared at the blank screen. I had access and certification to search criminal history, look for outstanding warrants, pull up vehicle information, and get fingerprints and other biometrics. But only when requested. Mostly mid-incident, for the officers I dispatched. Sometimes, for Glenn if he requested it. Never just for the sake of looking. The information was need to know, for official duties only.

My fingers floated over the keys, compulsion pulling me into its snare. How easy it could be to search for *him*. A whole slew of information sat there with a few clicks of the mouse.

However, all logins and transactions were recorded by the NCIC. I didn't have a good cover story to explain why I was searching on the scumbag. My mouth went dry.

Jason appeared beside me, quiet like a ghost, and I snapped out of the danger zone of temptation.

"Hey, Liv." Steam emanated from the mug in his hand.

"Hey." I jumped out of my skin and quickly turned my gaze to another one of my monitors. Typed. Moved around the mouse on a map.

"Mind if I use your terminal for a few mins? Glenn needed me to run a search."

"Sure, sure." I stood and stepped away to top off my coffee, which didn't need topping off.

I felt like a child caught red-handed. Well, I wasn't a child, but I was sure as hell about to look at something I shouldn't have been. I had *just* been internally commending myself for my good behavior. What the hell was I thinking? I had been so close to stepping over that edge. Heat flooded my chest. *What the actual hell, Olivia?* Thank God Jason interrupted me.

Come to think of it, I didn't recall Glenn requesting more scope work to be done today or this week. It was something he usually addressed in a team meeting.

Chloe's voice broke through my thoughts. "911, this is emergency operator one-four, Chloe. What is your emergency?" She was already pulling up the caller's location on a monitor. Listening, she clicked her mouse and typed notes into an incident box, then asked, "What is the address of your emergency? Can you hear me?"

Jason and I swapped spots, and I put my headset back on. I let the realization of what could have been just a moment before—me performing an unauthorized search in the NCIC database—evaporate from my conscience as I focused on the task at hand.

More typing. Chloe clicked mute on her headset. "Might need a phone ping." She pulled up the map on her screen. "Never mind. 112 Watson, Olivia."

Usually, call takers and dispatchers never spoke to each other mid-call, communicating via the CAD system only, but this was Caleb again. I sighed. The five-year-old at 112 Watson loved to call 911 while his mom was in the shower. After the police being sent there three times in the past two months, you would think his mom would figure out a way around this behavior, but who was I to judge? Even Logan called 911 out of curiosity when he was little—just once. Was this a rite of passage for all kids?

"Caleb. Can you put Mommy on the phone?" Chloe coaxed.

The call popped into my pending queue, and information populated my CAD monitors as Chloe shipped it over to me. A few clicks and I determined which officers were available and who was the closest to the caller's location. I glanced at units already assigned in the active box. Officer Lagana was going to have a field day with this one. Though I was ninety-nine percent certain this was young Caleb calling for fun, we still had to send a uniform over to check for that one percent. Never assume anything. Always be objective.

Chloe was still typing. "He hung up, but I heard his giggles. Calling back in a minute to notify an adult that an officer is coming over."

A few minutes later, I closed out an incident on a monitor. I clicked off a notification box on the CAD console and cracked my knuckles. Rising, I returned the BOLO binder I had been using earlier back to its shelf in the middle of the room. The hum of radio chatter and Sharon on her station behind us talking to the PD filled the small room as I organized my station for the shift change. Rich came in and we swapped places.

Glenn trudged into the room to make brief announcements and run through the updates from the previous twelve hours. "We had one hundred forty-two calls..."

I ducked out as he droned on; no need to hear my day's work on replay.

As I waited in Glenn's office, I chewed a nail and stared at the whiteboard of dispatch statistics behind his desk. I flipped through my phone to my daily funny cat GIF from Logan. Chuckling under my breath, I sent one back. That goofball would never succeed in convincing me to get a cat. Two unread emails from Irina about the race. *Enough about that race already, Irina!* I deleted both.

Glenn's heavy footfall on the linoleum corridor could be heard long before he reached the doorway.

"What's up?" I turned to him as he entered...and closed the door.

"Did you think I wouldn't find out?" he asked, his arms stretched in front of him, palms pressing onto his messy desk. Frank, brown eyes held mine. He looked haggard beyond his sixties; his frown lines were deep with distress. His tie was loosened around his thick neck.

"Excuse me?"

He slapped a report out in front of me. "We're being audited."

"We get audited all the time. It's routine." I glanced at the pages in front of me and raised an eyebrow. "Unauthorized use of databases?"

He just stared, waiting for me to say more.

"I only use the databases to search when you request it or if an officer requires it from me. You know this, Glenn. I can count on my fingers how often I've needed to do it. Our activity is logged. You can check my access. Jason runs most of the additional criminal checks. He's the senior scope operator. Shouldn't you ask him about these discrepancies? I'm confused." Guilty people rambled. I shut my mouth.

Though it was all truths...I had *just* been contemplating doing this very thing. A hundred thoughts raced through my mind. Had Glenn seen me? No. He hadn't been in the communication room. Had Jason reported me? I hadn't actually *done* anything.

He rubbed his pudgy chin. "I'm confused, too, Olivia."

I waited. He said nothing. The silence in the room made my skin itch. "Have you spoken to Jason?"

"I have. He has no reason to be performing unauthorized scope work."

I clenched my jaw but said nothing. Really? Once I had seen Jason running a report on someone not in our call logs. He claimed it was something Glenn asked him to do. I liked to believe that Jason wasn't up to no good, but you just never knew. I mean, even I had that momentary lapse less than an hour ago. Didn't we all have our moments?

I wiped sweaty palms on my jeans.

Glenn asked, "You think I don't know?"

An invisible hand closed around my throat. I sought the minuscule waft of evening air coming in through Glenn's open window. "Know *what*?" I began to stand, but my knees wobbled.

"Sit down, Olivia. I know about your visit to Marta Neil. She called the police department today to ask more about her B and E case. Apparently, an Officer Rose visited her a month ago..." He left the rest dangling.

"I can explain." Don't people always say that when they know they messed up and have a fat chance in hell of getting out of it?

"Do explain." A lift of a light brown eyebrow.

My tongue was broken.

"I thought we moved past this a year ago, Olivia. Have you been copying and taking home reports again, too?"

"No!"

He had a smear of marker down the side of his pinky, probably from writing on the whiteboard. I hyperfocused on it, my vision blurring with tears.

"Olivia, I've been patient with you. You've done well this past year. You met with the counselor here, took that leave...and have been *normal* again. But now we have call log reports being printed and unauthorized access to databases. Some personal stuff—criminal records, warrants, fingerprinting, vehicle IDs..."

"I swear to God, Glenn, that wasn't me."

He gritted his teeth. "I know how much it upsets you, but it's not our job to catch the bad guys."

I blinked wet eyes and licked dry lips. I knew that, but it was so damn frustrating.

Glenn went over to his water cooler, drew on the spigot, and then handed me the paper cup. I sipped like a person in the desert staring down at a rattlesnake. Less parched, I said, "I only visited Mrs. Neil, Glenn. That's all. Just that one time." Embarrassed, I added, "That attic incident in March...it just sent me back to an ugly place. But it was *one* visit. I have *not* misused any of the databases or printed any reports, I swear it. Please. You need to check with others."

Glenn fell into his chair. "How can I believe you after what happened last year?"

Mess up once and they always remember it. I was the easiest person to blame.

"Just now, Jason asked to use my workstation. Said he had to do some searches for you. But you didn't mention anything in the team meeting—"

"He was probably following up on something."

I swallowed. "I've seen him other times, too. A few that struck me as suspicious. Maybe you should look into that before deciding it's my fault."

He shook his head, like an upset father. The way my dad shook his head when I told him about being pregnant and dropping out of college. I lowered my chin to my chest and hugged myself.

Glenn pushed another set of papers over at me and handed me a pen. "Sign these."

What the hell was this? I sniffled, unable to read the words.

"If what you say is true, then this should not be an issue. The first page is a statement for the Feds declaring that you did not access any of the CJIS system—including NCIC, NGI, and NICS databases—illegally or misuse them in any way, including printing reports or bringing home information. The second is your..." Now he choked on the words.

Don't say dismissal.

My breath hitched.

I picked up the pen and scribbled my signature on the line of the first page. Then flipped it over to read the next page through blurry eyes. Not dismissal. I swallowed the hard lump in my throat. "Leave? You're putting me on leave?" *Unpaid* leave.

"Twelve weeks, Olivia. Just while the FBI does their investigation and to give you...some space. Maybe see that counselor again?"

"That makes me look guilty! I signed the other page. I didn't do it, Glenn. I didn't. Nothing under the scope of CJIS. One stupid visit to Marta Neil. That's it!"

"Which you should *not* have done. And you could use some more time off, Olivia. If the Feds find nothing, great—come back sooner. Maybe it *was* a data error or something else—there was that recent software update."

"Or some*one* else. Please, question others. Is Jason getting the same paperwork? The same treatment?"

"I will investigate others who had access. Regardless, this is for the best. I have a boss to report to, you know. They're going to dig up any past employee incident reports."

As in when I messed up last year.

His sigh was palpable. "No matter what we find about the CJIS misuse, *you* still did something you weren't supposed to, Olivia, and there are consequences."

Gone. Twelve weeks. What would he tell my coworkers? What would I tell Logan?

I signed the second page.

He took the papers and shoved them into a folder. "I won't mention this to anyone unless necessary. We can tell them you went on leave for personal reasons. They'll understand. This job gets to us." He paused, rubbing at a head that lacked much hair to drag his fingers through. "It's been two years since the incident, Olivia. And a year now that you've been on a good track. I'm disappointed in you."

Disappointed.

Same word Dad said. Same damn word.

"I can't allow you to abuse or misuse your position, however justified you think the behavior is."

I nodded, the chastised little girl in me unable to respond.

"We *will* investigate everyone, okay?"

But I was the only one being put on leave.

He dismissed me, promising to check in the following week. I knew he would.

I hiccupped on a sob as I left his office, opting for the side exit so nobody would see the hot mess my face probably was. I had been so good during the past year! Then that one visit to Marta Neil on the heels of that attic incident. Dammit.

I texted Logan. Not about this. Just a simple hello, letting him know I looked forward to seeing him this weekend.

I drove with bleary eyes as I contemplated where I could get a waitressing job or some other part-time employment. My phone rang and I mindlessly hit the green button on my car's console, hoping to hear Logan's sweet voice. If he knew...oh my gosh, I couldn't tell him. "Hello?" I croaked.

"Olivia! Glad I caught you at the end of shift."

Irina. Her voice pinched a nerve. Did she have my schedule memorized?

She dove right into her spiel. The race this and the race that.

"You could use the money, Olivia. And since you're not doing the vacation with Logan anymore, this trip will take you away for a little while, give you some fresh air... You still have vacation time, right? I suspect we'll be going to Maine this year. And what luck! We'll see some gorgeous places. Have a fun adventure!"

Maybe I did need to get away. Winning and getting the sixty thousand bucks per teammate was a long shot, but what did I have to lose at this point? It wasn't like I had anywhere to be this summer. And Irina said the race organization sometimes gave away cash prizes, gift cards, or even some nice material prizes from sponsors. I could use anything at this point. Unpaid leave sucked.

When she finally came up for air, I said, "Fine! I'll join your stupid race!" I clutched the wheel so hard, my knuckles hurt.

Nine

Holden

I'd boxed myself into a corner...and was literally sitting *in* a corner, *on* a box of floral supplies in the back room of Park's Petals. It was mid-June, the Great Garden Race was less than two weeks away, and my teammates were at each other's throats.

Jin bent forward—a hard thing to do with a leg in a cast. "Ini, what about Bryan Peterson?"

"No way," Irina said. "No alliances. None." She crossed her arms.

Jin, let it go, man. Let it go.

As World War III erupted in the back room, I shot off a text to Paul asking if he'd feed Pixie tonight.

Pixie was spoiled, but she was my leading lady. She hadn't given up on me when life got hard. I was grateful Alyssa and Paul agreed to take her in for the two weeks of the race. Jayla would love the snuggles. She even set up a pillow and blanket "nest" in the corner of her room for Pixie.

Paul responded right away.

> No prob. Anything else?

> She likes it warmed up. Fifteen seconds in the microwave.

> Should I give her some of the bass we caught this weekend, too? Have Alyssa broil it with a cream sauce?

> Haha.

He sent me a laughing emoji.

I leaned toward Zach and whispered, "Thought you said these two got along? Are they always at loggerheads with each other?"

"Huh?" he asked before scarfing down a second sugar-laden cranberry-orange muffin. From what I could gauge, the pressure of the race had Zach off the rails with his eating plan. Mr. Health Nut always had a green smoothie or thermos of herbal detox tea or açai bowl and usually declined Irina's confections.

"They're like water and oil?" I suggested, guessing my phrase was too old for Zach. Dude, I wasn't even that much older than him, maybe ten years? Forty wasn't old. I took off my glasses to wipe the smudges with the hem of my T-shirt. Conflict in any form sent the hair on my neck rising. I'd never seen such heated tension fill a room. Even when I was fired after the work accident, the tension hadn't been that bad—probably because I knew I was screwed, and it was best to walk away and put it behind me.

Zach shrugged. "Sort of? Don't worry, they'll work it out."

Jin wasn't coming along, I wanted to say, but like most things, I didn't say it.

Zach wasn't shutting down the heat rising from the other end of the table. Instead, he got up and walked out to...what? Flee from this Great Garden Debacle? Use the toilet? Vape? I'd seen Zach vaping a few times behind the dumpster. I suspected he hid the habit from Jin.

I pulled out the mini Rubik's Cube in my pocket that Jayla had given me for Christmas. The smooth plastic glided beneath my fingertips with each spin and catch. I licked my lips, trying to relax as I twisted and spun the cube. I never thought I'd like Rubik's Cubes, but they were fun, and Jayla had a collection of them. The pyramid was her favorite. I gave her a few for her birthday last year, and we attended a recent speed cuber competition at a high school. She loved it.

I settled my jiggling knee with my fist. Tash hated that nervous tic.

"Listen, Jin, I appreciate your advice, but I still think—" Irina was saying.

"This is more than advice, Ini. I have a stake in the game, too."

He didn't rattle her one bit. She straightened her posture while repositioning a chart. A chart of competitors. Some pages were even laminated. There were piles of lists and spreadsheets and whatnot all over the table. This felt like a military briefing. This wasn't war. It was a race.

She said, "I know you do. You've done a terrific job lining up sponsors and promoting and can continue to do it here from home base. You trust me, don't you? I've been doing this race longer than you, and I *know* the competition. Personally, not just professionally. Besides, the rules state we cannot form an alliance. I won't win by cheating."

"You know Tad and Dottie will."

"That's on their conscience," she said. "And, that is just a rumor."

Silence.

Ouch, dude. Know when you're beaten.

Jin took control to a whole new level, while Zach was the poster child of go with the flow, eager and ready, but also lost in his own world most of the time with the flowers. I saw it around the floral shop, and here it presented itself again. My stomach twisted.

We needed a diplomat in this mix. I could be the peacekeeper. Or Olivia, if she ever showed up for a meeting.

I came over to the table and sat beside Irina. She handed me a packet of logistics. I focused on the race rules, committing them to memory. That seemed to be the easiest place to start while the others squabbled. I was the driver for our team. I most certainly was not the team leader. Voicing reason, I said, "Shouldn't Olivia be here?"

Irina's cheeks pinkened, clearly embarrassed by her stepdaughter's blatant absence.

"Yes, she should, Holden." Zach returned, carrying a flower arrangement. He looked expectantly at me.

I thought I was done for the day. I didn't forget a delivery, did I?

"Why don't we go for a drive?" he said, his mouth wide in his signature smile.

"Come again?" Irina repositioned a teal linen scarf over a loose boho blouse and played with one of her gold hoops.

Jin's face wrinkled in irritation, and his dark eyebrows furrowed together.

Zach darted his gaze away from Jin. "Our fourth teammate isn't here, and she's due a delivery tomorrow. Let's deliver it early. Team pep rally at the Rose home?"

The lightness he was going for felt contrived, but I consumed it like it was a spoonful of sugar, or in my case, sriracha. *Yes, let's get out of here.* "Good idea."

Zach turned to Irina. "Unless you think it's too late tonight? Should we text her? She was supposed to come, but you said something came up."

"Ehm, yes, she said she had work. But Logan told me she was home." She flapped her hand. "Probably a mix-up in her schedule. So yes, she should be home. I'll text her now."

Without looking at his partner, Zach said, "Jin, you can manage closing the front end? Selena is heading out."

Jin tossed a pen onto the pages, scattering a few with a huff. I suspected this race went deeper than money for him.

Man, I'd switch places with you in a heartbeat. But the prize money was nothing to sneeze at.

I had until July fifteenth to send in my deposit for the final year at grad school. That was cutting it close. If we won, I could float the money from my credit card until the winnings showed up, then pay off loans, pay off the lawyers, and even throw some money Mom and Pop's way. With Dad being permanently disabled from work, their funds were tight, too. We had a one-in-thirty chance of winning this race, and that was a heck of a lot better odds than playing the lottery.

Irina was already gathering the spray of pages into a stack. She shoved them into an accordion folder, stood, and then grabbed her handbag. 'I'll bring the muffins."

Zach handed the arrangement off to me, and Irina and I hustled out of the back room, leaving him to talk to Jin.

Irina opened the door for me, and as we approached the parking lot out back, I fished in my pocket for the keys. A motion-sensing light turned on with our movement. I clicked the key fob. My SUV beeped. Oh, wrong keys. I shifted the flower bundle and patted the other pocket. Empty. I must have left the van keys inside, hanging them up for the night.

Balancing the flower arrangement in one arm, I asked, "Can you just wait with these by the—?"

She made her way over to Jorge's commercial van.

"Not that one. This—" I flicked my chin to the empty spot where the Park's Petals minivan usually sat.

It wasn't there.

What the—

My words did not come out. Plus, I tried to avoid cussing.

Zach came up behind me, clearly frazzled by his goodbye with Jin. "Did you move the van out front, Holden?" He scratched the back of his neck and pushed out that usual fake smile.

"No." The flower arrangement suddenly felt like a sack of potatoes. I needed to put it down but didn't, not in this dirty parking lot. A heaviness in my gut joined the weight in my arms.

Irina and Zach walked around the front of the building anyway, not believing me. Why would I park it on the curb? They came back a moment later, convinced I'd been telling the truth. Where was the van?

I had locked it, right? When I returned from my route, Zach had been outside vaping furiously like a teenager in a school bathroom not wanting to get caught. "You heard me lock it, yeah?"

He ran both hands through his short brown hair. "Not sure. You didn't move it or something? I only saw the spare keys by the door inside, not yours. Do you have them?"

I shook my head miserably. Had I left the keys in the van? They weren't in my pocket and weren't on the key holder. We'd never had any trouble at the shop, but last week

Carlos' Pizzeria down the block had reported a delivery car being broken into, though not stolen.

"There must be an explanation," Irina tried, but even she looked weary. "Did Jorge take it?"

Zach's voice rose a note. "No. Jorge went home sick. The explanation is, someone stole our van. What the f—" He shook his head, pinching his lips. "You've got to be kidding me. First Jin's leg, and now this? What's Jin going to say?" He paced, muttering a stream of words that showed he wasn't as opposed to swearing as I was. He looked at both of us. "This is fine. Everything. Is. Fine."

"I'm sorry, Zach. I may have left the keys in the van." My stomach dropped.

I never got distracted. I never forgot things. Or did I and just refuse to admit it? Geesh, now I was gaslighting myself.

Zach resumed pacing and shook his hands at his sides.

Seeing as I was standing there gaping and holding a flower arrangement and Zach was unraveling, Irina took action. "Zach, Sugar, why don't you go inside, tell Jin, and call the police."

He nodded and went in.

She turned to me. "Why don't you put that arrangement down?"

"Not on this dirty pavement." I fumbled for my other set of keys and unlocked my SUV a second time, then nestled the vase filled with honeysuckles and roses on my front passenger seat. I leaned against my vehicle, and Irina busied herself with looking for something in her handbag while also balancing a container of muffins.

Zach returned a few minutes later, looking like he'd just run five laps around the block but less panicked. "Let's take your SUV."

"Shouldn't you wait for the police?" Irina asked.

"Jin has it under control," he said, getting inside the rear door of my SUV. He clapped a hand on the back of the front seat. "Let's do this."

"You don't wanna sit up front? I can move the flowers." At this point, I was just rolling with whatever they said. Was I going to be fired now? For screwing up...again?

He shook his head vigorously. "Nah, I like the back seat."

I said, "Why don't I deliver these to Olivia tomorrow, and we can postpone our meeting?"

Irina gave me a side squeeze and whispered, "Let's do it now. Jin needs something important to do, so he can talk with the police. Zach needs a breather. We need a meeting. Now is as good as any time. She knew we were meeting tonight, and she bailed, but I know for certain she is home and perfectly able to meet."

This was going to be a blast.

Ten

Holden

Irina hopped into the other seat in the back. I clicked the front passenger seat belt around the pretty arrangement. It wasn't my business, but Olivia's monthly rose deliveries had me curious. Overzealous boyfriend, or some sort of flower club? Zach subcontracted a few of those flower-of-the-month plans from big companies.

We drove in silence, my mind replaying the afternoon's events. Had I left the keys on the dashboard? I'd done that before if I knew I was going to be in and out. Then I'd been waylaid by the team meeting... If the keys were nowhere to be found, then it was a no-brainer: I had messed up. Guilt and I weren't strangers.

Twenty minutes later, as I pulled into Olivia's driveway, Irina piped up. "We'll figure it out, okay, guys?"

Zach nodded, absorbed in texting.

I mumbled another "I'm sorry."

If the police didn't find the van, how would we travel in the race? My SUV could hold us, but that meant extra mileage, wear and tear, another oil change...more money. It was also overdue for new brakes and rotors. It sounded selfish, but I didn't want to offer it up. Jorge needed the commercial van for deliveries in our absence, and it wasn't outfitted with rear seats anyway. Maybe we could get a rental car for the two weeks, but even that wasn't cheap.

Irina rang the doorbell.

Olivia opened the door a long minute later. I pushed out a smile from behind the flowers.

"Early delivery!" Irina said cheerfully. "Logan said you were home."

That was weird. I thought Irina had texted Olivia directly, not her son.

"Uh...hi?" Pink crept across Olivia's high cheekbones, and she fidgeted with the hem of her sweater.

Irina began nattering about the race, the floral delivery, and what perfect timing. Then like a freight train, she barged in. Zach followed with some mumbled apologies for the impromptu visit.

I wiped my feet on the outside welcome mat adorned with daisies. I sneezed, knowing it was probably from something in the floral arrangement. My scent might be near null, but allergies still worked at full function.

"Bless you," Olivia said, fiddling with her sleeve now. Caught in a lie or just unhappy to see us on her doorstep?

I handed her the arrangement. "Thanks. Uh, hope we're not imposing?"

She took the bundle, to my arms' relief, and a half-smile tipped her lips up.

Her eyes reminded me of freshly tilled earth, a rich dark brown where the irises almost melded with the pupils. The color matched hair that today was swept up in a messy bun, revealing a graceful neck and turquoise earrings. A touch of pink colored her lips.

On our previous encounter in April, we had worked up to some cordial, "Lovely weather today" greetings and chitchat about the gorgeous flowers in the arrangement. Her son had answered the door for the May delivery. Tonight she seemed...weary...and caught in an awkward lie.

Before I could stop myself, I said, "What did the thirsty bee say to the flower?"

She gave a soft shrug.

"Hey, bud, when do you open?"

Another smile at the pun. A laugh, even. A little one as she snagged my look. I liked her laugh. She had chuckled at some silly pun I told her in April, so I deliberately looked a few more up and had them on standby.

It seemed to work. She leaned in closer and whispered, "As thrilled as me to be having this meeting?"

"Over the moon. Maybe we can hide in the kitchen and they won't notice our absence?"

The tension that had been sitting in my chest eased a bit. At least I wasn't the only one feeling the edge in the air today.

She directed us to the front sitting room, across from the other room where I'd carried her when she hit her head in March. She placed the flowers on the coffee table, then sat on the bay window's cushion seat. I remained standing near her, beside an armchair. Irina and Zach took seats on the couch. He kept checking his phone.

"Should I make some decaf coffee, Olivia?" Irina offered. "Or tea?"

Olivia popped up. "I'll do it."

Irina stood and shoved the muffins into my hands. "Why don't you help her, and Zach and I will spread out the information here on the coffee table?"

I followed Olivia down a creaky hallway.

She turned to me as we walked into the kitchen. "Now we can hide in here for at least ten minutes."

"Want me to start a kettle for tea?" I offered as she set up the coffee pot. "You know how Irina loves her tea."

"That she does. Thanks. Use the one on the stove. Tap water is fine."

While we waited on the brewing pot and for the kettle to whistle, she gathered mugs, spoons, sugar, honey, cream, and tea bags. I laid out the muffins on a platter she handed me.

"Why don't we add some fruit? Apples?" She patted her stomach. "Irina's baking is rich. I gain weight just looking at a cookie or muffin."

She had the soft curves of a woman in her forties. Attractive. Why did so many women self-deprecate? I didn't understand it. Tash used to moan every day about her weight, and if it had gone up a few ounces, the neighbors could hear her cries. She never could take compliments, and I'd meant them. She was beautiful. Olivia, too.

"I'll do that," I said.

She pointed to the bowl of Golden Delicious apples on the kitchen island and a cutting board beside a knife set. I sliced a few apples and spread them out on the platter. She watched the coffee pot brew, tapping a chewed coral fingernail on the table. "Need a splash of something stronger in your coffee?"

I chuckled but waved the offer away, as much as I could use something to wash down the sharp reality that I was doing the race. It seemed like neither of us were up to this challenge. "This is a nice house. Mid-nineteenth century?"

Her eyes brightened. "Yeah. You know houses?"

"Saw the witch's window. Not too many of them around here. I'm a sucker for unique New England architecture."

"I loved that window while growing up. As a girl, I pretended a witch lived in the attic. On Halloween, my mom would tell wicked ghost stories while I ate roasted s'mores. Afterward, we would climb out the window and sit on the roof, waiting for the witch to arrive."

"Sweet story."

She waved a hand. "Anyway, that window wasn't so easy to get out of...you know, back in March. Glad you showed up when you did. I was an idiot. Sorry again."

"You're welcome. And no more apologies needed. Life throws curveballs."

We carried the refreshments into the front room. I took the armchair between Irina on the couch and Olivia on the window seat.

After everyone helped themselves, Irina asked, "Why don't we start with talking about what to expect?"

We nibbled, we nodded. Zach still seemed a bit checked out, glued to his phone, texting. Irina poked him in the ribs, and he looked up, fixing a smile on his face. "Yes, let's. There's a lot to go over now that our team is all here. Time for us to get ready to kick some butt!" He tucked the phone into his messenger bag.

"That's the spirit, Sugar." Irina stirred honey into her tea. "Okay, so there are thirty teams, twelve clues, and twelve days. And one amazing prize!"

Zach had said by getting sponsors, we cut the five-thousand-dollar buy-in significantly. Most of that money went toward our hotel costs, but some went toward the prize and operational costs. According to Zach, even passing the jury process to be a team was a feat. Both he and Irina must have had some pull.

"Alrighty, let's talk about the clues. They tend to be riddles or puzzles. Each clue has four parts we must figure out to complete the 'find' for the day." She lifted a finger for each. "Location—as in the city or town, and the place within that city or town where it is found. The 'thing,' or item that contains the plant. And, the actual plant. An example would be Paul Revere House in Boston, vegetable garden, sunflowers, or John's Bakery in Portland, old china cabinet display, apple pie. And we snap a photo of us four in that exact spot. We need to know our plants, but we also need to be good riddle solvers. Thankfully for us, we know a bit of this and that about New England and have great brains."

"I grew up in upstate New York," I said.

"You live here now, and you know more than you think. Zach says you're good at tinkering and solving puzzles."

I nodded and figured I might as well tell them a bit more about myself. Two weeks together meant we would learn a lot about each other. "I do like to tinker. I was a construction safety officer at my old job and have been working on a master's in civil engineering. I know a lot about machines, instructions, regulations. I also have a thing for maps." I felt a blush come on as all eyes went to me.

"Fabulous! Plus, you're going to be our driving whiz. We each bring something to this team," Irina said.

I pushed my glasses up, relieved to have the conversation off me.

Olivia had yet to sip her coffee, which sat cradled in her hands. "Is the solution to the clue or, uh, puzzle always a plant or flower?"

Irina nodded. "Always a plant...in some shape or form. Anything that grows and is botanical in nature. It could be a tree, crop, shrub, seed, or fruit. In past years, we've had to find living specimens, dried plants, or a picture of one...like in a mural, statue, or photograph, or one as an ingredient in a blueberry pie, or whatever. Be ready to think outside the box."

Zach added, chowing down on an apple wedge, "You may think you know flowers, know landmarks, know the history, but believe me, it's hard. But four brains are better than one. Right, Ini?"

"Right."

Olivia looked at the spread-out charts and lists. "Can we review the rules?"

Irina handed a sheet of paper each to Olivia and me. "First, we have a vehicle."

Zach snorted, letting frustration leach into his expression. "Hardly."

I answered Olivia's confused gaze. "Something happened to the shop van." That knot returned to my stomach.

Irina soldiered on. "But we'll figure out another vehicle if the van's not available. Speaking of vehicles, a crew behind the scenes monitors our progress via GPS."

"Monitors us? Like, tracked?" Olivia interrupted.

"Not a big deal. We bring the vehicle to the approved mechanic the week before the race. There are waivers to sign, which we already submitted, except I need yours, Olivia..." Irina fluttered a dismissive hand. She looked over at Zach to elaborate, but he was sipping his coffee and just nodding along, his brain probably still stuck on the stolen van.

Olivia clearly had some weird vibe with Irina. It was time for me to speak up. Mom always said I had a placating voice—and I had already read the rules.

I directed my look at Olivia, because there was something in those dark eyes that calmed my spirit, and I wanted to calm hers. "Yeah, the GPS is to keep track of us since they're not like chasing us with cameras or anything like *The Amazing Race*. Simply put, we have these twelve puzzles to solve over two weeks. We're given a clue in the morning, and then we're set loose for the day. We have unlimited guesses until we get the answer correct. Once confirmed correct, they tell us what hotel to go to that night."

I waited to see understanding in her eyes. She offered a head nod, so I continued. "The race is really about how *fast* you solve each puzzle. None of the teams get cut on the first day—it's like our freebie day. But they eliminate one team each day during days two through eight."

Olivia sipped her coffee. "And after day eight?"

"For the rest of the race until the end—those final four clues—there are no cuts, no mandatory morning start times, and no required hotel stays. We can submit our answer via text message and, if correct, keep moving."

"Gotcha," Olivia said.

I turned to Irina. "That schedule is tight. Do people finish before the twelve days?"

"Sometimes, but we have compression points to keep us roughly along the same timeline." Irina sipped her tea like she wasn't even fazed by any of this. "After evening check-ins, we get a relaxed night at the assigned hotels, then remaining teams depart with the next clue in hand in the morning." She paused, looking for nods of understanding.

"Does everyone usually make it to the hotel by evening?" I asked.

"Usually."

"And if not?"

Irina shrugged. "They find alternative sleeping arrangements if necessary. But they make sure to get their tushes to the assigned hotel to receive the next clue at eight a.m."

"Alternative? Like camping or other hotels?"

"Mm-hmm."

Olivia furrowed her brow. "So, what happens in the final four legs if there is no mandatory hotel stay? Legs nine through twelve?"

"This is where the sleeping in cars comes in, or we camp or grab a quick snooze at a motel with our own money," Zach said. "With no rigid schedule, we're left to our own devices. Hotels are provided. If we want to just keep on going, we can. But there will be compression points, like Ini said. Like, if a museum or place is closed, we're forced to wait until the next morning, and then the teams are back on the same playing field."

"The way the clues are designed almost guarantees a day-eleven or -twelve finish." Irina covered a yawn. "You three are younger than me, and if I can do it, you can. Zach, you used to compete. Running or something? You're quick as a lick!"

"Yeah, or something," he said softly.

Olivia put her mug down and shared a look with me. I offered a commiserating shrug.

Irina assured us, "People have to sleep. You won't need a triple espresso to get you through it. Nobody goes the last four legs nonstop."

"Unless you're Tad and Doctie," Zach griped.

"Who?" Olivia asked.

Who? was right. Irina and Zach both kept mentioning this mysterious duo.

"Dottie owns another floral shop. Tad's her brother-in-law." Irina hesitated before saying, "They've never been caught but we've had suspicions about them cheating."

"How?" Olivia asked.

"They always place high, even though they seem to take a leisurely pace to solving clues. I'd never seen them frantically rush anywhere—I think they follow other teams and somehow overtake them in the end."

"Overtake them?" I asked.

Zach said, "More like backstab or sabotage the other team they're allied with."

Irina tapped his arm. "Now, now. There's no proof of that. My guess is that they follow other teams, and then just beat them in that final push. Make the other teams do the hard work of solving the clues."

Zach snorted. "And they trip their opponent right before the finish line."

Irina pressed her lips together.

Olivia and I shared a look.

Irina heaved a sigh, seemingly frustrated with this conversation point. "It wouldn't surprise me if they did buddy up with people and manipulate them."

"People have been disqualified mid-race," Zach added.

"Like for cheating?" I asked.

"Yes, for cheating or breaking a rule. A race can bring out the worst—or *best* in a person," Irina said.

Olivia tapped a finger on her mug. "Does this happen often?"

Irina waved the question away. "Enough that we should just...watch our backs. Nothing to worry about, Olivia. We'll follow the rules by the book."

"Alliances and backstabbing? And you mentioned camping, running all night? This isn't like *Hunger Games*?" Olivia said with a grimace.

"Only if you encounter a human-sized Venus flytrap, I suppose." Irina laughed at herself. "This is a scavenger hunt, not a fight for survival. The only thing on the line is a cash prize and a bruised ego or two." Irina put down her empty teacup. "This race is supposed to be fun!"

Zach said with way too much enthusiasm, "And it will be."

This whole cheating-competitors thing had my mind spinning. I cleared my throat and finished with the technicalities, mostly for Olivia, for she looked as tired as I felt. "So, phones aren't allowed. We're given a special phone with built-in GPS, just like the car, but the internet is disabled. Unless you are a good tech geek, you can't change that setting. Texts, photos, calls, GPS. That's all the phone has. We're not allowed to use computers or do internet searching even in public places like at libraries. We're given basic maps, too. The hotels have rooms with basic televisions, no Wi-Fi, and telephones have been removed. No tablets or tech of any sort. No phoning a friend. They'll know. We'll be disqualified. We can't ask the hotel staff for help finding clues or places, but we *can* ask locals, shop owners, and people out and about. But no asking them to look stuff up on phones. Common knowledge sort of thing."

"How will they know? We're not being followed by camera crews like you said," Olivia asked with a hike of an eyebrow.

Irina crossed her legs. "No. But they keep an eye on us the best they can. There are race staff in each town we visit, inconspicuous, but out. Always assume someone is nearby watching."

"We wear GPS watches," Zach added.

"God," Olivia mumbled under her breath. "A tracked car, phone, and watch?"

Irina blinked, unflustered. "It's just to keep us honest and safe. And so they know where we are."

Zach clicked a pen, then nibbled on the end of it as he looked at a chart. "The whole point is to do this as a team. We need to remain within twenty yards—sixty feet—of each other, except after check-in on days one through eight, when watches can come off and we have freedom to shop, eat, explore the town, whatever, until the next morning at eight. Otherwise, stay close. We need to end up together and we don't have a way to communicate with each other, except like whistles or hollers. No walkie-talkies are allowed because it's technology, even if primitive."

Irina picked up an apple slice. "Any more questions?"

Olivia nibbled on her bottom lip. "What if there's an emergency?"

"We can use the phone for calling 911 or the race organizers—there's an emergency number." Irina refilled her cup from the teapot. "If there were an issue back home, they would let us know, too. A few years ago, a team dropped out because someone's wife went into labor, prematurely. If one person needs to go, then the whole team is done."

Zach teased, "Nobody get sick or hurt, 'kay?"

Olivia scrunched her face.

"Information overload," I said to her.

"You can say that." She summarized, "Basically, stay together. No technology. Don't cheat. Nights are relaxing. Then we bust our butts those last four legs."

Irina smiled with approval. "Bingo. We'll be bosom buddies toward the end."

Or cats scratching to get out.

We sat, digesting the information.

Olivia shifted on the bay window seat, closer to me in the chair. "This feels complicated."

I said, "It does. But we'll figure it out together."

Her eyes softened with my acknowledgement. "I could really use this money, and I have some downtime."

"Me, too."

"It'll be fine. Go with the flow," Irina assured us. She clapped her hands on her knees. "How about I read the teaser again?"

Nobody responded, so she did:

"You may need to bike, swim, climb, or row wherever you go...

Be prepared to listen, touch, smell, or taste with haste...

Bring your skills to the table, all who are able...

Amateurs and pros join together in this endeavor...

Bring your flower power, horticultural finesse, and all the prowess you possess...

It's time for the Great Garden Race!"

Zach rolled his eyes. "Who did they get to write this stuff? A kindergartener?"

Even Olivia smiled.

"I think this year's race will be in Maine, given it being the twenty-fifth anniversary and the foundation and race began there." Irina rose and began clearing mugs. "It's getting late. Why don't we clean this up? We'll have more time to plan. I'll email everyone suggested packing lists. We can bring whatever we want so long as it's not electronic. Pocketknives, shovel, gloves..."

"Uh, we're not burying a body, are we?" I asked.

Olivia was the only one who laughed. A woman who liked my jokes was a special kind of woman. All Tash did was roll her eyes...or ignore me.

Irina piled dishes on the tray. "No, but you just never know, do you? Pack for rain and sun. Snacks, comfortable shoes, swimsuits, creature comforts, or camping equipment you may think we need."

Olivia was chewing a nail like it was nobody's business.

After a few more minutes of discussion and a tentative game plan, we said our goodbyes and shoved off.

The next morning, Zach texted the four of us.
Zach:

> The police found the van.

Olivia:

> The van was missing? I thought there was just a repair issue?

Irina:

> Great! The race is still on! Not that it wasn't not on.

Zach:

> Not great. It was stripped. Not salvageable.
> Jin's working with insurance. It might be a few
> months before we get it settled.

Irina with a sad emoji:

> We can take my minivan. Holden, are you okay
> with driving it? It's automatic and has plenty of
> space.

Bless Irina. Always the optimist, always ready with a solution.

There was a pause as three dots showed, then disappeared, then appeared as Zach composed his response.

> You sure?

Irina:

> Yes.

> It's cool. See you July 1.

Irina:

> Get some rest, folks. See you July 1!!

Eleven

Irina

Dropping my suitcase into the back of the minivan, I sang a cheery tune under my breath. It was race day! I just hoped this *petmobile*, as Logan so lovingly called it, would get us through. When the race mechanic installed the GPS this past week, he suggested I get new tires soon, but I lacked time. I'd take care of it after the race.

With a grunt, I rubbed my achy knee. Dr. Ziegler said I needed to take more vitamins. Didn't I get vitamin D from the sun? I ate a salad daily and got my steps in. I didn't need Ziggy telling me what to do. After Jerry's illness, my thoughts on doctors had curdled a bit.

My phone rang from the front seat, but I ignored it while nestling a crate of food in my trunk space.

Violet ran circles around me, her long tail flapping like a flag in the breeze. She chased a butterfly that fluttered around the bushes. "Race day is here, sweetheart! Are you excited to be going to doggy day camp with Lisa?"

She came to me and brushed my thigh. I scrubbed a hand over the goldendoodle curls around her snout and refastened the lobster-print bandana around her neck. She pawed at it. She still acted like a puppy at two years old but was mellowing out the more we worked on her training.

Midway through loading, my phone buzzed once in the front seat with a text message. Ignoring it, I muffled a sigh, praying it wasn't Olivia with cold feet. It was race day, and she was in this, come hell or high water! I'd pick her up, then we'd get Zach and Holden at the floral shop and be at the starting line in Worcester by ten o'clock. Her moodiness was understandable. Logan had told me about Olivia being put on mandatory leave at work—her second time in two years. Of course, she didn't know that I knew. Logan insisted it was just due to exhaustion. I didn't buy it. Try grief. I was here for her, if she would only accept my help. Maybe Father's Day had hit her harder with Logan being away.

If she only knew how much I could relate to some of her feelings. If she would just let me in. She wasn't the only one who missed Jerry. And I wanted a relationship with my stepdaughter. My first husband, Eugene, and I never had children.

She and I had never been the best of friends, try as I might. Her father's remarriage to me probably struck her as happening too soon after her mother died. She missed her. I understood that. I didn't want to replace her lovely mother!

The phone buzzed yet again. "Alright, alright!" I scooped it up and looked at the caller ID. It wasn't Olivia, thank goodness. "Hi, Lisa. Just packing the girls up to come over."

Fatigue put gravel in the voice of the Kibbles and Kisses's owner. "We have an issue, Ini I'm so sorry."

"Are you alright?"

"A pipe burst in the kennel area. The plumber's been here all night." She heaved the world's heaviest sigh. "It's a long story and a mess. Everything's flooded. Shoot...they're waving me over. Listen, I hate to do this, but I have to cancel my bookings this week. I'm sorry, Ini. Will you be okay?"

Lily brushed past me and hopped into the minivan. I stroked her light red golden retriever coat. Despite the early hour, she was already panting with the July heat. I was glad to see her eagerness. Ever since Jerry passed away, she had been depressed. Slower, too. *I know, sweetie, I miss him, too.* I'd never allowed dogs to sleep in my bed, but after Jerry died, it seemed to comfort her to sleep on his side of the bed. Comforted me, too.

Violet barked again beside me. "You know me. We'll be fine. You take care of the pipes and your pups." I swiped the call off. I looked at two pairs of eager brown eyes. My neighbor was already managing my gardens and had two dogs of her own. It'd be a lot to ask of Rhonda to watch them. I could ask my brother, Gus, who lived in Maine. That could be a backup plan if our race ended up being located there. Or maybe a kennel somewhere in Maine. I couldn't leave my dogs with just anyone, though.

A few furry passengers in my minivan would not kill us. In fact, my girls brought life to the party. Their stuff was packed anyway. Decision made, I went into the house to pack more of the necessities. Time to race.

As I pulled up to the floral shop, Zach looked ready to take on the world. His signature smile split his lips, and a travel thermos—likely matcha or something else overcaffeinated—was in his hand. He wore jeans, a white-and-blue-striped T-shirt, and an open navy-blue vest. With a single, smooth motion, he pushed his sunglasses from the bridge of his nose to the top of his head. He always looked sharp, refined, and confident.

The other two looked like I was marching them off to war. This trip would change their serious faces and slumped shoulders. Adventure lay ahead!

When I opened the automatic sliding doors, the light in Zach's expression dimmed. "Thought you already dropped the dogs off at camp. We're going to be cutting it close to starting time."

I unhooked my seat belt and got out to open the tailgate manually in case there had been any shifting of luggage. I smiled at him. Smiles went a long way. With a wave of my hand, I explained, "The doggy day camp had a flood. They canceled reservations. I only got the call an hour ago. I can't find anyone on such short notice. They'll be a great asset. Good sniffers."

"They're not hunting dogs," Olivia protested as she got out of the passenger seat. She had been a bit put out when I picked her up earlier and explained the dog issue.

I huffed. "They're good company, well-trained, and love car rides." That was a little lie on Violet's part, but now was a great time to drop her into the deep end. Lily was my mature dog and loved long car rides and hikes. Violet had endurance and youth on her side. What could go wrong?

Holden helped load his and Zach's bags into the tailgate. "Dogs aren't against the rules, are they?"

I winked at him. This man loved rules. "No. Dottie Jones brought her chihuahua last time. Violet and Lily are the best guard dogs, too, and they sleep all night. They hardly bark."

The dogs would be just fine in the hotel room I would share with Olivia. The race typically provided two rooms, each with two beds, per team. Zach and Holden seemed agreeable to sharing the other one.

My backup plan, if my busy brother didn't have room for them at his house in Millinocket, was to leave Violet and Lily at another dog care center in Maine. I had a few places I could call, but I planned to text Gus a heads-up before we had to turn over our phones today. That was *if* we were heading to Maine.

"Do we need to put anything in the Thule?" Holden asked, pointing to the storage container on the roof rack.

"I have camping things in there, just in case. Better to overpack than be left wanting," I said. "There is room in the trunk for the rest of our gear."

As Zach put his backpack into the trunk space, the gin and Zinfandel bottles clinked in my crate of travel luxuries.

"Ini, we've got enough booze here for a good time! What did you do? Break into the packie?

Olivia stiffened beside me, her look souring.

Poor choice of words, Sugar. But he didn't know about that awful night. I'm sure she already felt like the van being stolen was a bad omen.

"It's going to be a long two weeks. We might as well make it lively." I liked to be prepared. I readjusted the plastic container of assorted Greek cookies. The crate also held tonic and limes, instant oatmeal, almonds, peanut butter pretzel bites, apples and bananas, and bougasta, which we'd have to celebrate making it through the first day intact. Olivia didn't like to admit it, but she loved that custard pastry.

Zach poked his nose in, admiring the pastries. "Ini, you should open a bakery someday. Jin and I can help you figure out the logistics."

Even Holden smiled. "My sister would love some of your desserts for her restaurant, Irina. Really. She gets hers from local bakeries."

Though it was a fun idea, I waved it and the compliments away.

Holden was a handsome man. When he smiled, he looked like that actor who played the duke on *Bridgerton*, but with glasses and a bit older, wiser. I suspected he was in his early forties, like Olivia. His reserved nature was a good match to hers. Sometimes opposites attract, like Jerry and I, but sometimes we need a kindred soul. I'd make sure Olivia sat in front with Holden, and they could commiserate together—or perhaps find a nice friendship.

As we finished loading the luggage, my mind hummed with excitement for the days ahead. My goals for this trip were clear. One, have fun. Two, connect with Olivia more. Winning the prize was just a bonus. I had a good retirement account from my former career as an elementary school teacher. My parents had both immigrated here, and I'd spent my childhood watching my father struggle with his limited education, so teaching had called to me. Even though I was successful in a career I loved, my first husband and I were never blessed with children.

Sometimes, life delivered bumps in our desired paths.

Flashes of heat filled my chest, and I was suddenly sweaty. Not a hot flash, long since passed for me, nor one of my rosacea flare-ups. Something purely mental. I fanned myself as if it were the sun triggering the pulling sensation on my skin.

I looked at the group. "Ready for some fun?"

Zach gave an enthusiastic, "Hell, yes!"

Holden and Olivia...well, I would work on firing them up.

We got into the minivan, Zach taking the captain's seat beside me, Holden as driver, Olivia as copilot, and my sweet girls in the third-row bench seat. Zach gave Violet a rub under her chin. "We're going to slay this, right, you gorgeous pooch?" Violet licked his hand. "Love the new collar, Ini. Purple pansies. It's so cute."

Zach plugged in the conservancy's Worcester location into his phone's GPS and handed it to Holden, who placed it in the cupholder. "Everyone have their phone?"

All mumbled a yes.

"We need to turn them over at registration. They'll put them in a lockbox for safekeeping," Zach said.

"What's preventing a team from bringing secret phones?" Olivia asked.

"Integrity," I said.

Holden and Olivia shared a dubious look.

"Okay, time for a team-building exercise," I declared.

"Shouldn't we have done this before the race?" Olivia asked.

Well, I *had* planned to. She hadn't shown up to any of the pre-race meetings except the one where we barged in with her flower delivery! I understood being down and missing Logan, needing respite from the stress of work, but enough was enough.

Zach suggested, "First up, race names?"

"Race names?" Holden asked as he turned out of the parking lot.

Zach dipped a hand into his vest pocket and pulled out a stick of gum. "How about this year we earn them by what we do along the way? Or like, who we are. Our quirks?

We did that once when Jim and I joined a group hiking the Appalachian Trail. We got trail names."

I was grateful Zach was enthusiastic. "Good idea. Race names can wait."

Olivia chewed on a thumbnail and looked at her cell phone, probably checking in with Logan. Holden was silent, focused on the drive.

I consulted the pile of index cards that I pulled out of my handbag. "Let's each share three of our strengths. Our assets."

The two in the front literally moaned.

"Don't be such killjoys. We can do this. I'll go first." I considered my skills. "I love plants and know a lot about them. I'm a people person and have friends in all corners of the country. I've traveled a lot around New England, so I'm well acquainted with some lesser-known places. There. Not hard. Zach, you're next."

He scrunched his face, clearly giving it thought. He played with a pen in his hand. "Umm, I also know a lot about plants. I have a degree in botany and a minor in design. I've got good stamina and a killer memory. That's three, or four."

"Fabulous. Holden?"

He tapped a finger on the steering wheel while we waited for the light to turn green. "I like maps and knowing how things work."

"Great," I coaxed. "Two great skills for this trip. And?"

He gave a self-deprecating laugh. "I'm a good driver."

"That's a freebie. Pick one more," I said, glad he was getting into this.

He scratched his forearm. "I'm good with instructions and details, and not too bad at puzzles. I'm a visual person. I like to find patterns in things. Is that a skill?"

"It is to me," Zach said. He patted Holden's shoulder from behind. "Good skills, man. Remember that fridge issue you helped us with? You're a great engineer and tinkerer. I can't wait to be wowed by your brain."

I prayed an internal and abbreviated Hail Mary and then said, "Olivia?"

She fussed with her seat belt. "This is silly."

The sad thing about Olivia was that I knew she was a likeable person and pleasant to be around...she just saved her sour for me. Stepmoms never got a break, I supposed.

"We each have skills to bring to the table," I assured her.

We waited while she thought, coiling a lock of hair around her fingers. "I know first aid," she said.

"Great, and I have the first aid kit. What else?" I said sweetly, though honeyed words never worked with her.

"I don't know much about plants," she said quietly.

"So you say. You're a talented artist and you draw them in your sketchbook, don't you? Your monthly deliveries?"

"Sure, but—"

"No buts. That's a talent. You have an eye for detail, too."

It pained me to know that Olivia didn't get her first choice in life. I wished she knew I was proud of her no matter what she did. She was an artist and would eventually find her place. She loved art in all its forms, and she was so skilled at decorating those birthday cakes for Logan. Maybe if I opened this hypothetical bakery Zach suggested, Olivia could join me...decorating cakes or something. Would that be enough to fulfill her art dream, though?

"You and Holden have some things in common." I thought back to the days she'd left Logan with me for babysitting. "You keep great notes. You're meticulous."

"That's fire, Olivia. Really. I'd love to see some of your sketches," Zach said.

"They're just flowers."

He wagged thin brown eyebrows and tapped a canvas bag with magazines spilling out. "Flowers are my life, girl."

"*Faux to Fab*?" I asked, pointing to them.

"Don't you know it. Won't leave home without at least one, plus other regional magazines that might help us. And my botany books."

"Those are allowed?" Holden asked.

"Totally. Even encouraged."

I nodded. "We can use hard copies of old-school any-thing. Magazines, maps, books, any notes we compile ahead of time or during the race. I stacked a few of your old encyclopedias in the back, too, Olivia."

"You packed my *what*?" Olivia turned around.

"Jerry had your old books in the basement. I was clearing some things out this summer and came upon the encyclo-pedia set. He said how much you loved to read them—that you liked to play librarian." I cleared my throat to return us to the previous topic. "What else?" I asked Olivia.

"What else what?" She crossed her arms and stared out the window.

"One more of your skills."

Olivia's voice grew quieter. "My job requires me to be quick-thinking and calm under pressure, and...and I'm good with maps, too. I look at them a lot for work and can calculate response times, distances..."

"Didn't you and Chloe deliver a baby a few months ago? Talk about calm under pressure. I was in awe, really."

She shrugged. "That was Chloe."

Olivia never gave herself enough credit.

I blew out my breath. "Now that wasn't so hard, was it? Next up: team roles."

The teams gathered in the parking lot at the Francis New England Botanical Conservancy's headquarters in downtown Worcester. Food trucks, concession stands, volunteers in bubblegum-pink and lime-green T-shirts, tech crews, the mayor, and a gathering of onlookers over-ran the parking lot. The local news stations were here, interviewing. Music blared from speakers beside the stage, which was decorated with balloons, also pink and green. This year's over-the-top feel gave me a little high.

I rolled down the windows and left the girls in the minivan. After checking in, handing over our phones, and being given our bag of essentials, we waited while GPS units were double-checked in the vehicles. Not until the strike of ten would we get the first clue.

Teams milled around, eating donuts and breakfast bur-ritos, drinking coffee, socializing with each other—more like eyeing up their competition—or speaking with family or friends in the crowd.

A few newbies meandered around, but otherwise, I saw a lot of the same faces: Janet Brighton from the church consignment shop and her gaggle of flower-lov-ing cousins, Vernon and Trish Thebeau with their two sons, and Maddie and her group of Mainers. I waved at her. Good people, the lot of them. I'd be happy to share the podium with them.

The sky was bright blue, and the humidity a spot higher than I liked. Two of my teammates still looked less than excited to be here. By the end of the race, Holden and Olivia would be thanking me for this adventure. Finishing today would help their morale, I was certain.

Douglas Francis strolled toward me, his smile wide. "Irina, you look ready to take on the world. All set?"

I fanned my cheeks. It was too warm for the three-season scarves I used to draw attention away from my pink skin. I wore a lightweight teal neck bandana instead. "Set to win? Yes. Set to sweat? No."

He laughed, and I toyed with my earring, suddenly jittery.

Douglas and I made idle chitchat.

Tad Thurlow walked around with Dottie Jones, both hamming it up for the journalists present. I never understood Tad's reason for doing this race. He was an accountant working for his brother's tech company. Maybe it was the prestige. Same with Dottie; well, the exposure was good, too, for her floral shop.

A coordinator approached and tapped Douglas's arm. "Showtime," he said with a small laugh. He rubbed his chin, looking down at his shiny shoes. He had to be hot wearing a full suit today. "Irina, I was wondering if, uh, after the race is over, if you'd like to grab a coffee at the new café in Wellford."

Coffee? With Douglas? A bubbling sensation bounced in my midsection, and I could use a cold compress on my neck right now.

"I've been wanting to catch up for a while, but the race has kept me busy, and since you're a competitor...I can't...you know..." He looked down into his paper cup of coffee. How could he stand a hot drink on this hot morning?

"Yes, I'd love to," I said, saving him from any more awkwardness. It had been two years since Jerry's passing. It was time to at least entertain the thought of dating.

"Great, great." Delight pooled in his dark eyes.

Another volunteer waved vigorously at us.

"I need to go make the announcement. Good luck." He gave my hand a squeeze.

Zach approached with Jin—who arrived earlier—at his side on crutches.

Zach's gaze followed Douglas, who now walked toward the stage. "Does that man have a swagger in his step for you! What did you say to him, Ini?"

I blushed as Zach poked me in the side.

He rubbed his hands together. "Okay, what torrid secrets did you get out of him? My eavesdropping around Tad and Dottie got me nothing. They're just bragging about sponsors. But someone spilled their coffee on Tad's shoes and he almost lost his shit on them."

"None," I said with a casual air, fighting the urge to fan my face.

Olivia and Holden came over to join our group, each with a donut in their hands. Chloe and Yasmine, two of Olivia's coworkers, waved enthusiastically at us from the sideline. Olivia gave a soft wave back to them.

Douglas approached the mic. The music was lowered, and he greeted the crowd, but I heard little over the sound of my quickening heartbeat—snatches of introductions, rules, and sponsor announcements. People clapped and cheered.

"...we'll see you at the finish line! Teams, take your places!" Douglas said.

Zach squeezed my arm as we gathered with the rest of the teams at the tape markings, which were our starting lines. "We're going to slay this, Ini."

I swallowed. "Yes, we will."

Douglas walked down the line of teams, handing us our first green-and-pink envelopes embellished with the Francis New England Botanical Conservancy's logo of a simple pink rose and green stem. Adrenaline rushed through my veins.

"Good luck, Zee. I'll be following you on YouTube." Jin gave Zach a quick cheek peck and made his way back to the spectators. It was nice to see him in better spirits than a few weeks ago, now that he'd accepted the fact that he was staying home.

The big clock beside the podium began its countdown. The crowd joined in, voices ringing out.

"Ten...nine...eight..."

I cleared my head. We had this. I put my hand into the center of our circle. Zach put his on mine. Holden and Olivia stared at our joined hands. *Come on, you drags.* I looked at my stepdaughter expectantly.

"Four...three..." the crowd shouted, louder.

Olivia put hers on Zach's, and Holden laid his on Olivia's. "Go team!" Zach and I said in unison.

"One!" the crowd roared.

We lifted our hands in a cheer, and Zach tore open the first clue.

Twelve

Zach

With shaky hands, the anticipation around me palpable, I read the first clue aloud:

"*Ready, set, grow!*"

"Looks like we'll have some tongue-in-cheek titles for each clue?" Irina peered over my shoulder. Like a lavender pillow sachet, her familiar perfume felt like home, and it settled some of my jitters.

I read the rest:

"My neighbor to the west celebrates me yearly
with a Father's Day soiree,
But my blue cousin to the south glories in her charm
around Uncle Sam's payday.
My distant sister awakens while the rest of us are sleeping.
I was named for minerals wolfed from soil, but to the
contrary

My spiky peas help other plants feel airy.
Once you figure out my identity, to the sea—
To the Jewel of the Maine coast take thee!
To the building that has the most stories.
Children sit among the gathered spines—that have no bones—
The one next to Island Boy is my home."

Irina shook my arm. "Maine! I was right. Let's get to the minivan."

Thirty teams scrambled to their designated vehicles in a mash of energy and discussions as the DJ on stage played a tune. The crowd scattered with a few whoops of encouragement.

"Go Park's Petals!" Jin shouted. I blew an air kiss to where he stood alongside a few of the kids supported by the Flower Child organization.

"Watch me on YouTube!" I waved at ten-year-old Sofia, who was wearing a superhero costume with a pink tutu, and five-year-old Enrique, who showed off his new running shoes. Flower Child paid for extracurriculars like her ballet classes and his soccer fees. Jin and I had decided early on that a portion of our winnings would go to the organization. It would be great to have the chance to do more for them than donate flower arrangements. Flower Child's donors had grown sparse in the past few years, and I would hate to see the organization struggle due to lack of funding. Though my relationship with competitive sports had soured as an adult, I understood how meaningful it was for these kids, and I wanted to foster their passions any way I could. At one time, swimming had been my life.

We clambered into the minivan.

"Olivia, the map is there on the dash." I pointed. She grabbed it and tried to hand it back to me. "No, girl. You'll be our Map Queen."

"But—"

"You work with maps all the time?"

"Yeah..."

"Then you'll do well. Irina and I will be back here to work clues together. Here." I handed her a pile of additional maps from Google. "Just in case, I printed close-ups of Maine, and well, the other states. We can recycle those," I added, hating the waste of paper when a phone would have been much easier.

"Look at you! Mr. Organized," Irina said with a bright smile.

"What can I say? You must be rubbing off on me, Ini." The fine hair on the back of my neck rose as the rush of today hit me. I fidgeted with the vape pen in my pocket. I'd allowed it to sneak into my life during the past six months. Instead of using it, I popped another piece of gum into my mouth. Might help my motion sickness, too.

It was less bad in the back seat. Not sure why. I had taken an anti-nausea pill earlier, to be safe.

The dogs stirred behind us. Irina hushed them with a wave.

"They're easing us in," I said. "They want us to get to the right state and be on the same playing field tomorrow morning for the first elimination day. Maine! Like you thought."

We shared a fist bump.

"The coast is our first stop. So, I-95? What is this 'Jewel'?" Holden's soft-spoken voice matched his patient driving through the mass exodus of cars from the parking lot.

"Holden, time to go full throttle. If you wait for those cars to go, we'll be at the tail end. Push out," I said. "You can handle Worcester's rush hour, narrow roads, and steep hills. You can totally handle this."

"Today is no rush?" he asked.

"Correct, but the first teams get the nicest hotel," Irina said, then added, "Not that they're ever *not* nice, but... Well, it's kind of fun to stay in the upscale places."

"Bragging rights." I winked. "And everyone sleeps better on nicer pillows."

"We don't want to be in Boston traffic," Irina said. "Inland is better until we reach the Maine Turnpike." She gave directions.

Irina was chomping at the bit to lead. She was the veteran of these races. I preferred solving the puzzles over decision-making. Have at it, girl!

"Are people going to piggyback?" Holden asked.

I looked over my shoulder as vehicles dispersed left and right on the street. "They may. Drive fast or take some weird turns? Drift?" I teased.

"This ain't *Fast and Furious*. We agreed I'd stick to the speed limit...ish," Holden said.

"Okay. It's too early for jokes, I guess."

"I suggest we go up I-190 first, then Route 2." He turned again at a stop sign and looked in the rearview mirror. "Most are going east, probably taking I-290. Then I-495 to the Maine Turnpike."

The minivan was sweltering, and I adjusted the AC in front of me. "Ini, the AC? It's churning out heat."

She flapped a hand, but said, "Holden, can you open the rear windows? My AC is a bit moody."

Moody AC in July? I was regretting this minivan already.

Between the dog funk, heat, and nerves, I hoped I wouldn't upchuck. Irina's dogs were well-groomed, and I wasn't exactly allergic to dog fur, but my eyes were watering. As for my motion sickness, Holden was a good driver, his pressure on the pedal smooth. "Ini, let's break it down line by line."

Irina took the envelope from me. "You, drink some water."

I sipped obediently.

"'Neighbor in the west'?" she asked.

"If we're going to Maine, that's New Hampshire. Soiree could mean a festival or celebration," I said. "A blue 'cousin' to the south could be anything. Maybe same family of plants, but not same species?"

"Smart," Irina concurred.

"'Uncle Sam's payday' is Tax Day, April fifteenth, so that means spring," Holden said. "And Father's Day is mid-June."

"And this sister that is *far away*, but awake when we are sleeping?" My stomach gurgled. I never should've had that donut, and not only because too much road food would mean extra gym time once I returned home.

Irina licked her lips. "Somewhere far could be out of the country? 'Sleeping'...could mean something dormant currently or not blooming. So, if this distant sister is awake, something here is dormant, or vice versa." She tapped a nail to her lips.

"Right. Let's table that. The pea family...so that's Fabaceae."

"I love your botany background, Sugar. What's something that wolfs minerals?"

"Play on words. But it also says on the contrary." I chewed on my gum. Blew a bubble. "Why wolf? Canine...teeth...eat..."

I sipped more water as we sat pondering the clues.

I had a weird new feeling about this year. Relief.

I felt relieved because Jin couldn't come along. Was that horrible of me?

Maybe he and I needed space. The old saying was absence makes the heart grow fonder. And sometimes I wondered if Jin was onto me, that he suspected I was holding back from telling him something big. How could I, though? What would he think if he knew the truth? That I was a coward? How could he love a guy who hated jumping out of planes and scaling mountains and who cowered at the first sign of swimming? Our second date had been mountain biking at a terrain park with wicked inclines.

"Remember when we first met?" he'd asked last night, rolling a few of my T-shirts for the suitcase.

"Like it was yesterday." I nestled socks into sneakers, then shoved them beside a pair of jeans. "You couldn't tell a ranunculus from a peony back then."

"Zee, those two look a lot alike! You know how my dad never stapled the cards with the customer address to the arrangements, and had sloppy writing, so I had to guess who got what arrangement based on notes he wrote on a clipboard. And yeah, not everyone can be a walking flower encyclopedia like you."

He leaned over and rubbed my shoulders and neck. Ahh, his thumb massaged right where a knot formed from hunching over flowers. I said, "You've come a long way with flower identification."

"I still can't keep dahlias and zinnias straight." He laughed and returned to putting toiletries in my bag. He kissed my cheek.

When we first met, it *had* been interesting. Jin had come to my house with an arrangement meant for someone else down my street. 51 Sumac Road, not 81 Sumac.

The arrangement was gorgeous. As was he. Even flustered, he had this sweet smile that just took my breath away. I think it was his vulnerability that I found attractive. Take-charge Jin was admirable, but I loved when he broke down the ego wall and let people see his humility. Nobody was perfect. Especially me.

After some chitchat, what ensued was me deciphering the floral orders—matching each arrangement to its recipient—while Jin drove to the addresses. It was like a game of *Memory*.

"That was fun," I admitted. I'd ridden with him all over town, getting high off a van filled with the nectar of flowers and greenery and a very hot guy. I had been in between post-college jobs, and Jin's dad hired me a few weeks later.

"Then I invited you out for a coffee. That was also fun." He leaned in and kissed me. As he pulled back, leaving behind a warm tenderness on my lips, he said, "I'm sorry I've been a jerk. I can blame it on the broken leg, but I know it's more than that. I've been stressed this year. The books, Zee. And my dad hassling me, telling me we're not doing it right."

I hesitated before saying, "But winning isn't everything, Jin."

"It is to me." He smacked his cast, then flopped back on the bed with a groan of frustration.

What about me? Aren't I everything to you? Would Jin still love me the same if he knew how I felt about all this thrill-seeking? I threw an extra T-shirt into my suitcase. "Hey, we're getting good social media likes and comments already by just participating."

He sat back up. He looked at his cast like it was a twenty-pound weight. "I can't wait to get this damn thing off! Oh, maybe I'll follow up on a few of those excursions for

New Zealand while you're gone. I was able to score a good deal on spelunking."

"Good idea," I mumbled.

He tucked a baggie with little slips of folded paper in it under a T-shirt.

"What's that?"

"Just a little something for you. But don't open it until the first night, okay?"

"Oh?" Now my interest was piqued. Jin and his little notes. I loved that soft side of him.

He smiled.

Then he showed up this morning and brought along Sofia and Enrique. That had been sweet.

And another reminder of how important winning this race was.

There would be no second place for me. Not now, not ever again. Because this would be my last race of any sort. When I got home, I was going to tell Jin the truth. I had two weeks to figure out how. My throat tightened. I could not go into marriage with this dark cloud over me. And I was not going into the adrenaline-laced trip he was planning without full disclosure. New Zealand was a gorgeous country that we could experience without risking our lives. I once went there for an international swimming competition. The water was pristine, the beaches, mountains, people, flowers all stunning. We planned our trip for November because I wanted to see the lupine along the alpine lakes. I wanted to take night photos at the Church of the Good Shepherd surrounded by the purple and pink flowers...

"That's it!" I yelled, pumping a fist in the air and startling a dog behind me. She barked.

New Zealand could be the *far-away sister*, and it was winter there in the southern hemisphere, so plants would

be dormant during our summer. Or it could be somewhere in South America. Either way, I knew the plant!

"What, dear?" Irina looked up from a stack of magazines she must have pulled from my canvas bag.

"Ini, I got it!"

Holden took a hard turn, and our bodies swayed in the
minivan.

"Sorry, guys. You said to drift, didn't you?" he teased,
but I could tell he was bothered by something. "I think
someone was tailing us. I was trying to lose them."

"For mercy's sake," Olivia mumbled, holding on to the
handlebar above her passenger window.

"Sorry," Holden said. "I'll take it easier. Just, I had to
shake that guy behind me." He blew out a nervous laugh.
"They turned into the grocery store so it wasn't a tail.
Excuse the paranoia."

I tapped the back of his seat. "Good thinking, though.
No such thing as paranoia when you have cheaters like
Tad and Dottie. And their MO is tailing others."

"You were saying, Zach?" Irina coaxed.

The AC finally started to blow drafts of icy coolness,
and the sweat on the back of my neck slowed its descent
down my back. "Lupine."

She looked at the clue again. "Yes. A sleeping or *dormant* sister far away!"

"New Zealand lupine," we said in unison.

"Or Andean lupine," I added.

"Indeed!" Irina flapped a travel guide for Maine. "Camden
is known as the Jewel of the Maine Coast, Holden, in answer
to your earlier question." She skimmed the travel guide-
books. "Look, there's an annual lupine festival in mid-June
in New Hampshire. That's our neighbor to the west cele-

brating around Father's Day. What about the southern blue cousin, Zach?"

"Bluebonnets are found in Texas and peak in April—around Tax Day—and they're similar but different from the wild lupine seen in alpine regions. All the same genus, though. So, our 'cousin.' We've got lupine. We've got Camden. What about the rest of the clue? The actual location?"

Olivia said, her voice tentative, "A library?"

Irina read the ending lines again. "'To the building that has the most stories. Children sit among the gathered spines—that have no bones—The one next to *Island Boy*, is my home.'"

Olivia nodded with more assurance. "*Island Boy* is a children's book. Logan loved it as a kid. But it doesn't have lupine in it that I can recall. Maybe the library has some lupine on its grounds?" She chewed a nail. "*Miss Rumphius*. My mom used to read that book to me. I think it's by the same author as *Island Boy*. It has lupine."

"That's it!" I clapped a hand on the back of Holden's seat, and he jerked the minivan again. "Sorry, sorry." But we had directions, we had some ideas. "Let's go, Speed Machine."

He said, "No, man."

"Furiously Fast? Come on, everyone wants to be like Vin Diesel. You need a cool nickname as our driver and head engineer."

He lifted his gaze to the rearview mirror to give me an "Are you serious?" look. Always serious, Holden. We'd get him to loosen up.

"Torque?" I suggested.

Now he shook his head and laughed.

"How about Wheelman?"

Olivia said softly, casting a sidelong glance at Holden, "I like Torque."

He returned the look briefly, the most tender smile emerging. Oh, man, was he crushing on her?

"See? Come on. You're good with mechanical things. You're a good driver. Torque?" I looked around. Irina smiled. Olivia nodded.

"Only if you let me pick yours," Holden relented.

Ohhh, he had some sauce beneath that quiet exterior. "Agreed. Torque it is. We're gonna slay this, guys."

Thirteen

Olivia

As we drove north on scenic U.S. Route 1 through the holiday traffic, I let the breeze run its fingers through my messy hair. The AC had gone hot again, so we'd rolled the windows down. I swiped sweat off the back of my sticky neck.

As the navigator, I'd put us on this road because I wanted to see the coastline, the vacation I would've had with Logan. Consider it my consolation prize. I'd only visited Maine once. As a kid, our family of three camped in Acadia. Eventually, I'd get up this way with my son. I missed him so much already.

I banished those thoughts. No need to tap the well of grief.

There were no eliminations today, so we could relax a bit, and damn, did my nerves need relaxing these days. But belatedly, I realized why Irina had suggested the inland route, though on the map it seemed out of the way and slower. Route 1 was slower still.

As we wound our way along the coastline, traffic thinned in spots, then bottlenecked near notable turnoffs or in seaside towns. I relished my view of classic Maine, even though Bath and Wiscasset were bumper-to-bumper. A mob of people lined up on the downtown corner in Wiscasset to get lobster rolls from a little shack. My stomach gurgled. Holden smiled at me—a handsome sight—and I munched on a granola bar to temper my hunger.

After a long stretch of quiet, Zach handed me a stack of CDs. "Here, Olivia. I wasn't allowed to bring my earbuds, so I made mixes using an old burner. Every road trip needs tunes."

I slipped a disc into the minivan's CD player. Did newer cars even have CD players anymore?

Holden smirked. "This feels so 2002. MapQuest and CDs."

"Google Maps. None of this MapQuest nonsense," Zach corrected. "I put oldies on there for you two boomers."

"Dude, Gen X," Holden countered.

Though he and I might qualify as older millennials, I definitely related more to Gen X.

Zach clapped the headrest behind Holden. "The sass comes out!"

Holden smirked.

I couldn't *not* smile in response to Zach's energy—he reminded me of Logan, down to those sparkling baby blues filled with youth.

Music from the late 1990s and early 2000s began to play. Were these oldies now? Is this how Dad felt when I liked The Beach Boys as a kid?

Even Holden was tapping his fingers on the wheel. Suddenly, he said, "Pun time."

"Pun time?" I asked.

"What does a flower say when it's surprised?"

I was lousy at puzzles, so I shrugged, but he piqued my interest. I fed him the line, "What?"

"What in carnation?!"

We laughed. "You really like puns, don't you?"

"I like your laugh more," he said.

Warmth invaded my chest.

As we drove north toward Rockland, I inhaled briny coastal air. "Oh, I need to get saltwater taffy for Logan."

"Good idea," Irina chirped from behind me. "I promised my friend that I'd get her blueberry jam and whoopie pies."

I admired the inlets and harbors as low tide lapped lazily along marshy shorelines. Sailboats and fishing boats bobbed in the gentle current when we passed yet another idyllic seaside harbor. The sun speckled the dark blue waters of the north.

I wished I could send Logan a photo. Or text him.

Before I left, my now adult son, wise beyond his years, ordered me to have fun, to take it in, to enjoy myself. *I'll try, Logan.* I hoped I could keep my promise. However...

I hadn't thrown away my Scumbag sketchbook as I promised, nor the notebook with the WRECC call log records and pertinent notes from authorized searches. Yeah, I know, I had a sick obsession. Acknowledgement was the first step in healing. However, there were a billion other steps. Kudos to me for leaving both those notebooks behind, at least, back in the closet. Out of sight, but not out of mind. Was that step two on this journey?

Could I take it?

Yes, I could. I would.

After I saw the perp brought to justice.

Righting a wrong could easily become a slippery slope. I had never run unauthorized searches in the NCIC database, as I had sworn to Glenn.

But it didn't mean that I forgot what I saw while running a scope for an officer, or when Jason and I were authorized to do follow-up searches after an incident. When needed, we could unearth a lot in the databases. I had memorized the important facts about a few people we ran scopes on, especially those with B and Es or other criminal histories. I had a few names and addresses tucked away inside my mind of those that served their time and were released, or were never convicted for the case on file, but had prior criminal histories.

One perp just happened to have a Maine address, of all places.

Was it him? I didn't know.

If we so happened to drive past this man's residence while on the race, well, then...

I *was* the navigator. It was worth a check, right? Like my visit to Marta Neil, it was a long shot.

Heat tingled in my cheeks despite the cool ocean air whipping my face. I had messed up badly. So badly. Glenn said we'd have a meeting a week before I returned to work, and he would keep me abreast of the audit. Nobody else had confessed. Perhaps it was just a misunderstanding. I had seen Jason a few times...but I couldn't imagine my coworker abusing our access to the databases. That carried a hefty federal charge.

The fact that I hadn't been fired over visiting Marta Neil or my previous lapses in judgement was a miracle. Glenn had been my guardian angel the past two years. I swiped a tear beneath my sunglasses. I could do better. I *would* do better.

I would move on from the burglary, just as easily as Irina seemed to move on from my dad's death. She'd looked chummy with Douglas Francis.

Holden said as if he had been pondering it for a few minutes, "I've never seen a lighthouse." His soft words were a life preserver in a choppy sea.

"Really?" I asked, hiding a sniffle.

"Really."

"Well then, lucky for you, we're in Maine," Irina said.

Why did her voice sound grating?

Wow, I really was a bit of a cranky mess today.

A seabird swooped down into the inlet, diving for a fish. I took out my disposable camera. It abided by the no-technology rule. Logan would appreciate the pictures.

Irina tapped my shoulder after I snapped a few. She shoved a boxy camera toward me. "You might like this more. It was your father's."

Holding the old Polaroid 600 camera, I remembered shaking the film as it develcped—did that even help?—and laughing at the results. Tweaking the exposure or focus. Looking through the viewfinder while Dad stood beside a big balancing boulder like he was a superhero holding it up. Taking photos of Mom making her animal-shaped pancakes on the camp griddle.

"I haven't seen this in years," I said, pulling myself from my melancholy at being an orphan at forty-two.

"I found it with some of his other equipment. It's loaded with color film, and I have a few more cartridges—a black-and-white one, too. I had someone check it out last week. He cleaned the roller and gave me the new fancy film packs they use. And he said you don't want to shake it anymore. Just lay it flat to expose the picture. Go ahead. Oh!" She handed me a roll of tape. "So you can stick pictures in your sketchbook."

Irina sure thought of everything. Suddenly, her voice didn't sound so grating anymore.

"That's allowed?" Holden asked.

"Yes. I asked," Irina said.

I lifted the camera to my face, flipped up the flashbar, checked for the green light, looked through the viewfinder without making any adjustments—I'd refresh myself on those tweaks later—and took a picture. It instantly spat out, the sound making me giddy.

While the photo developed, I took out my flower sketchbook and tin of colored pencils to draw a picture of the seaside.

With my mind more settled after a few minutes of sketching, I inhaled deeply. "Doesn't it smell great outside?" I asked Holden.

He nodded, his eyes trained on the behemoth RV holding up traffic in front of us. When the opposing lane opened, he floored it and passed the RV.

"Go, Torque!" Zach said, a bit too loudly.

Holden shook his head, probably regretting agreeing to the race nickname. "Can't go that fast. The Thule on the roof rack has a bit of drag."

My sketch was done. I'd color in the details at the hotel. In fact, I would draw something every day and write notes. Irina mentioned something about a memory challenge in previous years, and drawing helped me reinforce my memory of things I'd seen. Though if the time came for a special memory challenge, were notes allowed?

I looked at the photo I took of the harbor. Not bad.

Holden took his gaze from the road for a moment. "That drawing is really good."

I closed the sketchbook and cradled it on my lap while fidgeting with the photo in my hand. "It's not finished."

"Even unfinished, I see talent. You're an artist."

"Not really. I just draw or paint in my free time."

"What do you like to draw or paint?"

"Flowers, landscapes. That sort of stuff."

"I like to sketch a bit, too, but not as well as you. Mostly mechanical designs, buildings with interesting angles. I love a ruler and graphing paper."

"That's still drawing, and it takes a technical mind. What do you like to do in your free time when you're not drawing? You mentioned grad school for civil engineering?"

"Apparently, I drive in garden races," he said, pushing his glasses back up on his nose. He had an attractive smile. He also had what my mom would call expressive eyes, with little crinkles showing around them.

"Apparently," I said with a flash of a grin.

"I'm on a break from grad school. For fun, I like to fish or hang out with my friend—he's my sister's husband—and visit breweries and stuff."

"That sounds fun. I've never been to one."

He stretched and cracked his neck. "I like to understand the process of it. My friend is the one who likes to do the tasting. He scouts new beers and wines for my sister's restaurant when he's not working."

Our conversation died off after that. I was good at getting the answers I needed from people in crisis but didn't exactly excel at chitchat. Maybe that would change with this race. We had a puzzle to solve after all. And many more lay ahead.

Fourteen

Olivia

Zach kept looking out the window, straining to see if any competitors had gained on us. Our vehicles were conspicuously covered in race decals and sponsor magnets—even Irina's minivan had some—so it'd be hard to miss one. My pulse quickened as we closed in on our destination. I flipped through a travel guide.

Camden had a library, so that was our first stop.

We were making good time today, even if there was no risk of elimination at the end of it. *Torque.* I chuckled, wondering what other layers hid beneath Holden's calm surface, alongside the puns.

"No, Violet!" Irina snapped from the back seat.

"Sorry, Ini. Didn't think she'd nose into my bag. I have just protein bars there. Is she okay?" Zach asked.

Irina was wrangling a dog collar and trying to grab something out of a dog's mouth. Too late. Whatever it was, was gone. "Violet, you know better! Even with her sensitive tummy she grabs food she shouldn't eat."

Traffic slowed as we entered town. Camden was beautiful. Quintessential coastal Maine. "Isn't it—" I began.

My words were cut off by the sound of a retching dog.

"Ugh..." Zach said, his voice muffled by a hand over his mouth.

My stomach lurched. If we had a puking person in addition to a puking dog, I would need out of this minivan, stat.

"Oh, Violet," Irina chided. "Zach, hand me those paper towels."

He did but was pale and forced his look out the side window as we drove along Elm Street. He flipped his polarized blue sunglasses down to shade his eyes, then pinched his nose. I shifted to the mission at hand, trying to ignore the stench in the minivan despite windows being open. For me, the sound of the hacking was the worst part, and that was over. Holden seemed unaffected.

Focus on the task. If my job had taught me anything, it was how to hone my focus. At WRECC, I would shift into robot mode, stuffing emotions into a filing cabinet in my chest. It was only after a bad call, usually one with a child or a heart attack, that I faltered and let pain leach in just a little—even then, only at home.

Details, Olivia. You're good with details.

Today's protocol: Find the library. Find the item. Submit a picture of the item, with the four of us in it, and text the name of the plant, item (if there was one), town, and location. Wait for confirmation. Relax at the hotel. Live to race another day.

Rinse, repeat. Times twelve.

Shops and restaurants abutted each other, crammed in like happy sardines along Route 1. I assessed facades, signs, and placards as we inched through traffic. An alleyway offered a glimpse of the harbor. Everything here had tourist appeal.

"Look, there!" I pointed to a brick building up the hill on the right, just as we were heading out of town. It matched the picture of the library in the travel guide. "Quick! Turn down this street before we pass it." I was the navigator, right?

Holden found a space halfway down the one-way road.

Zach stumbled out to the sidewalk the moment we parked. "Air, I need air!" He bent over, palms on his knees, gagging.

"Why don't you three go ahead?" Irina suggested as she whipped out a spray bottle and set to work cleaning up the dog vomit.

"We need to stay together, remember? Sixty feet." I waved my wrist, the GPS step-tracker watch heavy as a hand-cuff. It was sleek, but as a reminder of the rules, of being watched, it made me feel a twinge icky. At least we didn't have camera crews chasing us and recording our every move or mistake. But knowing there were race staff out there—literally keeping an eye on us—also made me uncomfortable.

To the right of the road sat a sloped harbor park. Below the luscious green hill, windjammers and various fishing boats, sailboats, and motorboats bobbed along the docks. Kids fed ducks on the seaweed-covered rocks. Brine, fried foods, diesel, and the pungent scent of ocean filled the air. I would draw this view tonight.

On the opposite side of the road sat the library beside a grassy amphitheater composed of old-looking rock terraces. "We'll wait over there." I pointed. With the knowledge of one of my free art classes on trees, I identified the old hemlocks and birches that stood over the grassy lawn.

Holden scooped up our assigned cell phone from the cupholder. I grabbed my notebook. Zach, wiping sweat from his brow, pulled the clue out of his messenger bag and read it aloud again as we ascended steps to the amphitheater. He popped a fresh stick of gum into his mouth and tented his hands over his eyes, looking around. "This is gorg. Yeah?"

"It is," I said. We spun around, taking it in. I had a quick moment of imagining a wedding or art fair here.

"Let's go!" Zach said, already bounding toward the steps at the side of the amphitheater that adjoined the library lawn.

I caught up to him. "Hold up. We need to wait for Irina."

"But...better digs. Perks for being first. Remember?"

"Ah yes, soft pillows." I nudged him in the side.

His face shone with that dazzling smile.

"Rules are more important. We need to wait a moment," Holden said, much to Zach's chagrin.

Irina locked the minivan, which seemed counterintuitive since the sunroof and windows remained open. The dogs barked from within. "Just a few minutes, sweethearts," she said, flustered. "Then a walk."

"Shouldn't we take them?" I asked. "And our stuff is in there."

"Maine is as safe as it comes."

I ran back to the minivan and grabbed my small backpack just in case.

Two more decaled team cars came barreling down the road looking for parking. Zach raced up the steps to the library, two at a time, no longer waiting for us.

I snapped a few mental photos as I hurried to catch up.

Zach was already at the door. Holden paused for a moment, hand on his chin, staring up. He shook his head and looked at me. "Sorry, I'm a sucker for good architecture. Had to take it in for a moment."

"You said. It is something, isn't it?"

His eyes twinkled. "It really is. Looks like the amphitheater was built on a bent axis to—"

"Come on, slow pokes!" Zach interrupted.

We went inside. Zach kept his head on a swivel, always three steps ahead of us. He whispered, "One team is upstairs, and I saw one come downstairs, but they went over to the main stacks. If we're off mark, so is everyone else."

"Let's look up the book in the computer database—wait, can we do that? It's electronic," I asked.

Uncertain looks crossed my team's faces.

"Let's ask an aide at the desk instead," Holden suggested.

We did and then made a beeline for the children's section.

Two girls were playing with building blocks in the corner, a boy lounged on a cushion with a book upside down, and a woman perused the board books with a toddler in her lap.

We located Barbara Cooney's book *Island Boy* on the shelf, but not *Miss Rumphius*.

Irina was the first to spot the display of books set in Maine. "Here!" she said in an excited whisper.

Holden said the obvious. "Uh, there are no flowers on it."

I said, "The cover has her on a hill, but look inside." Irina opened it and flipped through pages until I pointed. "Lupine."

"Those are lupine," Zach agreed. "Good job, Olivia. Gather in. Picture time. Holden, the phone?"

We squeezed together around Irina, who held the book up. I was so close to Holden I could smell his woodsy deodorant.

Holden handed Zach the phone, and he typed in the necessary info: *Lupine flowers*, Miss Rumphius *book*, *Camden Public Library, Camden, Maine*. Then, we waited. I wanted to flop into a bear bag chair and read. Zone out a bit. Play in the kid-sized lighthouse.

Holden placed the book back exactly where we'd found it, not hiding it from other teams.

"How long will this—" I began but was cut off by a beep.

Irina leaned over Zach's shoulder. "Pish."

"What?" I asked.

Zach scratched his head. "Incorrect. Let's go outside and read that clue again, think about what we did wrong."

My ears buzzed, embarrassed that I had messed up our first clue as I followed them outside a different door than the one we came in.

He went on, "...maybe check historical places, like museums or the town office, or search the grounds more. It could be like, I don't know, a nonfiction book on lupine? In the adult stacks? Or in a bookstore? Or a historical building? Are there any famous people here who had personal libraries...?"

"Slow down, Sugar. I think it's the library," Irina said. "Olivia was right. But we need to think outside the box, remember? It's got to be lupine, but they don't exactly grow on a street corner. They're usually in meadows and along roadsides. Oh, look." She pointed to a small outdoor sitting area surrounded by flowers. "That's a garden... How quaint! Like an outdoor reading nook." She paused on flat cloud-shaped pavers inscribed with quotes.

We gathered in the reading nook.

"There's no lupine here," Holden said, looking at the mid-summer blooms and small trees around us.

Green vines climbed a stone wall like a warm blanket. I inhaled the sweet scent of summer blossoms, not having a clue what they were—just knowing their beauty and fragrance.

Irina listed flowers as she inspected petals and leaves. "Daylilies, hydrangeas, geranium, phlox, salvia, daisies..."

The reading nook was made of granite benches that were held up by carved "legs" of...

"Books!" Zach and I said at the same time.

We crouched and searched the stone books. They were children's stories—*Charlotte's Web*, *Stuart Little*, and a bunch I didn't know. My pulse quickened as I came upon *Island Boy* and then *Miss Rumphius*.

Irina squealed with joy and Zach whooped. Again, we posed for a photo. This time, Holden and I sat on the ground, to the best of our forty-something bodies' ability. Irina leaned in from the side and Zach crouched on the seat above the books in a squat that would have had my knees hurting for days. Ah, to be thirty and flexible. He texted our answer, and we waited again.

Another beep from the phone, and Zach fisted the air. "We slayed this!"

"Yes?" I asked.

"Yes! Great job, Olivia! One down, eleven to go."

Irina clapped me on the back. "Anyone feeling peckish?"

"Huh?" Zach and Holden said in unison.

"Hungry. Sorry, British mother. How about we get lobster rolls and eat in the park before we hunt down this bed-and-breakfast? I'm starved, but first, I need to walk the girls."

"Don't we need to check in to secure our spot in the race?" I asked.

"This confirmation text counts. We just need to get to our hotel before we turn in for the night."

I took in the sun as it glistened upon the harbor waters. "Yes, lobster rolls sound great, Irina." This first win pumped up my mood. Maybe we could do this.

Fifteen

Irina

While my teammates dug into breakfast, I headed to the front desk. I needed to find somewhere to board the dogs. The B and B had made a concession to let them stay after I agreed to pay an extra fee *and* offered the owner a highlight on my radio show after the race. The owner drove a hard bargain for how little I was asking. My dogs behaved better than most children!

I spoke from experience after years of teaching second grade. Some days it was like the trenches of war as I herded the booger-nosed, muddy-fingered, wiggly students. But, oh how I missed those days. They brought me joy during a darker period of my life.

Life could be like the Cracker Jack box, morsels of sweet with salty. Sometimes the quality control team goofed up, and the trinket you dug for was missing.

In my case, the quality control messed up on me, my body, so children were never in the plan for me. At least I had my furbabies, Logan, Olivia, and my nephews. It wasn't the same as being a mom, though.

I wasn't sure why I thought about this now, of all times. I'd come to terms with it years ago. Maybe Logan leaving this summer had caused the old feelings to resurface.

Finding nobody at the front desk to help me, and with my bladder calling me urgently, I stepped away to use the bathroom.

The single stall in the ladies' room was occupied, so I tidied my face in the mirror over the sink.

The sound of a miserable retch and muffled sob came from within the stall.

Oh, dear.

Concerned, I did a quick looksie under the door. All I saw were designer tennis shoes on someone crouching in front of the toilet. I cleared my throat. "You okay in there? Can I get you anything?"

"N-no."

That sounded like... No, not no-hair-out-of-place Dottie Jones. "Dottie, dear, is that you?"

"Go away, Irina."

"My meal last night gave my tummy a run for it, too. What can I do to help?"

"Please. Go."

I probed into my handbag and pulled out some antacids, an anti-diarrheal pill—one could never be too prepared for road food—and breath mints and left them on the counter before departing. Though I secretly wished for Dottie to trip over her perfect self sometimes, I would never wish illness upon anyone, and now was the worst time to be sick.

I returned to the front desk after finding another bathroom. Waiting for the man working there to notice me, I peeked out the window to check on Violet and Lily, who were already waiting in the minivan, eager for our jaunt as soon as a race volunteer handed over our new clues at eight o'clock.

I cleared my throat to get the man's attention. "Excuse me, I was wondering if you could recommend a dog daycare in the area?"

The rail-thin and weary-looking man furrowed his expression. "Jeb Monroe has one in Lincolnville. I think he's booked. Holiday weekend." He turned his nose back to the computer screen.

I pinched my lips. *No, sir. I am not done here yet.* "I'm doing this race." I waggled my fingertips toward the dining area, where six teams ate breakfast. "My sweet dogs really need a place to stay during this race."

He pushed the phone over.

I pushed it back with one finger. "If you can inquire for me, that would be great. I'm not allowed to use a phone. Race rules."

The man huffed but dialed and inquired. He hung up after some back-and-forth. "Sorry, ma'am. Like I said. The holiday. He's booked."

"Thank you for trying." I could ask about others in this area, but this guy wasn't exactly forthcoming. I doubt they had a phone book available. I took one of the free pens on the desk and plopped it in my handbag.

Before returning to my crew, I circled around back to the B and B's lovely veranda. Once again, I came upon Dottie, who was pacing beside a cluster of spent azaleas and rhododendrons. Maybe she needed fresh air.

I fell back a step and hovered under a pergola with trellised hydrangeas, so she couldn't see me. She held a phone to her ear.

"...I don't care what your father says, I'm not backing out! He knows this is important to me. And it's my last race. Look, I'm not supposed to even be on a phone, and if they find out, I'm out of the race. Jenny, can't this wait? I'm feeling fine. Just fine. Better than I have been... Yes, yes. I packed all my meds." She tapped a manicured nail on the wrought-iron fence. "No, you can tell him for the hundredth time, I'm not going to discontinue my podcast. I don't care what the doctor said. I left you in charge of this. You field the emails and calls. He's supposed to be in L.A." Dottie paced as she listened to Jenny's response.

Before being spotted, I retreated inside. No more *Happy Hibiscus Hour* with Dottie? Doctor? Meds? And why was Dottie using a phone?

Hmm. Well, I had my own issue to contend with today. The dogs.

Gus was a last resort if we happened to travel through Millinocket, but that was hours away. I'd left my brother a preemptive voicemail yesterday before we handed over our cellphones. Violet and Lily would just have to tough it out for now.

I returned to our table. Sipping my ginger pineapple tea, a local blend, I smiled at our crew. Holden covered a yawn, and Olivia scooped generous heaps of sugar into her coffee. Was it too early for them? I knew Zach rose with the sun to run. Olivia worked unearthly hours, so maybe she had trouble sleeping last night as her body modified its circadian rhythm.

"Are we ready for day two? Smashing job, everyone, yesterday." I leaned closer. "We were one of the first teams to check in."

Olivia raised an eyebrow. "How do you know? They don't post a leaderboard."

"Based on the teams here, plus like Zach said, the lodging. This is a *very* nice B and B." Our room held the Victorian feel of the old home, with luxurious lace curtains and two four-poster beds. A pretty vanity table, dainty but elegant bathroom, and courtesy chocolates on our pillows added just the right touches. Olivia was a snorer, but it didn't bother me. My spirit was buoyed knowing we were in the top group right out of the gate.

"The best for the best." Zach thumbed toward Tad's team. Dottie hadn't returned yet. "They've always gotten in the top three each year, right, Ini? And the coordinators were here last night, interviewing a few teams. If you see them recording segments for their YouTube recap, then you know you're with top finishers."

Or an eliminated team, but I didn't voice that.

"That means we were one of the first—" Zach counted the tables in the room "—seven teams here."

I finished a bite of pumpernickel toast with orange marmalade and gloried in our little win. I'd take any perks I could get. A few nights of roughing it might lie ahead.

Zach had already scarfed down his breakfast and was fidgeting with a piece of paper in his hand. "What's that, Sugar?"

He refolded the paper and tucked it into his pocket. "Ah, just a note from Jin. Some inspiration to keep me going."

"Aww. That's sweet."

"Yeah. He sent me with a whole bag of daily notes of encouragement. I'm going to read one each night. Thinking I can probably send him a postcard or two. Let him know how we're doing. Not sure how fast they will get to him."

"Aww, now that's doubly sweet. I think he'll get some of them before the race is over, depending how long the post office takes. I have a few stamps in my handbag that you can use." It warmed my spirit to see that he and Jin had parted on good terms. Jin had been a real crank after breaking his leg.

I thumbed through my bag to pull out the stamps from my wallet. "Uh, oh. Olivia, I found that pair of socks you were looking for. I put them in the car."

Olivia rolled her eyes with a sigh. "Violet?"

I chuckled. "She's a sock thief. Not sure why. Just loves to gnaw on them. Prefers to play fetch with the tennis balls."

"Thanks, Irina."

I gazed around the room. Tad gave me a haughty look from his team's table in the far alcove, the spot with the best view, naturally. He and Dottie had been nicknamed Minion and Mastermind by other racers a few years ago. And it was Dottie who was the brain of the pair.

Dottie strolled into the room and took her spot at the table, as if she hadn't just been throwing up or arguing with her daughter on the phone. And this was her last race! If she was sick...

She ignored her breakfast and stared out the window. Her silvery-gray hair kept picture perfect in a choppy pixie cut, dainty lips, regal neck, and soft blue eyes came off unassuming, but intelligent. Her clothing choices were in line with Tad. You would think the two were twins, but instead they were business partners on a mission: win this race again.

Money didn't motivate Dottie. Prestige did. She wanted the limelight.

She looked thinner this year. Many of my generation were getting sick these days. Cancer, diabetes, arthritis, osteoporosis, shingles, heart disease. Not me. I kept fit! I walked five miles a day with my girls, ate my vegetables, and took my vitamins.

Regardless, I knew that health came down to genetics and luck as much as good habits.

For the longest time, I'd thought activity kept disease away. Then Jerry got sick. There was no stopping your cells from turning on you. We conquered it; the cancer had gone into remission. However, the treatments had left unseen damage. We'd kept both his cancer and the cardiomyopathy under wraps. Jerry had sworn me to secrecy. He insisted on not telling Olivia anything about his health, given that her mother died from cancer. I guess he believed he was sparing her more pain. Now it felt too late to tell Olivia.

But maybe I should. Maybe if we opened the door of communication more, we could...share in this healing. Maybe I had to take the first step. Logan was grown and starting college. It was just Olivia and me now.

I lifted the teacup, forcing vapors of concern to dissipate like the morning haze on the harbor.

My scrutiny shifted to Tad. One of their teammates arrived and sat down with a frazzled look on his face. He spoke to Tad, and the mask Tad wore broke for a moment, clearly irritated with something the young man told him. He snipped at the guy. A few eyes looked his way, including mine.

As if sensing my regard, Tad replaced his frown with a fake smile, rose, and sauntered toward our table. He was like a strutting peacock. He paused to flash his charisma at a team around a nearby table, giving me a moment to warn our crew. "Trust nothing he says," I said into my napkin while pretending to dab my lips.

Tad offered us a smile beneath a well-groomed silver mustache and beard. Didn't anybody else see through his masquerade of garish white teeth, rolled-up oxford shirt, and gray sweater vest? He looked more like a hoity-toity college professor than a racer. His thin, judging eyebrows and penetrating dark brown eyes would not make me squirm.

Tad was like a male mosquito—the big one—though he was lean in stature from those marathons he ran. The male mosquitos floated around, for all to see and panic about, but they were in fact harmless. It was those females, small and bloodthirsty, that nipped you. That was Dottie...and she could use a good swat. Though a ping of empathy twanged in my chest as I watched her slowly dunk a tea bag in her mug. Maybe life and circumstance had swatted her enough.

Tad's voice broke through the mist like a foghorn as he stood beside our table. "Good morning! Haven't had the chance to say hi. New teammates this year, Irina and Zach?" He looked at Olivia and Holden.

Don't you mess with my team, buddy.

Holden rose slightly from his seat, dropped his napkin beside his plate, and shook Tad's hand. "Holden James."

Olivia followed suit without the handshake. "Olivia Rose."

"Ahhh, another Rose? Welcome to the club. I'm Tad Thurlow."

This was not a club, and Tad needed to bugger off.

Sharp eyes turned to me. "Nice ride you have this year, Irina."

I clamped down on words that were better left unsaid. "Only the best for my team."

"Your team and your mutts." He scoffed. "Think they'll help you sniff out the clues?'

The man's brazenness was as transparent as the windows of this room. I laid my teacup down. "My *golden* and *doodle* are better behaved than some humans."

Zach quietly coughed while sipping his coffee.

"Good luck. Though we know luck has nothing to do with this," Tad said. He eyed Holden and Olivia. "Next year, consider joining a winning team." He spun on his heels.

Zach put down his mug. "He's such a hack."

I nodded, reminded of Dottie's illicit phone use outside. "They've won twice before, once by a nose, but the other time by such a huge lead, even the judges questioned it."

Olivia pushed her spinach and feta omelet around on her plate, having hardly eaten any. "What came of it? Did they find anything?"

"Nothing, and no. Eat up, honey. We have another long day ahead," I said.

Olivia rested her fork on the plate.

Tad knew a lot of people in high places. Could one of those places be within the race organization? "Don't worry about them. We'll keep an eye out," I said.

Holden sat stiffly, his brow furrowed. "Is Tad connected to Thurlow Technology?"

"His brother, Carlton, Dottie's husband, owns it. Tad just does the books. Carlton's no peach either, from what I hear. Tad is Dottie's accountant and brother-in-law, who just so happens to like flowers..."

"...and money," Zach said.

And Dottie's tilled soil. I tittered under my breath at that unfounded rumor.

Five of eight came around and we rose, eager to grab a good spot in the front parlor. Twenty-eight bodies crammed in, our running shoes literally on. One never knew if we'd be traversing rocks or beaches or hillsides. Murmurs of anticipation spread through the group. I gave Janet Brighton a friendly shoulder pat. "Good luck."

Her hazel eyes glowed beneath a baseball cap. "You, too, Ini."

Across the room, Trish and I exchanged friendly smiles. It was nice to see her here with Vernon after his heart attack last year.

The grumpy man from the desk walked around, handing each team a sealed green-and-pink envelope. My pulse quickened. *Day two, here we come!*

Sixteen

Irina

Finally, the grandfather clock chimed at eight a.m., and we tore at the envelopes. My hands shook, and little bits of paper fluttered to the ground.

"Got it." Holden knelt and collected the pieces, which must be... "A puzzle," he said, cupping the pile in his hands like a duckling.

Zach leaned over my shoulder and read the clue aloud:

"Seize the Daisy."

I poked his shoulder. "Another fun pun!"

Holden and Olivia exchanged small smiles.

Zach snorted and read on:

"Put the puzzle together,
Backing, blocks, and batting, not filled with feathers.
We are adaptable and vigorous, returning each year with fervor,

In numbers of fifty thousand or more, claim observers.
With each new day we arise, then fold at night.
We peak in July, but some come again during autumn with might.
Here, at the inn of specters, where your hosts greet with ghostly glee,
My neighbor has four branches, but it is not a tree.
So, get yourself twenty miles north of Bananas.
This is where you'll find me, a place so Green, so serene."

Holden went to work with the puzzle at a small table, Olivia at his side. "Zach, let's pick this apart while those two smarties piece that together."

Most of the teams shuffled out of the room, murmuring and chatting excitedly, while a few stayed behind.

"Second line, quilting?" Zach whisper-asked. "Rosamund Francis was a quilter."

I loved Zach's knack for knowledge, and he'd spent extra time this year preparing and studying. "Definitely. My yiayia was a devoted quilter. Me, not so much, but *blocks, batting,* that's quilt lingo. Fifty thousand? Varieties?"

"Daylilies," Zach and I said in unison.

Another team looked our way.

We lowered our voices.

Zach said, "I read recently they're could be upward of like a hundred thousand varieties."

The rest of the riddle supported our deduction: peaking in summer, and the come-again variety in fall. I smiled. "They're everywhere this time of year."

Zach nodded. "And OMG, someone needs to teach these clue writers how to rhyme correctly. Okay...'Bananas' is capitalized. It must mean something. It says twenty miles north... We'll look at the map, but I don't think that's a town name. I mean, who names a town Bananas? Or is it something *with* bananas? Or something yellow? What about the inn of specters? Someplace uh, like, haunted? What about 'My neighbor has four branches, but it's not a tree'?"

"Slow down, Sugar. Let's take this one question at a time. We can look in one of my travel guides or magazines."

"Guys, does this mean anything to you?" Holden said from the side table.

"Wowzer, you're quick." The assembled puzzle was indeed a quilt, with an intricate geometric design of bright orange and yellow daylilies. I clapped my hands. "Let's get this show on the road, folks!"

Holden grabbed a free magazine from a nearby table and carefully slid the assembled puzzle between pages. I looked to Olivia. "You have the tape in your bag?"

She nodded.

"Aye, aye, Guv," Zach said. "Ooo! Your race name, Ini? Guv? Like those BritBox shows you love so much, and your mom?" He scratched the back of his neck. "Or, uh, dad? Whoever was British."

"My mom." I shook my head, though fondly. "The Guv'nor is the one in charge. I'm not. We never picked a team leader, and if anything, it should be you."

"Me?" His eyebrows shot up. "No way. Plus, you love to lead the charge. You're always happy and ready to roll. I vote Guv or Guv'nor!" He looked at Holden and Olivia.

"I like it," said Holden.

"Sure." Olivia shrugged.

In the minivan, we mulled over the clue while Holden drove down the road. "I assume north at least, on U.S. Route 1 until we know where we're going?" he asked.

"Yes, north. I got it!" Olivia said.

Violet barked.

"Where?" Zach asked.

She pulled out the map. "There are lots of small towns twenty miles north-ish of Orono. How will we know which?"

"Why Orono?" I asked.

Olivia scrutinized the map. "Bananas T. Bear is the mascot for the University of Maine. Logan and I toured it last year. UMaine's main campus is in Orono, so twenty miles north of there must be our spot. There are a bunch of small towns. Olamon, Cardville, Greenbush, Costigan, Greenfield... How do we choose? What more is in that clue?"

Zach read the last few lines again. "It says, 'at the inn of specters, where your hosts greet with ghostly glee'—we think that's a haunted inn. We can't find that on a map, so we'll need to ask people about haunted places. Then, 'my neighbor has four branches, but is not a tree' and 'a place so Green, so serene.'"

"Green is capitalized. Greenbush or Greenfield?" I tapped a nail to my thigh.

Olivia asked, "What has branches but isn't a tree?"

"Family tree, a pedigree?" Zach suggested.

I mused, "Political branches...the state house? That's south in Augusta."

Holden turned onto another road. "Where are those two towns located?"

Olivia ran a finger along the map. "Greenbush is on the Penobscot River. Greenfield is more east."

"Greenbush," Holden said. "Four branches, but not a tree...that's a river. Does the river fork?"

Olivia traced it. "Hard to tell on this big state map, but it looks like it forks out in four places north of Orono."

I whooped. "Butter my butt and call me a biscuit! You've got a good head on your shoulders there, Holden. You, too, Olivia. Great job! Hand me that quilt puzzle and tape. I'll tape it together for your notebook."

My high deflated like an unknotted balloon escaping fingers. Gas-sounding whoosh and all.

With each passing hour, my blood pressure rose. It was the first cut day! And we'd had three strikes already on locations.

The fourth—heavens, the fourth!—inn we were on our way to see was way off the beaten path, and in the middle of nowhere.

Please be it.

I masked my frustration. If one domino started to tumble on our team, the whole lot would. I would not be that first domino.

First, we'd visited an inn that wasn't haunted and didn't have any quilts. Then another with numerous quilts, with subtle differences in colorations and design, but none an exact match to the puzzle. Old and unnerving, complete with some sort of gargoyle statues, that place had made my teeth chatter. On our third stop, we thought we had it! We submitted a location that was known for its friendly ghost, a lobsterman lost at sea, and the old home had one quilt with pink flowers that resembled daylilies, but we got pinged with a "No, try again." At least we weren't penalized for incorrect submissions.

I began to wonder if the race coordinators purposely set up those red herrings.

Leaving that one, I couldn't help but ask, "How many haunted inns are there in this part of the state?"

Zach snorted.

We'd piled back in the minivan and stopped for directions yet again. The gas station attendant suggested the Holloway Inn, rambling on about the ghost of some woman from the Civil War era. He knew nothing about quilts.

Now we pulled up to that fourth inn.

With a wave, an elderly couple greeted us from the front porch. Zach sprinted ahead and was first on the steps, seemingly more determined after the three false alarms.

I'd thought it would be challenging to keep Olivia within twenty yards of us, with her constantly wandering off to take in the sights—though I was glad to see her enjoying the scenery and using her father's camera. Instead, it was Zach with his fast legs who was going to keep me on my toes. His endless stamina was enviable.

Holden pointed to multiple tire treads in the muddy driveway. Recent ones. "Look," he said. "Those cars by the barn are probably the owners, and I doubt they would've driven over in this area. We're behind a bunch of teams."

Were we toward the end of the pack today? Nobody wanted to be the first team cut!

A bit breathless and glad that at least Holden kept his steps in stride with mine, we reached the porch.

"They can't say whether people have already come through," Zach said. "But they said we are welcome to check out the inn and walk the grounds."

The woman on the porch grinned. We knew they weren't allowed to tell us anything race-related. She and the man swayed on a porch swing that had a quilt hanging over the back of it. "Lovely day, isn't it?"

"Indeed. Did you make this gorgeous quilt?" I asked.

"Yes, I did," she said, sipping a glass that clinked with ice.

I pulled out the taped puzzle. No match.

"We heard the inn might be haunted."

The woman just smiled. "Tours are self-guided." She pointed to the entrance.

After depositing a few dollars into the donation box, we searched rooms that each had a variation of the same quilt. "My goodness, who did the organizers get to make these?" Finally, draped over a loveseat in the sitting room, we found the one that matched our puzzle. "Bingo!

Some taps on the phone—thankfully we had a few bars of reception here—and we submitted our required photo and information.

"Winner, winner, chicken dinner," Zach said, reading the confirmation a minute later. "Or fish and chips dinner? Either way, go, Guv!"

"Go team!" I corrected, breathing a sigh. If we had been right, but last, the confirmation would have come with a notification of being eliminated.

After thanking the couple, we loaded into the minivan to drive to our hotel in Orono.

As we celebrated at a local eatery with a fish and chips dinner, I raised my gin and tonic to their beers. "To the team. I think if we have race names, we need a team name, too. I know we said no earlier, but I'm feeling it. Aren't you feeling it?"

"Good idea." Zach downed a second beer.

"Aren't our race names enough?" Olivia gave us a skeptical look over her hardly touched fish.

"Technically we are called 'team sixteen,' but really, the numbers are randomly assigned. People eat this stuff up on the socials. Hashtag-anything will get us more clicks when the race admins post stuff." Zach raised a hand to order a third beer. "Another beer?" He looked at Holden, who shook his head. "We can add our hashtag to the next answer we submit."

"The Fearsome Four?" I suggested.

Zach sprinkled malt vinegar on his fries. "Eh. We need something a bit more unique this year. Something with pizazz."

"Fleur Four?" Olivia offered, a glint playing in her eyes. "It's a mouthful. But you like those, uh, what are they called—those *Faux to Fabulous* magazines? It made me think of that." She pushed her fries around, then finally settled on one and bit into it.

Zach's face glowed. "Girl, you get me already!"

"You're a hard one to miss, Zach," she said sweetly.

"Hashtag Fleur Four." He smiled with air quotes. "Plays on the French influence here in Maine, too. We'll sign our texts to the admins that way. What do you say, team?"

A round of yeses and nods.

Zach's cheeks were flushed. "Take that, Tad and Dottie, and their Happy Hibiscuses or Hibisci or whatever they call themselves! We're slaying this!"

"Speaking of M and M..." I began.

Olivia asked, "Who?"

"Mastermind and Minion." Zach's lips tipped into a frown. "I saw them, too. Right on our heels today, and I think I saw them come into the library soon after us, yesterday. That guy is as shady as a big old oak tree. Dottie seems quiet this year. But vipers can be quiet until they attack."

I nodded. "That's what I was going to mention."

"They certainly know our vehicle," Holden said grimly.

Zach clapped a hand on his shoulder. "Torque, you'll need to lose them tomorrow."

We chatted and dug into our dinners as I tried to shake the feeling of unease at being followed...and of seeing Dottie's distress this morning.

Holden withdrew a small bottle of hot sauce from inside his top pocket, splashed some on his fish, then put the bottle back. He must like a bit of kick. Who was I to judge? I traveled with my personal stash of gin, plus dog treats in my pockets for the girls, who were resting in our room after a long day of driving.

While the others gulped their beers, I sipped my gin and tonic. After swallowing, I said, "Zach, speaking of names, I have one for you. I need to run it by the teammates first." I gestured to Holden and Olivia, and Zach swigged his beer with feigned dismay. He was going to wake with a beastly headache if he didn't cut back on the pints. I whispered over the din, "Holden, I know you wanted to give him his name. What do you think of *Legs*?"

Holden smirked. "Love it." He looked expectantly at Olivia. She nodded approval.

"Great. You do the honors," I said.

Holden lifted his half-full beer and clinked it with Zach's. "Your nickname is Legs. Because, man, you gotta stop running ahead of us!"

"Legs it is. To Torque, Guv, and our yet-to-be named navigator extraordinaire, Olivia. Team Fleur Four!" Zach finished the rest of his beer.

We clinked glasses.

Olivia smiled and picked up her fork and dug into her fish. My plan to get my stepdaughter out of her comfort zone was working. I really hoped, with Logan gone and more time on her hands, she and I could finally connect. It was long overdue.

I drank in the levity at our table.

I counted our blessings on making it through day two. So long as we didn't unravel, we could do this.

Seventeen

Holden

Here we were, on day three, sweating in the hotel parking lot, talking about Christmas in July. One by one, teams departed as they presumably figured out today's weird riddle. The engine of an SUV beside us turned over, and that group zipped out.

A headache from the heat twisted around the back of my skull. My T-shirt stuck to the seat, and I prayed my deodorant and antiperspirant would see me through the day. Instead of running the AC and wasting gas, we sat here, windows down, not moving.

I was told that Maine wasn't usually super humid or hot, but for at least a few days per year, the state liked to remind people that it wasn't the tundra. That time typically fell around Independence Day. This week.

I gulped some water to moisten my mouth. I didn't think I had much skin in the game, but after the first two days, I was feeling the vibe, as Zach liked to say. If we placed first in this whole thing, I could contact the bursar's office immediately and put the worries of my tuition bill behind me. Suddenly, it felt real, attainable. I had something to hope for, to work toward.

Flying under the radar had become my new normal. Keep my head down, don't stir trouble or attract attention. It only takes one time touching a hot burner to tell a person not to go near it again, at least not without a potholder.

As if I didn't feel cruddy enough about the work accident back at Whitlock Construction, the shop van had been stolen last month because I left the keys in it. I had dropped the ball...again. I had been feeling pretty low.

But now, that feeling lifted a bit.

"We have candy cane and red and green," Zach announced. "What's more north than the North Pole? Caribou, Maine. A caribou is like a reindeer. That's it."

North doesn't always mean compass north, I wanted to say, but didn't. It felt weird to disagree with my boss. North could mean something physically above our heads, like the top book on a shelf. North could be a name, or something else...

Well, or "north" could just mean compass north. The simplest answer.

I scratched my head, overthinking it all, then wiped my palms. I could use an icebox right now. Was it colder in Caribou?

"What about the pub?" Irina reached back and pushed the travel water bowl closer to a panting Violet. The pooches weren't too pleased to be sitting here either, not with their heavy fur coats.

Not to be left out, Olivia said, "The eight dollars and seven cents has to be significant..."

She had given the Christmas-in-July idea a hardened sideways shake of the head. I was glad to have a voice of reason beside me.

"Every word is important." Zach popped a bubble and chewed gum like his life depended on it.

He sometimes felt like a panic attack waiting to happen. The funny thing about Zach was he put on a good front of enthusiasm, but every now and then I saw his façade showing signs of cracking under pressure. His excitement didn't always add up. After losing my sense of smell, I'd spent more time relying on other senses. I watched. I listened.

My head spun as we bounced ideas off each other. I thumbed the wheel, itching to be on the road. If we chose unwisely, we could be backtracking and losing time for another mistake.

Earlier this morning, I'd almost snorted piping hot coffee out of my nose when Zach read the clue. *Say Aloe to my Little Friend.* Now, thirty minutes later, we were no closer to solving it, so some of my appreciation for fun with puns had worn off. Something more specific than a compass direction would be nice. Should I drive to Canada?

Olivia held the map out. She had marked the locations of our previous two days.

"Why are you circling them?" I asked, leaning closer to once again consult the map. And alright...to be closer to her, too.

She shrugged. "I feel like they may be important at some point."

I nodded. "Good thinking."

"This is about wordplay. No word is insignificant." Zach clicked a pen in his hand.

I pulled out and fiddled with my mini three-by-three Rubik's. Only four team vehicles remained in the parking lot. Most had burned rubber as soon as they had the clues in hand. Had our beginners luck worn off? "Read it again?"

My suggestion elicited a round of groans in the minivan.

Olivia read it this time, accentuating specific words. Her voice was a blanket of calm over the rising tension between Irina and Zach.

Today's riddle was written more like a story than a poem with stanzas.

"As the cold Northern wind buffets his hair, a taxonomist walks into a pub called The Promontory. He stamps his heels on the red-and-green welcome mat and asks for the house drink. The bartender, Dawn. says to order the Candy Cane. 'Can you recommend a meal?' the man asks. Dawn responds: 'Vegetarian or meat?' The man says, 'No berries for me. I'm a carnivore.' Dawn slides a pitcher his way. 'Then I have the thing for you,' says Dawn. The man pays $8.07. Donning his bog-ready boots after his drink and meal, he asks for directions to the best view around. Dawn responds: 'Go down that trail, where carpet turns to wood, and look around: there are pairs of pink gems that like to hide. Go past the cotton waving hello, and there you will find something to truly quench your thirst."

Olivia said, "My brain is on information overload. This weird taxonomist wants a drink and a steak, then goes on a walk?"

"Why don't we first analyze based on the Christmas-in-July idea?" More like rule it out than consider it; but again, I wouldn't get confrontational. I twisted my Rubik's so each color had a row, like stripes of a candy cane. "Maybe 'candy cane' doesn't refer to literal Christmas candy, but to something red and white?"

"Barber pole?" Olivia offered.

"American flag?" Irina suggested. "It is the holiday week, after all."

"If we're going with Christmas in July, Caribou is far," Olivia said, her frustration palpable.

Irina finally joined Team Reason. "And a stretch."

That made our vote three to one against Zach.

"What about the pub?" I asked.

"It's not an actual pub." Irina crossed her arms. "We have a taxonomist. That must be someone famous to botany or biology, but who?"

"Now we need to know scientists?" Olivia spoke through her teeth.

A part of me wanted to squeeze her knee or hand, tell her that it was okay, to let the two botany brains figure it out, but I didn't. That was way too forward.

Zach fired off names on his fingertips. "Mendel, Darwin...but I want to say Carl Linnaeus."

Irina tapped a pink nail on the travel guidebook in her lap. She'd already donated the un-needed travel magazines to a recycling center yesterday. "Now, what about—"

Zach's boyish face lit up, and he fist-bumped the air. "Linnaeus! Twinflower! Its scientific name is...*Linnaea*... Lemme look in my old textbook." He skimmed the fat *Taxonomy of Plants of New England* tome in his lap. "Yes. *Linnaea borealis*. Of course!" He faced the book upright so we could see.

Irina nodded. "That explains the pairs of pink gems that like to hide—the twinflower. But I think they may be along our way to finding the flower, right? Because there is a lot more to this riddle." Irina pointed to the photograph for my and Olivia's benefit. "Twinflower looks like two pink bells hanging on one shared branch. Two pink gems. Let's try to figure out the rest. Location?"

Zach popped a bubble. "Maine is a big state. They could send us all over the place."

Olivia laid her hand on my arm as I was about to spin the cube again into a new pattern. "Stop! That."

"Huh?" Was I bugging her? The feel of her hand, soft but firm on my arm, sent a ripple of shivers to my chest.

"West Quoddy!" She brimmed with a smile that unwound the knot in my upper back. She squeezed my forearm, and I'd be damned if I was gonna pull my arm away.

Is there such a thing as liking a woman's smile too much? Not just because hers sent the blood flowing to *all* my parts, but she bore a brightness, usually hidden behind a serious expression and now revealed. I asked, "West what?"

She took the cube from my hand, and my arm hummed where her touch had just been. "Some lighthouses have red and white stripes like a candy cane." She re-read the clue, and her hand shook, just a smidge. "Logan and I planned to visit several lighthouses on our trip...before it got canceled. Anyway, one stop was West Quoddy Head. I picked it because I loved how it looked, classic, red and white striped, and it's the most northeasterly of the lights in Maine."

Irina, looking through a book, chimed in, "The word 'promontory' works, too. West Quoddy is on a peninsula. Yes, Olivia! You cracked the location. Let's puzzle the rest out on the drive."

A dog barked to remind us of her presence.

I turned the key, and the engine took longer than a moment to turn over. "Irina? Has it done this before?" I thought of the dysfunctional air-conditioning and the slow pep of the minivan with the Thule on top—but that was probably just normal aerodynamic drag slowing us down.

The minivan also handled a bit differently with the heavier top. The extra weight could be drawing on the engine, too.

She shook her head, not a hint of worry in twinkling blue eyes. "No. A fluke."

I pulled out of the parking lot while Olivia gave directions to the closest highway.

"West Quoddy Head is far to go if we're wrong. It'll be hard to backtrack," Zach warned.

"Caribou is farther," Olivia argued.

The rearview mirror reflected Irina's smile spreading to her eyes. Team Fleur Four had a new leader today: Olivia Rose.

Zach let down his own shield of cocky overconfidence, much to my relief. He admitted, "This does seem the most logical. Thoughts on the eight oh seven? Entry fee? The number of red and white stripes?" He looked over Irina's shoulder at the book. "Some of the lighthouse is obscured in the photo, so I can't tell, but it could be eight and seven. Who's Dawn?"

Nobody had an answer.

"It's boggy there. I bet the rest of the riddle is about the trail and plant," Irina said.

Halfway to Lubec, Olivia startled us out of our mired thoughts. "Dawn isn't a person! I think West Quoddy sees daybreak first. Looking at the map, the peninsula is the most easternly spot in Maine. Some people drive up Cadillac Mountain in Acadia to see the sunrise, but at certain times of the year, the sun rises earliest in Lubec, maybe. That gets into more science than I know."

Zach looked up from a book. "I've been reading about the ecology around the lighthouse. The bogs have red and green mosses. They can look kind of like a carpet. 'Wood' could be trees or a boardwalk? Either way, I think we're on target. Sorry if I doubted us earlier. It's just..."

Irina gave him a squeeze. "It's okay, Sugar. We're a bit excitable. Some of us more than others."

Zach added, "Other flora include bog laurel—those have pretty purple flowers—various Arctic berries like baked-apple berry, crowberries, and cranberries, cotton grass, and pitcher plants... Oh! Wait. Yes, that's it!"

"What is?" I asked.

"The trail in the clue mentions cotton waving. That's our cotton grass. The berries are the vegetarian option on the pub menu. But our taxonomist is a carnivore and needs to quench his thirst. That's the pitcher plant! It's a carnivorous plant."

Olivia re-read the clue again, and we all cheered as our answers seemed to align with the puzzle.

"I think that's it, Sugar," Irina cooed.

Zach said a few minutes later, "So did anyone else count the number of teams departing this morning?"

"Hmm?" Irina asked. "It's too early for me to do math. The race is down one team as a result of the daily elimination. They interviewed them last night for the YouTube recap." She shook her head. "The Slaters. They did so well last year."

"Not just that, a second team was missing from this morning's lineup. I counted, since we all stayed at the same hotel last night. I wonder what happened. Maybe a health issue? At breakfast someone mentioned something about an injury on another team."

Irina pursed her lips. "Well it does happen."

"I'm gonna ask around more, see who has the deets."

Olivia and I shared a look. This race was a bit more than either of us expected.

An hour later, we pulled into the lighthouse parking lot.

Zach tapped the back of my headrest. "OMG, this place is gorg! Talk about classic Maine coast. Dreamy. I could design the perfect arrangement to go with the vibes it gives off. In fact, Olivia, maybe when this is over, can I look at your drawings? It might be a good promo—arrangements based on the race's clues."

"My sketches? Sure, I'd be happy to let you look at them. I'm taping the photos into the book, too, and writing notes on clues and places and things we see along the route."

"Good idea." Zach was hopping out the door.

Three other team cars were already parked in the lot.

Zach walked ahead of us and said over his shoulder, "I hope the others were thinking Christmas, too, and are halfway to Caribou!"

"Eight plus seven." Olivia pointed to the round candy-striped tower, absolute delight in her voice.

Irina grabbed Violet, the young goldendoodle, and put her harness on. "Dog-friendly means she's coming with us. Be back soon, Lily, love." She stroked the older dog. We left some windows open.

Olivia snapped a photo with the Polaroid as we walked down the hill toward the lighthouse.

"Drawing this one tonight?" I asked.

"Definitely."

Last night, while Zach and Irina played a rowdy game of rummy inside, we sat on the porch of our motel, me listening to the bugs and soaking in summer, Olivia drawing in her sketchbook. I tried not to watch, but her talent was obvious.

Boldly, I asked, "Wanna get up tomorrow for sunrise? To take photos or draw it?"

Olivia's brown eyes met mine. "We can walk down to the water, too."

We were right beside each other, and in that moment, I wished I could smell her hair or the lotion she used.

I smiled back and dropped some cash into the honor system box for the park admission then turned to Irina. "Where to, Guv?"

"Good question." She studied the tower and grounds for a moment longer.

The white light atop the tower blinked twice. A moist wind battered us—what was that word in the riddle? *Buffeted*? Compared to the warmth in the minivan, the gusts were refreshing.

Zach flipped his shades up. "Info first. But let's be quick!" Zach speedwalked to the visitor center and museum, which looked like the former keeper's house.

Inside, an exhibit about Fresnel lights and lighthouse history snagged my curiosity, but he breezed past it. I'd come back later.

"Do you have trail maps?" he asked the woman at the counter. Without waiting for an answer, he grabbed one and we hurried out the door. He pointed. "The bog trail is off to the right."

Violet rubbed along the ground, pawing at her Gentle Leader. "Violet, no!" Irina handed Olivia the leash and bent down to fix it.

"Ow! Mosquito!" The leash slipped from Olivia's hand as she swatted at her neck.

The dog made a dash back to the minivan. "Violet!" Irina snapped, chasing her down before she got too far.

"Sorry," Olivia said, her cheeks flushing. "I'm not great with dogs."

I leaned in. "I'm a cat guy myself."

She smiled, and my insides did a little dance.

"Me, too. Well, a cat girl. Logan and I love to send funny cat GIFs or reels to each other."

We shared a chuckle.

Zach chewed the end of his sunglasses. Then, as Irina returned to our party, he said, "Let's hustle!"

A silver SUV adorned with sponsor decals and bright hibiscus flowers, to the point of being gaudy, whirred into the gravel parking lot.

"Strike me pink. They must have a sixth sense, or radar or something. This is the second time they conveniently arrived *just* after us." Irina pinched her lips. Violet barked. "Settle, sweetheart. I'm fine."

"Now you have me thinking he *is* tailing us." Zach's eyes narrowed.

"I didn't see them behind me on the past few turns." The hairs on the back of my neck prickled. A few times, I swore I'd seen the shiny silver SUV behind me, but if it was Tad and Dottie's group, they'd trailed just far enough to make me question my suspicions. Thing is, after Irina mentioned Tad's connection to Thurlow Technology, the company that got me fired, I started to wonder if he knew who I was. Did he have it out for me? Were they following us specifically? Ugh, my stomach knotted but now was not the time to feed paranoia.

"Oh, well. It *is* a race. Fifth gear, Ini. Let's go!" Zach bolted toward the trailhead.

We went after him, Irina heading the charge. The trail was dirt and gravel, and to our left there was a great view of the coastline. We passed a picnic area, an information sign, and a spot to turn down for a viewpoint. I made a mental note to check that out later with Olivia.

All the while, we walked along the coastal trail which gave us stunning vistas from a rugged cliff.

"Gorgeous, right?" Olivia said.

I nodded. The tree-topped bluffs were amazing. White froth churned in teal water in a cove. "Don't slip," I said with a light tease.

"I'll stay close to you," Olivia said, stepping away from a steep ledge.

Soon, we came to a fork in the trail, signs pointing to different routes. Zach forged ahead. "Bog is to the right."

The trees were moss-covered and timeworn. It was like we walked in an ancient place, like something primeval. We came to a few more decision points and found ourselves at a boardwalk. The forest opened up and we stood at the edge of the Arctic bog, which felt otherworldly. It was vast and open and eerie. And out of place for typical coastal Maine.

"So, we're looking for the pitcher plant, right? Not the berries or cotton grass or twinflowers?" Olivia asked.

I pushed my glasses up on my nose. "Right. How exact must the GPS reading be? Maybe any pitcher plant we come across is good enough?"

Irina's fashionable boots squeaked on the wet boardwalk. "Worth a shot, but let's pay attention to the clue. Olivia, what about the geocaches you did with your father? How close did you have to be to the GPS spot?"

Olivia swatted another mosquito. She said a bit gruffly, "Geocaches work with an app on a cell phone. I don't have a GPS in my nose, Irina."

Ouch.

"She's just trying," Zach said to her in a loud whisper. He pointed. "Look, some cotton grass. Red moss and green sphagnum are all over the place. I saw a few twinflowers earlier on the trail, but don't see any here. Looks like this boardwalk does a loop. Let's just find a pitcher plant."

He was ahead of us again.

Lining the loop trail, informative signs described the flora and geology of the bog. Purple flowers, which I think were the bog laurel, provided a splash of color in the predominantly green and brown landscape.

"Found some!" Zach waved wildly. "Come over here."

We met him and, sure enough, a cluster of pitcher plants, red, small, unassuming, and... "Uh, so these are like carnivorous?"

"Yup! They eat insects and hold water. They lure insects to their death! It's so rare to see them south of Canada, but this little Arctic bog is a unique ecosystem. And here is a signpost about them. Let's get that, the plants, and us all in one photo. Take a picture!"

There were, in fact, pitcher plants all over.

We snapped. Texted. Waited.

A ping and a whoop from Zach. "Got it! Whew!" He wiped sweat on his brow. "Now we can breathe a bit. Who wants to go down the coastal trail and check out the view of the lighthouse from the beach?"

Eighteen

Holden

On cue, the coffee pot began to gurgle at four a.m.

In place of the rich nutty aroma tingling my nose, the sound was a promise of a pick-me-up. Thankfully, I had slept dreamlessly, no weird nightmares about people fainting and me being immobilized to help them. Even now, a few years after the accident, those nightmares persisted.

I woke up feeling rejuvenated after three days of success in a race...with a group of people I hardly knew but was slowly beginning to call friends.

Despite this lightness in my chest, a storm swirled on the horizon. What if I messed up? I covered a yawn. Such thoughts were too heavy for the crack of dawn.

An alarm chirped from Irina and Olivia's room.

I swept sleep away from my eyes. My knees cracked as I felt my age. I preferred a bed over a couch. I searched around for the flashlight and then popped two ibuprofen tablets and munched on a granola bar. The doctor told me that the skiing I'd done in my teens and twenties had wreaked havoc on my knees.

Our accommodations at West Quoddy Station—a perk for top teams—was a cabin just down the road from the lighthouse. Last night, as rain settled on the peninsula, we stayed in and made a pasta dinner, then spent a quiet evening around the small table, Irina and Zach playing cards and psychoanalyzing our competition while Olivia talked about her son, Logan, and drew. I listened to her and sipped tea, appreciating the warmth and companionship.

The cabin had only two beds—Olivia and Irina shared one, and Zach claimed the other. I curled up on the couch.

I gave a sleeping dog a small nudge to retrieve my sneakers from beneath her paws. When the floor creaked near the opening bedroom door a few minutes later while I was filling two thermoses with coffee, I whispered, "Hey." The dog at my feet perked up but laid her head back down.

Olivia shut the door behind her and put on a light vest, then pulled her long hair back into a low ponytail. "Must...have...coffee..."

I handed her a thermos, which she nestled into a small backpack.

"Cream and sugar?" I asked, already noting the way I observed her taking it.

"Yes, thanks. Have you seen a pair of blue socks? I think the sock thief stole them again," Olivia whispered.

"Sock thief?"

"Violet."

I searched around the couch. Lily was deep asleep. Violet was perked up, wagging her tail, said socks in her mouth.

Olivia waved her hand. "Never mind. She can have them. Maybe if I let her have one pair, she won't keep stealing them."

I gave a soft chuckle.

We went outside. It was a quick drive to the lighthouse. Our steps crunched on gravel as we picked our way down the hill toward the tower.

"Want to sit at the picnic table here, then walk the path after the sun is up?" Olivia suggested with a point of her flashlight.

I agreed with an "mm-hmm."

Someone else had the same idea as us, as they were sitting on a bench on the other side of the keeper's house, bundled in a blanket.

"Hey, I see Nova Scotia," I said, shining my light into the vast dark blue of the Quoddy Narrows, which led to the Bay of Fundy.

Olivia laughed.

I liked her laugh as much as her smile. Time to get one more of each out of her. "Why do flowers always drive so fast?"

She wiped the picnic table bench with a towel she pulled out of her bag, then sat. "Why?"

"Because they put the *petal* to the metal."

She lightly snorted.

"They're lame," I said.

"Nah, keep them coming. I like them. I don't laugh enough these days." Her silhouette was backlit by the smallest hint of orange nosing up from the horizon.

"How's the drawing?" I assumed her backpack held her sketchbook and camera.

"Good. Taking a few notes, too. In case we need them at some point."

"I can't imagine a more perfect spot to draw once the sun rises."

Dark navy morphed into softer blue, and we watched in appreciative silence as the sun made its first appearance among wispy gray clouds. As more light threaded into the darkness, a click of the camera broke the stillness.

I turned to her. She giggled, a bit giddy.

"There's just something about an instant picture with a Polaroid. The simplicity of it. The sound of the photo ejecting. Dad loved it. I probably loved it more."

She looked cute with the bulky camera of her childhood slung around her neck.

"Maine is just stunning. It's the smell of the sea I'm enjoying the most. Is that weird?" She sniffed, inhaling whatever sunrise on a cliff surrounded by wildflowers and bog smelled like.

"I miss that," I said.

"Miss what?"

"Smelling."

Confusion creased her expression. "You can't?"

"Not really. Not anymore. Used to, like a normal person."

I hated talking about myself, but Olivia made it easier. Though she had only shared a little about herself with me, I got the impression that she understood bumpy roads.

"Know why I take my coffee black?" I raised mine and sipped. Flavorless heat ran down my throat.

"It's calorie-free?" she asked wryly.

"That's just a bonus. Actually, I can't taste it. I used to take it with cream and sugar. Now it serves as hot fuel."

"What do you mean? Coffee is all about taste, and that heavenly aroma..." She paused and placed a hand on my knee. "Wait, you can't taste either?"

I sipped again, wanting something to fill my throat so I didn't answer out of sarcasm or frustration. I settled on, "Well, more it's limited. Very limited."

"Were you sick? I've heard of people losing their loss of smell permanently after Covid…" She shook her head. "Never mind. Sorry. Nosy of me to ask."

I laughed.

She looked horrified. But my smile must have put her at ease.

"I wasn't trying to be punny," she said.

Now we both snorted.

I tapped the bridge of my nose. "Botched sinus surgery a few years ago. I had polyps and a deviated septum. It was supposed to be an easy procedure, but with every surgery, there's a risk. I fell into the unlucky few. I lost almost all my sense of smell and seventy-five percent of my taste. The two apparently go hand in hand."

"Holden, I'm so sorry. That must suck." Pencils rattled in the tin in her bag as she shifted in her spot while taping the snapshot of the sunrise onto a fresh page in her notebook.

"I deal with it. The more time passes, the less I miss it. My sister and I make a game of it. She tries to spice my senses back to life."

I massaged a fist on my thigh. If it hadn't been for my defective nose, I wouldn't be out of a job and up to my ears in debt.

The prosecution had alleged I had been unable to detect the natural gas leak at work and rightfully so. Ah, my lack of smell was the perfect scapegoat.

The irony that my father also suffered from an on-the-job accident years ago was not lost on me. What would he say if he knew that my inability had been blamed for an accident that left three other people disabled?

My lawyer had presented a solid case. I followed all the OSHA requirements for the site. I did the hundred things I was supposed to do as a construction safety officer, not only with setting up the site, but also investigating the accident. What didn't sit right, what caused suspicion to grow on my brain like a lichen on a rock, was how two coworkers, former friends, had spoken against me. They had not been onsite when the accident happened, so how would they know the details? I suspected corporate paid them to lie. But why?

My guess was that with a multimillion-dollar project put on hold, it was easier to dispose of one chump they showed to be incompetent than to risk the directors and CEOs of Whitlock Construction being negligent, a project being shut down, and hundreds unemployed. They blamed it all on me—I was the fall guy. I was fired, and Whitlock Construction got back to work on the Thurlow Technology project after just a six-month delay.

At first, I had blamed *me*, too. But the more my lawyer and I dug, the more we found potential evidence leading back to Whitlock. But it wasn't enough for our defense.

Now Carlton Thurlow's wife and brother were in this race against us. I'd vowed to lie low, but if they were as conniving as Irina implied, they'd already done their homework on all the teams.

Which meant they knew about my connection to the accident. Did Tad have it out for me? Why? They won their case. End of story. Why continue to bother me? I knew about their cover-up, but my lawyer and I never disclosed our information. Our evidence was not strong enough. Maybe Tad knew that I *knew*.

I squeezed the thermos, wanting to break the metal with my bare hands, wanting to toss it out to sea.

Olivia bumped my shoulder with hers, knocking me out of my ruminating. "That explains the hot sauce."

My ears warmed, and I put the thermos down on the picnic table, then cracked my knuckles. "You noticed?"

"Who doesn't notice a guy who carries hot sauce in his pocket?"

"Got me. I never was one for spicy food before the nose decided to stop working."

"I'm sorry. I can describe the scent of the ocean—of this moment—if you'd like, but I'm not a poet. Just a wannabe artist."

"Why wannabe? You look like an artist to me."

"I was in school for art, but had to drop out when I got pregnant with Logan. Earned my associate's in English and composition, but art, well...it wasn't in the picture." She paused and shook her head. "Another unintentional pun. Geesh. You sure are rubbing off on me. Anyway, I have my job at dispatch and do copyediting on the side. It works."

"People probably ask why you never went back." It was my way of asking without asking.

"Time, money. The usual culprits."

I get that, more than you know.

"I guess I could still pursue art in some form without the formal education. Plenty do it. Now I have more time, I suppose." She took a long sip from her thermos.

"Who's your favorite artist?"

"Huh?"

I tapped her notebook. "You've got to be inspired by someone. Monet? You like landscapes. Or do you like Van Gogh? Who was the guy with the fruit?"

"Cézanne." She tried to hide her smile. "You know art history?"

"Just the basics. I took one elective course in college. Oh, what about...do you like, uh, what was her name?" I scratched my short beard. "The one who painted the flowers, like up close?"

"Georgia O'Keeffe. She also painted desert landscapes, buildings, and abstracts. But she was most known for her flowers."

"That could be your race name—Georgia. What do you think?"

She chewed a thumbnail. "Guess it could work. I'm no Georgia O'Keeffe."

"That's right. You're Olivia Rose."

There was something about her eyes. Outwardly, Olivia was like a boarded-up building, but her side smiles and soft laughs opened a window, and her eyes opened a door. When she was irritated with Irina, a flash would reveal itself. Or when exhausted by Zach's energy, an eye roll. When happy, and I only caught snatches of that, her dark brown eyes softened. It was like she could throw open the shutters with a smile or unbolt the storm door and let the breeze in with a blink of an eyelid.

Flecks of sunshine glowed in her irises. I swallowed. "What's your favorite flower?"

"Why do you ask?"

"You must have a favorite. Is it roses? You get those deliveries."

A puff of breath came in with her easygoing laugh-sigh. "Actually, roses aren't my favorite. It's an inside joke with my dad. Last name Rose. People tend to think that's part of my first name, not my last name."

I thumbed my chest. "People think I'm James."

Her smile deepened for an instant before a shadow passed over her face. "My dad died two years ago, and he set up some rose-of-the-month-club delivery for me. Weird, huh?"

"Sweet." And here I'd thought the sender was a clingy boyfriend, though she never mentioned a man in her life outside of Logan.

She rubbed her palm against her breastbone. "Daisies."

"Daisies?"

"Roses are sentimental to me, but daisies are my favorite." Then she laughed. "I have the worst luck, and even though Irina planted some daisies in my gardens, they never survive."

We sat in silence as the sun rose higher.

To tell someone about my issue was freeing. I sensed that Olivia felt a bit unburdened in her sharing, too, even if I didn't fully know her story, and she didn't fully know mine. She understood my loss and regret.

"Did you mean it earlier? Can you describe this scent to me?" I waved a hand to the air, the teeny water particles that comprised the morning mist tickling my fingertips. "I want to smell it. This place, right now."

"Alright. Only if you tell me more about this lighthouse, too. I saw you checking out the exhibits yesterday before dinner."

"You got it."

"What scents and tastes do you still have?"

"Only a few. Sharp spices like cardamom or curry, or strong acidic foods and hot peppers. It sounds weird, but I associate a feeling or mood or other sense like texture with my scent memories." I pulled my fingers into a fist and rubbed my stomach. "Like Thanksgiving in the kitchen with my mom and sister. My brain knows the kitchen should smell like spices, warm, sweet, and savory, but I can't imagine it beyond a feeling. Or Sunday mornings with Dad and a newspaper. Newspapers should have that printer ink smell, but to me, it's a gut feeling of this, like uh, peace.

I think about the crispness of the paper in my hand. Of the leisurely enjoyment of just reading together. Does that make sense?"

"Think so." She closed her eyes. The wind fluttered the hairs that escaped from her ponytail. "The salty sea air is like sand. Not sandpaper, but like if you pick up a palmful and let it slip through your fingertips. Gritty but soothing. Awakening."

I closed my eyes, imagining. "I like that. What else?"

"A smoky bonfire on a beach at sunset is a luxurious blanket, soft, like a hug, but almost dizzying. Makes you sleepy and relaxed. Hmm...saltwater taffy sticks in your teeth, but the sugar sends a buzz to your brain." She laughed at herself. "That one was silly."

I cracked an eyelid. "Nah, not silly. Go on..."

"Fish and seaweed." She tapped a finger to her chin. "It's like a surprise punch." She paused. "I should stick to drawing."

"Nonsense. I like it. How about coffee?" I held up the thermos. "I used to love the smell of it when I woke up, but..." I pinched the bridge of my nose. "Now it's hot water that gives me a good-morning hello."

"Despite the caffeine, coffee is like...a sedating cuddle. This sense of comfort, coziness, curling up on a couch, my head rested on the shoulder of a best friend. No judgement, just acceptance."

"Dang, coffee is that powerful, huh?" I asked.

"It's love in a cup. You can swap tea for it, but to me, the aroma of tea is like...weeds. You're not missing much there. Don't tell Irina that. And breakfast food, pancakes and sausage, those are like..."

We sat for a few minutes longer, Olivia gifting me with her canvas of textures and emotions. I closed my eyes, working to make connections between descriptions and scent. With the sun fully up, we hiked to the coastal trail while I suggested more things for her to describe. Fresh white paint. Tidepool. Bog. Rain. Clams. Dirt. Pine forests. She employed textures, emotions, and added sounds, too. She was an artist with her words.

My steps felt lighter, my lungs expanding with fresh air, while new associations imprinted on my memory.

I had gone into the race with an open mind, and was getting paid for a vacation of sorts, but I knew the odds were stacked against us. Now, as we scrambled upon rocks, not searching for a clue and not cramped in a vehicle, just taking in the sights and sounds of the shoreline and the freedom of being out among them, my outlook brightened.

Oh, and I liked Olivia. A lot.

Nineteen

Olivia

"Go Team Fleur Four!" Zach's smile reached his ears.

Piling into the minivan after solving day four's riddle, we exhaled a unanimous sigh. Holden figured out "When is a flower not a flower?" was a riddle for the state flower of Maine, the white pine pinecone. The puzzle also included a cipher, which he flew through solving. He was an impressive man.

And after our pleasant sunrise walk together, my disdain about being dragged on this race had gone from lessening each day to completely dissipating.

However, a short while after we pulled away from the Saint Croix International Historical Site, the minivan jarred with a hard pull to the side while I was trying to circle the location on the map. My pencil skittered a line until the point broke, while my shoulder smacked the passenger door. Rubbing it as my head bobbed back to center, I winced.

"Whoa! Letting this win get to your head, Torque?" Zach righted himself with a wobble as Holden recovered control of the minivan.

"Ugh. The minivan is pulling a bit and making a weird sound." His eyes flicked to the mirrors. His arms were taut, hands gripping the wheel. A whine came from the engine, multiple lights on the dashboard flickered on, then off. Then the engine temperature warning light came on and stayed on.

Irina gripped the back of my headrest as Holden found his bearings. He brought the minivan to a halt on a patch of dirt along the road's shoulder. The engine sputtered like a marathon racer on the twentieth mile, but he kept it running for just a moment to assess the dashboard. After our eyes went over every light twice, and only the temperature warning remained on despite the others flashing earlier, he turned the minivan off. Grumbling, we got out to inspect the vehicle.

"You've got to be kidding me," Zach groaned as a bit of steam rose from the hood.

Irina fussed with the white-and-blue bandana tied around her neck. "The minivan might be old, but it passed inspection in the spring."

"Even the AC?" Zach lifted a brow.

"Yes!"

Her cheeks flushed, which could be a rosacea flare-up or embarrassment—or both Empathy squashed my frustration.

Irina fanned her face. "Well, that's not an inspection point. I didn't have time for a full-service appointment, but the race mechanics added more Freon for me. Maybe it's just out again?"

"You shouldn't burn through Freon that quickly." I chewed a thumbnail. "Something electrical?"

"The engine temperature warning light is on, but also, the battery light flashed," Holden said. "The minivan hesitated yesterday when I started it in the parking lot. Could it be the alternator or battery?" He removed his glasses and rubbed the bridge of his nose.

"Would a dying alternator or battery make the AC not work well?" Zach cursed under his breath with a look back toward the road. "Where are we going to find an open garage on July Fourth?" He scraped hands through his cropped hair, then settled them on his hips, turning to Holden for any answer.

Nobody said what we were all thinking. All these things happening to a minivan that had been checked prior to the race just felt convenient—to our opponents.

Who would have the skill and gall to mess with our engine?

Or was Irina honeying the truth about the minivan's condition? She and I might not see eye to eye on a lot of things—she was more carefree than my reserved nature—but she'd never risk the race with a dysfunction-al vehicle. No, she would have made sure, even if the minivan was old, that it was running in tiptop shape. But then again...she had said her AC was acting funky prior to the race.

"Bad luck," Irina voiced, probably seeing my furrowed expression.

Zach pumped a hand into a fist, then out again. "Wasn't there a construction area back at Saint Croix? Did you run over a screw there? The minivan was pulling pretty hard."

Holden crouched and inspected the tires. "Nothing looks punctured. I checked the tire pressure two days ago when we got gas. Besides, the issue is the engine."

I pursed my lips, watching the steam emanate from the hood.

Irina worried her earlobe with a manicured nail. "We need to call the race organizers." She looked at Holden. "I assume we can't drive it if it's overheating?"

He nodded.

Irina pulled out the race packet from her handbag and located the phone.

"Do you think someone tampered with it? What the hell was going on with the dash?" Zach cursed under his breath as he followed Holden to the front of the minivan.

"Dunno, man." Holden gave me an eyebrow raise.

I came over beside him to inspect the engine, not that I knew what to look for. "Should we let it cool off first? Will hot fluids splash at us?"

Holden crossed his arms with a half-smile. "Cool off—yes. Geysers of hot liquids—not if we don't open things." He turned to Irina. "We need a tow to a mechanic."

At that very moment, Tad and Dottie whizzed past, probably on their way to lodging in Calais. We didn't bother flagging them down. They didn't bother to slow down.

Irina passed a glance heavenward. "Thank God we already found the scavenger item and secured our spot in the race."

Zach kicked pebbles. "They're always conveniently nearby. I swear that rat planted a tracking device on us or something! And I bet he did something to our engine. Jackass!" He began to pace. "Dottie's husband works in tech and has the connections. Anyone else want to tear this minivan apart and look?"

As the idea of someone sabotaging us settled in my brain, I contemplated the whole Tad-and-Dottie piggybacking thing. I didn't understand their reason. Why would they follow certain teams? Wouldn't they want to get ahead of us? Why would they track us with a GPS tag? Were they tracking others? How would this strategy help them win? My only explanation was that it was to keep tabs on us. Or maybe if they were struggling with a clue, seeing where we went—or others went—would help them. Were they really this bad at solving puzzles on their own? This behavior seemed kind of desperate.

"A tracking device?" Irina asked.

"A GPS tag," Holden explained. "It's so small, like the size of a large coin, you can slip it into a purse or under a seat..."

"Oh, dear." She handed him the phone. "I plugged in the race emergency number. Maybe best if you explain what happened." As Holden hit dial and put the phone to his ear, she patted Zach's shoulder. "Let's get some fresh air. I'm going to walk the dogs. Join me?" She fastened the Gentle Leader harnesses and leashed the dogs and grabbed poo bags.

After they were out of earshot, and Holden was off the phone, I asked, "What do you really think of this? The dash? The flickering? Zach's theory?"

"Dunno."

I pinched my lips. I was certain he had a theory, too. Holden did not like to muddy the waters with his opinions, but he certainly had them. I'd ask him more later.

While we waited, we sat back in the minivan and rummaged around for snacks. The humidity today was like pea soup, and I readjusted my ponytail, loose hair sticking to sweat on my neck. I could use an iced drink right now, but all I had in the minivan was tepid water.

"If it had been a flat tire, I could manage that," I said.

"Oh?" he asked.

"Single mom, old car, older house. Repairs aren't cheap. My dad taught me."

A short while later, Zach ran back to us, not winded—but frazzled. "She's not here?"

"Who? Irina?" I hopped out of the minivan.

"No, the dog! Ini thought she might've run back here. Where are her treats? Ini said to look for the one with a special yellow label and her squeaky toy."

"Which one ran off?" My mind went to the Five Ws of call taking: what, who, where, when, and why. Get details; keep them calm. Bringing these dogs had been a bad idea, but that was a conversation for later.

"Damned if I know. The curly one, uh, the doodle that likes to run away."

Violet. Violet liked to wrangle out of her Gentle Leader. "Where?" It was best to stick to where she had gone missing rather than traipse all over the place and get separated or worse, lost. We were on a quiet stretch of Route 1. If you listened, you could hear the ocean, but our view was blocked by tall pines and a hillside covered in meadow flowers.

He pointed. "That way."

"How long ago?" Time gave me a search area.

He waved his hands, exasperated. "However long it took me to leg it back here. Like, uh, two minutes ago?"

I dug into Irina's labeled bins and found the treats. After grabbing a baggy of them, the toy, and my backpack with two bottles of water, I handed Zach a whistle. I hung a second one around my neck. They'd been purchased after an incident of Logan wandering off a trail while we were hiking with Dad in the Berkshires, out of reception. "Whistle if you need us or if she returns. I have one, too."

"I'll help Holden."

"Good idea, Zach." He seemed to be unraveling today, and staying here was probably the best place for him. On a whim, I also grabbed a pair of my socks, since Violet seemed to be so obsessed with them. Lure her out with the promise of a pair of socks she could nibble on? I almost snorted. Hey, whatever worked.

I made for the direction from which Zach had come.

I began calling Violet, shaking her bag, and squeaking her toy. I met up with an agitated Irina a few minutes later, as she was scrambling down a path toward the shoreline. Lily walked beside her.

"Violet, sweetie! Vi-Vi! Come!" Hope lit her light blue eyes when they fell on me. "Did she go back to the mini-van?"

"No. I'm here to help you search. Which way did she go?"

Irina pointed east. "She wiggled out of her Gentle Leader again and then Lily was distracted by a frog. I slid on mud, and she seized the opportunity. Violet never runs away!" Her voice was high, her breathing ragged.

Except for the time at West Quoddy Head, but who was counting? Violet was still young and learning. I patted Irina's shoulder. "We'll find her. She's a smart dog."

Irina covered a sniffle as we walked down the trail. "I thought she ran down the ocean path, but now, I-I can't remember. I got spun around and then she was gone."

I offered her a water bottle. She waved it away. "Drink," I ordered. I didn't need to add a dehydrated stepmother to today's growing list of crap.

I squeezed the toy, hoping it would lure Violet out as we got closer to the ocean. Violet loved the water. "Hey, Violet!

I have a nice soft sock for you to chew on!" I waved my balled socks.

"Sweetie! I have your treats!" Irina shook the bag. "Your toy," she said, quieter with another sniffle.

Not finding the dog along the shore, we circled back on another trail that led up through the trees. We emerged at a meadow, and I tried not to think about the ticks in the long flowers and grasses. Just when I was letting my mood heat up to worried, a whistle sounded. "That's Zach! Let's go to the minivan."

Lily was panting beside Irina. She bit back a sob. "Did he find her?"

I slid my hand in hers and squeezed. "I told him to whistle if he finds her. Let's regroup at the minivan."

As we crested the hilly meadow to reach the minivan above, we heard the barking. Lily barked in response.

"Violet!" Irina exclaimed. Despite her obvious relief, she paused for a breath, clearly winded from the ordeal.

The minivan doors were closed, but Violet was bouncing around inside, slobbering the window with her nose and tongue.

I released Irina's hand and offered a side squeeze. Irina loved physical affection, and she could really use a hug right now. "See? Smart dog. You trained her well. She came back."

While Irina scolded and hugged Violet in the back seat, I found Holden ducked under the hood, tinkering with wires and connections. Zach sat in the grass on a blanket playing solitaire, clearly needing a mental respite.

"What are you doing?" I asked Holden.

"Checking wires and fuses, but I don't know what to look for. Oil and tires are the scope of my car skills, too."

I leaned in to see what he was staring at. "Could it be an easy fix like a bad battery or alternator, like you said earlier?"

He took off his glasses to wipe sweat off the bridge of his nose. "Wouldn't a tune-up by the race mechanics have caught that?"

"You don't think Zach's idea holds water, do you? That someone messed with the minivan?" My pulse skyrocketed as I verbalized the idea.

"Maybe."

His words may have expressed indecision, but his slanted frown said yes.

Twenty

Olivia

We spent the holiday evening sitting in a greasy garage waiting area that reeked of fumes. Instead of celebrating with hamburgers, music, and fireworks, we munched on snacks from the minivan and vending machines.

I could really use a cold beer. I yawned. And a nap.

Holden and I decided to walk to a small coffee shop in midtown, hopeful for something baked or an iced drink, and maybe just for some distance from Irina's apologies and Zach's worrying. But when we reached the café, Holden tapped the "CLOSED" sign on the door. Spying a convenience store farther down, we kept walking.

"Want me to describe the scents of the garage when we return?"

He chuckled. "That I can do without."

"This bites."

"It does."

Cars drove past and looked like they were going to a celebration farther down in town. Loud celebratory music blared from somewhere in the distance. We stopped at a crosswalk and waited for a signal.

"Olivia?" We stood so close I felt him breathe on the back of my neck.

"Yeah?"

"Do you really think this was..." He left the rest of his question hanging.

I swallowed and rubbed my throat, trying to massage the ickiness out of it. "Sabotage? Kind of, yeah. This can't be a coincidence. Somebody messed with the minivan. Do you think it was a team...or someone within the race personnel who did this? One of the people who inspects vehicles? But wouldn't we have experienced problems sooner than day four if it was an inside job? And is it just us, or have other vehicles been tampered with?"

He shrugged. "I figured it was a team, like Tad and Dottie. Sometimes a pulled fuse or faulty wire can cause electrical or mechanical issues on a delay."

"How much do you know about them?" I preferred facts over postulating, but even the facts had my palms sweating.

We crossed the road. He visibly stiffened, shoving his hands into his pockets. "Just what Irina told us."

"Irina gets a bit tipsy, and very chatty, with her gin and tonics. Last night, after we turned in, she was gabbing more about Dottie's husband. He's a tech hotshot. He has *resources*, if you know what I mean. Like what Zach suggested. Who's to say he didn't put a GPS tag in our minivan...or he has somebody on the inside who hacked the GPS unit the race mechanics put in? But, why? You know? I don't get it." I rubbed my nose. "And...oh, never mind."

"And what?" He looked at me expectantly.

"Irina also had some gossip about his...infidelity—rumors only. She thinks Dottie is sick, too, maybe cancer or something, and that this will be her last time racing. So, she wants to win, more than normal. Maybe they're desperate to win and will stoop to that level." I sounded as bad as Irina. "I don't know."

"Gossip must start somewhere. People do dodgy stuff when love, reputation, ego, or money are on the line."

"As for Tad, he's Dottie's stooge. She's the one with the connections. Tad has a good accounting firm, but—again, this is by way of Irina—it's been in trouble. Fishy books or something." I exhaled a groan. "Take this with a grain of salt. Irina can embellish."

Holden paused, his eyes lifting toward the horizon. Evening clouds had covered the afternoon sunshine and now the sky was shadowy and bleak. Wind swayed the long stems of a rainbow of zinnias in the front yard of the house beside us.

"Is she usually right?" he asked.

"Usually." Shivers prickled my spine.

"This is my fault."

"What is?"

He waved around us. "Driving in a broken-down minivan. It's my fault the shop van was stolen. I left the keys in it for just a few minutes... And now here we are."

I squeezed his forearm. "It's not your fault. Mistakes happen."

We reached the convenience store.

He opened the door for me as we walked inside. Holden grabbed a small shopping basket, and I tossed in food: almonds, beef jerky sticks, more gum for Zach, flavored water, and some black jellybeans for Irina—gross, but they were her favorite, and sometimes hard to find. We had a small cooler with ice back at the van, so I also grabbed yogurt, cheese, and pepperoni sticks.

Holden pulled a notecard from his back pocket. "Hey, what do you call a grandpa flower?"

A smile tugged my lips. "You have a cheat sheet?"

"Nope." He shoved the notecard back into his pocket with a bashful grin.

I knocked shoulders with him. "You're too cute."

He cleared his throat and averted his eyes to the shelf in front of us. Somehow, we ended up by the uh, personal hygiene products, and tampons and condoms were right at eye level. We made our way to the register as if our shoes were on fire.

I nibbled my lip. "Hmm, a grandpa flower... A bloomer? Like a 'boomer'?"

"An elder-berry," he said.

I just shook my head.

"Too much?"

"Nah. I love it."

Holden piled the food by the register. I handed him a twenty-dollar bill to cover my stuff and asked the cashier, "Umm, do you have the bathroom key?"

"Entrance is outside, round the back." He handed it to me, and I motioned to Holden I'd be right back.

On my return from the bathroom, I reached the front door at the same time as a man dressed in work overalls and smelling of cigarettes and motor oil. Friendly blue eyes stared down at me, but my own eyes blurred over when I saw the tattooed path of flowers down the left side of his neck. He held the door open for me, and I stood there, my mouth open.

"Happy Fourth. Ladies first," he said in a Mainer accent, a bit rougher than the typical Boston or Southie ones.

I did not move. I think I blinked. My hands went clammy.

He shook his head with an eye roll and let the door swing shut behind him as he stepped inside. Belatedly finding my footing, I followed him. a shadow to his steps down the soda aisle. Same blue eyes, rounded shoulders, age, height, and tattoo location—and a floral design—as the man whose masked image was burned into my memory. My pulse sprinted. He met everything on my perp checklist. Was this *him*?

We weren't remotely close to the Maine address I had memorized from the NCIC database. Maybe the person I wanted to investigate moved. Would fate do such a thing? Plop this perp literally into my path?

A hand on my shoulder made me jump, and I knocked a few snack packs off the display I was apparently cowering behind.

"You okay?" Holden asked.

I knelt and picked up the wayward cupcake packs. "Th-thought Zach could use more snacks."

Holden held up two plastic bags. "I think we're good. And he's had way too much sugar. You look a little rattled yourself." He looked over my shoulder to the back of the store, where the stranger lurked. "You sure you're okay?"

It couldn't be him. Could it?

Holden stepped closer. "Olivia?"

"Yeah, uh. Just hungry. T-tired. Long day."

I watched the man walk to the front of the store.

"Hey, Drew. How's things at the shop?" the cashier said to the tattooed man as he arrived at the register. "Got plans tonight?"

"Quiet. Just some race folks needing a repair. Then I'm going to the fireworks with Millie. You?"

"Same. The kids love them."

I overanalyzed his voice. Definitely Mainer. Not Worcester. Not him.

Holden took me by the elbow, and we left, my mind reeling.

I walked in a blur. Drew. That wasn't the name of the perp I had planned to investigate. Had he changed his name along with his address?

And his accent?

When we returned to the garage, the mechanic working on the minivan strode out. He wiped oily hands on his jeans, then lit a cigarette and trained his eyes on Holden. "Battery was fine, but a faulty alternator was draining it. Looked like a chipmunk had gone under the hood and began disconnecting things. I'll be honest, you're lucky you got this far. Not quite sure why it pulled right, but the tires are all fine."

As he explained loose wires, connections, and fuses to us, blood pounded in my temples. The man with the tattoo. The deliberate sabotage of our vehicle. Two different things, both really shitty.

Irina paid the man in cash and tipped him an extra twenty with a sweet smile.

As the others made their way to the minivan, I feigned tying my shoe. Once they were out of earshot, I asked the mechanic, "Uh, we ran into the other mechanic, at the convenience store. Drew. Nice guy. Has he worked here long?"

"Oh, a long time. Been here since he was like sixteen. Why?"

Damn.

"He just looked familiar. We live in Massachusetts. Thought I'd seen him around."

"Drew? Nah. He's as homebody as they come. Doesn't travel much, except for his Army tour in Iraq and Syria two years ago. He's home now for good though. Done with his service."

Double damn.

The memories of that time, two years ago, blurred the edges of my vision as I nodded my thanks and followed my team to the minivan. A few splatters of rain hit the windshield.

Think of something else. My mind went to how I would describe that ozone bite in the air for Holden. Earthy, thick, but also cleansing. That was a hard one.

We pulled into the hotel parking area around nine o'clock.

Distant fireworks cracked and boomed in the night as we dragged ourselves to our rooms, lugging backpacks and rolling suitcases. Even Irina remained wordless—not a grumble, not a peep. Tad and Dottie's team was nowhere in sight, which meant, even though Holden had done well with the cipher, we were somewhere in the middle or even the back of the pack, since they seemed to always finish in the top group. Except today they'd passed us on the road, which would have meant they finished after we did.

All I knew was they probably were cheating. How was another question. And why this keen interest in our team specifically?

I was too damn tired to make sense of it—for now.

Twenty-One

Zach

I asked Irina to read the clue...again.

And again.

As the words found purchase in my mushy mind, my pulse raced away from me like one of her dogs off the leash.

I stared at the expanse of Seboeis Lake. Dappled by late morning sun, it was gorgeous yet terrifying.

Fake it 'til you make it was a dumb phrase, and one I had lived by for too long. How the hell was I going to fake it through *this*?

Though I had loved every one of Jin's daily notes of inspiration and encouragement he had tucked into my suitcase, no words on paper would get me through this mental challenge.

I clenched my hand at my side to suppress the tremors vibrating in my chest. It was day five. Almost halfway. A water challenge was bound to come up.

During the last race, our water-related challenge was a hike to Arethusa Falls in New Hampshire. But there was no swimming or anything. Just a hike to the falls. According to Irina, one year's water challenge had to do with a cranberry bog on the Cape. She and I knew to expect water challenges, just like hiking and memory ones. So why was I gawking at this ginormous lake in the middle of Maine?

Irina's disposition collapsed for a moment into a sigh and frown. Maybe even she was getting cranky on this race. After yesterday, I didn't blame her.

She flipped her frown into her patient smile. "Zach, we figured it out already. We're going to paddle in canoes to the designated island, which we think is Hammer Island. We assemble the correct rocks—those with the chicory stamped on them or something—into a cairn. Then we camp for the night and bask in the glory by fire and moonlight!" She flourished her hands and did a hip shimmy, reciting the clue again:

"Two by two you go, all must paddle with the flow..."

"Got it. I'm not dumb. Maybe that hundred-year-old lumberjack at the gas station gave us the wrong directions," I snapped. Gillian, from another team nearby, gave me a look as she readied their canoe and gear. Their presence meant we weren't off the mark. I offered her a weak grimace of apology, heat warming my ears.

Where had that come from?

This is not happening. This is not happening.

I popped a piece of gum into my mouth to cut the sourness. I could not upchuck here.

The distance to Hammer Island was less than two miles. Ten years ago, I could *swim* that distance easily. In fact, I did, on a regular basis, training for competitions.

After the incident, I swore off bodies of water in all forms: pools, oceans, lakes. Nobody knew the truth, not even my parents—not even Jin. Somehow, I worked around it each time he suggested a water activity. *The beach and pool are for sunbathing. Sand is gross. The water is too chilly. Let's hike this trail instead. I have an upset stomach. I have a migraine.* At one point, he suggested I see the doctor about my frequent "migraines." I was so invested in the lies that I even believed them and began to get legit migraines.

Jin, like everyone, thought I had dropped off the swim team because competition had lost its luster, and I wanted to take my education more seriously because a career in swimming was a hard reach. He and I met after my swim days, so he accepted that lie as fact.

Not a soul knew about *that day.*

I had been tapering off my practice distances to prepare for the prelims. I went for my usual pre-race practice swim—the two miles between Balboa Pier and Newport Pier that mimicked the annual pier-to pier-swim event—and I got a painful charley horse just short of Tower 20.

I could do that swim in my sleep. I could do that swim with a damn leg cramp! But not on that day.

And never again.

I'd nearly drowned.

I could still feel the burn of salt in my nostrils.

I chewed harder on the peppermint gum, returning Irina's look with a glare. Her cheeks flushed. I instantly regretted my unkindness. She didn't deserve it.

She probably thought I was being testy about the race and doubting our direction with today's clue, like I had with all the clues. For a plant expert, I wasn't bringing my A game. I mean, I was okay, but Olivia, Irina, and Holden had done a better job solving the riddles. I shouldn't care, but I did. I cared too much.

The problem was that today we were on target. There wouldn't be canoes and a guy waiting here with life jackets if we weren't.

The map included in this morning's envelope, a simple drawing with points indicated by symbols, shook in my hand. Even if, miraculously, we'd gone to the wrong lake—Maine had thousands—what I couldn't deny was the very clear riddle involving water. On our way here, watching multiple teams turn off onto other roads, we surmised that clues with different locations were given at random. Not everyone was at this put-in. The remaining teams probably went to one of the other boat launches we'd seen on the map: one on the northern part of the lake and one on another lake.

I puzzled the details in my brain one more time, grasping at obscure straws.

Irina swiped at invisible wrinkles in her T-shirt and inhaled, recovering her confidence in her usual fashion. "Grab your overnight bag, Legs. We'll paddle one canoe together—I need your upper body strength—and Olivia and Holden the other. Life jackets are there." She left to talk to the man standing by the canoes.

Following her, Olivia asked, "Irina, how are you going to paddle with two big dogs?"

Dark green pines flanked the V-shaped lake as far as the eye could see, and in the distance, I saw a brownish blur where sky met treetops. Was that Mount Katahdin? Jin and I hiked to the summit of Maine's kingpin last fall. Killer, but worth the push. I would hike three Katahdins over canoeing today.

The other team had already entered the water and was putting distance between us. Who knows if we were second or last?

My gaze fell to the lake. The water was clear close to shore...and looked dark and deep beyond. Really deep. Choppy white caps frothed from the wind.

The lapping of the smaller waves up the pebbly shoreline splashed my sneakers, soaking through to my socks. Was the water rising? Was it reaching for me? My throat tightened, and my vision doubled as trees beside me became arms, reaching out, pushing me into the lake.

"Zach, you're getting wet. Didn't you pack water shoes?" a voice asked softly.

Olivia? Holden? I didn't know. Jolted from my stupor, I clambered back a step, as if poison had seeped into my skin and not the fresh, cold Maine water. I bumped into something solid.

"You okay?" Holden asked, steadying me.

I shrugged.

Irina buzzed around, gathering the dogs, their treats, food, blankets, and whatnot. These dogs came with more stuff than we did.

She brimmed with satisfaction. "The girls are all set. I spoke with the boat guy, Ned. He'll motor the dogs over to us after we figure out the puzzle and submit our answer for check-in."

Olivia wrangled herself into a life jacket. Holden dropped their backpacks into a canoe.

Irina walked the dogs over to Ned, her new bestie, who handed her a walkie-talkie. "It has good range," he assured her with a wink beneath grizzly eyebrows. "To only be used to contact me, okay?"

"You betcha," she said.

"The clue said tents and dinner will be provided at our designated sites." Holden took the map from my hand and showed it to Olivia. "I assume these triangles are the campsites. We should hustle."

I moved like I was being pulled. Or I *was* being pulled. A hand was on my arm as someone spoke imperceptible words in my ear.

Numbly, I slid into the life jacket. Click, click. I pulled the straps as snug as my lungs would allow. Tugged twice. Dropped my backpack beside the canoe. Changed into the water sandals Jin insisted I get. They were tight, never worn. My fingers fumbled with the bungee laces.

With my and Irina's packs in the hull, Holden stepped forward to help us launch.

"You okay, Zach?" he asked. "You thirsty or something? It's been hot…"

I couldn't answer him. Inside, I shouted at myself, *Move, Legs*! So much for that nickname. The frog legs were no more.

"Water always finds a way," a plumber repairing a leaky sink for the umpteenth time once told me. Would it today?

I had a life jacket on, for eff's sake. I wasn't going to drown.

Reluctant body parts moved. *First, put feet into water.* The cold bit into my skin, and the current tugged.

"Zach, you sit in the back since you're stronger. You already know that," Holden said, holding the canoe steady by the gunwale while Irina got in front.

Water lapped against my calves. *Get in, you moron!*

I got in. Holden handed us our single-blade paddles and then gave us a shove. The rocky shoreline scraped against the hull. With a whoosh, my stomach bottomed out as I felt the canoe lift, untethered to the shore…free to float, free to sink. I trembled, but the desire to not flip over forced me to move my arms in the rhythmic motion of paddling.

A voice came through the roaring in my brain. "Zach, Sugar, we need to stay sixty feet from the other canoe, remember?"

I didn't look back. Just forward. I paddled us forward.

Water. Lots of dark blue water.

It splashed as the paddle sliced. My palms slickened with spray as we worked against the headwind.

"I can't paddle this fast, Zach. Remember, sixty feet. We're getting too far away from Olivia and Holden. Slow down, Sugar."

Eff sixty feet. Those two could catch the hell up. The less time I was crammed into a slender death boat, the better. What if it tipped?

Then you'd float, dumbass.

What if the life jacket broke? What if a rogue wave hit us—

—*in the middle of a lake in Maine?*

The water looked deep. Bottomless. Dark. And it was getting inside the canoe. Was that a hole in the hull?

"Water is getting in, Ini," I managed to stutter out. "Do we have a leak?"

"No. You're splashing a bit, that's all."

"How do you know?"

"Because I am getting splashed, Sugar."

I rested the paddle across my thighs to give my burning upper arms and shoulders a moment's respite, and we drifted backward a little with the headwind. Whose bright idea was this task? This wasn't *The Amazing Race*! This was a race with garden geeks! Test our brains, not our brawn!

Holden and Olivia caught up and passed us, their paddles slicing through the water in synchrony. The two couldn't be better matched. I missed J:n. If he were here, what would he say to my spinelessnes?

I allowed the water to rock me. I closed my eyes. *Make it go away. This is a dream.*

"We need to move, Sugar. I didn't mean to stop. I'm good, I can do this. They're waiting for us."

"I-I can't."

I peeled open an eye. Dizziness captured me. I clutched the gunwales. Then leaned over and lost my breakfast.

Chunks of cowardice bobbed in the dark water, then drifted away. I wiped my mouth, too queasy to even attempt to reach into my backpack at my feet for a sip of water. Not tipping was my top priority. "Bad breakfast," I mumbled.

Irina paddled a few strokes to steer us away from my upchuck, then attempted to turn around to look at me. "Are you seasick, too, like the carsickness?" She sighed. "Oh, Sugar..."

She twisted further. My head spun again as I wobbled on my seat.

"Don't tip the boat! We can't go in!"

Defeat rang in my ears.

Know what stinks? The fine details you remember most about the pivotal moment of your failure.

It hadn't been my parents' disappointed faces when my potential career came crashing to a halt during prelims that seared into my memory the most.

It was the cries in the crowd when I freaked out during the gun lap—the final two lengths of the pool—of the freestyle 4x200 relay. I'd already taken second in the 1500-meter freestyle. All that remained was this event. It began fine.

I never scratched in a competition before, and I wasn't going to let some little incident during practice get in my way. I had even hydrated, stretched, and took my magic duo of drinking some pickle juice and eating a mustard packet to keep my potassium at a good level and prevent any cramps. After my teammate tapped the wall, I dove off the block and propelled myself forward, slicing through water, not far behind the leader. I drifted behind Seth Rodriguez in the lane beside me, getting ready to overtake him.

I remembered the cheers when I did my flip turn.

"West-ie! West-ie!"

"The best in the West!"

"Westerlind for the win!"

"Go Froglegs!"

Something in me snapped. I swallowed water, chlorine singeing my throat.

A vise gripped around my calf.

Afterward, I told my parents and friends a leg cramp overtook me. They understood sudden cramps. If I admitted the truth, that my near drowning in the cold waters off Newport Pier the week before had crippled my confidence, they would have thought I was a coward. To this day, I liked to imagine it had been a cramp and not cowardice that had me frozen.

Cries, questions, shouts echoed off the walls of the natatorium as I treaded water, gasping and grasping in the middle of a race pool for anyone, anything. Swimmers passed me, each touching the wall one by one until the only person left was me. Then I sank like a bowling ball to the bottom. Someone jumped in. Pulled me up just like the lifeguard on Newport Beach. On the tiles beside the pool, I passed out.

Shame burned more than any chlorine or salt water ever could.

Telling my parents that I was done with competitions and focusing solely on my botany degree had been devastating—more for them than me. I liked flowers. I liked what I did now.

After my swimming years were over, I met Jin. But his insatiable hunger for adventure brought the pain back time and time again. We had built our relationship on this commonality: the thrill of adventure. I had lied to him since day one. How could I tell him the truth now?

The lake returned to my vision as black spots disappeared.

Irina proceeded with slow strokes, alternating sides while I sat there, useless.

Her words floated back on a breeze over her shoulder. "How long has it been, Zach?"

I blinked. "Huh? Been since what? Breakfast?"

"Not breakfast, Sugar. How long has it been since whatever happened that made you afraid of the water?"

"T-ten years."

"That's a long time to hold on to the pain." She paddled harder.

There was no way she'd be able to paddle us to the island on her own, but my arms were jelly, and my stomach pinched with another spasm, sharp as the astringent taste in my mouth. My spirit was soggier than the back of my T-shirt, slick with the sweat dripping down my neck.

"Jin's the adventure junkie, isn't he? You just go along with his shenanigans."

What could I say? I was glad she couldn't turn around and see me. I probably was as green as the pines along the shoreline.

Olivia and Holden halted their canoe ahead. I felt their questioning stares.

Irina said, "You can do this, Zach. I know you can."

"I-I can't, Ini."

"Unless you want to sleep here on the water in this lovely little canoe, I suggest you put that paddle back in your hand and do this."

I want to toss the paddle into the water.

"You have me, Zach. I won't let anything happen to you. I won't tell you to pretend we're somewhere else, but I can tell you that you're safe."

Her kind words reached through my panic and felt like more than I deserved after my earlier assholery.

"I'm sorry I snapped at you."

"Pish. Never mind that. Let's stroke together. I can see the island. It's not far."

Picking up the light paddle, a heavy weight in my palm, I began to stroke. *Smack, whoosh, smack, whoosh.* My shoulders burned, but I forced the strokes, making the blade slice through water and propel us forward. Meter by meter, we made our way across the lake. Water splashed as we picked up speed.

"Repeat after me," Irina said. "Today I am capable."

I repeated it.

"Today I am worthy."

I repeated it.

"Today I am enough."

I managed, but choked on the word "enough."

"Today I can love myself just as I am."

My voice broke further on those words.

Irina did her best to synchronize with my strokes, her voice so placid, so soothing. "Zach, you are capable. You are worthy. You are enough. And we love you just as you are."

Evergreens and mountains and distant sandy coves blurred to green and gray, brown and rust and tan. The choppy lake became a flat sheet of deep indigo.

Irina continued to encourage me. I didn't stop paddling until we struck something hard. Did we hit a boulder? Had I flipped us? Had I brought Irina down into the abyss with me?

Panting, sweating, I squeezed my eyes shut.

Multiple voices.

A hand on my shoulder. "Man, I didn't think this was that kind of race. I'm gonna feel it tomorrow."

I opened my eyes. Holden grinned at me. He was in the water beside us, guiding the canoe toward the shore. There, Irina and I got out. My legs wobbled, and I collapsed into Olivia.

"Whoa, there! You okay, Zach?" She palmed my cheek, then forehead. "You're burning up. Come here. I have an electrolyte drink for you."

"I'll stay with him here, Olivia. You and Holden go over there. I see cairns, less than sixty feet ahead."

"Is he sick?" Holden asked.

"Bad breakfast," Irina lied. "You two go. You've got this."

"Ch-chicory is blue, pink...or white. The petals have like, five-five teeth on the ends," I stammered. "R-ray flowers. Not discs. T-take the phone. We'll join for the picture."

I heard the crunch of shoes on pebbles as they hurried to perform the cairn task. Irina tipped a bottle to my mouth. Sweet lemon-lime ran down my throat.

Looking around, I couldn't see the other team. And there was no telling how far ahead the others had gotten that we couldn't see because they set off from different points on the lake. "I cost us the race. We're last, aren't we?"

She tapped, then squeezed my hand. "No, you did not."

"I-I cost my team the race."

"No, you did not," she repeated.

I cracked open my eyes. "No, before. When I was in swimming. On the team in college. Our relay team lost in the prelims because I panicked."

"You don't need to tell me about it. Let's get you a towel."

"No, I want to tell you about it. I haven't told anyone ever. Not even Jin."

She hugged me. "Later, Sugar. Rest first."

That evening, after checking in and securing our standing in the race, we gathered around a crackling fire pit. The other three ate chili, drank hot cocoa, and assembled s'mores. My stomach was still queasy. I munched on a graham cracker. Olivia and Holden were lost in their own bubble, she with a headlamp on and drawing, he sitting shoulder to shoulder with her to chitchat.

Three long, haunting notes wailed on the lake.

"Loons," Irina said to my questioning look. "In addition to his love of rocks, Jerry liked birds."

Lily came over and rested her head on my feet.

"She's got a tender heart. She knows when someone is hurting." Irina lowered her voice. "She doesn't nuzzle me in the armpit the same way as she did with Jerry, though. She's been...sad. Missing him."

I leaned over and patted the dog's head.

Irina wrapped a blanket around my shoulders. In a near-whisper, I told her about the leg cramp, the near drowning, the competitions, my parents' pressure, and about hiding the truth from Jin. Everything.

She tapped my knee. "Jin will understand. When you're ready, you'll tell him. He loves you, Sugar."

Her tenderness was a lighthouse in the fog.

Later, before bed, after using the outhouse, I paused in a cluster of pine trees a short distance from our tent site. Pulled out my vape. Inhaled. Closed my eyes to numb my senses. It didn't help my feelings about myself. Vaping was an escape, and I was tired of escaping. I wanted to toss the vape into the lake...but then my problem would be the lake's problem. I didn't want to litter.

I coughed and put it back in my pocket. Pulled out a piece of gum instead.

On my way back to my tent, I overheard Olivia and Irina talking as they got ready in theirs.

"Irina, this isn't working with the dogs."

"I know, dear."

The ladies' tent had to be the most crowded one with Irina, Olivia, Violet, and Lily.

Irina said, "Tomorrow, we'll take them to Millinocket."

"What's in Millinocket?"

"Who, dear. My brother. We can leave Violet and Lily with him."

"Why didn't you mention that sooner? We could've taken the boat back to shore and driven them to your brother's house tonight, after we did our check-in. Won't going there tomorrow delay us?"

"I wanted to be here for Zach."

"He's not your son. He's a grown man and can handle himself."

Dang, girl. Did Olivia know how much her words stung Irina? And besides, *was* I a grown man? Sure, I was thirty-two, but damn, I was still trying to please my parents, to impress my boyfriend. I felt like a kid.

"It's better if we go together, first thing tomorrow and hope that it won't delay us much."

I heard the fatigue in Irina's voice. I had tested her patience today, and in turn, she'd offered only compassion. I reached our tent. Holden was reading a book, illuminated by his headlight. "Did you hear all that?" I asked.

"Yeah. Guess we're taking a detour tomorrow."

What more was there to say? Exhausted, I pulled out one of my encouraging notes from Jin. I read the words through wet eyes:

You've got this! Every step is a victory. Embrace the challenge. Keep pushing. You're stronger than you think.

Love you bunches. – Jin xoxo

P.S. Grab me some saltwater taffy, you sweet thing. (Because if Irina is correct—and we both know she always is—you're in Maine somewhere!)

Twenty-Two

Irina

"The potato blossom festival!" Zach exclaimed. His energy had done a complete reboot during the night.

I glanced at one of my Maine magazines. "I think so, too. And, fortunately, Millinocket is on the way to Fort Fairfield. Thing is, that festival usually runs mid-July, and it's only July sixth, which makes me think our location isn't in Fort Fairfield but nearby. What about Presque Isle? That area is also known for potatoes."

"How about I read it again?" Zach said, without a hint of irritation at me second-guessing his conclusion.

I smiled. "Meanwhile, Holden, head north to Millinocket. I'll guide you as we get closer to Gus's house."

Zach held up the potato, yes, a potato that we were handed with our clue. There was no doubting the potato blossom was our item to photograph, but the question remained: where?

He read: "*Bloom where you are planted!*" and snorted. "These really are cheesy. Like blue cheese." Then he continued:

"Red, white, and blue, we root in spring, blossom in summer,
and in the autumn have a date with your plate.
Get thee to The County.
When you arrive, you'll find this in a road, and a decision you'll make.
If you find it in a drawer, you'll be ready for mash or latke."

He paused and wrinkled his nose. "That so does not rhyme." Sighing, he carried on.

"Maria will welcome you at the door—
Just around the isle lacking guile.
Then you will find the answer...
Locate my blossoms on this:
You cut it on a table, but it is never eaten."

He made a throaty sound in that way Logan did when being snarky. "I think the writers of the clues were stoned. This is a new level of confusing."

"I agree. Gobbledygook." I stuck out my tongue.

Uncertainty floated in my stomach like an iceberg. Stopping to see Gus before we solved this puzzle was a risk. I had no way of calling Gus to see if he was even home. I hoped he'd received the text message I sent before we turned over our phones. What I hadn't told the kids was that my brother worked as a ranger at Baxter State Park. His station was near Daicey Pond, a popular camping spot.

Record numbers of outdoor enthusiasts flocked there over the holiday week.

My brother and I usually spoke frequently, but I'd been remiss lately, what with the race to prepare for. I shot a quick prayer heavenward, and my lifted eyes spotted a stain on the ceiling. If we won the race this year, I'd get a new minivan.

Which turned my mind back to the race. I patted Zach's knee after a few minutes. "I think you're right about Fort Fairfield...but I do wonder if it's worth checking Presque Isle first."

He bounced the tuber in his hands. "*Isle* isn't capitalized in the poem, so it may mean something else. Like...aisle? A play on words? Like in a grocery store or island or a traffic median. Who the heck knows about *guile*? There's that part about a decision. I think it's a fork in a road. Fork makes sense with the mash and latke. So...a fork, a median?"

I hated to see the doubt crinkle his expression. Yesterday was hard for him, but I felt privileged to have seen that side of him...and now he was back in the saddle, trying to win this race. "I agree, Sugar, but Presque Isle is on the way to Fort Fairfield. Might we rule that out first?"

I stared at the magazine in my lap. There was a lovely two-page spread about the annual potato blossom festival. "Red, white, and blue...the colors of potatoes, plus a spin on this festival happening just after July Fourth. The County must be what locals call Aroostook County."

"Blue potatoes?" Olivia asked.

Holden said, "Yeah. My sister has used them in recipes. Weird, right?"

"What about something you cut on the table but don't eat? Not a potato," Olivia said.

Zach pulled his deck of cards from the seatback and flashed a brilliant smile. "You cut a deck of cards on a table."

"Bravo!" I said.

"And Maria?" Olivia asked.

I tapped a fingernail on my lips. "Maybe Maria is a vendor at the festival and we're looking for a deck of cards at her booth, but since the festival isn't until next week, my guess would be a local shop. Last time, 'Dawn' was sunrise, not a person in the clue for West Quoddy Head. So is 'Maria' a person at all?"

A little while later, we reached Millinocket. "Holden, turn right here. The driveway zigzags and is a bit bumpy, but we can manage." Thankfully, it hadn't rained last night, or else this road would be a sloppy chute of mud.

My brain thumped up and down along with the wheels of my minivan on this road. I couldn't help but be sad about leaving the girls here. I trusted Gus, though.

Please be here.

"Potatoes on a deck of cards?" Holden said, working to keep control as we bounced through ruts.

"Mainers like their potatoes. I wouldn't doubt it. But what seems more likely is to have potato blossoms on a deck of cards. They're pretty flowers that can be pink, white, purple, or yellow. Why not put them on playing cards? I have coasters with lighthouses."

"I have a magnet with garlic on it from Gilroy, California," Zach added, tucking the cards into his backpack. "They even make garlic ice cream there."

"Exactly. Anything is possible," I said.

As we drove around the final bend through pine trees and fifty-year-old maples, Gus's cabin came into view. I girded my loins. Having him keep the dogs for a week was a big ask.

A beautiful chocolate Labrador retriever came running to the minivan, and the ice in my stomach melted. I hopped out.

If Sly was here, that meant Gus was around, since he and his ex-wife, Angie, shared custody of their dog...unless she just happened to come by to take care of his chickens or something. Gus's sons, Nikos and Mario, both lived across the country. They were sweethearts. I kept in touch with them as much as I could.

His red truck sat parked in the open barn. How long would he be here? If he couldn't watch Violet and Lily, would Angie take them?

A burly figure walked out the front door. "Ins, how the heck did that rust bucket make it up the incline?"

My brother wore a splattered apron. A quick sniff of the air wafting out the open cabin windows confirmed he was making one of his delicious sauces. Peaches? I put my hands on my hips. ' My rust bucket is better than yours, Konstantinos," I said, using his given name. He knew I hated being called Ins.

"Aw, she gets me where I need to go, especially through Baxter." He lumbered down the stairs, his heavy boots thudding on each step, then wrapped me in a bear hug.

I almost didn't want to let go. I needed more hugs than the average person, I think. Jerry would wrap me in a hug while I made my morning tea. Nowadays, I snagged a hug from Logan or the occasional friend or a side squeeze from Zach. Olivia wasn't much of a hugger.

Gus smelled of brown sugar and cayenne. "Hmm...peach barbeque sauce?" I pulled back and tickled his side, triggering a girlish giggle from a giant of a man.

He danced away from my poking fingertips. "With a kick of tabasco. I was going to jar and ship some to you and to Nikos and Mario, but since you're here..."

Violet and Lily barked from within the minivan, and the rest of the team gave a wave, but didn't get out. Time was of the essence.

"I'm as pleased as punch to see you, Gus, but we can't stay.... I'm sorry to spring this on you. Did you get my text?"

Sly came back to us and brushed against my leg. I rubbed his head and behind his ears. "Hi, bub. Want some company?" I handed him a treat from my pocket, then lifted my look up at Gus.

"Yeah, I got your text a week ago...but...." Gus rubbed a hand through his curly salt-and-pepper beard.

But wasn't good.

"I tried to get out of my shifts this week but couldn't. It's been busier than normal. Great weather. And lots of hikers. We're short a ranger. Rob hurt his back."

My heart sank.

"I wish I could, Ins. I would ask Angie, but she's out of town. I've got my neighbor coming by to feed the chickens and to watch Sly."

I fidgeted with a gold hoop earring.

"Sorry, Ins." He gave me another hug, then pulled back with an apologetic smile. Sunshine glinted on bright teeth. Gus had inherited Dad's striking looks: dark curly hair, now salted with white, deep-set brown eyes, burly build, and a robust flare that could fill a room in both voice and being. Angie was a fool to have left him for that hippie masseuse.

I turned back to my crew, masking my disappointment. "It's okay. Guess they will stay with us." How many strikes was I going to get with dog sitters? Maybe these two were meant to tag along. Violet just needed to get her behavior under control.

We needed to skedaddle. Gus walked at my side as I returned to the minivan.

He greeted everyone with a wave. The side door window was open halfway and Violet tried to slobber his face through the opening. "How's my Curlicue?" Gus rubbed her ears, then peered behind her into the back seat. "Hey, Lils."

Olivia's window was down. She didn't hide her frown well.

"Sorry, gang. Gus has to work this week and can't watch them. And we have nobody else nearby to leave them with. I guess they're staying with us."

Zach was the only one to speak. "Well...no more running off or puking, Violet. Okay?" He rubbed the back of her head, then turned back to me. "Hey, Guv. If the dogs are staying with us, we need to get moving."

A deep laugh boomed from Gus's chest. "Guv?"

"Yeah, her race nickname. Short for Guv'nor."

"Well, I'll be. A perfect name for her! She's always been a bit bossy."

I swatted his shoulder, my cheeks heating.

One more hug with my brother and I was back in the vehicle.

Silence reigned as we bumped down the road. At least it hadn't been too long of a detour.

Nearing the end of the long road, we almost collided with a silver SUV bedazzled to all heck. Holden slammed on the brakes, and we stared into the faces of Tad and Dottie in the front seats. Dottie's brows shot up above her oval designer glasses.

"What the f—" Zach started. "OMG. Now we know they're following us!"

Olivia shook her head. "This isn't a smart strategy for cheating. Following people? This is crazy!"

Tad made the world's fastest two-point turn and whirled back to the main road.

"Torque?" Zach drummed fingers on the back of Holden's seat.

Holden peeled out, tailing them. However, the minivan wasn't thrilled about going fast, and we soon lost them in a maze of turns.

"Dammit!" Zach said. "They were totally following us. This confirms it. Why would they have come up Gus's private drive? Next chance we get, I want to check this minivan for GPS tags. Empty all bags. Everything. I know nobody here wants to really talk about it...but they *are* cheating. How...we don't know." He shook his head. "I agree with Olivia. That was stupid to follow us. I mean, that is risky! What if they're following one of the last teams, then they would be cut."

Holden scrunched his brow. "I'll help you search the minivan, although it might be impossible to find. You can drop a GPS tag in virtually anything or hardwire a unit into a minivan. Kind of like the GPS they installed in our vehicles. It makes you wonder..."

I know I had been the holdout on the cheating theory. Maybe I held hope for the good in all people, even them. "...if there are people within the race helping Tad and Dottie?" I said with some reluctance.

"Yes," Olivia affirmed. "We now know they're following us...and maybe others. The minivan engine issues felt quite suspicious. Plus, yeah. I wouldn't be surprised if they had an insider helping them, too."

A lot of money was on the line. Did Tad and Dottie really have it in them to do such things? "That's a lot of effort to try to win a race," I said, maybe still a bit in denial. And it didn't look good for the race organization.

Zach chewed angrily on his gum. "Ini, the prize is bigger this year. Though they've never been caught, you and I both suspected them tailing people before. But to use technology? To damage our minivan? That's low."

"And desperate," Holden added.

We drove at a fast clip to Presque Isle, passing through farmland and hillside in a blur, all too revved up from that interaction with Tad and Lottie. With the puzzle teased apart, there was nothing left to do. Lily shifted to settle in between our seats and rested her chin on my thigh. I rubbed her head.

After a pit stop for gas, Zach handed Olivia another CD to swap for his "classic 1990s tunes."

Holden slowed down behind a boxy, black buggy, clopping along on a quiet stretch of road.

"Whoa? Uh, did we go back in time or something?" Zach gawked out my passenger-side window.

"Those are Amish," Holden said. "I was reading in one of Irina's books about a settlement up here."

Giving the horse-drawn buggy a wide berth, Holden slowly passed, receiving a cordial wave from the driver. Then he sped up again.

Zach leaned forward. "Drawing more flowers, Ms. O'Keeffe? Leaning over that sketchbook in a moving vehicle would make me queasy."

"Her race name is Georgia, *Legs*," Holden corrected.

"Got it, Torque."

Olivia and Holden exchanged mouth quirks like bashful teens in summer love. She tucked a swath of long hair behind her ear.

I stared at her face reflected in the passenger-side mirror. Pink blotches danced across the bridge of her nose. Good for them. Holden was a kind man, and Olivia deserved to be adored.

She said, "Yes, I'm drawing more flowers, Zach. And landscapes, places we've visited. And just reading my notes." Olivia flapped her book up to show a beautiful drawing of yellow and purple potato blossoms in a green field. She flipped to another drawing of pink-tipped white roses. "One of your arrangements. I really loved this one. You're so talented, Zach."

His smile reached his ears. Zach gave me a shoulder bump with his fist. "Good choice on that one, Ini, like I told you. You're the queen of gifting!"

My stomach felt like it had dropped below the minivan's undercarriage, and Holden had just driven over it three times. Zach needed to shut his trap *now*. Where was the duct tape? I was already upset about not being able to leave the dogs with Gus, and now this? Olivia wasn't supposed to know I was the one sending the flowers.

It had been my idea, after Jerry's death. He once mentioned their inside joke about the last name Rose and his gifts of roses on her birthdays. I was the one choosing the arrangements. I was the one reading Jerry's journals and including a memory from them on each card. I was the one trying to help Olivia heal while keeping Jerry's spirit alive.

"What do you mean? My dad sends them. Rose-of-the-month club, right? They're preordered and you just fulfill the order?" Olivia looked over her shoulder at Zach. "I mean, he set it up, before he...before he passed away. All those messages included with them..." The color in her cheeks joined a raging wildfire across her neck. Then, she looked at me. No, *through* me. "Irina? Dad did this, right?"

I stumbled over my words. "R-right. Keen idea of his, hmm?"

Zach scrunched his nose. "But, Ini, you're the one sending the flowers—"

"Guys, I need your eyes," Holden interrupted. "We're here. Presque Isle. We need to look for this shop of Maria's."

"Look for other race teams, too," Zach said, nearly bouncing out of his seat. He scanned the boutiques that lined the main street.

I peered out my window, my stomach churning with guilt.

How was I going to fix this?

Twenty-Three

Holden

My mind hummed with the conversation that just happened. Irina was the flower-sender? Not Olivia's dad? Something deeper was going on, more than the low current of tension that already pulsated just beneath the surface with Irina and Olivia.

The rose deliveries, Olivia's dad...there was more there.

We had a task to complete, but I wanted nothing more than to reach over and squeeze Olivia's hand. Her cheeks blazed crimson and her eyes were wet.

"Hey, Guv! A place named after you," Zach said, pointing to a restaurant named Governor's.

"What about here?" I turned onto another road that led to a busy farmer's market along the river. "Lots of veggies and stuff."

We parked, got out, and canvased the market to no avail. Though some vendors had potatoes, none had potato blossoms or anything related to the potato festival. They were friendly in answering our questions, but none knew anything about anything.

I kept in step with Olivia, not leaving her side, and we hung back a bit from Zach and Irina. I brushed my hand against hers. She was receptive and threaded hers within mine. I squeezed. She squeezed back. I wanted to tell her that I totally understood being blindsided.

While Irina paid for a baggie of whoopie pies and some jars of blueberry jam, Zach said, "I don't see any teams here. Let's keep asking around. Someone has to know some-thing."

We moved on to exploring the boutiques along the streets.

Zach pointed to a shop. "There! Marie's Paws and Petals!"

The storefront windows were an explosion of cats and flowers. The door read *Purrfect just the way you are*, with a cat cartoon. As we entered, a bell made a meow-tinkle. We divided and searched aisles, cubbies, corners, and every knickknack known to man. I approached the woman at the counter, who must have been near ninety years old. "Do you have decks of cards with potato blossoms on them?"

She stared at me blankly through cloudy brown irises.

"Like poker cards? Playing cards?"

Again, a blank stare.

A middle-aged woman strolled in from the back room. "Grammy, your tea is ready. Come, sit." She guided the elderly woman to a rocking chair in the corner. The black cat that had occupied it leapt down, then back up to curl on the woman's lap.

This younger woman, who shared the same dark brown eyes as her elder, turned to us. "Hi, I'm Jen. What can I help you find?"

Maybe the older woman was Marie?

"We're uh, looking for a deck of cards with potato blossoms on it." I fought the urge to rub under my glasses. It was a nervous tic I was becoming too aware of.

She lifted a thin, dark eyebrow. "We have a few decks over here." She guided me to the counter and spun the display around. Lighthouses. Sailboats. Maine wildflowers and blueberries. Cats. No potato blossoms. "I was hoping to get some in time before the festival starts next week. They're popular in the shops in Fort Fairfield. You here for the festival?"

"Not exactly." I searched the carousel once more, just in case.

Zach appeared at my side, running a jerky hand through his cropped hair. "Have any other race teams come in?"

Jen's brow furrowed. "Race teams, hon? The 5k fundraiser was last week. All we got going on this weekend is the farmer's market."

This wasn't the place.

She tapped a finger to her chin. "Lemme look in the back for you. Maybe the order came in this morning. Everything is delayed from the holiday weekend."

She zipped to the back. The air conditioner above the counter hummed, cool air raining down. I drummed my fingers on the glass countertop.

"Lookie here." She returned, holding a deck of cards with potato blossoms on the box. "Is this it?"

"Score!" Zach grabbed it. "We're the first!"

Or last.

Or wrong.

This didn't feel right. If this were where the clues pointed, there would have been cards out of the back room, obvious to all race participants. This woman would have shown a hint of knowing about the race.

As we gathered around Zach with the deck, Olivia switched from being beside Irina to over on my right. Olivia's demeanor had done a one-eighty since the rose delivery conversation.

While waiting for confirmation from the race judges, we each paced different areas of the shop. Zach located the candy. He grabbed one box, then a second of saltwater taffy. "Olivia? You said Logan wants some?"

She nodded. "Thanks, Zach."

I found myself beside her and the mugs. I picked up one embellished with a brown-and-white cat wearing goggles and snorkel, swimming underwater.

Olivia's fingers traced over a mug with a beautiful flower pattern of daisies and lupine.

"You should get it. I'm going to get this one." I held up my mug next to hers.

"At least it's not roses," she grumbled under her breath. "All this time it was Irina..." Her voice cracked.

I hovered closer, wishing to comfort her, but it seemed too early in our friendship to offer a hug. Prickles danced down my spine at that idea all the same. "Do you wanna talk about it?"

She wiped her nose and shook her head. "Later." She pointed to my choice questioningly. "Why this mug?"

"I've got a moody lady waiting for me at home. She hates when I go away, and this is the longest I've been away from her."

Our eyes connected. A tug-of-war reflected in her chestnut irises. Curious, but sad.

"Your girlfriend's not happy with you being away, even if you bring back sixty thousand bucks?" She put the daisy mug back. "A funny cat mug as consolation?"

"Huh? Oh, no. Pixie is my spoiled cat, my moody girl. I love cat knickknacks. I haven't dated much since getting divorced." I scrubbed a hand over my chin. Guess I neglected to mention that in our chatting.

Her lips dipped into a frown. "I'm sorry. I haven't dated much either. Been too busy raising Logan."

"He sounds like a great kid. He has a great mom."

She responded with a soft sound of agreement.

"Also, with him at college now, you have more time to date." *Subtle, dude.*

She flashed a small smile. At me. Pun time. I searched my brain for one I could remember without my silly cheat sheet. "Why don't flowers ever get lonely?"

"Why?"

"Because they come in bunches."

Her chuckle was subdued, but there. I pointed to the bracelets with flowers and paw-print beads on another carousel. "I'm gonna get one of these for my niece. Which do you think an eight-year-old would like?"

She picked up a pink one with yellow flowers and paws. "That one is cute." She then flipped through the postcards.

I brought my cat mug, the daisy mug for Olivia, and the bracelet for Jayla to the register. "Can I get these?" I asked the woman. I looked over my shoulder. "Hey, Zach. Do you need another postcard for—?"

"Dammit!"

Zach's curse made the employee almost drop the mugs onto the counter.

He said, "Wrong guess. Time to hustle, guys!"

I paid. "Uh, do you happen to have a sister store in Fort Fairfield? A store with Maria in the name? You mentioned others that like these decks of cards."

She pressed her lips together and handed me my change. "Not that I know of. Most of the sellers are vendors at the festival. Sorry."

I pocketed the change and followed Irina and Zach, who were already dashing out the door. Olivia was at my side.

"Big fat negative," he said. "It's not Presque Isle. What about Fort Fairfield?"

"Sorry, Zach." A deep ridge carved a path down Irina's forehead as we hurried to the minivan.

"'S okay, Ini. It was worth a shot. We're now really behind the rest. Torque—"

I was already opening the door. "Yes, I know. Fast." This felt like the longest day: a detour to Irina's brother's house, now this incorrect guess.

"It's not over til it's over. Plus, I've never been eliminated until the very end," Irina said brightly, though her voice faltered. She buckled in, not looking at Olivia or Zach.

"There's a first for everything." The saltiness in Olivia's tone could compete with the Dead Sea. She pulled out the map.

When we got to Fort Fairfield, we peeled our eyes for Maria anything as we drove downtown along the river. Elm Street, High Street... It was a small town, just a hop, skip, and jump from the Canadian border.

"There! No. Wait, there!" Zach said, searching over every little thing like he was playing *Where's Waldo*. He practically leaned into Irina's lap to look out her side. "There's not much in this town. Wait! We just went through a forked intersection back there...but no median. Some small ones here at High and Bridge Streets... I'm not really impressed by these medians as 'isles.' Lame riddle."

"What if...not Presque Isle the town, but this road? This is Presque Isle Street," I suggested.

"This is nonsensical." Zach shook his head. "What if it's not potato blossoms? Like you said, Ini, the festival is next week. Maybe we didn't scour Presque Isle thoroughly enough. Maybe I'm wrong again."

"You're not wrong," she said. "I was wrong to suggest Presque Isle. It's here. We'll find it. You're right, Sugar."

I located a parking spot and contemplated, tapping fingers on the steering wheel. "I didn't see anything Maria or Marie."

"There's another race team." Irina pointed to a small building beside a church.

We hopped out of the minivan and double-timed it over.

"This is an icon and consignment shop." Olivia stated the obvious, pointing to the Jesus, saints, and Mary statues through the front window. "Like the one I donate to at home."

Irina beamed. "What if Mary is our Maria? As in *Ave Maria*? Let's look inside."

Olivia stopped abruptly just inside the door, waving a hand. "Phew!"

I nearly collided with her, instead grabbing both her shoulders before I tripped. I slowly dropped my hands, a little tingle exciting my fingertips at the touch. "Wanna describe it?" She was on edge today. People on edge could use distraction, and my puns were not hitting the mark.

"This scent? Strong." Then she furrowed her brow. "Incense reminds me of Sunday Mass with my parents when I was a kid. A spicy tickle on the nose. Awakening." Her frown became a side smile, revealing the smallest of dimples. "It's probably why I feel connected to the thrift shop at the local church. My mom always donated things there. I've been donating my rose vases."

"Good memories with this scent, then?"

She nodded. "Woodsy, rich, spicy. Smells like Christmas. Smells...reverential."

I pushed my glasses up. "Thank you."

Sun broke through the storm on her face. I liked this scent game with Olivia. I liked a lot of things about her, in fact. We reached Irina and Zach at the counter. Zach's eyes darted looks everywhere—over icons and all sorts of knickknacks—while Irina peppered the older woman with questions.

"Here!" Zach practically screeched. There they were. A deck of cards with potato blossoms on the box face. Such an unusual find in this unusual shop.

He was already typing in the information. It's not like we had limited tries. We just needed not to be last. Halfway through the race, we had only two more days of eliminations.

We gathered, he snapped, he hit send.

We went out to the curb and waited.

And waited. Sunshine and humidity smothered us, not a lick of a breeze in the air. Sweat trickled down my back. I much preferred the coastal breeze we had in Camden and even the blustery wind in Lubec. Plus, I'd enjoyed my sunrise excursion with Olivia. I was getting kind of sad our time would come to an end in a week...or sooner, if we got cut.

"Did it send?" Irina asked, hovering over Zach's shoulder to look at the phone in his hand.

The phone pinged and the color drained from Zach's face. "We're last. We've been eliminated." He dropped the phone, and it clattered on the sidewalk with a thwack.

Twenty-Four

Holden

Ironically, our first time being interviewed by the race coordinators for the YouTube channel would be our last. Somehow, we muddled our way through it. We pasted on smiles the best we could, answered appropriately, kept it chill. At one point, I opened my mouth to say something about Tad and Dottie—about our vehicle's breakdown—but I didn't. I had no proof of any wrongdoing. Speaking up got me nowhere before. Instead, I nodded numbly. Expressed my gratitude and tuned the rest out.

That evening, we did our own thing. Zach and Irina went to a local bar, likely to drown their sorrows, Olivia sat in the small motel room drawing, and I went out to the minivan to look for those GPS tags.

After dismantling everything I could think of or gain access to, I leaned back in the driver seat and used the hem of my T-shirt to wipe sweat off my forehead. Nothing was out of the ordinary. We would need to check our luggage and personal belongings next. I wasn't a tech guy, but I knew what to look for. I'd located the tracking system the race organizers had wired in, but that was it.

No evidence of tampering with anything.

It could be in Irina's purse for all we knew. Or in the undercarriage, and I wasn't exactly going to shimmy under there on the gravel pavement.

Tad and Dottie tracked us somehow. Maybe they had an insider reporting our locations. That could explain why they followed us to Gus's house.

I pulled out my Rubik's Cube and spun the dials around. At least I could solve *this* puzzle. Click, spin, slide. The colors lined up in ten seconds flat.

I felt bad enough about the shop van being stolen, and now I felt somehow responsible for this. Had they targeted us specifically? Because of me?

I shook my head. Tad and Dottie's duplicity wasn't my fault. Regardless, I couldn't let my team down again. I got out of the minivan and leaned against the side of it, letting a small breeze cool me and my thoughts.

As if to rub it in, Tad and his entourage walked by. If I had a sniffer that worked, I'd bet my last dollar he wore a fancy cologne that reeked of money. He seemed like the sort. At least there were a few positive aspects to losing my sense of smell, especially in this stagnant air.

"Sorry to hear about your team, James. Need some dinner?" He dangled a bag with a smirk.

I didn't respond. I clenched a fist at my side. *You're better than this. You're better than this. Don't stoop to their level.*

He looked over my shoulder, taking in the modest motel behind me. "This is where they put the losers, huh?"

God help me...

Maybe without onlookers and only his team around, Tad felt it was okay to drop the fake niceties and be a jerk. Well, I wasn't okay with being bullied.

The two young guys looked curious, while clear irritation wrinkled Dottie's expression. She seemed a bit pale, fatigued. "Tad, let's go," she said, her voice wobbly.

"You guys go. I'll be there shortly," Tad said.

Dottie pinched her lips, shook her head, but carried on down the sidewalk without him. Probably to one of the nicer B and Bs we saw a block away.

Once we were alone, Tad approached me.

"Good thing you got cut early. The race doesn't tolerate liars."

What?

What the actual hell?

"Excuse me?" I asked.

"Oh, don't pretend. We know what you did at my brother's construction site." He shook his head, tsking. "Just admit when you screwed up, buddy. Own it."

A nerve twitched in my neck. As I suspected, Tad knew about the accident and lawsuit. He was an accountant for his brother. Of course, he knew. "I'm not the liar. I know Thurlow Technology and Whitlock Construction not only caused the accident due to negligence but also covered it up."

"Last time I checked, it was your responsibility to ensure the safety of the site."

"I did. They didn't allow me to shut it down. They didn't rectify the safety issues I suggested."

Tad's laugh boomed in the early evening air, and it hurt my teeth. "Nobody will believe you. They didn't before. They won't now, so tell your lawyer to stop stirring up trouble."

What? My lawyer and I had ceased our efforts to pursue this further. Was that why Earl Bachman's office had been reaching out recently? Not about billing, but about our case? Maybe the evidence my lawyer and I found *was* strong enough to support our allegations... And Tad and corporate were worried. Could that be why he had been targeting our team? To scare me? I stuck my chin out. I wouldn't be bullied anymore. There wasn't more I could say on that subject, nor anything I could do, until I got home. Riding the wave of courage, I added, "We know you're cheating. Your team conveniently turning up a *private* driveway? That's bull, man. Who are you kidding? Don't get too comfortable. We'll find the evidence we need to bring before the organizers."

"You do that," he scoffed. 'And if you do, I'll tell your team about the 'accident' and your part in it. How your incompetence caused others to be hurt. In fact..." He waggled a finger. "I may tell the coordinators myself how lucky they are that you got eliminated. because—" He shot a look into the ransacked minivan. "—we found a suspicious screw in our tire. And Amir said he saw somebody who looked just like you messing around our vehicle. We also saw Irina ask that concierge at the B and B in Camden to use his phone and we heard something about a walkie-talkie being used, hmm? And then she goes and makes that little side trip to her brother's house? Tsk, tsk, tsk."

What screw? This guy had a screw loose himself! There was no screw in any tire. Not by our hands or anyone else's. If Tad and Dottie were as formidable as Irina and Zach proclaimed, no other team would dare try to sabotage them. No. I called bull on this, too.

"You're the cheat, Tad." My mind raced. Irina used a phone? No way. Every word out of Tad's mouth was a lie.

My throat tightened.

He lowered his voice, the words gravel between his teeth. "Oh, and if you cry wolf about any of this—the race, the accident—you'll be a flower delivery boy for the rest of your days. I don't make idle threats."

Did this guy have the power to get me kicked out of my grad school program, too? It's not like I had the money now to stay, but even so... How far did his hand reach?

While he walked away, I just stood there as if I had been punched. This is what I got: stand up for myself and be knocked down farther. Why bother? My soul felt like a beaten dog.

I should have said more to him. But this man clearly had it out for me. I needed to say something to the race organizers. But with what proof? Why would anyone believe me now, any more than they believed me about the gas leak? So, I kept my head down and mouth shut.

For now.

I unscrewed my jaw and unclenched my aching hands. Then I breathed.

I stood beside the minivan, staring into nothingness for a long time before a welcoming voice broke through the fog.

"Hey, whatcha doing?"

I turned to find Olivia behind me, two beer bottles in her hands and a laundry bag slung over her shoulder. A breeze rippled her loose pink T-shirt.

The outdoor lights flanking the exterior motel room door clicked on as sun set.

I blinked away my stupor. "I could ask you the same. Laundry? We're going home tomorrow."

"I'd rather come home with clean clothes. One less thing to do. Plus, the drum in my washing machine has been as loud as a percussion section—need to repair it or replace it."

"Ah, well, speaking of clothing…" I reached into the minivan and pulled out a pair of balled-up slobbered blue socks. "These must be yours. Found them wedged in a seat while searching. Looks like she really took a liking to this pair for some reason."

"Violet. Geesh. Those were the pair I couldn't find back at West Quoddy Head. I may just give her this pair permanently, so she leaves the rest of them alone." She looked at the minivan. "Search? Something else wrong with the minivan?"

"Nothing new." I stared at the dashboard through the open driver's window, considering what Tad said. I took off my glasses, wiped them clean, and put them back on. "I'm looking for a GPS tag."

"Why bother now? We're out of the race. Even if they were cheating, we have no proof, and it's too late. We did our best." She handed me a beer, the glass cold against my sweaty palm. Shivers formed beneath the perspiration dabbing my skin.

I took a sip. "I need to look for answers, something tangible. Just want some cold, hard evidence in my hand for once."

"For once?"

"Long story," I said.

"Believe me, I get that."

"Oh?"

"That's also a long story." Olivia sighed.

I took a big gulp of beer. Felt the fizz of bubbles, tasted nothing. I could use the heady release alcohol gave, tonight of all nights.

After I closed the rolling side door, she leaned against it, sipping, staring up at the brown-blue sky. The sunset matched our moods. I blew out a breath. "So...I kind of know Tad by association. And not in a good way. I think he has it out for me." *Not think. Know.* He made that very clear a few minutes ago. But I wouldn't sit quietly. Not anymore.

She crossed her arms, cradling the beer. "Wanna talk about it?"

I tested her. "Wanna tell me about the roses and this Irina thing?"

She swallowed. "Okay, but I need something stronger than this beer. And food. Something spicy? Indian or Mexican food?"

"Either."

We finished our beers and recycled the bottles. Olivia waited while I swapped out my sweaty shirt for a clean one, then we walked to the closest eatery—a Thai place. "Perfect. Mango curry or drunken noodles, extra spicy, sometimes cut through the nothingness." I offered her what I thought was my funny grin. "You can describe some of the aromas for me tonight. Memory-wise, Thai makes me think of my sister, Alyssa. She loves Thai food, and we used to get takeout a lot in college."

"You went to college together?"

"Yup. She only attended for a year, though. Switched to culinary school. She was originally a biology major, but gastronomy—the study of food and culture—called her name."

We walked into the restaurant, brightly decorated with orange and blue murals and slender bamboo lights dangling over each booth. The hostess escorted us to a booth in the back.

Olivia ordered a fruity alcoholic concoction complete with umbrella and cherry garnish, and I went for rum and cola. I couldn't taste the rum, but the bubbles of the soda burst and popped on my throat as heat rolled down.

As we skimmed menus, she asked, "So you knew Tad before the race?"

I closed the trifold. "Sort of. His brother."

The server returned and took our orders. "Three peppers," I said for the spice level.

The young woman raised eyebrows, one of them pierced, toward purple-tipped blonde hair. "You sure? That's—"

"It's good. Trust me. I have a strong stomach."

I elaborated once the server left to put in our orders. "I knew his brother through my work. Thurlow Technology was a client of my employer, Whitlock Construction. As a construction safety officer, I wore a lot of hats—training, audits, made sure everything was safe for the workers." I pushed out a breath. "My dad worked construction most of his life, but he was injured more than once, and that spurred me to become a safety officer. While working, I found myself drawn to the projects themselves, especially the designs. That prompted me to go to grad school for civil engineering. But..." I took a long pull on my drink. How much to share? "Grad school is on hold for a bit. I just can't afford it. I'm not going back, I guess. Not now."

She sipped her peacock-blue drink and didn't even ask why I wasn't a safety officer anymore. Instead, she said, "I'm sorry. I can relate to that. Education isn't cheap. Nor are home repairs—that's why I was doing this. My house is crumbling. Mold in the attic—"

"Ah, the attic..."

"The one and only. I was up there checking out my mold issue, got locked in, and then was rescued by you," she said in such a breezy, romantic way.

Mold, romantic? Where was my head?

Our order of steamed pork dumplings came out. The red sauce that came with them had kick.

Olivia released a soft moan after swallowing her dumpling. "A little bit of heaven. So, you took off time from work so you could focus on school?" she asked. "Will you go back now full-time?"

"Not exactly." I laid down my fork. "I was let go. There was...an accident." The word came out like the burn of acid reflux.

"Isn't it your job to manage accidents?" She dabbed at the corner of her mouth.

Here went nothing. "There was a gas leak...and explosion. Some men got hurt. Badly." I finished the drink. The bubbles had lost their appeal. "Thing is...all safety protocols had been followed on my end. The higher-ups thought otherwise." I clenched a fist under the table and rubbed it against my thigh. "The project was rushed. Corners cut. But I, personally, do not cut corners." My head spun. I waved the server over. "Another, please."

Olivia sat there, attentive.

"Cut me off after this, Olivia. I can't taste it, but this body feels it." What was that saying? Beer before liquor, never sicker? Though I thought that had been debunked. Too late now. At least we had more food coming.

She nodded. "I'm sorry, Holden."

"Me, too. Here's the kicker. They blamed me. My boss, the CEO, my coworkers. All of them. Their claim was I didn't smell the natural gas leak. They add in mercaptan so you can smell it—like rotten eggs, sulfur—if you can smell. It was after hours, and I was checking things one more time. I was the only one there when the leak had supposedly begun. By the time the workers arrived, it was too late. Some didn't get out in time." I pushed out a sigh. "Thurlow Technology couldn't afford to have their project put on pause for too long. So they, along with Whitlock Construction, felt the best solution was to blame me, let me go, pay off some inspectors, and move on with the project."

Her mouth dropped open.

"Good old Dottie's husband, Tad's brother, Carlton Thurlow. They covered up their negligence by throwing me alone under the bus, so it looked like an individual's incompetence. It meant they could get the project going faster. They knew about my smell issue yet refused to have a second safety officer on staff for detecting odors or leaks. They wouldn't ever let the project be put on hold, even when I pointed out safety issues. Like an alarm I told them to replace. They hadn't. The list is long. Lots of negligence."

"Oh, wow." She took a long drag of her drink. "So, this is what you meant by finding evidence?"

I played with the cloth napkin, folding and unfolding it. "They got coworkers to speak against me, to support the case against me, of my incompetence. Corporate lied about a lot of things. It's royally messed with my psyche."

She reached across the table and squeezed my hand. "I'm sorry they did that to you." She didn't let go. "I remember that call, at dispatch. My supervisor told me a bit more about the accident later."

I heaved a sigh. "They pinned it all on me. I'm still paying my lawyers." And divorce lawyer, but who's counting?

An angry dip formed in her forehead. "Sometimes life is unfair."

Our food arrived and we dug in. I asked her more about Logan, trying to move the conversation away from my sad story. She told me about his internship, his college aspirations. Her face lit up whenever she talked about him.

I was distracted alright. I wanted to hold her hand again, to feel her fingertips on my skin. Watching her lips move with each bite, the maternal love in her dark brown eyes, her way of wiping her mouth with the napkin...made me want to kiss her.

Man, how strong were these drinks?

"You asked about the roses," she said as we finished eating.

"You don't need to explain."

"No. You trusted me with your story, Holden. I'll tell you some of mine." With a fork, she pushed around the rice left on her dish. "My dad, he, uh, he died. Had a heart attack."

"I'm so sorry, Olivia."

She swallowed. "Anyway, he used to give me roses on my birthday. The whole Olivia Rose thing. And then, after he died, roses came to my house monthly. I never understood how he could have foreseen his death and planned this. He was healthy. It makes sense now. Irina was doing it. I-I... It's petty to be mad at her, but I am. She lied. Made me think they were from him."

Though well intentioned, it sounded like Irina still deceived Olivia. "You two aren't close?"

"No. She and Dad got married only two years after my mom died. That was over ten years ago, but I've never been close to Irina. I just..." She puckered her lips. "I didn't give her a chance. Maybe I'm just a brat. Stubbornness runs in the family. She and I also...just have different ways we approach life."

We split the bill and made our way to the motel.

Olivia went back to talking about Logan.

I stumbled on a step, and she grabbed my arm. Warmth spread through my chest.

Irina and Zach must have been back by now because the lights were on inside one of the rooms. We hovered outside on the covered porch for a long moment.

"Thanks for listening to my sob story, Georgia," I said, my words a bit slurred as the drinks caught up with me. I nudged her shoulder with a finger. "Your name suits you."

She shifted on her feet but leaned closer to me. "And yours, Torque. One would never think you had such a lead foot. Or a weak tolerance. You're a bit tipsy."

"I like my minivans fast and drinks strong."

She snorted. I laughed. We were so close that if I could smell, I imagined I would inhale the fruity sweetness of her drink on her breath. Then if we kissed, I could taste it. Something stirred inside me, and it wasn't the alcohol or fiery peppers in my stomach. Under the porch lights, shadows gathered around her eyes. I noticed the little freckles across her nose. The small uptick of her pink lips.

Her look snagged on mine. Olivia's soft exhale tickled my lips.

The door to her room flew open.

I jolted back from Olivia as if I had been zapped. Somehow, both my hands had been on her shoulders. My rocking brain regretted the sudden movement.

"Great! You're back! We have news," Irina said, breathless. Her blue eyes glowed, probably from a gin and tonic. Were we all toasted?

I blinked double and grabbed the doorjamb with my hand to steady myself. This was why I didn't have more than one drink. My stomach gurgled.

Olivia licked her lips, then broke eye contact with me. She crossed her arms and turned to Irina. "What news?"

"Good news and bad news. Come in, come in."

We crammed into the small room. Zach was flipping through channels on the television, our only allowed technology even after we had lost our spot in the race. Cut teams still had to hold to the no-technology standard, except for a television, until the next morning of the race.

I rubbed my lips without thinking, wanting to remember Olivia's breath on them. "What's he looking for?"

"The news. Though I doubt our little race will warrant coverage even on local stations." She waved a hand. "The good news first."

Zach threw the remote onto the bed and stood. "Team Fleur Four is back in!" He whooped.

"What?" Olivia and I said in unison.

"A team was disqualified! For cheating. The organizers didn't elaborate in the text message. But since they're out now, we're back in!" Zach's eyes glistened from whatever indulging he had done.

"Who was disqualified?" I asked. *Please let it be Tad's team.*

Irina thinned her lips. "We don't know."

"The bad news?" Olivia asked, knotting her hands together.

"There have been accusations made against us." Irina paced.

"Us?"

This room was suddenly crowded with four people and two dogs. My head spun and my mouth felt like cotton. "Irina, Tad told me you used a phone. He made threats.

The trip to Gus's house...and oh, wait, you also used those walkie-talkies..." Did Tad's threat hold water?

Irina waved a hand flippantly. "I had the concierge at the B and B in Camden call some doggie daycare centers. I did not use the phone, and the man can vouch for me. The walkie-talkie usage at Seboeis Lake was approved by Ned, the race guy. And if they ask about our detour to Gus, he can attest that we were just trying to drop off the dogs."

All those moving parts, though individually benign, together kind of made us look like we were bending the race rules.

"You used a phone!" Olivia snapped. "What else are you lying about?"

I know that Olivia didn't mean to be so hard on Irina, and that the root of this outburst had to do with the roses. I hovered close to her side, again, the urge to console her, touch her, overwhelming.

"It was no big deal. I did *not* use it, as I said. In fact, I saw *Dottie* using a phone out on the veranda in Camden, though I didn't want to mention it."

Zach looked taken aback. "Ini! Why didn't you say? If she has a phone, then she can be looking up answers on the internet."

I added, "And using a GPS tag." *Which I can't seem to find...*

Olivia just shook her head, a look of disgust painted on her features. Oh, she was steaming.

"It was nothing. She was talking to her daughter about...personal things."

Zach continued, "Yeah, but, Ini, if she had a phone, or a burner, or whatever, who's to say she didn't use it again on the race? You've got to tell them. The team coordinators are going to meet us here tomorrow morning at seven to speak to each of us individually before we are officially let back into the race."

Olivia's voice rose. "Who is accusing us? And of what?"

"One guess." I grimaced. "Tad and Dottie. They said we messed with *their* vehicle, didn't they? Tad lied and said we put a screw in his tire or something." Black spots danced before my eyes. "They're accusing us of doing to them what *they* did to us."

"We messed with *their* vehicle?" Olivia said.

"Yup. Meanwhile, I just spent half the night looking for GPS tags in our minivan."

Zach's face lit up. "You did? What did you find?"

"Nothing."

Irina asked, "What if Tad and Dottie framed that other team? What if that team is innocent, too?"

"That is a whole new level of effed up," Zach said.

This race was getting too cutthroat for me. My dinner sloshed in my stomach, and I was afraid I'd be praying to the porcelain god soon.

"They have to be tracking us some other way." He shook his head. "We need to check all our personal belongings. Luggage and stuff."

"If they are, you've got me. I'm not a tech expert," I said miserably.

"Right, but Dottie's husband is," Irina added.

Dizziness consumed me. This was getting out of hand. It was a garden race!

Oh, God. My stomach.

I made a mad dash to the toilet just in the nick of time.

Twenty-Five

Olivia

Turns out, Tad and Dottie's team wasn't the one disqualified for cheating. After a thorough interrogation and a search of our vehicle and belongings, the race coordinators determined we hadn't broken the rules nor caused any sabotage. Irina's actions were all acceptable. We contemplated telling them about Tad and Dottie, but with what evidence? Holden was right on that. We had no proof after searching through all our belongings. Nothing. Even the loose wires and whatnot under the hood was circumstantial at best. Irina's minivan wasn't exactly in prime shape.

As the day progressed, the horizon felt sunnier, despite the cloud of uncertainty hanging over us. The start of this race felt like eons ago. It was day seven, and we found the clue in record time.

For once, the eye roll-worthy title they assigned the clue—today's was *Gather Friends like Flowers*—tied in to the actual activity. We located the place, Bloomington Community Garden and Country Store, tracked down the plant—dahlias—gathered a bouquet, paid, and submitted our response before noon.

At least we got flowers out of it. I was eager to draw the gorgeous ray florets later. According to Zach, there were ten distinct types of dahlias and thousands of varieties. We had picked a rainbow of the pompon, ball, and decorative types. The Crème de Cassis was my favorite, and the one we were told to highlight in our bouquet. It had gradient petals, deep purple at the base, changing to a soft lilac, then creamy white.

Irina was avoiding me, her usual way to evade conflict. That was fine with me, as I wasn't ready to talk about the Dad-roses thing either. Zach was zoned out, a permanent ridge of worry carved into his youthful forehead. Holden was quieter than normal, probably with a splitting hangover—and I hoped he wasn't regretting our near-kiss last night, something I could not wrap my head around now.

After lunch at a flatbread pizza place beside the community garden—a beautiful maze of vegetables and flowers and small farm animals—we were back on Interstate 95, heading to our hotel. I circled the location of our seventh find on the map.

The quiet in the minivan gave me time to ponder a plan. Because...

Well, we were close to *the* address. the one I had memorized from an authorized background check of a similar B and E to my own. Even with his prior record, this perp had been let go despite evidence stacked against him.

After encountering the man with the tattoo at the gas station on July Fourth, my intentions to find the perp in Maine had fizzled. I was turning into a nutcase! This type of behavior had gotten me into hot water already.

So, a few days ago, I tabled the idea of finding him. I tried to heal. But then...between Holden's painful story and Tad and Dottie's cheating, the urge for justice awoke in me again last night. We had already traveled through this region of Maine once going to Seboeis Lake on day five, again when we went to Gus's house, and now a third time on day seven. Was I being granted another chance to confront this man? Was fate leading me here?

I thought about how to get away from the group. I only had one more day until we could no longer separate from each other daily after solving the clue. I could borrow the minivan and say I was going for a drive for supplies, but someone would offer to come along, probably Holden. A walk was more logical, but our hotel was too far from this man's home. He lived just off the highway. If I could delay the group...

The only idea I had to sneak away was irrational, crazy.

But the need for justice persisted! This man deserved to be put away for what he did to us and maybe to others. If I did find him, if I could see his face and that tattoo, then I could let authorities know. Get a burner phone and call the local police and have them bring him in for questioning. Do it the right way. Like Holden, I didn't have any proof to put someone away. I only had a visual reference, as a witness, of the man I saw in my home. It had to be enough.

What if I got there and he recognized me?

What would he do? What if he bolted or did worse...? The man I was looking for, according to his criminal history, had a violent past.

I'd cross that bridge when it came. For now, I had to delay everyone.

"Let's stop for a few more supplies here," I suggested as we came to a gas station beside a rest area not far from the man's address. I tapped Holden's arm. A subtle heat sizzled in my fingertips at the touch. Now was not the time to think about *that*.

"Good idea. I need to stretch my legs," Irina said.

I rubbed Logan's birthstone necklace at my neck, a small silver turtle with emerald and peridot gemstones. He'd bought it for me after the original necklace was stolen by the perp. "Holden, how about I drive a little? I know it's just to the hotel, but you look tired." And still hungover.

He cracked his neck and handed me the keys. "Thanks."

"Yeah, and I can drive tomorrow if you'd like, too." I pushed out a smile. "That means you'll need to be the navigator."

He followed me to the gas station.

"I'm going to hit the bathroom."

"Want me to grab you anything?" He brushed a gentle hand on my back, and not only did I like it, I slowed my step to lean into his palm.

"An iced tea, thanks." I made my way to the bathrooms, a separate building outside the station. A growing heat rose within my chest and my pulse quickened. *I could do this.* Irina followed me into the bathroom. She was a creature of habit. If we lost her keys, I was certain that she kept a spare set in the mini backpack left in the locked minivan.

We could call for roadside assistance from the race cell phone, like we had when the minivan overheated. The race organizers or roadside assistance could break into the minivan and get the spare keys. *Everything would be fine. Everything would be fine.* I clenched and unclenched my fist. We had hours before nightfall. We had time.

It was a stretch. It was ridiculous.

Irina stopped at the counter, opening her handbag and pulling out a compact. "You go first, dear."

A woman exited the stal , a bit frazzled. "Careful there. This toilet has a mind of its own. I swear it would not stop flushing while I was sitting.'

Fortune was cutting me some slack today. I nodded and let the keys jingle in my hand, making their presence known.

"That's nice of you to give Holden a break from driving." Irina was reapplying lip gloss.

I stood in the bathroom stall for a long moment, my heart beating at the rate of a race car. Irina's key hung in the balance, clinging to my conscience and the keychain by a bent and flimsy ring. Losing it would buy us time. I could go for a "walk" and check out this perp's house.

The key could just happen to get loose and...

No. This was bonkers! I was not doing this.

With shaky knees, I sat down to do my business. What was I thinking?

The healthier thing to do was to get back in the minivan and forget this shady digression. I couldn't do this to my teammates, because what if it *did* delay us more than a few hours? What if the roadside assistance couldn't come right away? Once when Logan was camping in Vermont and his friend had lost his keys—which is where I got the idea from—the roadside assistance couldn't come out for like six hours.

Holden needed the money. Zach, too. Me, three. But it was more than the money. We all needed a win in life. This race could be it. But if I followed through with my plan, it could cost us the race. We could be disqualified. Delaying my team was one thing but getting us booted for illegal phone usage was another.

After I got home, I was going to call a therapist. The trip to Marta Neil this spring, this irrational justification right now, were enough to make me realize I was not on a good path. Maybe there was a more logical way to pursue this. Take it up with the police again...or well, I didn't know what. They had all but given up on my case.

I breathed a sigh. *Good job, Olivia. Making the right decision for once!*

I stood up and my shoe touched something slippery on the floor. "What the—?" I fell back, bracing one hand on the metal toilet paper dispenser and the other on the toilet tank. I heard a jingle. A splash.

The toilet roared and flushed. "Gah!" No, *no, no. I changed my mind! Damn it. Damn, damn, damn!*

But the key had already gone down.

"Irina! Ugh!" I pulled up my jeans and spun around. It was too late to stick my hand in with a burst of courage. The keys were gone. I stared at the refilling basin.

I flung open the stall door.

Irina was quick to my side. "What is it?"

I held up the keyless keychain. "The little ring must have bent or something. The key and fob fell in!"

"Oh, dear."

Could thoughts cause something to happen? No. But, damn if I didn't feel guilty about this. "I'm so sorry, Irina. Please say you have your spare!"

She patted my shoulder. "I do but left it in the minivan in my backpack. Let's call the race organizers and then roadside assistance. I have the phone at least in my handbag."

We reached the guys at the minivan and told them what happened.

Zach blanched. "Fell in...what?" As Irina pulled out the phone, he added, "We're not too far from the hotel, and we already checked in. This is just a minor delay."

Irina gave him a side squeeze. "Love your optimism, Zach. I agree." Her eyes flitted skyward. "Plenty of daylight left. Easy peasy." She tapped on the glass of the minivan window and Violet slobbered it. "And the rear windows are cracked open, so the girls are okay."

Still in my purgatorial headspace, I said, "It's going to be a while before they get here. I'm going to walk." I pointed to a maintenance road that ran behind the service station, then did a quick overarm stretch for emphasis. "This driving is making me creak in new places." Surely, the key falling in was a sign for me to pursue this.

One last time.

Says the crazy lady.

"I'll come with you," Holden said.

"No-no. I mean, it's okay. I'm okay on my own."

"Olivia, dear, you shouldn't walk alone—" Irina began, dialing the race coordinators on the phone.

Holden approached. "I'd feel better if I was with you. We promised to have a buddy system on this race."

"Okay. Uh, I'll be just a minute. I'm going to uh, grab a candy bar."

Holden waited by the minivan. I ran into the gas station, and without giving it another sane thought, I put a candy bar and a burner phone on the counter. I would need it to call the authorities when I got to the house. After ripping open the packaging and tossing the plastic, I began walking, too disconcerted and determined, the feel of the phone in my back pocket a reassurance, a lead weight.

Fate gave me this chance. I was going to take it.

"We'll just wait here for you," Zach called pointlessly. "Be back soon?"

"Sure."

Holden wasn't part of this plan. How could I explain my reason for turning down a specific street? I mean, the keys flushing had been a sign, right? To follow through? Oh God, my head spun with audacity.

He kept in stride, quiet for a few minutes. "You like to walk?" he asked as we turned into the neighborhood and in the direction I had memorized from a map before the race.

"Not really. I-I just needed some air, some time away from her." That was a truth.

We walked another five minutes before he spoke again. "Should we head back in about ten minutes? We don't need them to send out search and rescue." He shoved his hands in his pockets as our pace slowed.

I had no energy to smile back, even though Holden had a beautiful grin that reached his eyes. "Feeling better today?" I asked, eager to move the conversation off me and my erratic behavior.

He scrubbed a hand through his short hair. "Much. This is why I don't drink often. Alcohol hits me hard if I overindulge. Sorry about last night."

Sorry about getting sick or about almost kissing me? I didn't ask. I wasn't sorry. I'd felt the chemistry that bubbled between us.

I began to sweat as we approached the address I had memorized. There it was. A small white ranch-style house with light green shutters, as Zillow had showed. No orange hatchback in the driveway. In the garage?

Was I really doing this?

I froze and stared. Now what? I never rehearsed this part. Do I just knock on the door? This was different from visiting Marta or the others, people whom I wanted to help. Now I was confronting a known criminal. I could get fired for this. I could get in bigger trouble than I had with Marta Neil. This guy could press charges. Or worse. And I would cause my team to be disqualified if I used the phone.

I ran my fingers over my back pocket, questioning my ill-conceived plan.

"You okay, Olivia?"

I shook my head. I most certainly was not. My knees locked.

He followed my gaze to the house. "Do you know these people?"

My skin heated and I rocked in place, rubbing my thumb and forefinger over the turtle pendant at my neck. "No."

"Then why are we here?"

The response clogged my throat. How could I explain?

"This wasn't just a walk, was it?"

I shook my head, hugging my arms to myself. "No."

He squinted at the front door. "Need me to—"

"No. I-I..." I dragged leaden feet to the front door, sensing Holden's presence behind me the entire time. I blinked, swallowed, and then rang the doorbell. Once. Waited. Twice. Waited. Nobody came to the door.

"They're not here," his whisper-quiet voice said from behind me. He laid a hand on my waist and applied gentle pressure as if wanting to guide a kid away from a cliff edge.

I shook my head. "No. He has to be here." I whirled around and made for the garage. I cupped my hands to the clear glass windows and peered inside. A silver sedan sat beside an empty spot. No bikes or bike rack. No hatchback.

I shook my head, an ache flooding my chest. "Stupid. So stupid! How did I ever think I'd find him?"

I practically ran back to the sidewalk. Holden kept up. Half a block away, I leaned over, gasping. He pressed his hand into the small of my back and rubbed in a circular motion.

I sniffled and righted myself.

"Do you wanna talk about it?"

"It's a long story." Pain choked my words as we resumed walking.

"I have time." He cautiously slid his hand into mine. "We're good at long stories."

I swiped tears with my other hand. "Remember how I told you about my dad?"

He nodded.

"He...his heart attack..." I hated crying. I'd rather have anger and remorse chew me up inside than shed tears. I hadn't cried when Eric left me to raise Logan on my own. I cried a little when Mom passed away, but we had some time to say goodbye first. Then Dad ten years later...my fortitude was a half-assembled beaver dam and the grief was a raging river. Keeping busy with work, with friends, wasn't enough to distract me. And now my baby was off to college. I felt so alone, insignificant.

Holden's fingers and palm squeezed my hand tighter. "It's okay to not be okay."

I sniffed. "My dad died during a home break-in. We came in on the intruder. The guy had pushed in the air conditioner. Dad confronted him. The guy was carrying away Logan's gaming computer..." I fluttered my hand, sobs snagging my words. "Dad had a heart attack. I couldn't save him. The guy wouldn't let me call 911. I can still hear his voice, telling me to stay put. He got away. He wore a mask. Don't know who he was, just saw the tattoo on his neck, his blue eyes, and the car he drove. It had been parked on the street. I never got a look at the plates...so, well, any other perp that I find out about through work that might resemble this guy...I've followed up on."

"I'm so sorry, Olivia. That must be hard for you."

He flicked his thumb over his shoulder, back toward the neighborhood. "This guy is—"

I shrugged, feeling small. So small. "I don't know. I suspected it was him. And, at the gas station the other night...I saw a man with a similar tattoo. Thought it was him. It wasn't. Guess I won't ever know. I just wanted—" A fist clenched my heart.

"Justice." Pain infused his voice. "Sometimes we have to just let things go. Finding closure can be hard without answers. But sometimes the bad guy wins."

I released my hand from his and dug into my pocket for a tissue. "Too often they do. I'm not crazy...just..."

He stopped to face me. "Grieving. You miss your dad. You want to see this guy caught."

"And I couldn't save him. My dad. I did CPR and he still died. And...I should have known better than to put that damn AC in the lower-level window. With my job, I know these things." More than catching this guy, I wanted to forgive myself. *I'm sorry, Dad. I couldn't save you. Now I can't even find the perp who ruined our lives.*

"We can't do it all perfectly. The AC in the window—not your fault. Your dad—even the best doctors lose patients. Not your fault. Look at my defective nose. I did all the safety things I could, and an accident still happened."

My lips trembled. I wiped my eyes. Squeezed the soggy tissue in my fist. Then, I wept harder. My body shook. Holden scooped me into his arms, right there, on the sidewalk in the middle of Maine, and I cried into his T-shirt. "I hate that he's still out there. I hate that I couldn't save my dad."

Holden stroked my hair.

He understood remorse. He understood not seeing justice served.

Here, Holden held me while I cried like a baby.

As warm arms embraced me a moment longer, I allowed myself to contemplate what it would be like to truly give up this need for vengeance and to free myself from guilt.

When we reached the gas station parking lot, I slipped the phone out of my back pocket and tossed it into a trash can.

Twenty-Six

Olivia

There was something about crying. You get all that pent-up emotion out and then can breathe again. Maybe it had been sharing my story, or at least some of it. Maybe it had been the physiological release. Maybe it had been Holden's arms around me. Whatever it was, I felt unburdened today. One step closer to emotional freedom. I was still steaming about Irina and the roses, though.

I wasn't surprised when I caught myself humming along to a nineties hip-hop tune as we weaved our way through the mountains of western Maine. "Another great mix, Zach," I said from the driver's seat—giving Holden a much-needed break this morning.

Zach beamed.

Today was day eight, and the last elimination. From here on would be an unrestricted final push. No more mandatory check-ins at a hotel after solving the clue. They would immediately give us our next one. This also meant we had to be together 24/7.

"Drive 'til we drop!" Zach exclaimed as we drove to a gourmet chocolate boutique near Jackman.

Long stretches of no sleeping? Give me that and a bag of chips. No problem for this insomniac.

Irina pointed to a directional signpost. "What a hoot! They really have a thing for Christmas in this race."

Even I laughed at the signpost, which had directional arrows showing the border six miles away, New York, Miami, Fenway, and the North Pole.

We were just shy of nowhere, deep in the western Maine woods, flanked by ancient mountains worn down by time and weather. We passed an old railroad station and a place called Moose River.

Holden opened the map again and spread it across his lap. He stared at it intently for a solid minute.

"What's up?" I asked.

He folded the map to show our route.

Zach leaned forward. "Don't hold back, Torque. What's itching you?"

"It's—" Holden scrunched his face.

"Don't say silly," I cut in. Holden was a second-guesser, like me.

"Can I draw on the map?" he asked.

He might be a man of few words, but I loved watching his mind work. "Sure. Are we close?"

He traced the map with a pointer finger. "We already passed Long Pond. To the east is Little Big Wood Pond. Stay on U.S. 201, and we'll keep an eye out for this 'Lavender and Lily' shop. Another shop. Makes me think they finagled their way into the race for free publicity."

"Oh, definitely," Zach concurred. "It also helps the organizers to have a business as a location, so they can coordinate around liabilities or permissions. Sending us to a random meadow in the middle of nowhere leaves too many loose ends. Not that they don't do that, too. Okay, guys, let's read it once more to piece cut the rest." He shook the clue.

"Lavender and Lily
Long...then Little.
A touch of gourmet just shy of the border.
Don't worry, you won't need your passport.
Four by six.
A baker's dozen.
Sweet and savory.
Pick the right combination, like the turn of a Key, and you score:
A treat and on to the next feat."

"A combination lock?" Irina asked. "So we need to figure out the numbers... Four, six. ."

"Four times six is twenty-four." Holden scratched his head. "A dozen is half that."

"A baker's dozen is thirteen," added Irina.

We all looked a bit puzzled.

Our answer revealed itself when we walked into the chocolate shop a short while later. "A box of twenty-four!" Irina said cheerily. "Now...which?"

I leaned close to Holden as we looked at the case filled with decadence. "Oh! Perfect for you. Cayenne chocolate? That's gotta have some zip."

He pushed up his glasses. "Worth a shot."

He flashed a smile that was sweeter than the aroma in the shop. The tight quarters gave me an excuse to shrink the gap between us. I brushed my shoulder, then forearm, then fingertips against Holden's arm, then slowly dropped my arm to my side.

I kept my eyes glued to the chocolates in the display case. "My mouth is watering," I said, my cheeks heating at my choice of words. Our fingers danced, the backs of mine against the backs of his, as ripples of pleasure shot up to my elbow.

He moved his hand, clasping mine.

I squeezed. "W-want me to describe the scent? I'm getting high on the sugar in the air."

"Sugar, even though I can't taste it, hits the happy spots in my brain. Like alcohol, if I consume too much, I'll get a bit of a buzz before I know it."

"Like the other night?"

"Ha, yeah." He closed his eyes for a moment, breathing deep, as if trying to inhale the buttery. nutty, roasted aroma of the shop. "My mom's kitchen on Easter. She always made chocolate cake and peanut butter chocolate eggs. Pure sugar rush. Her secret ingredients in the cake were cinnamon and coffee."

He licked his lips in memory, and I watched the motion, hypnotized, wondering what his mouth tasted like.

"Sticky frosting on my fingers...the heat of the oven...my mom's hugs."

I closed my eyes, too, imagining his happy home. I inhaled, then opened my eyes to find his look hanging on mine. I said, "That memory is a hundred times stronger than the smell or taste of this shop and better than I can describe."

Zach's voice broke our moment like a bucket of water on our heads. "Georgia and Torque! Stop inhaling calories and get over here! We're torn on the last chocolate."

The pulsing thrill in my belly dissipated as we let go of each other's hands. I whispered, "We're not being helpful, are we?"

He chuckled that soft, velvety Holden chuckle. "Nope."

We shuffled over to Zach and Irina, who pointed to the candy box filled with chocolates that were more art than food. She said, "Lilac, candied violet, rose petals, lemon balm, coffee, cardamon, maple, hibiscus, raspberry, hazelnut, orange mint..."

"Dang, they really do have it all, don't they?" Holden peered into the box. "Pretty much anything here can be botanical when you think of it. So how did you choose which twenty-four?"

"We just started requesting a bunch. We think we need to just be sure we get one of the correct kind," Irina said.

Zach fidgeted on his feet as another team entered the shop. He whispered, "Which one is the one we *must* have, though?"

Holden and I looked at the clue in Zach's hand, then each other, then said in unison, "Key lime."

"Key is capitalized," Holden whispered.

"Oh! Key lime was Rosamund Francis's favorite pie." Zach grinned.

"How do you know this?" Olivia asked.

"It's on the conservancy's website. A whole page all about the founding family."

Irina added, "Plus Douglas Francis mentioned it in his radio interview."

"How many limes does it take to make a pie, Ini?"

"It varies by recipe. Maybe eight or a dozen or so."

"How many of the Key lime do you think we need? Just one? Twenty-four? The amount used in a pie recipe?" Holden asked.

Irina's brows lifted. "Hold on... The clue says a 'baker's dozen.' Maybe thirteen of the Key lime?"

We agreed, removed some of the other flavors to make room for thirteen of the Key lime, each of which had a green lime-looking garnish on top, and took our group photo. While Zach texted the judges, Holden turned back to the counter, ordering more chocolates to go. "My mom and pop would love some of these. Alyssa, too."

"Don't forget the cayenne," I said.

He smiled that melt-my-insides smile over his shoulder and threw in a wink for good measure.

Irina pulled me aside, pointing to the display of pre-wrapped candies on an antique white hutch. "How about you bring some back to the crew at work? For when you return in a few weeks from your, uh, break?"

My face tingled. "You mean from vacation?"

She fluttered her hand. "If that's what you want to call it."

"What do you mean?" I balled my hands at my sides.

She twiddled with a gold hoop earring and pointed to a box. "How about that one?"

"What did you mean, Irina? Did Logan tell you?"

She clicked her tongue and heaved an exaggerated sigh. "Yes. Logan told me you were taking time off work. Some sort of...*respite* leave." She drew me closer. "Personal leave," she whispered as if saying it would conjure demons out of the woodwork.

My son wasn't great at keeping secrets, but then, Irina was cunning at extracting information. "Yes, personal leave. Things have just been...getting to me." Admitting that aloud to my interfering stepmother was hard, but at this point, I wasn't going to lie.

A lot of healing was owning your part. I had screwed up by visiting Marta Neil—and my gosh, yesterday. What I had almost done. I was not better. Not yet.

Glenn had scheduled a meeting next month to talk about my job moving forward. I still wondered if someone else had misused the databases or if it had been just an awful mistake. And I began to wonder: did I even want to go back?

Irina came in closer, clearly wanting to side-hug me, but not doing so. Her perfume competed with the scent of chocolate around us. "Everyone needs a break now and then. It's good to know when you need to step back."

"Score!" Zach gestured for us to leave as the employee behind the candy counter handed him the next green-and-pink envelope like it was a gold medal. Holden held the door open for me, a plastic bag filled with confections hanging from his arm

Irina hurried to keep by my side as we walked to the minivan. I walked faster, my pulse speeding along with my legs. The hairs on the back of my scalp prickled.

"Olivia...please don't be mad at Logan."

I stopped and fired my look at her. "I'm not. It's just... He adores you, and tells you everything, but some things I wish he didn't tell you. Some things are private, for family." I regretted the words as soon as they came out.

Hurt flared in her eyes, and pink circles formed on her high cheekbones. "At least I share. You're a closed book, Olivia."

"But somehow you know everything that's going on with me. Do you know *why* I'm on leave?" I said in a raised voice, not caring if I drew the looks of passersby. All I saw was Irina and my own shame.

"You're tired. Let's rest a bit before we go find the next—"

I could not keep this bottled up anymore. "No. Let me tell you the real reason. A year ago, I couldn't get *that* night out of my head. So, I followed up on other similar cases from work, trying to find him...because most perps strike again and again until they're caught." I gulped, hating the memory as it flooded my senses. "That *man* broke into our home! How could I not follow up on those leads? Try to find the person who ruined our lives, who ended Dad's, too!" I exhaled through my nose. "I got put on leave. I got better. Felt better! He gave me a second chance. Then this spring, this spring—" I ran angry fingers through my hair, scrubbing my scalp, as if doing so would erase the memories and pain. My eyes burned. "I got locked in my attic, and opened the door to..."

My vision sharpened and I saw Holden standing there beside Irina. I looked at him, at his handsome brown eyes, at the concerned crease diving down his forehead. "...to another person I didn't know, standing there in my hallway. It triggered me. I found myself walking down that dark path. And Glenn put me on leave *again*. I thought I was better, but maybe I'm hopeless. Two strikes now. One more and I'm out."

Holden came near, squeezed my hand. "I'm so sorry, Olivia. This is my fault."

"No, it's not." I returned the squeeze, realizing how blaming my words sounded to him.

Irina's face was sad, pitying, shocked. "I'm sorry you're going through this. I didn't realize it affected you so much." Her teeth tugged at her bottom lip.

I shook my head, sniffling as tears welled and plummeted. "It's my fault, Irina. Yes, that perp needs to be caught, but ultimately, I let Dad die." From the air conditioner being installed in that lower-floor window to the chest compressions, Dad's death was my doing.

"It wasn't your fault. There was no helping your father."

"What do you mean? I'm certified in CPR." The pressure built behind my ribs, and I began to hyperventilate. I needed gulps of air.

"Your father had a heart attack, Olivia."

"I know that." *I couldn't resuscitate him.*

"I-I..." Unable to hold my eyes, she turned away to get in the minivan.

Cold raced down my limbs. I grabbed her shoulder. "What are you not telling me, Irina?"

Irina called me a closed book, but she avoided difficult subjects, too. First the roses then how she knew about my leave, and now...?

She blinked, a tear falling down her pink cheek. "Your dad was sick, Olivia. He had cancer. The treatments weakened his heart. That's why he had a heart attack. Not because of the incident. He-he already had one six months prior. He was living on borrowed time. He didn't want you to know."

She lied to me.

He lied to me.

Dammit, Dad.

I swallowed a cry. How could he not tell me about it? I wasn't a fragile flower whose petals could be crushed if you held it too hard. I could hand e bad news. To find out in this way...

That was crushing.

As my knees wobbled, Holden scooped me into an embrace. Wordless, he brought me to the minivan, took the keys from me, and then buckled me in. The hole in my heart had broken open like a bottomless ravine.

Holden drove. I hugged my arms to my chest and stared out the window, only half listening to the others solving the next riddle. I napped. The sunlight had dimmed.

"The park's closed for the day," Holden said. "We'll have to find the item tomorrow morning."

Zach's bubblegum pop was like a shot, snapping me to attention for just a moment. "We'll need to stop for the night and go in the morning when the access road is open. Sounds like a pinch point."

Doors opened, closed. I stayed in the minivan.

They returned.

"They only have one room, two beds," came Zach's words.

Holden's voice, steady like a heartbeat, said, "I can sleep in the minivan."

"Nonsense," Irina said.

I got out of the minivan to stretch. My legs felt like bags of flour, and a painful kink radiated from my neck. "I'll take the minivan, too."

Zach put his hands on his hips. "We passed that campground a few miles back and it's closer to the access road. It even had some glamping options. We have all your camping gear, Ini."

"This is fine. Zach, why don't you and Irina and the dogs take the motel room? Olivia and I will stay out here." Holden shot a look at the clear, blue-purple sky. "No rain is forecasted."

Irina was quiet as she removed her overnight bag from the minivan.

"We'll pop in and use the bathroom after dinner," Holden said to Zach.

Later, showered and fed, I situated myself in the passenger seat. Water dripped down my back from my air-drying hair, and I shivered despite the day's residual heat in the vehicle. We rolled down the windows and opened the sunroof. I pulled out my pencil box and flower book to draw something tonight, but I wasn't feeling it.

Holden handed me a small blanket. I was braless, dressed in my navy-blue T-shirt and plaid pajama pants. I brought the blanket up to my chin as the air cooled.

Holden swapped the remains of my dinner for a to-go cup. "Decaf. You can spread out on the back seat," he offered.

Despite my cry-induced stuffy nose, I could smell the citrus and mint of Holden's body wash and the hazelnut creamer he splashed into the coffee. I shook my head. "I can lean back in this. Besides, it smells like dog, and the fur propagates back there."

He chuckled.

Somehow, the passenger seat had become my safety zone. The shape of the bucket seat molded to my tense shoulders and wrapped my weary spirit.

"Do you wanna talk about it?" He clicked the driver's seat back for more leg room. It stuck, but he gave it some push.

No way could he sleep there, beside me, with that steering wheel in the way. Holden was tall, and lean, though his well-fitting clothes highlighted admirable muscles.

"I thought yesterday at that stranger's house was *it*. Rock bottom for me. Closure. That I was done with tears. Guess not." I sipped the warm coffee. "I bought a burner phone yesterday at the gas station. I was going to use it to call the police once I confronted that guy. I was willing to risk disqualification, my job, and possible harm by this known criminal, all for this vendetta. I was willing to let you all down, all for my own selfish reasons! How screwed up is that?"

"Everyone has demons they need to work through." He spoke between pauses, thoughtfully choosing his words. "Closure is hard. Acceptance is harder. And forgiveness is the hardest."

He cleared his throat and took off his glasses, laying them on the dash. He reclined the seat a bit more and stared up through the sunroof at the sky as stars began to emerge. Irina had removed the Thule storage container this evening to access some of the extra supplies.

"After the accident...I used to drive by the construction site. Watched the work continue after the lawsuit wrapped up. They hardly delayed it. It's like what happened was erased, hadn't existed...and I never existed either. I felt insignificant."

I was quiet, watching his mouth move as he spoke. A nearby streetlamp poured yellow light into his window. I was wrapped in shadows.

"I get it, Olivia. I reached out to coworkers. Tried to rework the pieces to figure out how, what, and why." He rubbed his palms along the short hairs of his beard with a soft scraping sound.

"I'm sorry that happened to you." My fingers prickled, wanting to feel those hairs on my skin, on my fingertips, against my mouth. I wanted him to rub his chin along my neck, sending a riot of shivers down my body. I wanted to console him. I wanted us to kiss each other's pains away.

He turned to me. Deep pools of dark brown stared at me. He looked tired. Not just sleepy, but mentally spent. As he drew his mouth into a smile, a sad one, small half-circles wrapped the bottom of his eyes.

I reached forward and found his hand.

He whispered, "I never got closure. Sometimes, we don't get it. I'm trying to be okay with that."

I licked my lips. "I haven't always been this unhinged, you know. I thought I had worked through most of this junk last year, but I guess healing is a bumpy path." I wanted to pull my eyes away from his gaze, but the words poured out. "I have another book. I used to draw *him*. The guy. Over and over. He wore a mask, but I remember his icy blue eyes. The tattoo on his neck." The last words came out in a sob, and my face crumpled. Acid rose up my throat. "Here I am, chasing the man with the rose tattoo. I'm hopeless. Chasing roses."

He took my other hand in his and pulled me closer. Hugging in a minivan was no easy task. He pushed his seat completely back and reclined as fully as it would allow. He drew me over to him and I sat on his lap, losing the blanket along the way. I leaned my head against the warmth of his chest. A steady heartbeat thumped into my cheek.

"You're not hopeless, Olivia. You're hurting. Grieving. It's a twisted path. And it can be bumpier than this minivan on Gus's driveway."

I snorted.

A long moment passed, just me in his embrace. I cleared my throat. "How do you know flowers are capable of kissing?" I asked, giddy with fatigue and emotional drain.

"Uh?" Now he looked perplexed.

"I found a flower pun...framed on the wall of the country store next to the Bloomington Community Garden where we picked the dahlias."

"Hmm, how *are* flowers capable of kissing?" he asked.

"They have tulips!"

We both laughed.

I took a breath. "Do you know your own scent?"

This kind of talk ventured into uncharted territory. But I was in his lap, for crying out loud. We were already in that territory.

He didn't answer.

I released a bashful sigh. "Citrus...like a freshly peeled orange. The kind that just wakes your soul. Mixed with smooth mint, like spearmint, not tangy like peppermint, but the kind that releases this calming sensation through your whole body." I nosed his neck. "Fresh linen."

I swallowed as he stroked my damp hair. More shivers danced across my skin. "Your scent is an invigorating feeling, but also a soft comfort. Like when a friend brings you homemade cookies or soup when you're sick. I like your scent, Holden." I lifted my head from his chest and looked into his eyes. So, so close. Unable to control myself, I rubbed his beard. Prickles zapped down my skin, raising gooseflesh.

"Is that what I am? A friend?" he asked, his voice hoarse, his hand stroking my back.

I bit my lip. "Maybe we can be more?"

I angled my face to level our mouths.

He closed his eyes and kissed me. Featherlight at first, then deeper. I lost myself to the sensations of his lips hot on mine, his arm around my waist, a hand stroking my spine, and our shared sigh. He tasted even better than he smelled.

I awoke to sunshine in my face and my flower book and pencils sitting in the driver's seat. Holden was gone—off to grab morning coffee, perhaps. My clothes were rumpled, and they felt sticky in the stuffiness of the minivan. I tugged on the collar of my T-shirt to smell down my chest. Holden. Though our kiss had gone no farther than a bit of making out, my body smelled of our embrace. Citrus, mint, him.

I picked up the sketchbook and saw the roadmap beneath it, folded into a square and with our route outlined. Holden had connected all the locations in a shape that looked like a boat propeller with three elongated blades in marker, and then he'd added two more blades in dotted pencil. Did propellers have five blades? I followed the curves with my finger. No, wait, it looked more like a five-petal flower. A lot of flowers had five petals. I flipped through my sketchbook, full of drawings and notes from the race.

Didn't Zach say something about wild roses having five petals? Just like the marked-up route on the map.

Roses were all around me. My name, the deliveries, the man with the tattoo, and this race. Now, in front of me was a five-petaled blossom. Yesterday, I would have found the flower-shaped route of the race to be a sign, bringing me back to the same location time and again: where that perp lived, at the center junction of all five petals.

But this race wasn't about me finding the man who broke into our home.

A five-petaled flower could be so much more. The five elements, the five stages of life, the five senses. Or simply, the race organizers thought it would be fun to have our race path end up being a wild rose flower outline.

Regardless of meaning, we had a rough idea of where we were heading next. And a renewed sense of hope filled me.

Twenty-Seven

Irina

These rubber boots lacking good traction probably weren't the smartest shoe choice. Pebbles skittered under my boot again. "Pish!"

Holden grabbed my elbow as I slipped on the trail. He righted me and I smiled in thanks. At least today, July tenth, was moving along. Yesterday's item—moss on a glacial boulder connected to an outrageous picnic table sculpture in Peaks-Kenny State Park—was an unusual find. Thankfully, our trail had been relatively flat and easy.

Today's, not so much. We were climbing. And still climbing. Lily was by my side, moving at a slow but steady pace. Zach walked ahead with Violet, her new favorite toy—Olivia's balled socks—in her mouth.

We were closing in on securing item ten. Today's clue included a copy of a painting with a viewpoint from a mountain summit. Zach had deciphered the rest about the blue spruce, tower, and state park.

I loosened the patterned bandana from around my neck. It was too hot to wear my scarves in this weather, so I had brought a few of my favorite bandanas, which were great for dabbing at sweat. Jerry had gotten me this one. It had black and white paw prints on it.

This mountain hike was more strenuous. Were the race coordinators sadists? Zach had wanted to go all-in yesterday and do a double-header hike, but by the time we'd gotten here, sunset and closing hours were upon us. Instead, we set out at sunrise after sleeping in a nearby motel.

After my confrontation with Olivia two days ago, I just wanted to go home. Winning the race could not come at the expense of our relationship. The race was never about money. I had extra in my pension. All I wanted was to help her, be part of her life. Jerry was gone and we only had each other.

A sigh came out as a hiccup. Olivia was a grown woman and didn't need help. Don't we always need parents, though? I missed mine terribly, and I was sixty-two. She and Logan meant a lot to me. I kept in touch with Gus's sons, but being an aunt was different and they all lived far away. There was no deadline for connecting with Olivia on a deeper level, but Jerry showed me that life is short, and I had to act now. I wasn't getting any younger.

She had every right to be angry with me. I'd known about her leave of absence, and I'd hidden the truth about the roses and Jerry's health from her. I grew up in a household where we didn't talk about emotions. We put on smiling faces and held our cards close to our chests.

I hurt her with my actions, and then she had hurt me with her words and cold shoulder. My face warmed, and not from the rosacea or the heat of the morning as we trekked up the trail in Mount Blue State Park looking for some viewpoint and tower and blue spruce. There were gobs of evergreens here. Flowers were more my forte than trees.

I dabbed sweat from my eye and then smacked my neck. I wiped the smooshed remains of a mosquito from my palm onto my bandana. Up we climbed, each step more trying.

About a mile from the trailhead, we took a breather, gulping water and eating granola bars beside an old, abandoned cabin. I poured water into the portable doggy bowls and gave them to the girls. "Lily, you're a real champ. Us old ladies need to stick together." I was grateful dogs were allowed in the park and on this trail.

Zach said this trail was a bit over three miles round-trip, and four hours total to hike. If we were wrong...

We resumed, and I lugged my tired thighs up another steep ascent. Where were the flat parts? My breathing heaved. My knees were not thrilled. But I could do this!

My pulse was kicking. With Jerry's illness and heart scares, we'd adopted the habit of walking at least a mile or two each day on the local trails or around the neighborhood. I missed our walks. I missed him. So much, my heart ached even more than my thigh muscles burned on this dreadful climb.

Fortunately, we were on the right path. I counted at least three teams coming down, brimming with satisfied smiles, and two that passed us on the way up. The teams seemed to be bottlenecking late in the race. It could be a run to the finish.

"Hi, Ini!" Janet Brighton said cheerily. "The view up there is incredible!"

I liked Janet but wasn't in the mood to chitchat, especially if her team was ahead of us. I pushed out a smile.

No Tad or Dottie so far. Good. I didn't need them to see me huffing and puffing like an old dragon who'd lost its fire. Our team was only as fast as its slowest hiker: me. Once we all returned home, I was making it my priority to do more hill climbs with the girls. Some ladies from the garden club could join me, too. But meanwhile, I refused to be the person who cost us the race. I kept going.

If Dottie was sick, I wondered how she was handling this mountain? Cheating aside, my heart went out to her.

Look at me, losing my competitive edge.

I bent over, hands on hips and breath heaving, once we reached the summit. Thank God!

A tall observation tower greeted us. I didn't cringe at heights, but the idea of climbing it made my knees wobble. "Another point for you, Sugar. This is the spot."

Zach waited for me to catch up. Violet ran circles around him on her leash. 'Thanks, Ini."

It was nice to see the true Zach emerging. Genuine enthusiasm and pride glowed in his expression.

Zach framed the vista with his thumbs and pointer fingers, turning to take in a blue spruce and the tower. "Here!" he exclaimed, bouncing on his feet. "We need the tree, tower, and summit signpost in the picture."

We gathered, squeezed in, and snapped our photo.

While waiting, Zach and Holden explored the modern radio/viewing tower that Zach said was modeled after a former fire tower. I rested on a granite boulder, allowing a gentle breeze to cool my overheated skin and urging my thudding heart to settle itself. To my surprise, Olivia sat beside me and handed me a water bottle. Lily sat between us, and Violet on my other side. She gnawed on the ball of socks.

Olivia hugged her knees against her chest as she stared off into the green hills and valleys, topped with a cornflower-blue sky and puffy clouds. Birds soared. It was a picture-perfect view.

"I'm sorry, Irina," she whispered, turning to face me.

I almost choked on the water I was gulping. "Nothing to be sorry for," I said with a wave.

"There's plenty." She kept her gaze forward, on the horizon, clearly musing over what to say next.

"Plenty on my end, you mean. I should've told you about your father. I'm the one who owes you an apology. I didn't think you would be so hard on yourself. It wasn't your fault, Olivia. Not one bit."

Olivia picked at a loose string on the hem of her capris. "Yeah, I'm trying to tell myself that." She sniffed.

Lily came in closer and nuzzled Olivia under her armpit.

My heart squeezed at the gesture. "She only ever used to do that with your dad."

Olivia looked down at Lily, rubbed her nose and behind her ears. "Really?"

"Mm-hmm. She'll rest her chin on my feet, and she likes to sleep on your father's side of the bed, but she never does that with me. She knows when someone is hurting, too." I blew out a breath. "Your dad wanted to protect you by not telling you. I didn't agree but honored his wishes. After he died though...I should have told you." I finished the water and still felt thirsty. "The flowers were my idea. He and I...we had talked about it. But we never had a chance to follow through on it while he was still alive. I set it up after he passed away. I'm sorry for misleading you to think they were from Jerry. I thought it would..." I shook my head. "I didn't think. He always gave them to you on your birthday, and I thought you would miss them. And well, now I see that I went about it the wrong way."

She nodded. "I do enjoy the flowers, you know? And I like the notes from Dad. How did you choose them?"

"Now *that* was all Jerry He kept a journal with his favorite memories about you. I copied from those. His words. My—" I cleared my throat. "—management? I'll give the journal to you when we get home."

She rubbed her nose and dabbed at tears from either the crisp wind or the pain of sharing. I wanted to hug her but didn't.

"Logan has a big mouth," she said with a chuckle.

"He loves you. He was worried about you. He wanted to make sure you were okay after he left."

She slid her hand into mine and squeezed. "I guess...I just wanted to control the narrative. I was ashamed about what I had done last year, and then this spring...I was slipping back into bad coping mechanisms."

"Sometimes we make questionable choices out of pain. Like how I held on to that journal because it was a piece of Jerry. But a piece I should have shared with you upfront. It wasn't my place to keep it."

She shrugged. "When my mom died, I was crushed. Then Dad met you so quickly, and moved on...I was angry, jealous even. I'm sorry, Irina. Instead of being more open, I pulled away. I didn't give you a chance. I'm stubborn."

I snorted. "You get that from your father."

She nodded. "I've been a brat."

"I can't replace your mother, but...I can be a friend."

She squeezed my hand again, then released it. "You're more than a friend, Irina. You're a happy light in my and Logan's life."

My heart welled with emotion. Fighting tears...and los-ing...I sniffled. "I really want to be your family, Olivia. I wanted kids, you know. Biology had other plans. I was married before Jerry. We, or rather I, couldn't conceive." I waved that scab away. "A career was it for me. And I was truly content. Time passed, we divorced, I met Jerry, and by then, I was far too old to even contemplate children. Then God brought me my answer to a family, just on a different timeline than I had hoped. He brought me you and Logan."

"I miss him."

She squeezed my hand again. "I know. Me, too. You gave up a lot to raise him."

"What do I do now?"

"Anything you want. There is no wrong or right way. We can jump around in careers, even in our forties or fifties or beyond. I'm here to support you, financially, or in any way you need, while you figure that out."

We weren't too different, she and I. Her education and career had been cut short by motherhood; my dream for a family was dashed, and I threw myself into a career instead. Olivia would never unwish her life with Logan, and I would never regret my years as a teacher and now the fun I had as a radio host.

I instinctively went to fiddle with an earring, but I forgot to put them in today. I'd been out of sorts. I ruffled the sweaty bandana around my neck instead. I needed a show-er, badly.

Olivia's lips parted, then closed. Her eyes shone with tears. Blotches of pink dotted her enviable, flawless com-plexion.

I bit my quivering lip. "Oh, sweetheart. It'll all be okay."

She nodded, then leaned her head on my shoulder. "You mean a lot to us. Can we...start over? Next week, after this is done, want to come over for tea? Maybe teach me one of your favorite Greek recipes? Logan loves your kourabiedes. Those are melt-in-your-mouth delicious. I'm more into decorating cakes and cookies, but I don't mind dabbling in some baking, too."

"Tea for me, coffee for you. And yes, I would love to do some baking with you. Zach suggested I open a bakery or something after the race. Silly, huh?"

"Not silly," she said.

I smiled. "Well, if I open this hypothetical bakery, will you come and decorate the cookies and cakes?"

We both laughed. "Deal." She played with the hem of her T-shirt. "I can do better. I really am sorry."

We dabbed at our tears. "I love you, Olivia."

"Love you, too." She dug into her pocket. "Oh, I found this. Reminded me of the rocks and minerals you have at the radio station." She placed a small, flat gray rock with white striations in my hand. It was smooth and heart-shaped.

"Oh, wow. Thank you, Olivia."

After a long moment of staring at the vista, I said, "We better find the guys."

As I rose, my body rioted with aches everywhere after resting for too long. I was going to be sore tomorrow. But my heart was full.

We picked our way down the mountain, my steps extra careful. Wasn't it true that more people injured themselves on the descent? Or did that only apply to mountains like Everest?

Olivia walked beside me. Having spent our emotions on the summit, we made our way down quietly, reflectively. Zach led our group with Lily by his side—it was like my old dog got a burst of energy while on the summit—and Holden was a few yards ahead of us with Violet. Our text message confirmation said to look for the man at the trailhead with the hot-pink baseball cap for our next clue. We had two more puzzles left to solve. Could we pull this off?

Halfway down, Olivia spoke up. "Holden, what's your theory on the next two locations?"

He paused in his step and turned a contemplative look over his shoulder. "I have a few ideas, but I'm not a hundred percent committed. You?"

He smiled at both of us, but it lingered on Olivia.

"How would you know?" I asked.

Olivia said, "Holden connected the locations on the map, and if the next two are where he thinks they may be, the entire race route makes a five-petal flower. That must be significant."

Holden shrugged. "The locations could be totally random. I was just doodling, trying to connect the dots. Maybe seeing something just because I wanted to."

"No, I think it's significant," Olivia said.

I quickly made the connection. "Rugosa roses—also called beach roses or wild roses—were Rosamund Francis's favorite flower. Wild species have anywhere from five to nine petals."

"Zach said as much before." Olivia sipped from her water bottle.

Holden added, "He's a smart guy."

With super ears. "Say what? Someone is reflecting upon my botanical genius?" Zach halted ahead of us.

As we caught up to Zach, I asked Holden, "Where does your proposed route land us next?"

Olivia pulled the map from her backpack. She flipped it open and folded it to show our route so far.

"Strike me pink." That was indeed a five-petal flower. I drew a finger east from our current location to the general area just north of I-95, west of Bangor. "This could be our next spot. How delightful!"

Violet and Lily were pacing around us. Lily, in her unusual perkiness, decided now was a perfect time to play tug-of-war with Violet. They both had their jaws clamped on the balled socks. "Lily, no! Those are Violet's," I said sternly.

I cleared my throat and fluttered the map. "They've had a few Rosamund-themed finds already—the daylily quilt and the Key lime pie."

Zach peered over my shoulder. He wasn't even panting, and the sweat on his forehead was more of a sheen. Ah, youth.

"And the canoeing," he added. "They loved racing. And didn't her husband row competitively? It's not a coincidence that several of the clues have to do with Rosamund Francis. It's perfect, Ini."

I chuckled. "Sugar, this is Holden's deduction."

Another team of four ascended the trail. I quickly pressed the map against my chest so they couldn't see. "Hi, Trish and Vernon...not too far. Keep at it!"

Their huffing made me feel better about my own subpar endurance. I liked Trish and Vernon and their two sons—who barreled ahead of them, gliding over rocks like they were flat pavement and ducking under limbs without a care. Their family lived in Peabody. I met Trish Thebeau at our regional garden club, and this was their first year participating in the race.

Vernon pulled a handkerchief out of his back pocket and mopped his face. "If you say so, Ini. Boy Wonder up there insisted on oatmeal. My gut is not too thrilled." Sweat dripped from the peppered white sideburns poking out from a Red Sox ball cap.

"Take it easy," I encouraged as they continued up the trail. Vernon was pushing seventy.

Once we were alone, I drew everyone back in. "Psst! Fleur Four. What do we think the next two spots will be based on our Rosamund theory?"

"The Francis estate is near Rockland, on a smaller island. Uh, Brookhaven. That would enclose the final petal," Zach whispered. He raised his voice. "Let's do this!"

Olivia refolded the map and tucked it into her backpack.

Violet growled beside me, still trying to get her socks out of Lily's mouth. "Lily, let it go!" I said firmer this time. "Really, you two. My patience is wearing thin."

This was good. Olivia and I were...better. I could smell the finish line. Now we just needed to tackle the next clue and then—

In a blink, Violet pulled back hard, the sock ball unraveled, and she collided right into Holden. He went down with a surprised grunt as pebbles skittered.

The sound of something plastic hit the ground. It bounced, and the round, one-inch white object came to a stop at my feet.

So much for sunshine and roses today. "What in heavens is that?"

Holden winced, but more than pain furrowed his brow. His eyes were glued to the small object near my boot. "A GPS tag."

Twenty-Eight

Olivia

"It's just my wrist. I'll be fine," Holden said for the third time.

I was far from being a paramedic, but I knew his wrist was not fine. No bone protruded or anything, but it needed an X-ray. "We should get it checked."

"No," Holden insisted with a wince at my gentle prodding. "Ice, wrap, ibuprofen. Nothing feels broken. It just needs time. You can drive." He wiggled his fingers for emphasis.

"I agree," Zach said, climbing into the back seat.

I scoured the first aid kit, shaking my head. "No ibuprofen or acetaminophen. And I don't have any in my backpack." I used a few wipes to clean the scrapes on Holden's hand and gave him a bandage. Maybe it was just a twist.

Irina pulled out her small handbag and shook a pill bottle. "Here, dear. Take one of these pain pills. I keep them...in case. Pulled my back this spring. It's gentle."

He swallowed one with some water. Looked at me. "See? I'll be fine."

Holden let his injured hand rest on his thigh while he rolled the GPS tag in his other hand. "I'll be damned. It was in those socks the entire time? God, why didn't I look in those?"

"Uh, because they were chewed up and slimed with dog drool?" I tried to remember the last time I had seen those pair of blue socks before they had "gone missing" and ended up wedged in a seat in Irina's minivan. It was at the lighthouse, on our third day. But maybe they had been missing longer. Then Holden found them on the night he was searching in the minivan. Had someone from Tad's team gone through my luggage at some point? We had left the minivan open and unattended a few times on this race.

"That weasel!" Irina said.

I had other not so kind words to describe Tad right now. The violation was just...ugh!

Zach waved the clue envelope. "Okay, team. We need to focus on the clue. Hold on to that tag, Holden. I would say toss it out the window, but we need to nail those cheaters!" Zach tore into the clue and read it aloud.

I didn't pay attention, protocols from work flying through my mind. I'd already assessed Holden the best my non-medical-professional self could, and he was calm as a clam, even though he kept hissing through clenched teeth when he prodded his injury. And mumbled things about Tad under his breath.

"Stop touching it," I ordered. "We really should—"

"Punch it," Holden said.

"Woo-hoo, Torque! That's what I'm talking about." Zach whistled.

Bristling, I shoved the keys in and turned the minivan on. "Where to?"

Holden whispered, "It's not even my dominant hand. I can wiggle my fingers. It's fine. Can I get the map from your bag?" He pointed to my backpack at his feet.

"Sure."

"Olivia's sketchbook, too," Zach added, reaching for it.

"Huh?" He wanted to look at my drawings right now?

"It's a memory task!" Zach tapped the side of his head. "Mine's perfect, but I want to read your notes for anything I didn't notice at the time." He skimmed the sketchbook. "Meticulous. This is fire. You're sharp, Olivia."

Irina said, "The coordinators love to throw a memory task at us, usually for the twelfth leg, but maybe they're doing it sooner. And it even said on the clue to leave our notes at the door. So cram as much into your noggin as you can before we reach the door, Zach."

"There are like a hundred and one details from this trip," Holden said.

I gave him a placating squeeze on his thigh. Hurt Holden, it seemed, was a cranky Holden. All the more reason to get him seen by a doctor... What if a bone was broken?

Irina said with her coy smile, "I bet Olivia wrote all one hundred and one down in her notebook."

Zach flipped pages. "She sure did."

I rolled my eyes and shrugged. "I'm taking Holden to an urgent care center."

A resounding "No!" came from my three passengers.

"We'll get ice at a gas station, okay? I'll be fine. We're so close, Olivia. I'll navigate." He buckled in a bit awkwardly, pushed his glasses up, and nodded. "It's fine. Really. A twist."

I heaved a sigh. "Where, then?"

The three of them chatted briefly over the clue.

"This is too straightforward," Irina said, her voice wary.

"Read it again, please?" I asked, tapping a frustrated finger on the steering wheel.

Zach did:

"Have you been enjoying the race?
How is your mind's eye?
Head to Daisy's Paint Your Own, Waterville.
Sometimes three hands are better than one.
Time will tell you your next clue.
A dozen spots await,
See what's in store—
But leave your notes at the door."

He said, "Uh, we have eight hands total. Why the three? Like a three-legged-race kind of thing? Will someone have a hand behind their back? And why the dozen? Is there only room for twelve teams? We had seven teams cut on days two through eight. One team had to leave due to a health issue and another was disqualified for cheating. So, from the original thirty, we now have twenty-one."

Irina spoke up. "We'll see when we get there, I guess."

Holden folded the map. "I'll guide you out of here, south on Maine State Route 4, then U.S. Route 2, and Interstate 95 near Waterville."

I still didn't fully understand how memory came into play but trusted my team. Off we went. But first, ice for Holden.

We made it to the studio two hours before closing time. Four other teams were here. Tad and Dottie's was set up in the far corner, diligently painting something. The clerk at the counter did a thorough search—it came close to a TSA pat-down. After confirming we had no material to assist us, we were escorted to a table. A folded note sat in the middle of the table, much like a place card at a wedding.

Zach grabbed it. We read over his shoulder:

Is your mind's eye ready?
Time will tell.
Bring your skills to the table.
Work your way around the garden.
Don't get dazed in the eleventh hour.
Awaiting you at midnight is Rosamund's favorite flower.

Zach shook his head. "I'm confused. I thought...we'd have to like, match stuff and be timed. We have to do a craft or something?" He eyed the other teams, wielding paintbrushes on wooden objects.

Irina squeezed his shoulder. "Don't fret. We have our resident artist."

"Yes, Georgia!" Zach's face lit up. They looked at me.

Warmed by their affirmation, I wiped sweaty palms on my shorts. "What exactly am I doing?"

Holden pointed to the corner of the shop, where shelves were lined with a mishmash of ceramics and wood carvings. "Let's check and see if there's a clock. Many clocks have three hands: hour, minute, second. Though not all of them have the second hand."

Zach's blue eyes widened. "For real, you're a genius, Holden. Twelve clues. One for each hour?"

We canvased the shelves. Before I knew it, I was sitting and looking at a blank wooden clock face. Holden sat beside me, riffling one-handed through the kit components to assemble the mechanism that would be mounted on the back. A small set of tools, which looked like tweezers and tiny screwdrivers, was provided.

"Simple," he said at my questioning gaze. "We have all the parts needed: the movement—uh, that's the motor with all the gears and working parts in it—the dial, hands, battery, and you have the face there If I need help, I'll ask."

"So, we have one try, Olivia. Don't mess up," Zach said, the scent of his mint gum zesty on my nostrils.

Holden's face was set with concentration as he tinkered. "She won't."

"I'm painting each flower at each hour? Just the plant? Not like the items...like the children's book or the quilt?"

Irina's brow wrinkled. "The clue says to work around the 'garden.' I think plants only. Zach?"

He nodded. "Maybe the other elements will come into play on leg twelve. Or not at all."

I dipped into a purple paint and held the brush at one o'clock, nervous to start, nervous to screw up. "Lupine?"

Irina and Zach nodded.

I took a cleansing breath Around us, people spoke in hushed voices. Ceramic, wood, and brushes clinked and clacked at a dozen tables.

"They're filing in. Maddie's Mainers...Team Thebeau..." Zach said with a look around as all the tables now had teams at them.

Irina looked up. "Oh! Vernon and Trish. Good for them."

Twelve spots on the clock, and twelve tables. The remaining teams would have to wait until we finished, or worse, work on this tomorrow. We lucked out today, as the studio was only open for another hour. Would we power through tonight or be able to sleep? I yawned. "Hope you can steer me on the answers for eleven and twelve."

Holden said, "You know number eleven."

"Huh?"

"The paint studio's name. Daisy. Plus, in the clue, they said 'dazed.' Wordplay?" He smiled at me, and my cheeks heated. Did he remember daisies were my favorite flower?

I swallowed. "What about midnight?"

"'Awaiting you at midnight is Rosamund's favorite flower,'" Irina said. "Rugosa rose." She clapped her hands together giddily. "Those sneaky buggers will still make us solve a puzzle to locate the actual rose for our final task, of course."

"Zach, hold there," Holden asked as he fidgeted with parts.

I wiped extra paint off the fine tip of the brush, then began. I summoned my inner artist. No, not inner artist. I *was* an artist. One sidetracked for eighteen years, but here I was.

Each spot around the ten-inch clock for the plants was, uh, small. At least I had good eyes and a steady hand.

While Holden and I worked, Irina grabbed a pencil from another canister and wrote on the craft paper protecting the table from spills.

"One—lupine. Two—daylilies. Remember the colors, Zach?"

"Orange and yellow."

Irina continued. "Three—pitcher plant. Four—white pine pinecone. Five—chicory."

I paused in my strokes of green leaf spirals and looked at my lupine stalks of mixed purple and blue. "How's it look so far?"

"Great!" Irina went back to the list. "Five, oh I did five. Six—potato blossom. Seven—Crème de cassis dahlia. Eight—Key lime. Nine—moss. Ten—blue spruce. Eleven—Daisy. Lastly, at twelve—rugosa rose. I'll show you what the stem and leaves look like, Olivia, plus the color of the blossom."

She was already drawing a rose on the brown craft paper and wrote "pink" beside it.

Zach twiddled his thumbs, his blue eyes darting around the room.

He grimaced. Irina patted his forearm. "We're ahead. No nerves, dear."

I let my peripheral vision grow fuzzy, focused on painting the second flower. Zach's knee bobbed beneath the table, shaking the water cup. Small metallic pieces rattled in a ceramic bowl as Holden worked. "I'll need the clock face for a moment to finish assembly."

I paused and took a moment to review Irina's notes and sketches on the craft paper while he did so.

Irina took Zach by the arm. "Let's walk. Grab some teas or coffees next door at The Java Joint."

"Sixty feet, Irina?" I said, not looking up.

"It's connected there, through the doorway. You've got this, Olivia. Your sketchbook was spot-on. You're so talented. Can I get either of you anything?" Irina pushed her wooden chair out with a loud scrape.

"I'd love a latte and muffin. Thanks," I said.

"Ditto," said Holden.

He sat patiently as I worked my way around the clock. Three and four o'clock done. On to five. Then six. He spun the GPS tag on the table, shaking his head. "What are we going to do about this?"

"You have your evidence now."

"Think it's enough?" he asked.

"Yes. And who knows. I bet they tagged other teams, too. I know Tad has some warped vendetta against you, but I wouldn't put it past them to have been tracking other teams. This answers the question about an insider. There wasn't one. Not if Tad and Dottie had a phone, which Irina saw them use. And this tag. That's how they were tracking us."

He was quiet for a long moment, then pocketed the GPS tag.

He pointed at the clock. "Hey, that's the night I puked."

The paintbrush skittered in my hand but didn't mess up the potato blossoms. I chuckled. "You definitely can't hold your booze. We've had quite the adventure, haven't we? I keep wondering what else will happen, then something does. How's your wrist?" I rinsed my brush, then grabbed a smaller one for the yellow stigma.

"It'll be fine. I'm gooood." He scooted closer, allowing his thigh to press lightly against mine. The soothing scents of citrus and mint reached me.

"That was also the night I knew I wanted to kiss you."

Was he trying to mess me up?

I blinked and refocused and moved on to day seven, the dahlia. They were becoming my new favorite flower.

"That one is pretty."

"Thanks. I liked the burst of color in that community garden."

"I liked the trellises and supports. Like the way they grew tomatoes on those long twines. Those were impressive." Holden leaned in even closer to me.

All the places we visited were memorable, even with the minivan issues, dog mishaps, cheating competitors, detours, disagreements, and injury. I'd need to come back to Maine with Logan. Maybe for a long weekend during leaf-peeping season. "A lot has happened on this race."

"And not all bad." His mouth was beside my ear, and shivers raced down my neck with his warm breath.

"...and that's the day we kissed," he said as I painted the Key lime.

My pulse quickened.

"That was good. I want to kiss you again." He nosed my neck.

Who was this Holden? I didn't mind his flirtations, although it messed with my concentration. The man was so close, he could be in my lap.

"I like you a lot, Olivia." His voice slurred a bit.

There they were, his fingertips on my spine. His touch became playful, gliding just above the waistband of my jeans, on the small of my back. Electricity zapped me through my thin T-shirt. "Listen, Torque."

He smiled. The one he saved for me. My insides turned to jelly.

"Yes, Georgia?"

My concentration was crumbling—I dipped in orange instead of yellow to highlight the Key lime. I laid the brush down and turned to him. I grabbed both his wandering hands, despite myself. "You're acting goofy, Holden." I searched his dark brown eyes. They looked okay, not dilated or anything. When he fell, he'd landed on his butt, bracing himself with his wrist. He hadn't bumped his head.

He scratched said head. "I'm feeling loopy."

"Are you a lightweight with medications, too?"

"Yup. Alcohol and pills." He scrubbed his chin. "I thought Irina said this was gentle pain relief?"

I said firmly, "I need you to—"

"How's it going?" Irina asked, returning with a cardboard tray holding several hot beverages and muffins.

"He's loopy, Irina. What was that pill you gave him?"

"Just a muscle relaxant."

I gritted my teeth. "You said a pain pill."

She flapped her hand. "Same thing."

"Not really." I wrestled with self-control. "Can you get some drink and food in him and keep him, uh, entertained?"

Just then, Holden reached for the paintbrushes. His unsteady hand tipped the cup, spilling brushes and then water all over the craft paper. "Oops!"

Lightning fast, I picked up the clock to save it from the flood.

"Dear me. He's a lightweight, isn't he?" Irina said, blotting the mess with paper towels. Once she was done, she escorted Holden out.

"Sixty feet!" I hollered after her. She waved my words away.

Zach eyed my work. "Almost done. Go, Georgia!"

I messed up on the moss, which looked more like a blob, and had to wipe it away with a wet paper towel.

As I was finishing the rugosa rose with Zach's guidance, noise erupted from the far corner. Zach glared at the source, another team finishing up and hurrying out the door. Tad and Dottie's group.

I laid the paintbrush down. "There. Good enough?"

"More than. That is beautiful! The detail reminds me of the Insta reels I watch. Teeny tiny brushwork on cookies. I love to watch videos of bakers. But watching food videos makes me hungry, so I go back to flower reels." Laughing, he ran his finger around the edge of the clock, careful not to touch the drying paint.

"I love to watch baking and cooking shows. Maybe it would be fun to take a cake decorating class. I mostly do watercolors or acrylics on canvas, or colored pencil drawings in my sketchbook, but I do love food decorating, too."

"You should. Oh! And maybe you can also run a floral drawing workshop at my store with Ini. Follow your dream, wherever it may land you."

"Thanks, Zach. That sounds like fun."

He was already moving toward the counter. "Come on! Let's pose with our team."

Holden was still a bit loopy, with glazed eyes and a dopey smile, and I kept fighting yawns, but we took the picture and submitted it. And waited.

Zach whooped when the text came in. He grabbed the next pink-and-green envelope from the studio owner, and we bolted out the door—neck and neck with Tad's group.

No rest for the weary.

Twenty-Nine

Zach

Anticipation churned within me as I looked out over the railing at the vast ocean. We were so close to the finish line, yet it felt surreal. I counted ten teams on the ferry. Cars had been instructed to be left behind, but the dogs were allowed to travel with us. Yesterday at the pottery shop, we had simply been given an envelope with tickets and a departure time of seven a.m. on the Rockland to Brookhaven Island ferry.

Shortly before disembarking, a race volunteer handed out envelopes, and I gestured to Irina. "You do the honors, Guv."

We found a spot to sit on the outside deck, away from the other groups. The dogs were well-behaved, claiming spots right next to Irina. My stomach lurched as the ship shoved off, and a waft of diesel from the ferry smacked my nostrils. I stared at the horizon to ease my seasickness. Hopefully the breeze would diffuse the odor because it didn't help my queasiness. Though the sun was low in the sky, I dropped my sunglasses from my head to my eyes.

Irina pulled out her reading glasses from her bag, smiled, and read:

"Flowers never fade.
Revel in Rosamund's favorite pastime.
Only one can take the crisp plunge.
Abandoned long ago by Lewis and William, now a swimming hole.
Buoy your lead in the Great Garden Race.
North or South?
Only the name will tell."

A hard rock joined the whirlpool in my stomach. A swimming hole. A second water challenge?

"One of Rosamund Francis's pastimes was doing foot races, correct?" Holden scrunched his forehead. He looked worse for wear.

"She also loved to swim," Irina added.

My pulse quickened to a gallop. All eyes turned to me.

Holden said the obvious. "I would do it, but I'm queasy, and my wrist hurts."

"I can dog paddle." Irina mimicked the movements. "Never was one to join the ladies at the Y in their water aerobics classes. Olivia, think you're up for it?"

I appreciated Irina protecting me on this, but I knew the team would want me to do it.

Olivia was quick to say, "I have my swimsuit underneath my clothes in case. I just had a feeling, you know? Want me to try? Though, Zach, you're the strongest. You don't break a sweat when you run."

"Sounds like we need to find a buoy." Holden plucked off his glasses and rubbed tired eyes. "This makes no sense. What flower or plant are we going to find attached to a buoy? Seaweed? And where?"

Irina pulled out another pamphlet and kept her voice low. "I grabbed this at the ferry terminal. According to the historical society, Scottish brothers Lewis and William Norbury had a quarry that's now a popular swimming hole, named North Quarry." She traced a finger on the map on the back of the pamphlet. "One mile on foot to get there." She ran her finger the opposite way. "There's another quarry, closer, also at one time owned by the brothers, named South Quarry. I'm not sure if it's a swimming hole. Only one person can do the swim, and we can't divide and check both at the same time. It'd go against the proximity rule."

"So which quarry? North or South?" Holden asked.

"I think the farther one. North." I fished around for my water bottle in my backpack. We had all packed for one day and night—in case. Fortunately, I'd tossed in my swim trunks—brand new, tag still on. Jin had insisted I pack them. I had planned to use them as spare shorts, but something about this clue, even before we got it, told me to bring swim trunks. I mean, we were going to an island for the last puzzle.

"Why?" Holden asked.

I said, "It says 'North or South. Only their name will tell.' Their last name is Norbury, which also means northern fort or, like, northern town. Nor and bury. So I think going with the one that is most like their names is the correct choice."

"How do you know all this?" Olivia asked.

"I took Latin in college. Latin comes in handy in botany."

"Hopefully nobody else found the pamphlets at the terminal. I didn't see anyone else grab one." Irina fluttered the pamphlet and tucked it back into her bag.

My pulse wouldn't settle. I'd survived canoeing on Seboeis Lake, but this was different. A swim.

"I agree. That sounds like it. And it is the farther one, so why make it easy for us, right?" Olivia offered. Holden and Irina agreed.

"Anyone need to stretch their legs?" Irina pulled me aside.

I shook my head. "I can do this."

"You can. You are capable, Sugar," she whispered, giving my hand a squeeze.

I exhaled through my nose. I had forty-five minutes to psych myself up. Sink or swim. Literally.

I drank more water and munched on salted peanuts, knowing water and salt would help prevent cramps. Wished I had some pickle juice or mustard packets, my preferred cramp preventative. I pulled out today's note from Jin and read it:

Do your work with your whole heart, and you will succeed.

Be it first or thirtieth place I love you to the moon and back, Zee.

Jin

Folding his note and tucking it back into my pack, I repeated the affirmation from Irina.

I am capable. I am worthy. I am enough.

I could do this.

We discreetly disembarked while simultaneously trying to haul ass. Tad and Dottie's group bolted off the ferry with no regard for anyone in their path. Tad nearly ran over a little kid. Dottie looked as green as Holden and was having trouble keeping pace with her team.

As we made our way past them, I overheard Tad saying something about a car and driver.

Tad and Dottie's group was one of six that made a mad dash toward South Quarry. Good. Two teams turned right toward North Quarry. Another went somewhere else. It gave us a moment's pause, but we looked at each other in unspoken agreement. North Quarry was it.

Psyching up hadn't worked. I wanted to hurl my peanuts.

"It'll be okay," Irina said softly.

At least the weather was favorable, a delphinium-blue sky with hardly a cloud above us. A terrified guy had to focus on anything positive. The sun and ocean breeze dried the sweat on my neck into a desiccated salt.

Holden and I walked a bit ahead of Irina and Olivia, keeping a decent pace. The women chatted as they power-walked, their voices drifting to us on the wind. Each had a dog on a leash.

Holden said, "I still can't believe the GPS tag was in those socks the entire time." He shook his head. "Violet for once did something right. Even if by blind luck. I guess it's good they stuck it out with us on this race."

I snorted. "Yeah." Though I wanted to nail that cheating team as much as the rest of my group, my mind couldn't focus on this kind of conversation right now.

A mile later, we made it. Sunlight glistened on the water. A handful of children splashed and played while a lifeguard looked on. He stood close to the granite steps. A few families sat on towels, eating snacks and basking in the beautiful day. Small pines, large boulders, and stacked granite slabs surrounded the idyllic-looking swimming hole.

I peeled off my shirt, having already changed into my swim trunks in the ferry bathroom. I kicked off my sandals and made my feet find purchase on the flat, smooth granite. I began arm swings, not even looking at the water. In fact, I spun to face the other way, toward the parking lot. The one-mile walk had been a good warmup to get blood pumping, so I could skip jogging in place.

Swallow the fear, Westerlind. You can do this.

This was it. Like, *it*.

Irina squeezed my shoulder. "You're going to slay it. And look, there's a lifeguard here, too." The young guy looked distressed, his brow wrinkled, as he watched the water. He stood beside a pile of green-and-pink life jackets and an orange rescue ring.

In case I freak out again? I wanted to say but didn't. I nodded.

Irina picked up a life jacket and handed it to me.

The lifeguard approached our group, and the two others that had arrived a moment before us. "All racers must wear a life jacket and enter and exit by the granite steps, here on this side, or on the far side. The quarry walls are steep and hard to grip. The swimming hole is about fifty feet deep. Everyone understand?" he said, pointing to the steep granite lining the swimming hole. He looked a bit pale.

We all nodded.

Violet barked and I noticed Irina taking a firm grip on her leash. "No water for you today, love."

Olivia peeled off her shorts to reveal a one-piece swimsuit. Holden's eyebrows shot up, then back down as he not so subtly checked out her neckline, bottom, and everything in between. The man was crushing hard. She held on to a life jacket in case.

I threw a look over my shoulder when I heard splashes. The other teams were already sending people into the water. Colby from Team Thebeau and Gillian from Maddie's Mainers made a beeline for the buoy, slowly, as the life jackets slowed them down.

I steeled my breath.

The lifeguard moaned. "Ugh..." He blew a whistle. "Need everyone out for a minute, please!" He waved at Colby and Gillian and the kids swimming. "Out! Need. You. Out." He gripped his stomach and bent over.

"What's wrong?" Irina asked.

"My, uh...freaking sushi!" As soon as Colby and Gillian popped out of the water on the other side of the swimming hole, and the four kids in the water scrambled up the granite steps to safely exit, the lifeguard dashed to the nearby porta-potty.

My teeth chattered, and not from the outside temperature, which was at least seventy degrees.

A few of the children whined but sat with their families nearby, appeased with snacks and drinks.

Younger Zach would have loved this place. Me now? I didn't care how clear the green-blue water looked near the steps. Danger lurked in the deep, dark blue center of the swimming hole.

The buoy bobbed closer to the other side, which felt infinitely away, but really it wasn't that far.

I transitioned to wide arm swings, one forward and one backward in tandem. Then I leaned over and did some chest hugs. Lastly, a few leg swings and squats before I tiptoed to the steps. It was overkill to do these warmups, but there would be zero chance of a cramp.

No more procrastinating. As soon as the lifeguard returned, I would go in. I slid on the life jacket. I was safe. I was fine. Fear would not control me anymore.

The edges of my vision blurred. I closed my eyes. The lifeguard was still MIA.

After a deep breath, I opened my eyes.

Irina smiled at me in that nurturing, supportive way, and Olivia stood by my side as well. "You've got this, Sugar."

They were such patient friends. Friends? Yes, they had become close friends over these two weeks. They didn't judge me. They took me for who I was. I clung to that sentiment. I blinked through wet eyes.

A loud splash snapped me from my thoughts. Then another. Two kids had jumped back in. The lifeguard hadn't returned yet and they must have gotten fed up.

"Breathe through it, Zach. You've got this," Olivia said softly and firmly. Was this her dispatcher's voice?

I pressed my fingertips to my eyes, taking a few deliberate and deep breaths.

"You don't understand."

"Want to tell me? We have a minute."

I glanced at Irina. Her stalwart smile was a life raft. No pun intended.

My knees wanted to buckle. I stood as immobile as a statue. The water lapped against the granite slabs in front of me as another kid jumped in. He broke the surface and laughed, splashing at his friend. Colby and Gillian looked irate, still waiting on the opposite side of the quarry, sitting on large slabs of granite. The race organizers had been strict in their rules. If safety was an issue, we could not proceed. We had to wait for the lifeguard.

I coughed, dislodging the frog in my throat. A frog in Frog Leg's throat. Funny. "D-did Ini tell you?"

"Tell me what?" asked Olivia.

Words could ground me. They came in a quick flood. "I used to swim, in-in college. Competitively. On a team. I had an accident once, while training in the ocean. Almost drowned because of a leg cramp. Then I clammed up during a meet. Had a panic attack in the middle of the pool. Dropped out of the team. Lost my scholarship. Switched majors. Disappointed my parents. All this adventure crap...I lie. I don't like any of it. I'm a fraud." My voice shook. I swiped tears from my cheeks. "Jin doesn't even know."

"Those are some big things. I'm sorry, Zach. You had trauma. It's normal to feel this way." Olivia's hand rubbed a circle on my back. "I can do it, if you need."

I sniffled at her soft, understanding voice. "No. I'll do it." Talking about this for the second time helped. The pressure in my chest eased as I stopped bottling up the fear, as I stopped pretending. True confidence washed over me. "I can do this." I stopped shaking. I stood firm.

Irina hugged me from the other side. I felt seen, heard, believed all in one moment. Sharing with them didn't make me weak. It gave me courage. I could do this.

A scuffle ensued a few yards to our right. Tad and Dottie snapped at each other, like two people who had spent too much time together. When did they get here? And how did they get here so quickly?

Dottie sounded tired, irritated. Tad, frustrated. They stood close to the edge of the water on a granite slab beside a steeper drop-off. How long had I been standing, rooted to the granite? How many minutes had passed? Did that lifeguard fall into the toilet?

"I can't swim," Tad grumbled, taking a step back, closer to the edge as a kid ran past him. "Hey, you little brat! Watch where you're going!" He shook his head.

"I don't feel well. Amir?" Dottie panted.

Amir knelt to untie his boots.

I wiggled my toes and bent my knees. Steadied my breath. I had to do this. Even after Irina's and Olivia's pep talk, I wasn't a hundred percent ready yet. But I was getting there. Deep breaths. I had a life jacket. I was not going to drown. I moved down a step, letting the cool water hit my ankles. I waited, ready when the lifeguard returned.

He finally emerged from the porta-potty. "Please, every-one, just be—" He gurgled and grimaced. "Ugh! Wait! You c-can't go in yet!" He dove back in, slamming the door behind him.

"You've got to be kidding me," I said. Seriously. I clenched and unclenched fists at my side. Instead of relief at another stay of execution, my heart pounded. I could not take much more of this tug-of-war.

Undeterred by the lifeguard's warning, a little kid ran by, bumping into Tad. "Gah!" A loud splash, and Tad fell in the water, fully clothed, shoes included.

He flailed, sputtered, and then went under. Broke the surface again. Clawed at the steep edge of the quarry and found no grip. Amir knelt and offered him a hand, but Tad's kept slipping out of it. Tad had to get to the steps, where I stood, but they were yards away from where he'd fallen in.

"Help!" He flapped his arms and went under again.

Up.

Under.

And he didn't come up again.

Dottie hurried over to the pile of life jackets which were a good distance away, and grabbed the orange life ring, shouted, "Watch out!" and feebly tossed it in. Her aim sucked. The ring plopped yards away from where Tad had vanished.

Unlike the life rings we'd used in my college training, this one didn't have a line Dottie could use to tug it into a better position. It floated and bobbed, useless.

Not giving my fears one more inkling of my thoughts, I pulled off my life jacket, knowing I'd be faster without it, and I would need to go under. Tad would sink like a rock in this deep water.

I dove in.

Thirty

Olivia

Zach glided through the water like a merman. Once he reached the spot where Tad had fallen in, he dove under. It all seemed to happen in like three seconds.

Belatedly, from across the swimming hole, Colby jumped in, life jacket still on, to assist Zach. All the remaining teams stood nearby, transfixed.

A crowd gathered at the edge of the swimming hole. Everyone just watched, mouths agape. I watched, too, in awe at this heroic and huge moment for Zach. To put fear aside and just act. It was very brave.

"I'm sorry, Mommy," one boy said, the one who accidentally pushed Tad in.

"Amir, jump in and help him!" Dottie said, her voice frantic.

Amir approached the edge but Irina put her hand on his arm. "Zach's got him. And Colby's going to help."

I wasn't a rescue swimmer, so I waited on the steps. I'd be needed here, on dry land. Despite my inability to resuscitate Dad on that night, I'd kept up with my CPR and first aid classes religiously.

I stood on the lowest step, waiting to help, wanting so badly to jump in, too, that my muscles twitched.

We waited. Seconds? Minutes? No, not minutes. But it felt like it.

My pulse pounded in my head, my gaze rapt on the water.

Finally, two heads broke the surface, and the crowd of bathers and teams cheered.

Zach immediately turned to swim backward, his arms under Tad's armpits as he towed him to the steps.

Colby reached him, dragging the errant life ring. He swam on the other side of Tad, while Zach pulled Tad along, effortlessly, like he was a rag doll floating on the surface.

I knelt on the submerged bottom step as they reached me. Colby shoved the life ring under Tad to give support while Zach pushed Tad out of the water. I grabbed one of Tad's arms and helped lift him. Using his good hand, Holden helped on the other side of Tad. Amir also assisted.

"Thank God!" Dottie said.

We laid his lifeless body out.

I tapped his shoulder. "Tad. Can you hear me?"

Unresponsive.

I tilted his head back and put my ear to his mouth while also checking for a pulse on his wrist. I was too amped up to be sure if that was a weak pulse or the sensation of my own jitters.

No breathing.

Holden hollered to one of the onlookers, "Call 911! And someone get that lifeguard out of the porta john!"

I started with chest compressions. Then I administered two breaths. Thirty more compressions.

My arms began to ache with the force of my work. I blinked through the sweat on my forehead. Flashes of *that* night erupted behind my eyes.

Dad on the floor. Me working on him. The sirens of the ambulance and police. The feeling of the rug and shattered bits of the broken air-conditioning beneath my knees. The desperation in my soul as time ticked and there was no response from Dad.

No. This was not then. This was now. Tad was not my father. Tad was just a man in need, and he needed me. I could at least do this until the paramedics arrived. I focused on compressions and breaths. I focused on my current surroundings: the whimper of a child, the sobs of Dottie, the feel of the sun against my back, the water lapping against my feet, the hard stone beneath my knees. I was not at home in my family room. I was here on a granite slab step in Maine. Nobody moved, but I felt their presence, a ring of bodies around me and Tad, like a protective blanket.

Beside me, Zach began to shiver, rivulets of water dripping down his face and shoulders. "Is he dead?"

I shook my head as my arms worked. I was growing short of breath with the labored movements. "No!"

The lifeguard finally reappeared and took over the chest compressions while I did the breaths. I don't know how much time had passed. It felt both infinite and fast.

After another set of compressions and breaths, Tad coughed.

"Get him on his side," the lifeguard ordered.

Water dribbled out of Tad's mouth.

I fell back. Holden caught me before my palms hit granite. I panted and blinked. "He's okay. He's okay."

With the crisis over, Gillian jumped back in the water and headed for the buoy, followed by Amir. Colby stood beside us, looking tired from his efforts in assisting.

A distant siren wailed. Holden and I stepped away while Irina sat with Tad, propping him up. She handed him a towel to mop his face and hair. Lily sat at Tad's feet, seeming both curious and concerned.

Dottie sat on his other side, her hands shaking. Her face was blotchy and pink.

I looked at Zach who was standing over Tad. "Good job, Zach. Good job." I squeezed his hand. It was clammy and cold.

His blue eyes darted around, as if watching for other dangers. A young kid wobbled close to the steep edge and Zach straightened, opened his mouth. The mother grabbed the boy, and Zach's shoulders softened. He looked at me. "You, too."

"You okay?" I asked him.

"Uh-hmm. Will be. Just kinda feeling, you know..."

I nodded. "Me, too. You did well. Take a moment. A lot just happened."

"'Kay."

I suspected Irina knew about his water fears, but she hadn't told a soul. My respect for her grew exponentially in that moment. She'd only asked me during our walk here to be an extra set of hands on the shoreline "in case the object he had to retrieve was heavy." *Oh, Irina.* Still looking out for others in her own way.

None of our team considered going in for the clue, too overwhelmed by the moment. It was like we finally reached our breaking point. Between the minivan issues, Tad's cheating, the dogs running off, getting eliminated, then reinstated, and all the emotional and literal mountains we climbed the past two weeks...

I hugged my stomach, suppressing shivers. There went my adrenaline. I was emotionally and physically tapped dry. I just couldn't dash off, not now. Like when working at dispatch, I had to make sure the case—the person—was handed off to the proper support before I closed out the incident on my end. Tad needed to be seen by a medical professional.

My teammates sat or stood in bewilderment, in reflection, while we waited for the paramedics. Was winning, even with all that money at stake, really that important? Both Zach and I were in swimsuits and could easily jump in... But we didn't.

Holden was the first to speak. "Should one of us go in? Get the clue? While we wait on the medics to clear Tad."

I loved that he understood my need to stay.

Amir came over to us. "No need. I got yours, too," he said, handing a canister to Holden.

Gillian was beside Amir, also with two canisters. "Here's yours, Colby."

"You can't do that," Dottie snapped, but with less steam.

"Bite me," Amir said, wet and his shoulders heaving. "Tad nearly died. What the hell is your problem? It's just a race."

A deep V dug down her high forehead, but she said nothing. She looked as depleted as us by this incident.

Amir moved to Zach's side and patted his back. "Thanks for saving him, even if he's an asshole."

"Even assholes deserve a chance," Zach said quietly.

"Is he okay?" Colby asked.

We nodded. I added, "Thanks for getting that life ring, Colby."

Tad teetered to stand, much to our protests. "Let's go. We have a car waiting." He looked at Dottie, who had risen, but was a bit stunned to move. He collapsed back on the ground, cursing and shaking. Dottie dropped beside him to help, though she looked weary. She might put on the angry bitch front, but I saw how this incident affected her. Tad could have died.

"You need to be looked at by the paramedics." I crouched beside Tad, but he brushed me away.

Mason, the fourth member of their team, knelt beside him, too, laying a hand on his shoulder. "Maybe we should wait, Tad? The ambulance is nearly here. It won't take long."

"No. I'm fine. We need to go."

Tad nearly drowned, and all he cared about was getting to the next location.

Which was the finish line.

Holden handed me a small towel. I wiped sweat from my brow and dried my cold hands.

Tad stubbornly, and with some effort, stood on wobbly legs.

"Tad..." Dottie said, her arm on his elbow. "I agree with Mason. Let's get you checked out first."

"We...will...finish first!" he puffed out. "I-I've got the driver nearby."

Leaning heavily on Amir and Mason, Tad stumbled away from the quarry. I just shook my head.

"Can they do that?" asked Holden.

Irina, who had been quiet, perked up. "Do what?"

"Get a car or something? A driver?"

"No. We're not allowed to get a vehicle."

Vernon and Trish came to stand beside their son Colby. "Ya'll going to be okay?" Trish asked. She wrapped an arm around Colby's waist, and he leaned into her, his sigh audible. He was young. This seemed to really affect him.

Irina said with forced cheeriness, "We most certainly will be. Go kick their butts! Win it for us!" Violet barked her enthusiasm.

Gillian squeezed my shoulder. "Good job."

Teams scattered, departing for the finish line, or of the few that seemed to have arrived in the past few minutes, for the buoy.

I shook my head. "Tad still needs to be checked. If we know where we're going, we can direct the paramedics there."

"Well then, Fleur Four, let's find out." Irina shook the canister and opened it. Pink petals and a notecard fluttered onto the wet granite.

Zach bent down and picked up a handful of petals.

Irina swiped the notecard from the ground and read it. "Rosamund's estate."

By the time the paramedics arrived, Tad and his team were out of sight. One paramedic insisted on giving Holden's wrist a quick look while he was there anyway.

After getting a thumbs-up, Holden smiled at me. "See? Fine. Now let's go."

We directed the paramedics to Rosamund Francis's estate.

"I know a shortcut. I've been to Brookhaven before. Only locals know about the shortcut because the map shows it as a dead end, but it's not," Irina said. "Think we can walk extra fast? It's about a mile or so east."

We nodded and shoved off. At least her dogs were fast walkers.

We still had a chance to place on the podium. Maybe. Maddie's Mainers and Team Thebeau had departed shortly before us and took the longer route. We'd been here, way-laid, for who knows how long. *Did* we still have a chance?

Though our route did shave time off the walk, we didn't get to the estate first.

Or second.

"There it is!" Irina pointed to an oceanside estate a few hundred feet ahead of us.

Flowers and vines scaled the stone walls bordering the property. Pines lined the interior of the walls, obscuring the view of the mansion. Excitement bubbled within me.

As we passed through the arched stone entranceway, cheers tumbled down the long winding driveway. Tired, but exhilarated, we ran up the driveway to see dozens of people converging on the expansive front lawn: former teams—though eliminated, they were probably here to be good sports and cheer us on—race staff and volunteers, and a video crew. People cheered and clapped. Music blared from somewhere. We quickened our pace.

I blew out my breath, glad I'd haphazardly tossed a T-shirt and shorts back on over my bathing suit as I took in the massive stone mansion ahead. It was sprawled out on a hillside, with the ocean beyond it. Manicured shrubs, white trimmed windows against a gray-stone façade, numerous chimneys, ornate fixtures, and patios with vistas as far as the eye could see...it was gorgeous.

Holden slid his hand into mine as the pebble walkway took us through a rainbow of fragrant flowers and lush green shrubs. The roses held center stage. Pale yellow, vibrant red, and blushing peach, they were exquisite. Close to the mansion's front doors stood a raised platform with a giant pink and green balloon archway in front of it.

At an uptick of cheers from the onlookers, I glanced over my shoulder. Another team turned onto the long driveway a few hundred feet behind us—looked like Gillian's crew, Maddie's Mainers—so we picked up our pace.

Irina whistled as Trish and Vernon Thebeau and their sons crossed the finish line—just under the balloon archway—a hundred feet in front of us. Tad and Dottie's team already stood on the platform, flanked by the broken ends of the pink and green streamers that marked the finish line. A handful of men and women dressed to the nines—probably race organizers and sponsors—stood on the stage, grinning from ear to ear.

Zach, still in wet swim trunks and a damp T-shirt, had slowed his step beside us once he saw we placed third. He looked...disappointed. I gave him a side hug, the way Irina liked to hug me and Logan. "I'm proud of you." I suspected he didn't hear those words enough.

"I cost us the race."

"No, you didn't. You did the right thing," I said firmly. "You saved a man's life."

He dropped his sunglasses onto the bridge of his nose, putting his mask back on. "You, too, Olivia."

He straightened his posture and practically cat-walked around the broken finish line tape and onto the stage as the crowd whooped and clapped. He brandished his hands and egged them on, knowing the cameras were turned to us. Nothing like going out with a bang.

Holden raised his voice to be heard over the din as we crossed the finish line, securing third place. "Scent?"

I could describe the sneeze-worthy fragrance of the roses and other perennials, the briny oceanside breeze, the smell of fresh-cut grass or seaside pines. I closed my eyes for a moment. "Friendship."

"Uh, that's not a scent," he teased.

I cracked open my eyes. "No kidding, wise guy. Remember, we're describing scents by moments, feelings? Friendship is...a hug to your heart. Like the tightest squeeze that makes you squeak."

"Friendship, then," he agreed, squeezing me so that I did squeak.

I returned his smile. "Here's a memory to go along with our feeling. You're trapped in a minivan with friends who are *hangry*, and it reeks like a locker room or wet dog, and the air is stagnant because the AC is broken, and your butt is sticking to a hot seat, and you're driving through the middle of nowhere on nothing but a hope and a dream...but you wouldn't trade being anywhere else in the world for it because you're with friends."

The creases around his eyes deepened. "Uh, so this whole party here smells like wet dogs or stinky feet?"

I bumped his shoulder with mine. "No, silly. That's joy. That's friendship."

He squeezed my hand again.

Delight danced across his handsome features. I could look at his face for days. I had. Almost a dozen of them, in fact.

Over those days, Holden had become a trusted companion, a friend...and more. Or at least, I knew I wanted more.

These past eleven days had been more than just a race adventure. It had been a turning point for me.

Fate hadn't guided me on this race to locate the perp who had forever altered my life two years ago.

No, this race had been a chance for me to let the matter go instead.

Ever since the flushed-key incident and emotional breakdown in front of that stranger's house, the flame feeding the vengeance within me had dimmed. In fact, this break from dispatch was a breath of fresh air. It was rewarding work, but maybe not the best work for me anymore. So long as I worked there, temptation would continue to linger. I needed to remove myself from it. I was done chasing the man with the rose tattoo.

Standing beside my teammates as celebratory music played, the tether holding me to the past released in a wave of acceptance. I felt rooted in the here and now. I felt pure joy in the moment.

As we gloried in the cheers with the other top teams, Holden leaned into me and whispered, "What did the flower say when it won a medal?"

My smile widened. "What?"

"I rose to the occasion!"

I practically snorted. He slid his hand around the back of my waist, settling it comfortably on my hip. It felt right. I really liked him and couldn't wait to get home to explore our relationship more. For the first time in a long time, genuine excitement for what lay ahead rushed through my veins and warmed my soul.

Thirty-One

Zach

Third place didn't feel as bad as I expected. I always said I wouldn't get second this time. With a snort, I laughed at myself. Third definitely wasn't second.

Honestly, I felt okay. Like, really okay. We had run a good race. One with integrity. One with highs and lows. I came out feeling...different. Better.

Heaviness still weighed my limbs down after the post-adrenaline rush from saving Tad. Despite this, the water on my skin had felt familiar...felt *right*. I had always loved swimming, not for the competition. Just being in the water. I missed it, honestly.

I needed to sit down, have a moment.

I weaved through the party on the front lawn. This place was rocking. I wished Jin could be here, but with the secrecy of the race, nobody outside of the racers, sponsors, organizers, or hired staff were allowed. The conservancy always threw a huge bash a few days later down in Worcester at the main location, so all could attend the after-party. What I had to do couldn't wait until then.

I escaped the celebratory energy and found a quiet corner of the mansion to make my phone call. The room looked like a library with floor-to-ceiling bookshelves and old armchairs. A vase of resplendent peach roses sat on an antique glass table. Before I lost this newly gained courage, I had to call Jin. Tell him everything. I propped up the phone against the vase, sat in an old armchair, and video-called him.

I took the vape from my pocket and rolled it around in my hand against my thigh and out of the camera's view. The metal was smooth against my palm.

"Zee! I'm so happy you called! Oh my gosh, I've missed you. What a race!" he practically screamed into the phone. His words were so fast and filled with exuberance. His face was alight. It had felt like ages since I'd seen him.

My ears buzzed with his contagious energy. He rattled on for a long while, rehashing all the details I already knew, or highlights I missed from being out of touch with technology. I listened, just enjoying the sound of his voice and seeing his animated expressions.

"...and that race was intense! You guys were in the top teams so many nights. Ther. that one day, hmm, day six, when you were last—wow. That team that got cut! The organizers downplayed it, but that team cheated, didn't they? There was no YouTube interview with them."

I couldn't even get a word in because the man was on fire.

His tone reduced to a simmer, his words coming out slower. "Zee, I can't wait to see you. I missed you. I watched every night. I visited some of the kids at the hospital...we watched in the TV room together a few times. Oh, Zee." His voice cracked with emotion.

Not one word of jealousy for not being on the team, nor disappointment for us placing third. Only love. Jin only spoke with happiness—this was the Jin I loved so very much. When he could put the work and pressure aside. When he could just live life vicariously. Maybe that's why I always lied about the thrill of adventure. I loved this side of him. I envied this side of him.

I didn't feel the need to apologize for once. Our team *had* given it our all. Maybe we didn't claim first or second, but we had won in other ways.

"Zee...I'm so proud of you. I just heard about what happened at the swimming hole. You...wow, Zee, wow. You saved someone?" He sniffled.

Now I felt the tears beginning to well. Jin wasn't one for tears, but I could see his eyes glistening. "Yeah. It was Tad."

"No way!"

"Way."

"That was incredible. How do you feel? About like, everything?"

"Good. The race felt different this time. Your notes got me through on the tougher days."

"They did?"

"Yeah."

"I got one of your postcards. Loved it. The lighthouse with flowers...it was beautiful, so were your words." He paused. "The kids and I, we had so much fun watching the race from afar. I-I...I know I can get caught up in it all, and I'm sorry I can be a hothead. I know that winning isn't the end-all, be-all. I'm sorry I put that pressure on you."

"It...yeah. I understand. Hey, how's the publicity going?" Okay, this was me stalling, but I legitimately wanted to know.

"Really good! Lots of new followers on the socials. More orders coming in. Jarvis Funeral Home reached out to me a week ago. They loved the arrangements you made in the spring for Eleanor Campbell—like I said they would—and they want to continue to contract with us. Isn't that great? Oh! And there's been interest in the new fall workshops you put together. It's going to be a good season for us."

How I hoped so, in more ways than one.

He finally took a breath, then said, "Your parents texted me a few times."

"They did?"

"They watched the highlights each night. They didn't explicitly say so, but I think in their own way, they're proud of you. Your mom was, like, nice to me. I am so freaking proud of you, Zee!"

Mom? Nice? More tears wet my eyes. Dammit. Words I had longed to hear for so long. *Proud of you.* Maybe they didn't say them, but my parents' actions meant a lot. I pushed out a breath. "So, Jin. I need to tell you something."

And then I did. Everything. From the near drowning in the Pacific, to the incident at the swim meet, to all the adventures I pretended to relish as much as he did. Now it was my turn for the words to come out in a rush, like a waterfall. Maybe three was becoming my lucky number. Third place. Third time telling someone about my swimming incident, my fears, and the façade I had worn for the past decade.

This was Jin. My soulmate and partner. He had deserved to hear this first, not third.

He listened, attentively. My eyes clung to him. For so long, he had been my support, holding me up. But I had to hold myself up now. There would be no more pretending. Only truths.

Emotion crinkled his forehead. "Oh, Zee. I'm so sorry you've gone through this. I don't want you to be fake around me. I'm sorry I've pressured you to do things you weren't comfortable with..."

We talked for a few minutes, the fist of anxiety in my chest loosening. Freeing. I felt so free. Free to do anything I wanted. Free to take on the world. "I love you, Jin."

"I love you, Zach."

I tossed the vape pen into a nearby trash can, leaned back in the chair, and offered Jin my signature smile. "Now, tell me more about the Jarvis contract."

Thirty-Two

Holden

As the remaining teams crossed the finish line through-out the afternoon, the party kicked into high gear. People swarmed the grounds, chatting, eating, and drinking. I made myself a hot dog with sauerkraut and sriracha. Everyone had their phones back, so they were making video and phone calls to loved ones, who we would see back at the conservancy in a few days for another party.

Snatching a moment of calm between people asking questions about the race, I pulled Zach aside from where he'd been bobbing his head to the music.

Some of his beer sloshed onto the grass. "Torque! It's party time!" he protested over the music blaring from speakers on either side of the stage.

"Hey, can we talk a moment?"

"Yeah. What's up?"

I scrubbed a hand through my beard. "First, are you okay? I'm sorry we didn't win. I know that it was important to you."

He flipped his shades up. "I'll be okay. We were a fab team, Holden. Third place is nothing to sneeze at. And no more saying sorry, okay? You and me both." As he spoke the words, the glint of acceptance and realization brightened his smile more—if that were even possible. He truly believed what he said. This felt like the real Zach, no more putting on a front.

Good. Good for him.

We *had* been a great team. The four of us had accomplished this huge challenge—together. That felt good. Shivers raced down my spine. It had been so long since I'd felt accepted, been part of something.

"Are you, uh, okay? Like okay-okay? After the swimming hole?"

"Yeah. I'm good." He sipped his beer.

"What you did...to save Tad. Man. That was..." I found myself short on words.

He smiled, the light in his eyes sparkling from pride.

I heaved a sigh. "Well, speaking of Tad..."

"Yeah, we need to say something. You got the tag?"

I tapped my pocket.

He shook his head. "I wouldn't doubt that other teams were being tracked by them, too. Probably several of us, so if they saw a pattern in our movements, then they knew they were on track and they would follow us or the other teams. They also used a car here on the island. We all heard him say 'get the driver' and that went against the rules. We had a suspicion about them cheating in previous races, but they were pretty blatant this year."

"Yeah. Plus, Dottie's phone usage, which Irina saw. Though nobody saw them tamper with our vehicle, that mechanic was sure convinced somebody had messed with our engine. Maybe at one of the race stops, Tad's team got under the hood, or overnight while we were sleeping. Olivia and I don't think it was a race insider. This was all Tad and Dottie. GPS tags, following us, phone usage, vehicle usage, sabotaging our minivan... We have a good case."

This whole thing felt surreal. I'd been screwed over before with the work accident. But this was different. And I wouldn't let Tad's threats deter me.

"I agree. We need to nail those cheaters." Zach passed a look over the crowd. "Oh, and I learned who the cut team was. They were a top team. And they're not here."

"Even more reason to report Tad and Dottie's team. Who's to say they hadn't set that team up to fail? To eliminate a threat?"

Zach nodded. "I agree. They're slime and need to be put in their place. This is not fair."

Irina appeared and clanked her glass with Zach's. "Great job, Sugar! You, too, Holden." She sipped. "Did you guys know one day we lost first place by a nose? I was chatting with Douglas, and he shared the daily leaderboard recap with me. It'll be in the YouTube montage later. Oh, and they want to interview us in a few minutes. Fleur Four!" She seemed a bit inebriated, but holding herself well.

Zach's grin widened. "Sweet."

"Where are the dogs?" I asked, looking around. They had been real troopers in this race, and if it wasn't for Violet, I wouldn't have the evidence of Tad and Dottie's cheating in my pocket. Sure, we had all the other things, but those were circumstantial. This was physical proof.

"They're in a lovely screened-in porch off the back of the mansion. They needed a rest from all this excitement."

I shoved my hands into my pockets as the two of them carried on. If we were going to talk to the race organizers, we would need our last teammate.

She sat quietly on a bench under a willow tree that offered a view of the shore below the estate. I sat beside her and pulled her in by her elbow, getting right to the point. "Hey, so we gotta tell the judges about Tad and Dottie. It's been gnawing at me for days. Zach agrees. We have the evidence...and time now."

She twisted a lock of her hair around her finger. "The race is over. What good will it do?"

"I don't know, but we can't do nothing. It's not about coming in third. This is about integrity...and justice." I swallowed and admitted, "To be honest, this scares me. Last time, with my work accident, I was played the fool. I can't allow another bully to win." Of anyone, Olivia could understand this sentiment.

She stared at the crashing surf, nibbling the bottom of her lip. In a low voice, she said, "Look at what seeking justice did to me."

"I know." I slid my arm around her shoulders. "But we need to keep trying. We have a lot of evidence against them."

She smacked her knees and stood up. "Okay. Let's do it."

We managed to cajole Zach and Irina away from the small group of people they were celebrating with. Could they be higher today? High on the limelight, that was.

"Hey, before we go, I just wanted to..." Zach's eyes glistened as he paused. "Thank you, all of you, for accepting me for who I am. I am so proud of our team."

We wrapped in a great big group hug, and Irina started crying, too. She wiped her nose. "Okay, gang. Let's do this."

The four of us made our way to the judges' area, Team Fleur Four...one last challenge, together.

Spurred by our actions to go to the organizers about Tad and Dottie, I called my lawyer later that evening.

"So good to hear from you, Holden. In fact, I have some great news. Been trying to reach you," Earl Bachman said, an undercurrent of excitement in his tone.

"Oh?"

"They're reopening the investigation into the incident at the Thurlow Technology construction site."

"What? I thought our evidence wasn't enough?"

"One of your former coworkers came forward. Carlton had bribed him to lie. I guess the man's conscience couldn't handle it anymore. Plus, with the evidence we have about Whitlock ignoring safety regulations, we have a good case. I've been talking to one of the inspectors, too, who is a bit reluctant, but seems willing enough to come forward."

We talked for a few more minutes and scheduled a meeting to go over notes and the plan moving forward.

As soon as I hung up with Earl, I called my parents. If I had learned anything in this race, it was to tell the truth, no matter the outcome. I couldn't just give up and let the bad guys win. I needed to tell them about the work incident. It had weighed too heavily on my heart these past few years not to say something.

Later that evening, my mind still buzzing from my phone calls, I spent time alone with Olivia. Our shoes crunched on the pebbly shoreline of the mansion's private beach as dusk cast vibrant hues of yellow and red across the ocean.

"Telling the race officials about Tad and Dottie felt good," I said.

"It did. Just knowing they're going to investigate it is a relief. It's interesting to hear that they had Tad and Dottie on their radar already. We're not imagining things."

I nodded. "So, seeing as how Zach talked to Jin about the stuff that was on his mind, and we told the race coordinators about Tad and Dottie, I felt compelled to call my parents after dinner. I was tired of the shame, Olivia. Turns out my mom knew about the work accident all along. Kinda hard to hide the court case, you know? It...felt good to get that weight off my chest, too."

Olivia threaded her fingers with my good hand as we walked. "I'm glad that helped."

"It did. And I spoke to my lawyer." My heart still pounded with the reality of what he said on the phone.

"Oh?"

"They're reopening the investigation." Pumped up from this day, I scrubbed a hand over my face.

"Oh, wow. How do you feel?" she asked softly.

"I dunno yet. Good? Trying not to get my hopes up too much. A bit sad, too. Wish my coworker had come forward sooner. But maybe in this case, the bad guy will see justice served after all." I paused. "Damn, it feels good to know I wasn't completely at fault. I mean, I knew, deep in my bones that it wasn't just my poor sense of smell. Yes, that was some of it. And I own that part. The accident could have been prevented. A big part is on them. The cutting corners, ignoring safety regulations—like not having another officer on with me... They manipulated the fallout, too. The cover-up, the lies...yeah, well... We'll see what happens."

She squeezed my hand. "I hope they get those bastards." Then she laughed. "I guess I'm still on Team Justice."

"That's not a bad thing."

She lifted an eyebrow. "I just need to go about it in the right way."

We watched the ginger sun fade to a deeper red as it slipped below the dark blue horizon.

She chewed on her fingernail. "Guess it's my turn next."

"Your turn for what?"

"It's time I talk to my boss. I understand why he suspected me of unauthorized criminal searches. I really screwed up...in other ways. I think it's time I step away from dispatch."

"But you like it, don't you?"

"I do. I love helping people. But it's not healthy for me to stay there. I'll be okay with whatever I do. Just need to remove myself from a situation where I may still be tempted, you know?"

He nodded. "I'm sorry you didn't find the man who broke into your home."

"Me, too. But that man will get his comeuppance. Crime always catches up with you. But it's not my responsibility to make it happen. It sucks, but it is what it is. I'm going to move on."

We continued our walk along the shore, holding hands, bodies close.

"What are your plans when we return?" Olivia asked. "I mean, after the big party at the conservancy." She toed off her sandals and wiggled her feet in a sandy spot among the pebbles.

One bonus for the top three teams: we got special lodging here at the Francis estate. My room was right beside Olivia's. I knew where I wanted to be tonight...but did she feel the same? I sucked my teeth. "My deadline for paying the rest of my tuition for grad school is the fifteenth." I shrugged. "Don't have the money now...but maybe I can still figure it out. Loans are not ideal, but they may be my only option."

"I'm sorry, Holden." She picked up her sandals and resumed walking.

"Eh, it's life. I'll figure something out."

"I'm thinking about going back to school or taking more classes, too. I don't know. Irina offered to help me out. I hate taking money from people...but she and I are in a better place. I'm ready to get *myself* in a better place now. Imagine me in college at the same time as my son?"

"Look at us, two old geezers talking about college—"

"Who are you calling old?" She stopped and turned her chin up to me.

I waved my hands defensively, laughing. "Nobody!"

She poked me in the ribs. I captured her hand and placed it on my waist. With my other hand cupping the small of her back, I drew her in closer. Our thighs touched.

She said, "I love your smile." The last ember of daylight danced in her brown eyes. The surf played in our ears, and the wind ruffled her hair.

"I love your kisses."

"Don't you have a pun for this moment or something?"

"I do, but I'd rather kiss you." I pulled her in even more, hooking my fingers through her belt loops. The lovely swell of her breasts met my chest. I angled my head down and kissed her lips, a feathery soft tease.

She released an audible sigh and leaned into me.

We kissed long and slow, hands roving along backs, bodies pressed longingly together. Electricity fired in all parts of my body. I wanted so much more than a kiss.

I scooped my hand below her chin and rubbed her cheek with my thumb, relishing the feel of her smooth skin.

Pulling back just a little, I nuzzled her neck. Gooseflesh danced on her skin, and I planted a kiss on her collarbone. "One more scent I'm dying to know."

"Yeah? What?"

"You. Your hair." I brought a strand to my nose. "Describe it to me."

She chewed on her lower lip, pondering her response.

Finally, she said, "I call it Olivia à la Rose."

My laugh bubbled up. Then I caught a whiff of something...spicy?

My nostrils had to be playing tricks on me.

I kissed her neck and inhaled her again. Cloves? Lemon? I always had better luck with the strong scents of spices like ginger or turmeric. Was this her scent? Was my sense of smell awaking from its hibernation? I shook my head, not caring. Beauty, inside and out. That was her scent.

With a soft giggle, she stepped back to climb up the beach toward the house. "Are you up for one more chase? A rose awaits you at the end." She shot a teasing smile over her shoulder.

I followed, a warmth expanding my chest. Now this, *this* was a race I could get on board with. "Hey, you do know they call me Torque, don't you?"

Olivia squealed in delight and bolted up the path.

Epilogue

Olivia

"Hey, about time you picked up! I was starting to think you were stuck in the attic again," Holden teased.

I put him on the speaker phone while I bustled around the kitchen. I had an important delivery to make. I topped off my coffee in the daisy mug he'd given me after the race two summers ago. It was my favorite. "Going to hold that one against me forever, are you?"

"Maybe..."

"*You're* the one who is running late. I'm just here, waiting for my driver. Get that fine booty over here. We have a three-hour drive, and the Francis New England Conservancy waits for nobody!" I tossed last-minute items into my canvas bag, my creature comforts for the hotel—some instant coffee packs, a few snacks, my water bottle. The cookies and cupcakes were boxed up and ready to go.

"Yes, yes, my cookie goddess. I'll be there momentarily. Traffic..."

"Don't tell me that engineering brainwork you do every day means you forgot to be fast and furious with the pedal, Torque? It's after the morning rush hour."

He laughed, that chuckle I had come to love. "Actually, Georgia, I had to first drop Pixie off with Alyssa to cat-sit, then I had to stop by Park's Petals. Selena and Amir were fretting about a few logistics and something with the fridge making a weird sound. I think they're just nervous about managing the shop while Jin and Zach are in Vermont."

"They'll be fine." I grabbed a dish towel and wiped away crumbs from my kitchen counter. "What did Alyssa think of our latest delivery?"

"She loved the semolina custard with the phyllo and uh, citrus syrup...forget what that was called."

"Oh, the galaktoboureko?"

"Yeah, that and those lemon cookies, too. She wants to increase her order for the restaurant. She knew you were busy this week but said she'd reach out to Irina next week."

I blew out a breath. "Fabulous."

"You'll never guess what Zach and Jin did yesterday." Holden's words came with the blare of a horn through my phone.

"What?" Zach and Jin went yesterday to set up the flowers and balloons.

"Paddleboarding."

Way to go, Zach. He still went on adventures with Jin, but took on a more active role in decisions, keeping it within his comfort level. Easier hikes, skiing, bike rides on flat rail trails.

Holden lowered his voice. "Hey...so...last night was...good."

I licked my lips, a rush of warmth racing through me at the memories. "Oh?"

"Not that. Well—" He cleared his throat. "—that. Yes. I meant the fire. How do you feel about it?"

Ah. Logan, Irina, Holden, and I had a cookout, complete with s'mores by the fire pit. A tradition I'd grown up with for Independence Day, but had stopped after Dad's death.

Apparently, sketchbooks made great kindling. It only took me two years to finally find the courage to burn them, but to give myself credit, I had kept them boxed up this entire time, not looking at them once. Watching the flames consume the last part of *that night* I had been holding on to had been cathartic.

The only journals I kept now were my flower and Maine sketchbooks and my dad's diary of memories.

"Great," I said. "I feel really great. Be here soon? Irina and Logan left a few hours ago, so they should be there by now."

"Oh, the Guv's just getting there early to see her squeeze, Doug."

We laughed once more and disconnected.

Next, Logan texted. He went with Irina to set up the entertainment. Some of the radio station DJs signed up to participate.

Just got here. Love you.

I wrote back quickly.

Love you, too! See you in a few hours. Just leaving now.

I liked having him home for the summer, but he had another internship right after the race. He was a busy guy. Life was good. More normal.

Then another text came.

It was Chloe. Yes, I replied, I was still coming to her barbecue next weekend. A lot of the dispatch team would be there, and it would be good to catch up with them again.

After my return from the race two years ago, I'd immediately submitted my resignation, even after Glenn told me the audit had found no misdoings on my part. It turned out our senior scope operator Jason *had* been the one, just as I suspected. He wasn't just looking up criminal backgrounds, vehicle information, warrants, fingerprints and other biometrics, but selling the information to others. He was fired and criminal charges were pressed against him. I thought Jason was an okay guy. It just went to show how easily we could slip from right to wrong. I knew that too well.

I still saw Yasmine and Chloe for our girls' mornings out. As for Glenn, Irina and I were contracted to make the desserts for his upcoming retirement party. That's right, I was a baker now. Well...Irina was the baker. I was her decorator.

I stared into the dozens of boxes on my kitchen island, filled with pink and green embellished cookies and cupcakes. After signing a thorough nondisclosure agreement, I became the sole person the organizers trusted with the answer key to each clue this year. I had made unique designs in royal icing and fondant to tie into the theme of "Botanical Alphabet." The twelve clues all had answers that were the first letters of the alphabet, A through L. I had fun designing the unique floral toppers.

The race organizers, who had prepared intentional compression points on the final two legs to determine the approximate time, shared in confidentiality that they expected the first teams to cross the finish line tonight.

As for our own race, Tad and Dottie's team had been disqualified after Dottie came forward and confessed, disclosing their use of phones and placement of GPS tags on multiple teams' vehicles, use of a vehicle on Brookhaven Island, and their sabotage of our minivan. Neither admitted to having cheated in previous years, which made me think that they had either been more subtle in their tactics in prior races or they truly never cheated before our year. Dottie had been ill with cancer, and a bit desperate to win, with it being her last race. Tad would deny his involvement forever.

Dottie had turned a corner and was in remission and more cordial to Irina than before. Definitely not besties, but they weren't enemies anymore. Life sure could change your outlook after serving a wallop of a punch.

Once they put to bed the matter of cheating, the Great Garden Race of New England had one more surprise in store.

Not only had Trish and Vernon's team moved up to first place to claim the two-hundred-fifty-thousand-dollar grand prize, but we got bumped up to second place. And that year, in honor of the race's twenty-fifth anniversary, second-place winners were awarded a one-hundred-thousand-dollar prize!

What a person could do with twenty-five thousand dollars.

Irina started her own catering business and continued to host her weekly radio show on the side.

Zach and Jin invested more in the floral shop, donated to the Flower Child organization they adored, and expanded workshops and community work.

Holden re-enrolled in graduate school and paid off his lawyers. Also, the re-opened investigation into Whitlock Construction and Thurlow Technology and subsequent trial found them guilty on multiple charges.

Me? I got the attic repaired. Then I attended a culinary arts program, supplemented with fine arts classes. Turns out, I was wicked good at decorating desserts. It was more fun than I could have imagined.

Irina did the baking and managed distribution—Park's Petals and Alyssa's restaurant were our biggest clients. And just a few months ago, Irina hired an assistant to handle the books. Plus, of course, she hired me. I guess Zach's idea of Irina and me running a bakery together took root.

I yawned as I finished a second cup of coffee. My sleep had become more consistent, but this body still loved its jolt of caffeine at sunup. Besides, I'd been up way too late putting the finishing touches on the cookies for The Great Garden Race.

The doorbell rang.

I went to look at the doorbell app on my phone but stopped. I really needed to cancel the subscription. It had been on July's to-do list, but I got waylaid by other things.

My muscles relaxed and breathing eased as I swung open the door, trusting whatever lay on the other side. It would be okay.

"Delivery!" Holden said from behind a gigantic spray of yellow and white daisies mixed with lavender. "We won't be here for the fifteenth, so I brought them early."

My standing order of roses from Irina had long since ended. Holden no longer delivered flowers for Park's Petals, but the man loved romance. We'd made a new tradition. Holden insisted on delivering me flowers on the fifteenth of each month. It reminded him of the first time we met in what we called The Attic Affair. The flowers varied, and he even gave me roses from time to time.

"My favorite," I said, taking them and inhaling their fragrance. "Herbaceous. Cheerful." I turned my eyes to him. His grin could not get any brighter.

"I can smell the lavender just a little," he said.

Some of his sense of smell had returned after the race. It wasn't completely back, but more than before. It was fun to explore aromas with him, test his limits, and see what he could smell now.

He scooped me into his arms, and I dropped the bouquet on the entryway table. I lifted my chin and kissed him. We lingered there at the threshold.

His hand slid down and squeezed my bottom. "Do we have to leave right away?"

"Afraid so."

"I booked us a cute B and B. Ready for another race?"

My knees still wobbled with his smile.

"Ready."

Acknowledgements and Author's Note

I live in Massachusetts, but I adore Maine—it's called Vacationland for a reason. I got married in Camden, have family who live there, and I just cannot resist the beauty the state holds on each and every visit. I have probably been to Maine at least thirty times in the past twenty years.

I love all plants (too much. Ask my friends). I also enjoy a little bit of competition and love *The Amazing Race*. Maine, road trips, flowers, and races: Why not put that all together? And that, folks, is where The Great Garden Race of New England began its journey.

With it came research. Lots of it. The astute observer may notice my story has sprinkles of both real and fictional places. It's a mashup like most of my novels. It is fiction after all. As an outdoors person, naturalist, former scientist, lighthouse lover, and plant enthusiast (okay, okay, I am a plant whisperer who is in love with my gardens; just check out my Instagram and you'll see), I did my best to capture each location and plant with authenticity and accuracy.

Thank you, Bobbie, for your wisdom and love when I was setting up my first perennial gardens in my home eighteen years ago.

Thank you to authors Janet Raye Stevens and Sharon Healy-Yang for their friendship and support as we discussed book ideas (or commiserated) over coffee and ice cream, and collaborated at many book-signing and selling events.

I would like to thank Patrick and Kelsey for their help with all things related to emergency communications and response. Thank you to Rachel and staff for giving me a tour of the Central Massachusetts Regional Emergency Communication Center and for answering all my pesky questions!

Thank you, my good friend and author Tom Ingrassia, for allowing me to sit in on your Motown radio show. What a blast! As a fellow botanophile, he "gets me."

And thank you to Shandi for guiding me in bringing Holden to life on the page with authenticity and sensitivity.

And, last but never least, *Chasing Roses* would not be here without the thoughtful guidance of my critique partners (Lorraine, Anette, and Rebecca); editor, Therese; and talented cover artist, Angela. Thank you, all!

ABOUT THE AUTHOR

Jean has a penchant for the misunderstood, be it sharks, microbes, or wounded characters. A scientist by training, she now spends her days as an author and champion for her children. She draws from her interest in history, science, the outdoors, and her family for inspiration. She serves on the local library board of trustees and is an advocate for community, inclusion, and diversity.

A nature enthusiast who adores the national parks, Jean also writes for family-oriented travel magazines and websites. When not writing, she enjoys gardening, tackling the biggest mountains in New England, and going on adventures with her husband and children, while taking snapshots of the world around her and daydreaming about the next story. If she were stuck on a deserted island, her three essentials (besides family, food, water, shelter) would be: coffee, lip balm, and endless pink sticky notes.

Find out more about her books by visiting her website: www.jeanmgrant.com

www.ingramcontent.com/pod-product-compliance
Lightning Source LLC
Chambersburg PA
CBHW020550120726
47903CB00001B/208